AND POINTS BEYOND

*Other Books by Percy Marks*

A TREE GROWN STRAIGHT

THE PLASTIC AGE

MARTHA

WHICH WAY PARNASSUS?

LORD OF HIMSELF

A DEAD MAN DIES

THE UNWILLING GOD

THE CRAFT OF WRITING

BETTER THEMES

# AND POINTS BEYOND

A Novel by

PERCY MARKS

FREDERICK A. STOKES COMPANY
NEW YORK        MCMXXXVII

FOR
MY FRIEND
THOMAS G. GOODWIN

AND POINTS BEYOND

# AND POINTS BEYOND

## CHAPTER I

THOMAS BEAMISH GRAY turned into Fifth Avenue, waited for the green light, and then crossed to the west side so that he might walk in the bright autumn sunshine. Girls hurrying to offices, women out to shop early, turned to look at him. Other men passing were as good-looking as he was and some of them were better-looking, but they were merely a part of the mob, city pale and city nervous. Tommy's eyes were bright and expectant, his face was richly tanned, his lips slightly parted in a smile. His gray topcoat was open, and his step, as he threaded a quick way among the throngs of people, was full of eagerness and spring. It was his vitality, his healthy aliveness, that attracted the women. He seemed to be going toward something far beyond his gaze and going gladly.

He was happy in his feeling of aliveness, and most happy because he hadn't expected it. Only the night before when he returned from New Hampshire, the city had seemed hard and bleak and empty. He had been almost painfully aware of the gasoline fumes, of the pallor of the people in Grand Central Station, and of the rumble and clangor. That, however, had been last night and he had been tired. Now it was morning. He was rested, and the city no longer seemed grimy and raucous. Instead, the rumble was like a mighty pulse throbbing with purpose and power.

He felt re-born. For the first time in more than four years there was an eagerness bubbling in him, an expectancy. It had taken him all those years to free himself from the past, from Freda, but now at last he had the freedom. It was most precious because he had won it fearfully. To gain it he had to relinquish a memory that even when it was most painful seemed necessary if he was to live at all. But now in spite of himself he was free. Time and Polly had brought him peace, and tonight he would see Polly. He had written and asked her to telephone. She would. That was one of the grandest things about her—her understanding, her dependability. Lord, he could hardly wait! Six weeks . . .

Ten minutes' walk down the Avenue brought him to a tall building. Here Winchester, Winchester, and Tucker had their offices. It was a conservative and dignified firm of attorneys, and Tommy was proud of his four years of association with it. He liked and admired the partners, and it meant a great deal to him to know with sureness that they liked and respected him.

The elevator carried him rapidly to the fifteenth floor. He strode down the corridor, turned a corner, and stopped so unexpectedly that he almost stumbled. He shouldn't have been surprised, but he was—completely surprised and unexpectedly moved. A month before when he had left for his vacation the letters on the door had spelled Winchester, Winchester, and Tucker, Attorneys-at-Law. Now they spelled Winchester, Winchester, Tucker, and Gray.

He took a step forward and stared, another step and another. His lips, tense with effort, fought futilely with the smile that pulled at them. Close to the door at last, he succeeded only with conscious effort in withstanding his childish desire to trace with his fingertips the black G-r-a-y. He wanted tactile assurance that the letters were real.

"Winchester, Winchester, Tucker, and Gray . . . And Gray . . . And Gray. . . ." There it was! No doubt about it. And lower down on the door the partners were listed by name: Jonathon R. Winchester, Frederick T. Winchester, Martin Kaynes Tucker, Thomas Beamish Gray.

He ought to have known that his name would be on the door, but it had never occurred to him that it might be. He thought of his last conference with Mr. Jonathon Winchester. He had called Tommy into his office and asked, "You're leaving for Canada today, aren't you?"

"Yes, sir. I'm going to spend a week up there with a friend in the woods. Then I'm planning to lie around and play tennis and golf the rest of the time."

"A good idea." The old man smiled then, rumpled his thick white hair, said, "Hrrumph," and smiled again. "Er, er—er, Tommy," he began. "Er—I have some news that I hope will be pleasant to you. Let's see; you're thirty, aren't you?"

"No, sir—just twenty-nine."

"That's young, very young, but youth is desirable sometimes. One grows old very fast, and all of us here seem to be growing old. I'm sixty-eight, my brother is only two years younger, and Martin Tucker is forty-seven. No, I'm not sorry you're young—and you haven't youthful faults. You haven't been really upset by our conservatism, have you?"

"No; I like it—most of the time."

Mr. Winchester smiled at the momentary hesitation. "I'm glad you don't like it all the time. But I think you have learned that conservatism in a firm like this pays. It has saved us and our clients during this depression, and it has added to our standing. But a firm can be too conservative. We know that. We have known it for a long time, and you are only the last of a long line of young men we have brought into the office in the last twenty years. But the others didn't fit. Some of them missed the drama of the courtroom; some of them were irked by the very quiet of our offices; some of them found us stodgy; some of them wanted to go into politics, and so on. And, of course, we didn't like some of them. But we do like you. You fit. We like your name, your background, your character—and, needless to say, we like your work. I confess we wish you were married, but," he added smiling, "time will probably take care of that."

"I have been married, you know," Tommy said. He was confused as much as he was pleased by Mr. Winchester's remarks. He had had no hope of being taken into the firm for at least another five years. Therefore when the invitation was offered him, it had been a complete surprise.

Now a month later as he stood in the corridor and stared at his name on the door, his admittance to partnership became truly real to him for the first time. There was such significance in those painted letters that he almost feared to open the door and leave them behind, but he could not spend the day staring at them. He leaned forward, glanced guiltily over his shoulder, ran his fingers quickly over his own name, opened the door and entered the reception-room.

The telephone girl smiled at him. "Good-morning, Mr. Gray. Have a good vacation?"

"Grand, Ethel."

"You look it. My, you're brown."

"I ought to be. I've lived in the sun. Has Mr. Jonathon come in yet?"

"Oh, no. None of them have come in yet." She smiled and added coquettishly, "You're the first *partner* this morning, Mr. Gray."

Tommy blushed. "I expect more reverence from you now, Ethel. I'm heavy with dignity. Will you let me know when Mr. Jonathon comes in?"

"Yes, indeedy."

He passed into his own office and busied himself with his mail. Five minutes later the door opened. Tommy jumped to his feet and held out his hand.

"Good-morning, Miss Vadney. Did you have a good vacation?"

"Well, you did, that's sure." She held his hand and looked him over. "With that tan you'd pass for twenty in the sunlight. What a child you are to be taken into this firm!"

"I know it," he confessed. "I feel just the way I did when I was a kid and dressed up in my father's clothes. I'm afraid somebody'll catch me."

Miss Vadney chuckled and sat down. She was fifty years old and looked fifty years old. She was Mr. Jonathon's secretary and the queen of the office. Deliberately old-fashioned, she twisted her thick gray hair into a complex knot at the nape of her neck and then complained bitterly because she couldn't find a hat that would fit. She was given to dark blue silk dresses, lace collars, and sensible shoes. Now her blue eyes smiled at Tommy through her horn-rimmed spectacles.

"Well," she said, "I told Mr. Jonathon you'd do, and I'm sure you will." Her eyes grew serious. "I've been with this firm thirty years. It means a lot to me. I came in to congratulate you, but I don't think I will. I'll congratulate the firm instead for getting just the right man."

Tommy was touched. "Thank you, Miss Vadney," he said. There was a little huskiness in his voice and he cleared his throat. "Thank you."

" 'Miss Vadney'?" She stood up. "My lad, you're a partner." She left the office without looking at him again. An instant later the door opened and her head appeared. "Mae to you," she said gaily, wrinkled her nose, and vanished.

Tommy grinned at the closed door, leaned back in his desk chair and tried to relax into his contentment. Mae Vadney's approval meant a lot, more than he had realized. What a grand old girl she was, anyway—strict as a schoolma'am with the other girls; guide, counselor, and friend to the partners; Mr. Jonathon's right hand, left hand, and memory. And she was a long way from being a fool. She knew . . .

The telephone rang. "Yes?" said Tommy, leaning forward and picking up the instrument.

"Miss Pauline Beeman calling," said Ethel.

"Put her on."

"Hello, Polly," he cried once the connection had been made. "I've been waiting to hear from you. How are you? When am I going to see you? Did you save tonight?"

Polly laughed and said, "This is a call from my office to your office, remember. Or are you remembering?"

"I'm afraid I wasn't," Tommy confessed, "but I am now. How about tonight?"

"Yes—oh, yes. I—well, I particularly want to see you to-night. I should have called you even if you hadn't asked me to."

"Why, what do you mean? Is there something wrong?"

"No, not wrong, Tommy—but important. I'll tell you when I see you. About eight?"

"But dinner," he protested. "I was counting on dinner with you."

"No—sorry, but I can't make it. I'm going to be busy. I'm busy now. There's an author bouncing up and down in the reception-room. I've got to see him. And you must be busy, too."

"I ought to be, but I'm not. I'm just wasting time feeling good, and—oh well, this is an inter-office call, isn't it? You imagine what I'm thinking."

"I'm a lady. I refuse to. At eight, then. Good-bye."

"Good-bye."

Again he leaned back in his desk chair and let his thoughts drift. It was nice to hear Polly's voice. She was nice; her voice was nice—she was nice all over. Great girl, absolutely the best ever . . . Something important, she said. What could be bothering her? Surely she wasn't going to . . . Oh no, she wouldn't—not Polly. If she were going to start any-thing, make any demands, she would have done it long ago. She wasn't that kind—never was, never would be. She was an absolute trump.

And what she'd done for him! He was the luckiest man in the world, and he wouldn't half appreciate her, either, if it weren't for the others he'd hunted with, and after, before he'd met her. There wasn't one he wanted to remember, not one . . . He'd get to thinking of Freda and when he couldn't stand it any longer he'd hunt up a girl—and then later he'd wish to hell he hadn't hunted her up. How many times he had promised himself never to have another casual affair—and then he'd get to thinking about Freda again. . . .

But Polly, bless her! had changed all that. Their companionship had been wonderful, and he wouldn't cheapen it by calling it an affair. That was a cheap word for a cheap experience, and Polly was never cheap. She gave everything to him and asked nothing. Mentally, physically, emotionally he and she were in step. He wondered why they had never fallen in love, why they didn't want to get married. He didn't know about how she felt, but as for him—well, she brought him peace, made the responsibilities and agonies of marriage unnecessary. It had been great to hear her voice. Just the sound of it made his happiness complete.

Tommy did no work that day. Mr. Jonathon arrived and wanted to see him; Mr. Frederick Winchester wanted to see him; Martin Tucker wanted to see him. The partners shook his hand, told him warmly how glad they were to have him a member of the firm, spoke admiringly of his healthy appearance, told him that their wives wanted him for dinner as soon as possible. Flowers arrived from both Mrs. Winchesters, from Mrs. Tucker, from the girls in the office. Then as a kind of climax the three young lawyers who had been Tommy's associates a month ago and who were now his subordinates called in a body. Red-headed Charlie Lovett came first, followed by Craig Sherman and Teddy Winchester, Mr. Jonathon's grandson.

Charlie advanced to the desk. He was trying hard to look reverent and solemn.

"Hrrumph," he began, clearing his throat noisily, *"Mister* Gray, my associates and I—hrrumph, we the workers in the firm of Winchester, Winchester, Tucker *and* Gray; we the drones, the unsung, the unnamed, the anonymous; we,

we humble ones, we have called on you, *sir,* to offer our
congratulations on your—shall I say well-merited promo-
tion? No, no, I shall not say it. Probity is the motto of the
firm, care, accuracy, *truth!* No, no, I shall not say it. But,
nonetheless, you have been promoted. You are now a partner. No longer a good egg, no longer one of the gang, no
longer—ah me, one of the boys, no longer good old Tommy
Gray. Tommy is dead and Mister Thomas Beamish Gray
has risen from his ashes. We, the office peons, the esnes, no
less, we know our place, and we know our onions. We are
taking no chances. We intend to get in right with the new
partner at once. At once!" he cried, turning to his grinning
colleagues. "At once, gentlemen. There is not an iota, not
a scintilla of evidence that we are any longer safe; the gray
wolf of the depression still howls at our doors. Therefore,
*Mister* Gray, we have invested a large sum which we could
ill afford—ill afford, I repeat, sir—to get on the right side
of you." He held out a package and smiled. "Tommy, you
old slob, take this and like it."

To hide his emotion Tommy smiled and busied himself
with the string and paper. Opened, the package revealed a
long flat cigarette-case, ivory with his initials set in gold.
He looked at it, fingered it gently. Then he looked up.

"Fellows," he asked softly, "would you like to see me
bawl?"

The three shouted then, crowded around him, shook his
hand, clapped him on the back, made over him with generous enthusiasm. He was touched by the gift and by their
unenvious delight in his success. The day through they
ragged him with mock reverence, and when the office closed
they carried him away to the Yale Club for drinks and dinner. It was Tommy's day, and as he walked rapidly that
evening toward Lexington Avenue he thought that surely
it was the most beautiful day in his life. Everything that
had gone before had led up to it. Only one thing more
was needed—Polly, and in a few minutes more he would

have her. He thought back to his despair four years before. He would never despair again.

He turned into the vestibule of the apartment house where Polly lived and pressed the button under her card. The lock clicked. He opened the door, rushed up one flight of stairs. Polly was waiting in the hall, her hand out. He seized it, pulled her into the apartment, kicked the door shut, and took her in his arms. Then he kissed her long and thoroughly.

Polly struggled, forced her right hand up to his chin and pushed his head back.

"Let me breathe, you abysmal brute, you," she commanded. "And unhand me. I want to look at you." She laughed when he shook his head and brought his lips to hers again while he muttered hungrily.

"No, sir," she cried. "Not now. You let go. Let go, I say!" She kicked his ankle sharply and broke free. "How dare you maul me?"

She was laughing, and Tommy laughed with her, though he hardly knew why. It was kisses that he wanted, not laughter. As she drew away, he caught her hands and held them firmly.

"It's good to see you, Polly," he said. "You don't know how good."

"It's good to see you too, Tommy, and how fine you look. The change is marvelous. A month ago you looked twenty-nine; now you look about twenty. Those tight little lines around your mouth are gone, and the tired look has gone out of your eyes. You are so hard and brown, and you look so happy."

"Happy!" Rough with eagerness he pulled her close to him again and bent his head for another kiss; but she struggled, freed herself. Confused, Tommy clung to her hands and stared at her. Was Polly turning coy on him? What in the world was the matter with her? He didn't want to talk —not now.

She saw his confusion and laughed at it. "Give me a chance, will you? And control your mad, mad ardor. I want to hear you talk. Please let go, Tommy. You're hurting my hands."

Instantly he released her, ashamed to have been cruel. For some reason she didn't want him to kiss her; yet she had responded to that first kiss as ardently as she always had. Well, if she wanted him to he could wait, but he wondered what was in the wind.

She dropped into a chair and smiled at him. "You said you were happy. You look it, too. Are you really?"

There was nothing else to do; so he sat down in a chair opposite her. "Happy?" he said. "I should say I am. Polly, I've had a day—the kind of day you dream about and it never comes. But it did."

"Tell me," she commanded.

So Tommy told her. "Everybody was wonderful," he concluded, "and Charlie and Craig and Teddy never let up on me all day long. One of them was always popping into the office mistering me and sirring me until I threatened to knock their heads together. I felt an awful fool, but I liked it."

Polly's smile deepened. "I like it too, Tommy," she said softly. "I'm so glad for you. It means a lot when you can be promoted and not make other people envious. It means they really like and admire you. You're settled now, and I'm glad; I can't tell you how glad."

Tommy knew she meant what she said. Polly always meant what she said. That was one reason they had always got on so well together. She was, he thought, the grandest girl in the world. Not beautiful, not even pretty, he supposed, but honest and intelligent and fine. And all woman. Broad in the shoulders and hips, deep chested, there was a strong, primitive look to her that he loved. And he loved her big, generous mouth and thick brown hair. Her nose was unevenly modeled, her skin too dark, but her brown eyes behind her glasses never evaded his. There was no evasion in them; there was no evasion in her. Yet now she was evading. For the first time . . . There must be a reason, a *good* reason. He pressed his lips together with determination. If Polly wanted him to talk, he would talk.

"I know you're glad," he said gratefully, "but somehow I wanted you to tell me you were. I wanted your congratulations more than anybody's. Your letter was fine, but I wanted to hear you *say* you were glad. I thought Mr. Jonathon told me at just the wrong time. You were out of town and I was leaving right away. It seemed a pretty empty honor when I didn't have a chance to share it with any one. But he knew what he was doing. It's better this way."

"Yes," agreed Polly; "yes, it's better."

Tommy settled deeper into his chair. Temporarily his excitement was subsiding into contentment. The room was acting like a drug on him, as it always acted. Polly and the room; to him the two were one—they were peace. With a few pieces of good furniture, a few pictures, wisely chosen draperies, and a plain rug, she had made a harmony that soothed him like good music softly played. Many, many times in the past year and a half Tommy had found physical and spiritual solace in that apartment. Now he felt as if he had come home. He could wait . . .

The silence lengthened. Tommy looked at Polly and asked, "What were you thinking?"

She laughed. "You would never guess. I was deciding that you were really a very good-looking man. I've always thought you were *nice*-looking, but now you're better than that; you're really good-looking."

Embarrassed, Tommy grinned. "Woman," he said, "you're nuts."

"No, I'm not. You've got a grand build—long and slender and strong. It's not that, though. It's your face. There's always been a tightness in it before, a strain. Any man with decent features and all his hair is pretty good-looking, of course. You've got good teeth and nice brown eyes and your nose will do, but that stern, tight look has always been more noticeable than anything else. Now it's gone, and you're really something for a girl to be proud of."

Tommy ignored the compliment to consider its implication for him. "I don't know how I look," he said slowly at last, "but I know how I feel. I don't feel tight. I feel free."

"Maybe you've escaped Freda at last."

"Yes," he agreed thoughtfully; "yes, maybe that's it. Yes, I think I have. . . ."

Freda? Of course, he'd escaped. Why, not for a month—two months. . . . Why think of her at all? Polly was . . . He sat up and looked at her, his eyes very bright.

"What's the matter with me, anyway?" he demanded. "Here I am parked across the room from you—after six weeks. It was certainly mean of you to go on your vacation just before I went on mine. Two weeks and four make six. Six long weeks—and I have been faithful to thee, Cynara, in my fashion, and my fashion is faithful."

He half rose and then sank back into his chair. Polly did not smile. She did not look at him. For some reason she refused to see what he meant. She seemed to be studying her hands folded in her lap as she asked softly, "You've always been faithful, haven't you, Tommy?"

He nodded. "Yes, though it's no virtue. I didn't need any other woman. You made me happy."

She looked at him then, and he knew that he would not make another move toward her until she gave the sign. Her eyes were so soft, so sad, and when she spoke her voice was so tender that he could not break into her gentle mood with passion.

"It's sweet of you to say that," she began a little hesitantly. "I—I'm glad you said it. But I wish—" She broke off suddenly and stood up. "Wait a minute. I'll get you a drink." She disappeared into her tiny kitchen. Tommy looked after her wonderingly. Something wasn't quite right. Polly wasn't the same. She seemed curiously gentle and somehow withdrawn. She'd said there was something important. In her own time she would tell him what it was, but now he felt confused and uncertain. The atmosphere was strange.

She returned with a tray that she placed on the low table beside his chair. There was only one glass.

"None for you?" he asked, pouring whisky.

"No. No, not now." She sat down and waited until he had prepared his drink. Then she asked unexpectedly, "We've had a good time, haven't we?"

"Good time? The best ever!" He lifted his glass high. "Here's to many more of them." He drank, placed the glass on the tray. "You know," he said, "it's really wonderful how we've hit it off—how our interests have jibed, I mean. Music and books and hockey matches and galleries and hikes and prizefights."

"Not the prizefights," objected Polly. "I'm never going to another one. I don't like them. But everything else. Yes, it's been perfect—perfect agreement, perfect freedom. I suppose the freedom made the perfection possible. But—"

She hesitated, and suddenly Tommy was suspicious, uneasy. He leaned forward and studied her. "But what?" he demanded. "What are you thinking? What's the matter with you tonight? Has perfection palled? Is that it?"

"No—no, it hasn't palled. It's just that—well, oh, Tommy, I can't be tactful. I have to come right out with it. I didn't want to make you stop kissing me. I wanted you to keep on the way I've always wanted you to. But I couldn't let you —I can't—  Tommy, I'm going to be married."

*"What!"*

She smiled sadly at his amazement, at his rigid posture, his open incredulity. It was cruel to take him unawares this way, but there had been no chance to prepare him, and a clean, sudden break was best.

Tommy stared at her. His mind refused to accept the meaning of her words. Polly married? Married? The word didn't mean anything.

"Don't look so dumfounded, please," Polly said at last; and then trying rather pitifully to ease the strain, she added, "It isn't very flattering, you know."

Flattering? Polly getting married? Flattering? Tommy shook his head, blinked his eyes, and frowned. "Say that again, will you?" he demanded. "I didn't get it, did I?"

"Yes, Tommy, you got it." She fluttered her hand nervously toward him. "Please sit back. Take a drink. Do something; just don't look like that. You look as if I'd hit you with a blackjack."

Tommy took the drink, blinked at her once more, and then said rather crossly, "That's the way I feel. What are you talking about, anyway? Did you say you were getting married? Who to?"

"To somebody you don't know. Please sit back and let me tell you."

Tommy dropped back in his chair. "All right," he agreed. "I'm ready, but I still don't believe you." He sat upright again. "Why, Polly, I *can't* believe you."

"Yes, Tommy, yes—you'll have to believe me." She lighted a cigarette, puffed at it deeply, crushed it in a tray. "You're making this harder than I thought it was going to be. You see, our perfection can't continue indefinitely. It isn't real, you know."

"Why not?" he demanded hotly. "Of course, it's real. It's wonderfully real."

She shook her head slowly in denial and smiled at his boyish indignation. "No, perfection can't be real. Our perfection is based on our freedom, and that is the unrealest thing in the world. Oh, I've been doing a lot of thinking about us. We've been true to each other because we're like that; but if either of us wasn't, the perfection would have gone long ago. We've had a kind of instinctive trust that's saved us. But, Tommy, we've been happy in a vacuum, and life has to have meaning for me."

Confused, Tommy studied her. "I don't understand, Polly. Have you fallen in love with somebody? Or are you just tired of me and making a philosophy out of it? Don't tell me I've been in a vacuum with you. I tell you I've been happy."

"Maybe, but I don't think so. Tell me, Tommy, have you been as happy with me as you were when you married Freda?"

"That's not fair!" he cried, hurt and indignant. "I've never pretended, and neither have you. I wasn't looking for ecstasy like that with you. I didn't expect it. I didn't ask for it. You don't have to be mad with joy to be happy. Is that what you're looking for?"

Again she shook her head. "No, I'm not asking for that. I had it once, too, when I was a senior in college. When I lost him—oh well, why talk about that? No, not ecstasy. This is something different. I'm not even expecting the peace I've had with you—and I don't know whether I really want peace like that or not. Maybe I won't even get the physical joy. No, Tommy, it's something more; I'm expecting life, not an imitation of it. Maybe that doesn't mean much to you, but it does to me."

She paused as if to order her thoughts. Then as he waited, obviously impatient, as obviously confused, she went on:

"Listen, Tommy, I'm twenty-eight. I've been out of college seven years. I came to New York all worked up about a career. I was going to be a distinguished woman. Well, if I do say it, I'm a damned capable woman. I'm a good editor. Anybody'll tell you that. I'm making good money, and in a few years I'd be making more—and that's just where I'd end, with more money, I mean. Career? Where's the career in that? For a woman, anyway? I get to meet interesting people, certainly, though I want to tell you that an author bellyaching over a comma isn't the most engaging creature

in the world. But what does it all come down to? Days,
sometimes nights, of work that go to make somebody else
distinguished. In the end, I'm just earning a living. The
book doesn't bear the imprint of my name. I'm Miss
Anonymous forever.

"If I had some kind of special talent it might be different.
If I could write a book of my own, I might feel differently.
I might feel I was fulfilling myself in my work. I might feel
useful to myself and the world. But I don't, Tommy. I
merely feel capable. That's not enough. And my contentment with you isn't enough, either. We can't go on forever
being unselfish. Sometime one of us will want a part of
the other's life, and that will be the end. We promised each
other freedom, and we've kept our promise wonderfully;
but the freedom is unnatural, it's unreal. It means friendship, not love—and friendship isn't enough. If you fell in
love, it wouldn't be enough for you either."

"But," Tommy objected, "I don't think you've fallen in
love. You don't sound at all as if you had. Why can't we
go on as we are until you do?"

"Because I've been offered love and because I think I
can love him. Maybe I do now. I'm not sure; that's all. You
know who he is. I've mentioned him often—John Bruce. I
met him years ago when he was teaching at N.Y.U. I liked
him enormously, and I thought more than once he would
ask me to marry him. I know now he would have if he
had had more money. Then he got his chance at Harvard.
Now he's been promoted. His last book did that. We've always corresponded, and he came to see me at Sunapee almost
as soon as I arrived. He stayed the two weeks I was there.
A week ago I wrote that I'd marry him. I'm going to tomorrow. I put it off until you came home so I could explain."

"Tomorrow?"

He still looked confused, unbelieving. The total unexpectedness of her news had stunned him, and he could not

yet realize that she was taking herself out of his life at a time when he had been most sure of having her an essential part of it.

She was unhappily aware of his bewilderment and tried to dissipate it by speaking crisply and quickly.

"Yes," she said, "tomorrow. We'll spend our honeymoon getting settled. Listen, Tommy, and try to understand. I've thought it all out. John loves me, really loves me. And I can't have a career of my own, only a pretense of a career. But I'm lucky. I'm a woman. A man has only one chance, and if he can't make a career for himself, he has to be satisfied with earning the best living he can. But a woman has two chances. If she can't make a career of her own, she can have a part of her husband's career. She can help make it. No matter how tiny his success is, she can have a part in it. And that's a career, I think—being a wife, I mean. And being a mother is a career too. I want children, Tommy. I've fooled myself long enough. I want a grubby little boy who'll come to me with his hurts, and I want a little girl to dress all up in something dainty for a party. I want to curl her hair and put a ribbon in it. I don't want freedom any longer. I want human responsibilities. I want to be loved, Tommy. I know that love means pain, but I'll welcome it. It'll be reality."

There was a warmth in her voice, a glow in her eyes that disturbed Tommy even more than his loss of her disturbed him. Polly didn't know that pain she mentioned so glibly. He knew it only too well, but how could he tell her? How could he ever make it clear?

He searched for words to express his confusion, his distress. He wanted to tell her that he knew how she felt. Hadn't he dreamed dreams, too, once? Didn't he know that longing to make yourself a part of another person? How he had longed to merge himself with Freda, to be literally one with her! And the longing had brought him what? Three months of heaven, three of purgatory, and years of hell. When you tore yourself wide open to let another person in, you had no defenses left. There your heart was—so pitifully unprotected. He and Polly gave each other perfect companionship, brought each other peace. Men and women shouldn't ask more of each other than that. More demanded a price too great to pay. He cared for Polly. He didn't want her hurt. She would be. He was sure of it. She would be hurt terribly and probably never even glimpse heaven; yet if he tried to tell her so, he would sound like a dog in the manger.

"I know what you mean," he said slowly; "of course I know what you mean, but are you sure, *sure,* Polly, that you're right? I know Cambridge. I was there three years in law school. I can't imagine you in that atmosphere. It's so old-fashioned, so academic. There are ten thousand tabus. And, tell me honestly, can you imagine yourself at a faculty tea?"

"Yes I can," she replied flatly. "I shall hate it, I suppose, but it won't be any worse than a literary tea, and it will be a damn sight less noisy. Oh, there'll be things I'll hate—but when you hate, Tommy, you're alive; you're feeling. And Cambridge is a community; it hasn't the horrible emptiness of New York. People live in Cambridge. Maybe they don't live my way, but they live. And John loves me; remember that. It means a great deal to be loved, Tommy —at least to me, it does. If you loved me, I might feel differently about getting married, but you don't. We've been lovers, but we've never been in love. I think you've forgotten how much love means."

Tommy hadn't forgotten. Try as he would, he couldn't forget; but he couldn't talk of the memories and the pain even to Polly. Besides, discussions of love got nowhere; love was too intimate, too personal. To escape the discussion he asked her if she would have married him if he had asked her to.

"No." Her answer was disconcertingly quick and assured.

"I'm female all through, and I wanted you to ask me. My vanity wanted you to. But I've always known you didn't love me. You couldn't have left me so free if you had. You'd have been suspicious and probably jealous sometimes too. But you never were. Oh, no, Tommy, I've had the right association with you, and I've always known it. I haven't a single regret either. If the Mrs. Grundys in Cambridge ever find out about you they'll think I ought to die of shame, but I shan't wilt even a little bit." She motioned toward a fine copy of a Corot landscape. "The picture goes with me."

"The one thing you ever let me give you," Tommy grumbled. "You're so damned proud."

"I oughtn't to have let you give me that, but I couldn't resist it when you surprised me with it. I love it for itself and I love it because you gave it to me. No, I haven't a regret, and I hope you haven't either."

"Regret?" He looked at her in astonishment. "Regret? Oh, no! But what am I going to do without you? I can't imagine what life will be like. You don't know how important you've been to me. Why, you've been like a wife without any of the faults of marriage."

Then Polly laughed. "What an ideal relationship that would seem to lots of people! We haven't given each other a single responsibility, have we? I haven't cost you anything, and you haven't asked me to darn your socks. We've been really free, and that's what so many people want—but me," she quoted, "me this uncharted freedom irks. I think maybe I've grown up."

Tommy didn't know whether she was entirely serious or not, and he didn't care. No more discussion; he didn't want any more discussion. His passion was forgotten, and his mind was numb. Suddenly he was aware of being almost unbearably tired. Polly's announcement coming after the exciting day had drained him of strength. He had been shot unexpectedly to an emotional peak, as unexpectedly been dropped to an emotional depth. He felt weak, depressed, lost. He couldn't talk any more.

Rising slowly, he said, "I think I'll go now, Polly. You must be busy and I—well, I'm all mixed up. But you know how much happiness I wish you, don't you? And you must know that if you ever need me, I'll do anything in the world for you. I shan't stop caring, you know."

Polly's eyes filled with tears, brimmed over. She came close to him. "I know, Tommy," she whispered. "Please kiss me good-bye."

# CHAPTER II

## I

As Tommy walked slowly eastward, the last gleaming shred of the day's happiness dropped from him. He felt utterly alone in an utterly empty world. The let-down had been too sudden, too complete. He had gone to Polly tingling with life, eager to see her, hungry for her felicitations, more hungry for her kisses. A month of play and rest had given him surging vitality, a healthy animal vigor that cried for release in love. The excitement of the day had made his nerves sing, but the key had been too high, the emotion too long sustained. He had expected to relax in Polly's arms, to climax the excitement with ecstasy, and then sink with her into dreamless peace—and now, now denied the happiness he had so naturally expected, his body ached with weariness. He felt too tired to move and, at the same time, too nervous to rest. And worst of all, he felt alone, pitifully, inescapably alone.

His apartment was a block from the East River in the Fifties. He left Third Avenue behind. There were fewer people about him now, fewer taxicabs in the street. The shops seemed grimy, the people sitting in the doorways all dark and unkempt. Ugly, New York was really ugly. Back of its lights and towers—only a block or two back of them—there was nothing but ugliness. And emptiness. A taxi honked; somewhere above him a child screamed. He shivered. . . . An emptiness; that's what he was living in—an ugly emptiness broken with painful sounds.

Another block and the street was almost deserted. The buildings lifted blank façades toward a dark sky, and the occasional rectangle of yellow light only stressed the blankness and the darkness. His depression sank deeper into him. The world was empty.

Somebody was there, though; in a vague, subconscious way he knew that somebody had been there for a full minute. Somebody had touched his arm, moved away, touched it again. He turned his head. Only a pace to his right there was a girl looking up at him with bright questioning eyes. She was very young, even pretty. The lights of a taxi flashed across her face, and the prettiness was gone. Nothing was left but the mascara on her eyelashes, the rouge on her cheeks and lips. For an instant she looked more like a badly painted mask than like a girl; then the lights were past and she was pretty again.

She smiled and Tommy paused.

"Keep on walking," she said softly. "There's a cop on the next corner."

"All right, sister," he agreed. "What are you working an empty street for?"

"It's not empty; you're here." She smiled at him pertly. "And you look lonely."

"Don't all men alone look lonely?"

Tommy didn't know why he was talking to the girl, but at the moment even a chippie off the streets seemed better than the blankness.

"Oh, no!" she exclaimed. "Lots of 'em are on their way somewhere, and lots of 'em are coming from somewhere. You know what I mean, doncha?"

Tommy grinned. "Yes, I know. My mind is pure, but I know. And I take it that I don't look as if I'd been anywhere or was going anywhere. Well, you're right. I haven't and I'm not."

She moved closer to him so that her arm touched his. "You're a nice guy and would treat a girl right," she said softly, her voice urgent. "And I'd treat you right, too. Honest I would. How about it, mister?"

Tommy stopped in a shadow and studied her. She was a soft little thing, not up to his shoulder. In the darkness her eyes were luminous. Was it desire, really desire? He wondered. Her slightly parted lips promised everything. And why not? Women like her were made for lonely men like him. There was no one for him to be loyal to, no one to care what he did. And he was so damned tired of trying—trying to be loyal only to lose what he was loyal to. He was tired of everything, tired all over.

Again a taxi passed, and again her face was lighted. Once more the girl was transformed into a painted mask. She moved and a wave of cheap perfume offended his nostrils. Why fool himself? He didn't want this girl. He didn't want any girl. . . .

"No, sister," he said almost regretfully, "it's no go. But I'm glad you spoke to me. You wouldn't understand, and maybe I don't—but I'm glad." He put his hand in his pocket and drew out his wallet. "Will you have a drink on me?"

To his surprise, she drew back. "Aw, I ain't no beggar. I like you, mister. You look nice. Honest, you won't be sorry."

"That's just the point. I would be. But I like you, too. I've disappointed you and I'll feel better if you'll take a little something for a drink or maybe a pair of gloves. I know you aren't begging."

"O.K., then, if that's the way you feel." She took the bill without looking at it. "Thanks." Then she smiled. "I bet your girl took a walk-out powder on you."

Startled, Tommy asked, "What makes you think that?"

"Lots of young fellers live around here. 'Bout every so often, a guy says to me, 'O.K., kid; to hell with her.' That's the way you looked."

Tommy touched her arm. "You've got brains above your job. Now I've got to be going. I hope you have better luck with the next fellow."

She seemed to wilt a little then as she looked vaguely

up and down the street. "Maybe I won't like the next one," she said, wistfulness in her voice. "I liked you."

"Maybe you wouldn't if you knew me better. Well, goodnight."

"Goodnight, mister."

Tommy left her standing in the shadow. Had he realized it, there was more life in his step now, more lift to his head. The little street-walker had given him something when he needed it—not much, but something. She had filled a small spot in the great emptiness, given him for the moment a feeling of personality, an awareness of his humanness among others who were human. She had liked him. It wasn't only his money she had wanted, but her hungry little body had actually yearned for his. He had a vague regret that his hadn't yearned equally for hers, but he was so damned tired—and, oh well, a girl like that . . . But it was comforting, just the same, to hear her say that he was nice, to have her feel that he would be kind.

He hadn't really wanted her. He wondered why not. It was his background, he supposed, his upbringing—something of the sort that always acted as a check whenever a prostitute approached him. But what would it have mattered if he had brought her along? He belonged to nobody; nobody belonged to him. There was nobody in the past to injure and nobody in the future. Surely his body was his to do what he pleased with, and the girl had really liked him.

Then, smiling grimly to himself, he shook his head. He was arguing like a child tempted to snitch a piece of candy. He didn't believe a thing he was thinking. If he had taken that girl, he would hate her and hate himself. Background, upbringing, whatever it was, he was like that. There were standards he couldn't escape; obligations he had formed with himself that were more binding than moral theories ever were. He could argue moral theories away, but no argument would touch the obligations. They had nothing to do with arguments; perhaps they were even irrational. He didn't know and he hardly cared to know. They were a part of him, stern, inescapable.

In a way he envied the men who weren't bound as he was. They took their satisfaction where they found it and had no regrets. Life, he thought, was simpler for them. Oh well, what was the use of thinking about it? He was feeling low; that was all, or he wouldn't have been tempted. He couldn't leave Polly and take to a girl in the streets. He was a fool even to think he could.

When he switched on the lights in his apartment, its perfectly neat, somehow alien atmosphere struck him more forcibly than it ever had before. He sometimes wished that Maribelle's eye were less accurately geometrical. She saw to it that he had a place for everything and that everything was in its place. The magazines that had accumulated during his absence were laid on a table, one overlapping the next with perfect precision. The pillows on the davenport had been plumped and smoothed until they seemed cast out of metal, and each chair was in its appointed spot. Everything was ordered, dustless, impersonal. For four full years Maribelle had taken care of that apartment, and day after day she carefully erased any evidence he might have left of his own personality. With becoming modesty she never left any evidence of her own; yet, though he had never seen her, he felt that he knew her well.

When Tommy had first rented the apartment, the janitor had come to him. He was a grinning black man, slovenly and amiable.

"I'm Charlie," he explained, "an' I takes care of the furnace. You got somebody to take care of this 'ere 'pahtment, Mr. Gray? Mebbe you takes care of it yo' own self."

"No," Tommy said. "No, I don't want to take care of it. Do you know of somebody? Do you want the job?"

"No, suh, I don' want no mo' jobs. I got all the job I wants, but my sistah Maribelle, she takes care of 'pahtments, Mr. Gray, an' she takes care of 'em good. An' she won't 'sturb you none, neither. She comes when you ain't heah."

Then and there Tommy engaged Maribelle sight unseen. Charlie told him to leave any messages on the ice-box, and the money too. "Maribelle's gennelmums allus leaves the money on the ice-box," Charlie said. "She gits it. You leaves pencil an' paper there, an' Maribelle writes effen she needs anythin'. She don' come Sundays an' holidays, Mr. Gray. Is that all right wif you?"

Tommy assured him that it was quite all right, that he liked to sleep late when he had a chance and preferred not to be disturbed. So it was arranged, and so Maribelle entered his life—a black jinnee who came from nowhere to disappear into the somewhere, absolutely efficient, totally invisible. The owner of the apartment house had long ago dismissed Charlie, and so the pad and pencil on the ice-box formed Tommy's only link with Maribelle. When he had left town for his vacation, he scribbled a note saying that he was going and that he would be back on a certain date. He had returned to find the apartment in its usual perfect order. His unpacking the night before had been hasty and incomplete. Now his suitcases had disappeared along with the dirty clothes he had left strewn over chairs. Once more the apartment looked like a hotel sitting-room just after an especially conscientious maid had finished her job.

Yet tonight the apartment, as it sometimes had in the past, reminded him of Freda. Somehow those pieces of furniture had carried with them from Albany some faint memory of her. More than once he had wished that he had been less economical and had sold every chair, table, and bed that she had bought; but he had been guided by the spirit of his frugal New England ancestors and refused to take a needless loss. The furniture was good, he had argued; so why sell it and then buy more just like it? Besides, it suited his taste. Freda hadn't bought so much as a doily without consulting him. And how she had worked to furnish those four rooms! Timid, inexperienced, unsure, she had visited every model room she could find in Albany and New York. Even then, she had turned to Tommy for guidance and reassurance. In the end, she had done well. Every one had thought the apartment charming.

Well, thought Tommy, throwing his hat and topcoat on the davenport, *this* apartment wasn't charming. Polly's two rooms were half the size of his, her furniture had cost half as much; yet she had made a lovely home, while the best he and Maribelle together could do was to make an offensively well-balanced emptiness. Even Freda, scared as she was, had done better. She'd had a way with flowers, and, then, she was so exquisitely decorative herself.

The rooms seemed hollow with silence. He switched on the radio. A torch singer was howling like a lonesome coyote. Hastily he turned the dial. Ah, that was better. Brahms. . . . Good orchestra too. "Now," he decided, "what I need is a drink. Then maybe I'll relax and get some sense. I've been acting like a fool kid."

He went to the kitchen. Habit led him to look at the pad on the ice-box. Good! Maribelle had had something to say. He ripped off the top sheet and read:

"Dere Mr. Gray, you sure come back dirty. Them kakee pance stink awful, you must of set in sumthing rotten or sumthing. I called yore laundrey and gave the man everything cause I nowed you dident want them stinkin things round here, I bawt soap, 50 cents. You needed it bad. Verey truley, Maribelle."

Tommy chuckled. Maribelle's spelling and her respect for punctuation always amused him, and he suspected that her humor wasn't always as unintentional as it might seem. He placed a half-dollar in a glass that always stood by the pad as a money-holder, picked up the pencil, thought a moment, and then wrote: "Dear Maribelle: Here's the money. Thanks for taking care of the laundry. The smell came from honest sweat. I'm going to invite three friends in for an evening next week. We'll want sandwiches. If I ask them for Monday, can you take care of things for me? T. Gray."

The question was merely a formality. Maribelle was a true jinnee; she needed no warning, no time. A scribbled request always brought something better than he had hoped for. There would be sandwiches in the kitchen Monday evening—delicious sandwiches covered with a slightly dampened cloth. There would be beer in the ice-box, napkins laid out—a siphon of soda water, and probably a note; but there wouldn't be a crumb visible to indicate that Maribelle had labored in the kitchen.

Tommy prepared his drink, returned with it to the living-room, and slumped into a chair. He was really fond of Maribelle. He had tried to be kind to her, and she had returned kindness with kindness and humor. Once he left a note asking her if she knew any one who could use a couple of suits he was ready to discard. "I've got a husband skinney from settin," she wrote in reply. "He needs new pance bad." From that time on Tommy's old clothes went to Maribelle, the Christmas ties, the extra boxes of candy. He paid her what she asked, no more, but at Christmas his present was generous. He hoped Maribelle understood that he gave it out of liking and not for services rendered.

The Brahms symphony ended. What was that the announcer was saying? Ravel's Bolero? He scrambled out of his chair and reached for the dial. God, he couldn't stand that tonight—anything but that. He turned the dial experimentally. Jazz. No, not that either. "We are conquering this depression—" No, and not the depression or talk about anything. Ah, here was something—chamber music. Just right. . . .

He returned to his chair, sipped his liquor, and tried to relax. Strange, he had always been glad to get back to the apartment before, especially after a busy day. There was something comforting about being alone. He always felt as if he were collecting his personality to him again, reassembling himself, slipping back into himself. But now he felt caged. The doors were no longer protecting him from problems and people; they were shutting him off, barring him in, isolating him. They made everything and every one, like Maribelle, seem doubtful, not quite real.

Oh well, he told himself, this was just a mood. He'd been through a tremendous day, been lifted clean out of himself—and then Polly had dropped a brick on his head. It was foolish, though, to be so depressed about her. It would be different if they were in love, but they weren't, never had been, and it was too late now even to pretend. Just the same, he was going to miss her terribly. There was no denying it; he would. You didn't find some one like Polly every day—not with her brains and her humor. Lord, what good times they'd had! He'd liked pictures long before he knew her, but her passion for them had intensified his liking into a passion equal to hers. The hours they had spent in the galleries, in the Metropolitan! And how they had fought about Cézanne. That really had been a noble fight. Strange, how long it had taken him to see what she had seen all along. Well, she had been really pig-headed about Sibelius. She could understand Finlandia, but that was all. That kind of music didn't move her, though he had explained and explained, played and played. But she really did care about music, really understood most of it. She could have a grand time at a concert and a grand time at a hockey game. She was all around. And the nights . . .

"Oh, damn!" he cried aloud, jumping to his feet. "Damn!" There was no use trying to fool himself. He was going to have the devil's own time trying to get along without Polly. He *needed* her! He needed a woman, her kind of woman. He couldn't be happy with this girl, that girl, and the other girl. He wasn't made that way. He'd tried it often enough, the Lord knew. Each time he'd think— He snapped off the thought in disgust. He had fooled himself too many times not to know that he might fool himself again, but he had no desire to contemplate his own weakness. There was no girl there to tempt; there was nothing but the thought of Polly. And at that moment he wanted her as he had never wanted her before.

He wanted Polly Beeman, no one else—and somebody named John Bruce was going to have her because he said he loved her. He could have said he loved her, too. Damn it, he did love her. Of course, he loved her. Did she think that John Bruce loved her more than he did just because he said, "Marry me"? As if something the city clerk said or maybe some minister or other would make her Bruce's wife any more than she had been his. He could say, "Marry me," too. Why not? He'd never find another woman like Polly. Never!

He bumped into the davenport in his rush toward the telephone. His finger touched the dial when he noticed that he had brushed a cushion off the davenport to the floor. He stared at it. Freda had made the cover for the cushion. He could see her making it, her fair head bent over the green tapestry. The memory made him dizzy. He had tried to take the tapestry out of her hands so that he might kiss her. There had been a little struggle, laughter, and then she had dropped the tapestry and turned to him.

Slowly he lifted his finger from the dial. "No," he whispered. "No, I couldn't—not even with Polly." He dropped to the davenport and held his head in his hands. Freda . . . Could he never forget her? . . .

II

The night was bad and the return to the office the next morning almost worse. Yesterday's excitement was all gone; the business moved on. It was like the fifth of July, he thought, when he was a youngster; the quiet was downright

audible. There was almost a weakness in the let-down, almost sadness in the anticlimax of just living. The roses,
more than full-blown now, reminded him of the exploded
firecrackers that had littered the walks, and they reminded
him too strongly of yesterday. They weren't quite gone. He
called the office boy and told him to put them in the reception-room. Then he opened the windows. He wanted the
office and his memory washed clean. He turned toward his
desk and thought wryly, "Now that I've got rid of the
flowers, maybe I can bury the corpse."

As the day wore on, his depression lightened. There were
a hundred threads to pick up, old problems that still needed
solving, new ones to be considered. He went to lunch with
Frederick Winchester and discussed business, to dinner and
later to a prizefight with Teddy. It was late when he returned to his apartment. He tried to read, but soon threw
the book aside in disgust with his own inattention. He felt
restless and irritable—and most irritable with his restless-
ness. "I'm foolish," he told himself sternly. "I can't expect
to rearrange my life in a day. What I need is sleep."

He did need sleep, but he got far less than he needed.
Thoughts whirled around in the darkness, futile, fantastic
thoughts that refused to order themselves into ideas. And
through all the broken fantasies one thought darted back
and forth, back and forth, appearing, disappearing, reap-
pearing: "I'm just where I was four years ago. I'm just where
I was four years ago. I've got my name on a door and some
more money; that's all. I'm just where I was four years ago."

He felt better the next morning, however, and a busy
day at the office cleared his mind of worry. Squash with
Fred Homans in the afternoon, dinner at the Harvard Club,
a movie with some one he met there, kept him occupied and
in good spirits.

"That's the idea," he thought on his way home. "Keep
busy. There's no sense sitting around mooning and feeling
sorry for myself. I've got my work and my friends. There's

no need to be lonely. If I give myself plenty of exercise and half a chance, I'll be settled in a routine before I know it." But the instant he closed the apartment door behind him, the bleak feeling of aloneness returned.

In the weeks that followed, though he worked and played hard, it always returned. He could fill his days and evenings with work, exercise, and pleasure, but he could hardly endure the loneliness that descended on him once he had left his companions. At first he had attributed his mood entirely to the loss of Polly, but the arrival of the announcement of her marriage proved to him that the cause went deeper. When he was opening the thick envelopes, Polly had not been in his mind. Thick envelopes were a commonplace in his life. They came from fraternity brothers, college friends, people he met in clubs and in homes. He had read the announcement from Polly without at first taking in its import; then as the finality of the message reached his consciousness, the curious, unexpected emotion that he was experiencing held him rigid. "Why, I'm glad," he whispered in amazement; "I'm just glad." And he was—glad that Polly had had the courage and the wisdom to take what she wanted.

Why, then, was he so wretched, so lonely? He had little sympathy for neurasthenic people and none at all for his own neurasthenia—if that was what it was. He didn't know; but whatever it was, it came from a weakness in him; of that he felt sure. A healthy-minded man didn't have to have every moment occupied with work or pleasure; he didn't have to spend every waking moment in association with people. And the kind of introspection he was indulging in was probably unhealthy; at any rate, it was certainly juvenile.

Of course, he was forced to confess, he had suffered like this before. The experience was nothing new. He had known nothing but loneliness for two years and a half, and at that time he hadn't expected to know anything else ever again;

but he'd been so numb with pain then, so confused, that he had hardly cared. Then he had met Polly, and before he had realized it, the loneliness had gone.

He wasn't numb now, though—and he did care. Before, there had been an understandable reason—Freda. All his life he had looked forward with joyous eagerness until he came to New York and left Freda behind. Dreaming, planning, hoping had ended with her, and only hard work had given any significance to his first years in New York. But he couldn't place the blame on Freda now, not after a year and a half of contentment with Polly.

Did he merely need a woman? Offended, he rejected the idea instantly. He wasn't that much a slave to his body, and he wasn't so shallow either that the satisfaction of an appetite alone could make life significant. He couldn't ignore the appetite; it was too strong, too persistent, but he refused to believe that it alone was controlling his life. After all, Polly had been more than a body to him, a thousand times more. There were plenty of women to be had if that was all that was troubling him, but he made no move to try a cure in which he had no faith.

He knew well enough what Polly had meant to him, but he disliked to put his knowledge into words. The fact was complimentary neither to him nor to Polly; it made him meaningless and made her into something far less than she was in her own right. He could not progress in his thinking, however, until he put the fact into words, and so at last, unwilling and resentful, he formed them in his mind: "Polly was just an escape for me; that's all. If I'd been in love with her, she wouldn't have served her purpose. As it was, she quieted me and kept me from thinking about Freda and myself. As long as I had her I didn't have to plan. I used her as a kind of narcotic, as an excuse for living." He thought that over. "An excuse for living?" No; that wasn't it. As an excuse for *not* living; that's what he had used her for. He had held her like a shield between him and life.

Then he paused. Life? Living? What did he mean by living, anyway? What did any one mean by living? Most people did just what he did—worked and played, slept and ate. They earned money and spent it, saved it, lost it, worried, worked, earned more and spent it. Yet most of them seemed to think they were going somewhere; most of them were terribly earnest about living, and most of them thought they were living. They were always saying, "I'm going to—" and went doggedly or gaily, sometimes efficiently, sometimes clumsily, about doing it. Well, he had worked hard and he had got the partnership as a result. What now?

It had been a long time since he had thought, "I'm going to do—" well, anything. He hadn't thought when he returned to be alone in his apartment; he hadn't planned or dreamed. No, he had merely relaxed and rested. His contentment with Polly had been a false mortar that seemed to connect the bricks of experience that he called his life; actually, of course, it hadn't really been anything but an escape from a purpose, an evasion.

He tried to look at himself honestly, and the longer he looked, the less sympathy he had with his loneliness and despair. "I've got more than most people," he admitted to himself. "Why, I've got economic security. I've always had it. That alone would be enough for millions of people these days. They would think they were in heaven if they had that, and probably they'd be right, too. Well, I've got it. I've got health and strength. That's more than most people have, too. I can enjoy games, and plenty of people can't. I know enough about pictures and music to enjoy them, about books and shows. I have more friends than most, too, and lots of them are interesting. What's more, I'm not bothered by bores. I can always get away from them. I belong to clubs; I have more invitations than I can accept. What more does anybody want?"

He didn't know. There was no justification that he could find for his loneliness, and he had no respect for morbidity.

To him it seemed unhealthy at best, and he suspected that it was the result of timidity and weakness.

He read an article in a magazine that asserted that the blues were invariably due to a physical disorder, and so, feeling rather ashamed of himself, he went to a specialist for an examination. It was lengthy, complete. When it was at last over, the doctor said, "Mr. Gray, you come close to being the healthiest specimen I have ever examined. For a professional man, you are in amazingly fine condition. I suspect that you could run a mile in good time right now. Why, your body is a good five years younger than you are. I mean that I should think you were twenty-four or five if you hadn't told me you were twenty-nine. What was worrying you, anyhow?"

Tommy flushed with embarrassment. "The blues," he confessed. "I felt all right physically, but I read somewhere that a really healthy man doesn't get morbid. I thought I'd take a chance."

The doctor looked at him keenly. "I'm not a psychiatrist, Mr. Gray, but I am a diagnostician and I know that a sick mind can live in a healthy body. Your body is healthy. If you are morbid, you probably know the reason and refuse to admit it to yourself. I don't hold very much with most psychiatric theory, but I do agree that you can't remove the cause without discovering it. Maybe you need some one to help you find it, but you look to me like the kind of man who can find it for himself."

For a moment Tommy thought of confiding in the doctor, though exactly what he had to confide he did not know. Besides, it was his instinct to keep his troubles to himself. Later he thought of that momentary impulse and smiled. Suppose he had said, "Doctor, as near as I can make out, I have pretty nearly everything in the world to make me happy; but most of the time I'm lonely and blue and despondent." Why, the man would have thought he was crazy—and with good reason too.

Or maybe he would have just thought he was a cry-baby, that's all. "Probably," thought Tommy, "that's just what I am—but I wonder if there aren't perhaps a lot of cry-babies like me keeping a stiff upper lip in public and feeling all lost and aimless. Maybe not, though. Probably those people know what's wrong. . . ."

# CHAPTER III

## I

TOMMY liked Mrs. Wallace. She was one client he enjoyed entertaining, and he felt that she had enjoyed the evening with him. But, then, Mrs. Wallace had a gift for pleasure, a zest that he envied. In spite of her sixty years and her widowhood she went gaily into new countries, new experiences, and found something delightful or interesting wherever she went. She and Tommy had seen a good show and then gone to the Waldorf for supper. Now she glanced at her wrist-watch.

"I really must go to my room, Mr. Gray," she said. "I've had a grand time, but at my age I have to rest if I'm going to have more grand times." She smiled at him. "You're really quite wonderful, you know. No one would think you were just doing a job. You've made me feel that you've enjoyed the evening too, and that has added a great deal to my pleasure."

Tommy leaned against the table and looked her in the eyes. "Mrs. Wallace," he said earnestly, "please believe I'm telling the truth. I *have* enjoyed the evening, every minute of it. Of course, entertaining clients is a job sometimes, but sometimes it isn't. You are always good fun, and I should enjoy an evening with you if neither of us had ever heard of our firm." He noticed the waiter, signaled, asked for the check and laid down the necessary money. "I know how you must feel," he went on when the waiter had departed, "and I suppose you think I feel like a gigolo. Well, I don't. I didn't have to be with you this evening. When I saw you with Mr. Jonathon, I suggested this party to him myself."

"Really!" she exclaimed. "Oh, how nice of you to tell me
that. Honestly, I don't know when I've been so pleased.
I'll be back from San Diego in May. Will you be my guest
then?"

"Indeed I will." He paused to collect the change the
waiter had placed beside him. "But I know you're tired.
Shall we go?"

As they made their way through the tables, a bright head
caught Tommy's attention. He had seen hair like that only
once before in all his life. It was pale gold, as silky and alive
as a child's hair, and it curled softly at the nape of the
woman's neck. He stared. The woman turned.

"Tommy!" she cried.

For the moment he forgot Mrs. Wallace entirely; the
woman held his complete attention. He felt frozen, incapable of thought or movement. The woman, too, was obviously disturbed, but her poise was better than his; she re-
covered quickly and held out her hand.

Almost automatically, Tommy took it and bowed.

There were six people at the table. She presented all of
them, but after the first, Tommy heard not a single name.
She had said, "My husband, Morton Ballard." Morton Ballard her husband? But—but he couldn't be. It didn't make
sense. Why, she was— He acknowledged the introductions
mechanically and then said, "I'm sorry but my guest is
waiting. You'll forgive me?" bowed again, and hurried after
Mrs. Wallace.

"I'm sorry," he apologized when he found her, "but I was
stopped by an—an acquaintance."

"It's quite all right. It's too bad you left them so quickly.
After all, I only have to go to the elevators. How beautiful
that girl is! I don't think I've ever seen any one so beautiful. Do you mind telling me who she is?"

"Mrs. Morton Ballard."

"So that's the girl he married! I remember there was talk
when it happened. She came from upstate somewhere, I

believe, but I can't remember what the talk was. Oh, now I know. It wasn't anything against the girl. It was just that everybody was astonished when Morton Ballard married somebody outside of the Social Register. She looks like a child. He must be a great deal older than she is."

Ballard hadn't looked old to Tommy, not much over thirty, but his mind wasn't really functioning, and, besides, he didn't care anything about comparing ages. "He's been married before, hasn't he?" he asked because something had to be said.

"Yes, eight or nine years ago. His first wife was a Van Orsten. She was a cold, haughty girl. I knew her a little. They never got along, I believe. They were divorced in a year or two and she married an Italian prince. Well, his new wife is lovely, lovely. Have you known her long?"

"Yes," said Tommy; "yes, for a long time." They had reached the elevators. "Goodnight, Mrs. Wallace. I hope you have a pleasant winter in San Diego, and I'm grateful for a delightful evening. Please believe I mean that."

"I do believe it." She held out her hand. "And I'm so glad to believe it. Thank you, Mr. Gray."

Tommy took a taxi home. He wanted quiet to think, and he wanted it as quickly as he could get it. Mrs. Morton Ballard? How in the world? And why hadn't he heard? Of course, he'd seen mention of Ballard's marriage in the papers, but Ballard hadn't meant anything to him and so he hadn't read the stories. And where was Oliver Fleming? What had become of him? God, how beautiful she was! He'd never dreamed it would shake him like this to see her.

Once in his apartment, he undressed quickly and got into his pajamas and dressing-gown. He wanted physical freedom for his thoughts—freedom from formal thoughts, formal clothes, a stiff collar and a stiffer shirt.

Freda? Freda was Mrs. Morton Ballard! That was an ermine wrap hanging over the back of her chair—the jewels!

And how she'd carried it off! It was perfect. Not one word
of explanation, just "Mr. Gray." And she'd been just as
startled as he had, just as flabbergasted. Oliver or somebody
had certainly done a damn fine job of teaching her the
tricks.

But where was Oliver? He hadn't died; of that Tommy
felt sure. Oliver was rich enough to rate obituaries that
could hardly have escaped notice; besides, there were friends
in Albany who would have written. No, Oliver was certainly
alive. He was somewhere, and Freda was here in New York
—Mrs. Morton Ballard. How neatly it all worked out. Poor
as dirt, just poor, comfortable, rich, very rich. . . . One,
two, three, four . . . Just like that! But who would ever
have thought it of Freda?

He fell into a chair and lighted a cigarette. So she was
just a gold-digger! He'd never guessed that for a moment—
just a shrewd little climber on her way up. Well, she could
certainly climb; he'd say that for her. One, two, three, four.
. . . She'd hit the top. The Ballards had everything, the
right position uptown and down, in Newport and New
York, in Lennox and London. Imagine it! Little Freda Carlstrom from some hick village in Minnesota wearing the
Ballard jewels, swimming at Cannes, taking tea with the
Duchess of this and the Princess of that.

A revulsion shook him. The honest emotion he had
wasted, the tenderness, the pity—and the regret! All of it
on a climber. God, what a fool he had been, what a damn,
dumb, blind fool. She had seemed so soft and innocent and
genuine, so tender and brave, and all the time she was just
on her way up. Well, she had made it in three steps, but he
wished with fierce intensity that her first step hadn't been
on his heart.

## II

He had been out of law school only a year when he met
Freda. On his graduation he had been offered a position

with an excellent firm in Albany and accepted it. A few months later a new stenographer was engaged. Her name was Freda Carlstrom, and from the moment Tommy saw her he thought she was the loveliest girl in the world.

She was, he learned later, four inches over five feet; but she seemed smaller, there was something so exquisite about her, a manner so gently feminine, so delicate and fine. Her hair was braided and wound in a coronet around her head, but little silken tendrils broke away and curled softly at her temples. From the first Tommy hunted for similes and metaphors to describe her hair. Being no poet, the tropes he found were trite. He compared it to ripe wheat, but no wheat ever held that sheen. He thought of it as palest gold, but gold was metallic and hard, and Freda's hair was soft magic. Honey? Yes, but honey suggested something all wrong. No, there were no words to describe that hair; it was uniquely beautiful, uniquely her own.

Her features were small, prettily shaped, her eyes very blue with brown lashes. And she used neither rouge nor lipstick. It would have been a crime against all beauty, Tommy thought, to hide the rose pink of her cheeks or the deeper pink of her lips under cosmetics, and he admired the taste that made her refrain. Soon after he knew her he told her so, and she replied naively, "It isn't that. I know I look country this way, but I can't afford rouge." She couldn't afford to have her long braids bobbed, either. Bobbing meant haircuts, and she had to have stockings.

Tommy's capitulation was immediate and complete. Her beauty captured him; her directness and simplicity held him. She had been born, she said, in Minnesota. Her grandparents had been Swedish immigrants, farmers with no thought other than toil and no aspiration greater than ownership of their small farms. But her father had been a wanderer, going from place to place, changing from job to job, going everywhere and getting nowhere. When she was fourteen her mother had died, worn out with poverty and discouragement. She never talked much about what happened then. Evidently her father, never too reliable, had taken to drink. For no reason that she understood they came to Albany, and for no reason they stayed there. Sometimes her father worked; sometimes he didn't, but by some miracle of effort and economy she managed to graduate from high school.

That had been two years before. She had gone to work immediately as a waitress and found herself supporting her father. She was determined to escape into something better. She was never able to explain her determination; it seemed only a blind instinct. It was like her cleanliness, as much a part of her as her voice or eyes. Sometimes Tommy thought it was her yearning for cleanliness that had driven her forward, her need to live in surroundings as sweet and clean as she was herself. But for a year her father baffled her; then one night, more drunk even than usual, he fell under an automobile. His death was a release for Freda, and she never pretended that she thought it was anything else.

In the next year she worked as a waitress during the days and attended a secretarial school at night. She felt, she said, that she had reached heaven when she was accepted as a real stenographer in the firm for which Tommy worked. Well, said Tommy, if the offices were heaven, she had arrived where she belonged, because if ever there was an angel on earth, she was it. Freda had smiled and shaken her lovely head. No, she wasn't anything like that, but it was awfully good to get away from the steamy kitchen and the tough talk of the other waitresses, though they'd always been nice to her. And it was wonderful to work sitting down; her feet used to get awfully tired. And waitresses' feet always got ugly. Had he noticed that? Well, they did, and she hated to think of hers flattening out that way.

Tommy was wooing her long before he was consciously aware of being in love. Her humble ancestry, her work-worn mother and drink-sodden father never mattered to him. So far as he was concerned, Freda had no past existence before he met her. She merely *was* in all her adorable simplicity, her flowerlike beauty.

When he asked her to marry him, she at first refused. His surprise was complete, and there was no vanity in it. He had built a mansion of dreams around her, and it was so real to him that he could not believe that it wasn't real to her, too. It seemed as if she must have dreamed the same dreams.

"I couldn't," she said shyly. "Oh, I couldn't."

"But why not, Freda? Why not? Don't you love me at all?"

"It isn't that. I—I think— You're everything—I mean—" She stumbled hopelessly, the pink in her cheeks deepened to the warmest rose, and her eyes shone with tears. Finally she whispered, "You'd be ashamed of me."

"Ashamed of you!" Ashamed of her? Of the loveliest, sweetest girl the world had ever seen? How could she think such a thing? Whatever had made her think it?

"*Ashamed* of you?" he repeated. "Why, I'd be so proud of you I'd bust. Freda darling, haven't you any idea how lovely you are? Don't you know you're brave and beautiful and honest and fine? Well, you are. How could anybody be ashamed of you? What is there to be ashamed of?"

She met his incredulous stare unwaveringly. "I'm nobody," she explained softly. "My grandparents spoke funny English, all of them, and my mother did, too, sometimes. 'I bane,' you know. And Papa wasn't any good. We lived in awful places, and I don't know about nice people. I just know about waitresses and the men who ate in that restaurant, and you don't know how tough they were. Why,—"

"That's nonsense!" he broke in hotly. "You're a brave girl who's worked her way up, and I'm proud of you for doing it. Any halfway decent man would be. And what do we care about your grandmother? I don't want to marry her.

I want to marry you. And you know all about nice people because you're nice yourself, the nicest person I've ever met—lots the nicest."

She shook her head. "No, I don't know about being nice. I—I don't know about forks and things like that. Oh, I want to be nice. I do. I do. I want to more than anything in the world. I love nice things. You don't know how I love them." Her fingers caressed the sleeve of the silk blouse she was wearing, and she smiled shyly. "I love this. It isn't very nice, I guess, but it's the nicest one I ever had, and I love it. But you've always had nice things, you see, and you know nice people—lawyers and professors and people like that. I wouldn't know how to act, and I don't know about books and things. You'd be ashamed of me, and it'd be awful."

Tommy took her hands in his and pleaded with her. "Listen to me, sweetheart; please listen. The things you don't know about don't matter. Forks? We'll buy all the kinds of forks there are and use them every day until you pick up the right one without looking. We'll buy the right books and go to the right shows. I'll help you if you'll let me. You would let me, wouldn't you?"

"Would you?" she cried. "Oh, would you really?"

"Would I? *Would* I? Why, I'll be a regular schoolmarm. I'll be a walking book of etiquette, though I don't know so much about etiquette, at that. But I can pull off this kind of thing all right; you know, like this: 'Darling, a lady doesn't need to rise to greet a man, but I think it's nice of her to do it if the man is her guest—but she ought to rise always to greet an older woman.' How's that? Let's see . . . Oh, yes. 'She may offer her hand to a man or not, just as she wishes. When making an afternoon call, she leaves three cards—one for herself and two for her husband.' I remember my mother always used to do that and I thought it was cuckoo. There's nothing to learn but a few things like that —honestly, and you can learn them in a week."

She studied him earnestly and then asked again, "You'll really teach me?"

"I will, darling; I will."

"And you won't laugh at me when I make mistakes?"

"You won't make mistakes, and I'd cut my hand off before I'd laugh at you."

"And you'll try not to be ashamed? I don't think I'm very smart, you see, and maybe—"

But by then Tommy knew that he had won and he stopped her questions with kisses. They were married a month later as quietly and unobtrusively as possible and went to Lake George on their honeymoon. They came back to settle down in the four-room apartment that Freda furnished with such fear and care. Tommy was touched by her rapture. She seemed to have a deep, passionate love for every chair, picture, dish, and spoon in the apartment. And he was touched, too, by her childlike devotion to him. To her he was a god, as beautiful as Apollo, as wise as Jove. She came to him with her social problems and listened, frowning with concentration, to his explanations. She learned quickly, deferred to his taste in everything; and being both modest and beautiful, she won her way into his particular group so easily that she was suspicious of her success.

"They're just nice to me on account of you," she said in her frank, self-distrustful way.

"Nonsense, darling!" Tommy reassured her. "You ought to hear what they say about you to me. If one person has told me you're beautiful and sweet, twenty have. They all love you. Nobody could help loving you. And you know I do, don't you? You do know it, don't you?"

She had gone to his arms then, whispering, "Tommy, oh, Tommy. . . ."

A month of perfection passed and a second month. The problem of forks had been mastered along with other social niceties, and they progressed to books, music, and pictures.

Then there were some difficulties—not important ones, they seemed to Tommy, but difficulties. Patience was needed, he told himself repeatedly, patience, patience. He couldn't expect Freda to learn in a month or six months what had taken him twenty-five years. Besides, why shouldn't she like popular songs better than Schubert's? He liked popular songs himself sometimes; but he had been well educated in music, and her indifference to even the simpler classics baffled him. He was a good pianist, and he felt that he must bring some understanding of really beautiful music to her. Her singing voice was better than his, sweet and true, and he dreamed of accompanying her while she sang for their friends. He could see people admiring her, wondering at her beauty and gifts. It was a dream that could come true, that must come true. Freda sang whenever he asked her to and whatever he asked her to, but he felt that she sang without pleasure.

The pictures on the walls were his, and she believed they were good because he said they were. He took her to New York to the Metropolitan and walked her up and down corridors for hours while he lectured earnestly on Raphael and Leonardo, Constable and Gainsborough, Memling and Rubens. She trudged after him, listened intently, and said nothing. Finally he asked her what she thought of a Rembrandt.

"Should I like it?" she asked. "It seems awfully old and kind of dirty—not nice and clean like Maxfield Parrish's pictures. I love them."

Because he wanted her to be perfect, Tommy was irritated. But only for an instant. Understanding came before he gave any sign of his disappointment. He had no right to be superior. After all, every one had to pass through the Parrish stage. He had had three Maxfield Parrish prints in his room in college, and he had had them there because he had thought them beautiful. And lots of people turned up their noses at the prints just because they were popular. Freda might have a lot worse taste.

She read the books that he asked her to read, but he knew that she enjoyed few of them—and she didn't quite see why she should enjoy them. She was very careful of her speech, eternally wary of her grammar, but the books Tommy selected bored her. She couldn't understand why he found them enthralling or why he scorned the books she really enjoyed. She showed her confusion but made no effort to defend her taste. She took it for granted that it was bad.

Her very pliancy began to make Tommy afraid. If she had stood up to him and defended herself, he would have accepted her for what she was and made the best of it; but she had no faith in herself and absolute faith in him. He knew everything; she knew nothing. She was utterly humble and almost pathetically eager for him to make her into whatever he wanted her to be. He tried to be patient; he honestly thought he was patient, but after three months a strain came into their relationship that cast a shadow on the happiness that had been so marvelously bright.

Yet it had never occurred to Tommy that his marriage was anything but a success until Oliver Fleming came to him and said with surprising candor, "I want to talk to you about Freda."

Oliver was thirty, a bachelor, and an esthete. He made a fetish of fine and delicate living. Tall, slender, perfectly dressed, with his unusual refinement showing both in his face and his manner, he succeeded somehow in suggesting perfect culture without giving a hint of effeminacy or preciousness. He had inherited thirty thousand a year and saw no reason for adding to an income so ample, and so he pursued a number of artistic hobbies and found apparently complete satisfaction in them. Tommy had met Oliver soon after his arrival in Albany, and, although they were very different in temperament he enjoyed knowing him and felt that he had learned a great deal from him.

The request to talk about Freda came as a complete surprise. Oliver had been very kind to her, and she had accepted him with unexpected ease. Of all his acquaintances, Tommy had thought that Oliver would frighten her most.

"Freda?" Tommy asked. "Why, what about her?"

Oliver smoothed his gloves over his knee and then looked up. "I hate emotional messes. I've never been in one, and I've come to you because I don't want to get into one. Besides, I like to think of myself as an honorable man. I am going to tell you exactly what I think and how I feel. If you tell me my assumptions are wrong, I promise you that this conversation will be the end of the matter."

"Honestly," Tommy said, "I haven't an idea what you are talking about."

"I suppose not, but, you see, Tommy, I've been more or less outside of life always. I've kept myself apart. Probably for that reason I've taken more than normal interest in other people's lives. I've become, I believe, rather unusually sensitive to atmospheres. In the last few months I've felt a strain in your house. Every time I come I feel it more; I feel the strain in Freda." He held up his hand. "Wait, please. I know you are angered, but hear me out. I'm not intruding because I want to. You must know me well enough to understand that. Please listen . . . I've studied Freda for months now. I have thought about hardly anything else, and I've become convinced that you and she can never be happy together. It isn't your fault or hers. You've both tried, and Freda has tried too hard. Her spirit is breaking; she is acquiring a sense of inferiority that will eventually wreck her—wreck both of you. And I've come to you because I think I understand her—and, well, Tommy, because I love her."

Tommy boiled with astonishment, pain, and rage. He was only twenty-five years old and for a few months he had known happiness even beyond his dreams, and he still dreamed of capturing that happiness again. He felt no diminution in his love for Freda, and he had not been consciously aware of any in her love for him. They could still find rapture together, rapture that erased all the strain and made such things as books, pictures, and music seem of less than no significance.

Hot words rose to his lips, broke forth. He denied everything that Oliver Fleming had said, accused him of having made love to Freda, called him a liar and a false friend, and declared passionately that nothing in the world would make him give Freda up.

Oliver's pale skin flushed and his lips quivered. Long after, Tommy realized a little of how much Oliver had suffered during that interview, but at the moment he had no understanding of him and no pity for him. Tommy knew how to use his fists, and he had an aching, primitive desire to use them on Oliver, but it would have been like striking Freda. Oliver did not know how to fight and would not have fought even if he had known how. No emotion could strip him of his civilization, of his control.

He heard Tommy out and then said gently, "I'm sorry, Tommy—I give you my word, I'm sorry. But everything you say is wrong, and down in your heart you know it is. I admit you've tried, but you're temperamentally incapable of understanding Freda. You must know that you don't understand her. The child's miserable, filled with a sense of futility and failure. I told you I was in love with her. I am. But remember, Tommy, I haven't told Freda. If you say so, I'll take the next boat to Europe—but think it over before you say so." He got up. "Don't damn me, Tommy, until you've had time to calm down. Maybe some day you'll thank me."

Tommy took a long walk. He had to be by himself. He had to think. But he couldn't think. He could only feel and fear. Eventually he thought he was sufficiently in control of himself to face Freda. His hand trembled when he inserted the key in the lock of the apartment house door. He had no feeling of anger now; nothing remained but terror.

He looked at Freda and then looked away. Oliver had

opened his eyes, and in a single glance he saw too much. He saw Freda's weariness, the child-like contrition that seemed to envelop her. It was agony for him to speak, but he lacked the courage to delay speaking. And so, with his voice so husky and broken that his words were hardly intelligible, he asked her if she was happy. Her lips trembled and her blue eyes filled with tears. Tommy needed no other answer. He left the room.

Later they talked and he tried hard to persuade Freda that she had not failed. Six months, he said passionately, meant nothing; it was absurd to think that six months could mean anything. There were years before them, all their lives. How could she think she had failed when he had been so happy? If he had been harsh or impatient, he was sorry. Maybe he had asked too much. If he had, everything was his fault. Besides, he loved her. She knew he loved her, didn't she?

Sadly, she exonerated him of all guilt. He had been wonderful. The fault was all hers. She was stupid and common, and that was all there was to it. Tommy cried angry denials, but he could not touch her conviction that she wasn't fit for his kind of life.

Fearfully he asked her if she knew that Oliver was in love with her. Yes, she knew. He hadn't said anything, but she couldn't help knowing. Then because ignorance was more terrifying than any knowledge could be, he asked her if she loved Oliver. She didn't know—oh, she didn't know.

Tommy tried hard and in all honesty to show her that marriage with Oliver would be far harder for her than with him. Oliver, he said truthfully, cared a thousand times more for books and the arts than he did; Oliver was a thousand times more sensitive; his standards were a thousand times higher.

She admitted everything, but Tommy could not fail to see that she had some kind of faith in Oliver that he had failed to kindle. She seemed to feel that Oliver understood something essential—something that she could not put into words but which was basically, fundamentally important.

Tommy was beaten, but he didn't know it; for two weeks he struggled. He couldn't give up his happiness; he simply could not. Then one day it occurred to him that it had already been taken away from him, that there was no longer any question of losing it; it was already lost. Then he struggled no more. He permitted Oliver and Freda to make whatever arrangements they wished. Numb, unthinking, incapable of thought, he merely stood aside. Fortunately the offer from Winchester, Winchester, and Tucker came just in time to save him the embarrassment and humiliation of making explanations to his Albany acquaintances. He accepted the offer immediately. Freda remained in Albany until he was free to go to New York. That same day she left for Reno. Three months later he noticed in a New York paper that Mr. and Mrs. Oliver Fleming were sailing on the *Berengaria* for France. They were spending their honeymoon abroad.

That was the last Tommy had heard of Freda or from her until the accidental meeting in the Waldorf. Now she was wearing ermine, diamonds and sapphires; she was Mrs. Morton Ballard. Well, maybe she would stay Mrs. Morton Ballard; she could hardly aim higher.

The first few months following the separation had been blind, nerve-shattering agony. He had loved Freda so fiercely, tried so hard, that he could not believe that she *could* leave him. And he still didn't know why she had. Oliver? What was her faith in him? She had said she was too common; yet she had left a healthy animal like him to go to an esthete who approached every act with the critical care of an artist putting paint on canvas. Round and round his thoughts went in the same futile circles until loneliness and despair made all thoughts impossible. In losing Freda he had lost all his plans, all his dreams—everything but his hunger for her. That remained, ever present, never satisfied.

Until he met Polly Beeman he could find meaning in nothing but work; otherwise life had no zest for him, no sting. With Polly he had at last found a kind of peace, a rest from pain. Now Polly was in Cambridge married to another man, and Freda whom he had loved and for whom he had suffered had turned out to be nothing but an amazingly agile climber.

He shook with rage. For the first time in his life he truly experienced hate, felt loathing that made his gorge rise. He had worshiped that girl, trembled—literally trembled—at her touch, at her beauty and sweetness. She had seemed to him more angel than human. Angel? That was a good one! Well, Oliver had been right, though he'd never believed it before; he hadn't understood her. But, by God, neither had Oliver. What a shock *he* must have got. She was the lowest kind of low-class slut—but she had certainly taken two good men for a ride.

### III

Though at the time he did not in the least realize it, it was the meeting with Freda that made him turn when he saw Harriet Carrington on Madison Avenue the following Saturday afternoon. Usually he would have been glad that Harriet had not seen him and gone quickly on his way. He had seen her often in the days before he met Polly, and he had been willing enough to forget her.

She was a lawyer, well known to the profession and to the press. She was in the forefront of all movements for the advancement of women, and in the courtroom she showed a shrewdness and an implacable aggressiveness that had intimidated more than one male opponent. Her quiet sarcasm was famous, her cold, cutting contempt. Her skin was dark, her features sharp, her hips far too broad for her narrow shoulders, but she dressed so well that most people thought of her as a rather handsome and certainly as a distinguished-looking woman. Her age was a secret, but Tommy suspected that she would not again see thirty-five.

He turned. "Harriet," he said; "Harriet Carrington."

She glanced over her shoulder, stopped at once, and held out her hand. "Why, Tommy Gray. It's been literally years, I think. I supposed you had left the city."

Tommy knew perfectly what she was thinking and so he evaded neatly by saying, "Don't make me feel guilty, Harriet. I have a New England conscience, and I hate to have it disturbed. So let's just leave it alone, shall we? Tell me, how are you doing and how are you feeling?"

"Splendidly, thank you, to both questions. You look so well that I needn't ask. Instead, suppose I ask if I'm ever going to see you again?"

"There you go taking a jab at my conscience. I knew you would." Tommy grinned at her and received a pleased smile in return. "You're going to see me just as soon as you'll see me. I'm supposed to be one of a thousand or two at a shindig at the Ritz tonight, but I shan't be missed if I don't turn up. Want to break a date to have a date with me?"

"No. Or, rather, yes, but I can't. I've got to go to a meeting I can't avoid."

Ah, the old game was on, Tommy thought. One always had to play ring-around-the-rosy with Harriet. One always had to pretend that the game was new, that they had never played it before with each other. They would be just pleasant acquaintances who happened to meet, happened to make an engagement, happened to return to her apartment for drinks and conversation—and then, ah then! Then the flesh deceived them. After all these years, Tommy thought, Harriet ought to be a little suspicious of flesh so consistently unreliable, but her faith was so perfect that she never escaped the joy of seduction. If he even hinted that what would certainly happen might happen, she would be out-

raged. Her dignity must be protected with social subter-
fuge.

Therefore after a great deal of needless conversation it
was agreed that Tommy was to call for her at eleven o'clock.
They would go to a night club, see the midnight show, and
then, they both pretended to believe, they would call it a
pleasant evening.

The next afternoon Tommy sat in his own apartment
and damned himself for a fool. "Now, why," he asked, "did
I have to start something with Harriet? I knew what she
was like. I was well rid of her, and I knew I was; now I'll
have to get rid of her all over again."

Her coyness in love, he thought, was as sickening as her
mental dishonesty was unforgivable. Harriet Carrington the
lawyer was hard and keen and admirably realistic; Harriet
Carrington the woman was sentimental and deceptive and
unrelentingly selfish. She was so afraid that she might love
a man enough to lose her emotional independence that she
gave nothing. Yet she expected everything. And if he met
her an hour hence she would pretend that last night had
never happened. Once more they would be merely pleasant
acquaintances. Oh, to hell with women like her!

He knew well enough, however, that his feeling of disgust was more for himself than for Harriet. She would not
bother him. If he didn't want to see her again, he didn't
have to. And he was the one who had taken the lead, not
she. He had made the engagement with his eyes wide open.
He had known well enough what to expect. There had been
an opportunity and he had taken it. He had no one but
himself to blame.

Besides, he always felt depressed and self-condemnatory
after a casual affair. He wondered why. There wasn't any
reason that he shouldn't have casual affairs if he wanted
them. He hurt nobody. There was nobody to hurt. The last
thread that had tied him to Freda was severed now, and if
he'd thought he was hurting her by spending a night with

Harriet, he was fooling himself, that's all. She wouldn't give a small-sized damn what he did last night, tonight, or any other time. Nobody would give a small-sized damn. Then why in God's name did he feel so low?

It wasn't conscience; he felt sure of that. Conscience had nothing to do with it. His conscience, he told himself, didn't trouble him any more than Charlie Lovett's did him or Fred Homans' did him, and they played around with one girl after another. Yet he felt something close to shame, a kind of despair with himself. There had been no joy in his night with Harriet, only a kind of fierce feeding of an appetite that had been too long denied. With Polly there had been joy; with Freda there had been. But never with any other woman. Was he never to know that joy again? Must he always have this feeling of having broken faith with himself?

A sexual experience wasn't that important. It was absurd to say it was. Miserably he ran his hand through his hair and shook his head. It was to him; there was no denying it, it was to him. Maybe he lacked the pagan spirit, maybe he was an idealist; he didn't know. But he did know that he was so made that he could not take physical intimacy happily unless he shared something that might be called a spiritual intimacy with the woman too. He had to care for her, trust her deeply, and feel sure that she shared the trust. Once in marriage he had found it and once outside of marriage. Despairingly he wondered if he would ever find it again. If he failed he was doomed to more nights with Harriet or with women like her. There was no sense in fooling himself. This depressed mood, this hour of honesty with himself, would pass and once more he would find himself undone by his hunger—once more depressed, once more for an hour honest.

Suddenly, thought, control left him. He leaped to his feet and strode wildly up and down the room. Muttering the words, he cursed Freda; damned her with obscene epithets for what she had done to his life, done to him, made of him. He wasn't reasoning any longer, seeking explanations or evasions. The words came from his emotions, and his emotions had no need to seek for understanding; they knew.

IV

After the meeting in the Waldorf Tommy did his best to forget Freda, and in spite of the Harriet incident, which might well have made him dubious, he thought he was going to succeed. Loathing was likely to prove a lot better mental eraser than regret and longing had been. One instinctively put people one loathed out of mind.

He was busy with a client when an office boy entered and handed him an envelope. Tommy made the necessary apologies and opened it. The note was brief: "Dear Tommy, Please see me. It's important. Freda." He stared at her business college handwriting; felt his face burn, his heart pound; and tried hard for composure.

"If it's something important," said the client, "I'll go now." He glanced at his watch. "I really ought to go, anyway. When would you like to finish this?"

Tommy suggested a date, noted it on his calendar, shook hands, and watched the door close after the caller. Then as if shot upward by the spring of his taut nerves, he leaped to his feet and raced back and forth across the office with tight, quick steps. He couldn't see her! He wouldn't see her! What had made her come here? Couldn't she leave him alone? That was all he was asking: to be left alone, and it was little enough. Suddenly the tenseness left him and he felt weak and impotent. He walked to the window and stared down at the traffic. He didn't want to see Freda, but what could he do? What would he accomplish if he sent out word that he was too busy? Not a thing. He'd hurt her perhaps, but there wouldn't be much satisfaction in that. Besides, he had no desire to hurt her; he just wanted to forget that she'd ever lived. She was waiting in the reception-room. . . .

He turned, shrugging his shoulders. "Oh, hell," he thought, "what difference does it make, anyway?" He picked up his telephone. "Will you send Mrs. Ballard in, please?"

In the old days her beauty had always come to him as a surprise. If he merely walked out of the room where she was sitting and returned two minutes later, her beauty startled him. Now it was a shock. It had attained perfection. She was wearing a woolen suit that even to a man suggested Paris. So did her small hat, her purse. And there were sables on her shoulders.

She walked to his desk, but did not offer her hand. "I had to come," she said. "I had to explain."

Tommy's throat felt painfully constricted. There was a pulse beating that seemed to echo all through his body. He managed to motion to a chair. She looked at him, then sat down. He was glad to sink into his own chair and feel its firmness under him. "Yes?" he asked softly.

She bit her lips to keep them quiet. Tommy saw her hand tremble, and there was a quiver in her voice when she spoke. "I know I embarrassed you the other night," she began, "and I'm terribly sorry. I shouldn't have spoken; I know that, of course, but I was so surprised that I spoke without thinking."

Her nervousness gave him assurance, and sudden, new anger gave him poise. "I understood that," he said with cold politeness. "There is no need for an apology."

She placed her purse on the desk, rested her hand on it, and studied him. She was, he knew, only twenty-five, and she looked hardly older than she had when he first knew her; but she had changed. The timidity had gone. She was nervous now, but it was the situation that upset her, not the old lack of faith in herself.

"I don't blame you for speaking that way," she said at last. "I expected you to, and I know what you think. I couldn't let you think it. I can't. That's why I've come. I

don't care whether any one in the world understands but
you, but you've got to. I can never have a day's happiness
until I know you understand." The hand on the purse
trembled, and her blue eyes grew bright with tears. "You'll
let me explain, won't you, Tommy?"

Her emotion angered him further. He didn't believe in
it—not after her poise in the Waldorf. Once upon a time
—yes, but not now. She was putting on some kind of act.

His anger showed in his eyes, in the soft intensity of his
voice. "I don't know what you can have to explain to me.
The explanations were over long ago. If you want my congratulations you have them."

"Tommy, please!" Her voice broke and her hand moved
toward him imploringly. "Oh, please. Please give me a
chance. Be kind—please be kind. You were always kind. You
don't know how important this is to me."

Tommy looked at her long with his anger and contempt
clear in his eyes. "I don't know whether I can be kind or
not, Freda," he said, measuring his words. "When I saw
you with your new husband, I'm afraid I lost my kindly
feelings."

"I knew you had! I knew it! That's why you must listen."
She leaned forward and spoke rapidly as if she feared he
would leave her before she said what she must say. "I know
what you think, what anybody would think. Oh, listen,
Tommy! I'm not what you think I am. I'm not bad. I'm
not! You wanted me to be something I just couldn't be
when—when we—when we were married; you kept pretending I was something I wasn't. I tried to be it for you. You
don't know how hard I tried—and I'd have kept on trying
forever if you'd really wanted me to, but you didn't. You
know you didn't. You liked to look at me and—and sleep
with me, but that was all. You know it was. And you
wouldn't admit it, but down in your heart you thought I
was vulgar and common. You tried to hide it, but I could
see. I thought I was common too, but I couldn't bear to

have you think it. And I couldn't help loving all the beautiful things. You didn't know what they meant to me. You thought it was stupid to love things that way. You didn't understand; you didn't understand a bit. And you were jealous of them. You thought I loved the things more than I did you."

His face remained so stern that she dropped her hands into her lap with a movement of utter defeat. "You're not trying to understand!"

"Yes, I am," he said with careful control. "I'm trying, and I know there is some truth in what you say. I don't know how much, and I don't know why you bring it up now. But I'm willing to listen. I am listening. Go on."

She studied him fearfully, breathed deeply, and then continued. "I have to bring it up. You'll see why. You see, Tommy, things meant so much to me because I'd never had them. I never could believe I did have them. I still can't. And I didn't like the things you did. I tried and tried to, but I couldn't—and I knew you despised the things I liked. When I made myself into a stenographer, I felt proud; but you took all my pride away—and the kinder you were, the more ashamed I felt. Can you understand that?"

Tommy felt his sternness slipping from him, his anger, and he tried to cling to it. Without anger, he would be lost. It was his only defense, but he couldn't hate this beautiful girl whom he had once loved so tenderly. Besides, it hurt to learn that he had stolen her pride.

"I think I understand," he said, his voice rough with his emotion. "I'm trying. Go on."

Freda noted the change in him and spoke with more assurance. "Oliver understood all that. He explained it to me before I could explain it to myself. That's why I trusted him. And I wasn't afraid of hurting him. I knew I couldn't hurt him, and I'd hurt you terribly. That was the worst thing. I just couldn't go on hurting you. I didn't care for him like I did for you, and he knew it, but I was lost,

Tommy; I didn't know what to do—and he *did* understand.
He always understood. He understands everything. Sometimes I think he understands too much. But you don't know
what a comfort that was to me, and he was having a grand
time. That was a comfort too."

She smiled reminiscently and shook her head. "He was
more like a teacher than a husband, and it was the teaching
he enjoyed. He—he isn't very emotional. He took me to
Europe and we stayed there more than two years, and he
trained me. He said he was modeling perfection. Once he
told me a story about Pygmalion and Galatea. You know it?"

Tommy nodded.

"Well, that's the way he felt, I think; anyway, it's the
way he made me feel. Sometimes I really did feel almost
like a statue. But he was always kind and gentle and understanding. He even understood my liking for things, though
he said I liked the wrong things, and he tried to teach me
what the right ones were. He says I can give the right lip-
service now in the right spots every time, but it's only lip-
service. He tried for three years and in a way we were happy
—not really happy, you know, but he was doing something
he liked to do, and I loved going places and seeing things
and *having* lovely clothes and things like that. Besides, Oliver can be lots of fun.

"Then he got tired of it. He said he had failed, but that
he had enjoyed trying. Do you know what he said? He said,
'Freda, you'll always be a beautiful little Swede with common tastes, but I'm the only person in the world who'll ever
guess it!' And he said it was time I went back to the emotional life I was fit for. Morton was in love with me, and,
of course, Oliver knew it. He practically arranged our marriage—honestly! He said Morton was the one man in the
world to make me happy and that I was absolutely perfect
for Morton. Nobody is as pleased about the whole thing as
Oliver."

Tommy couldn't help smiling. Unknowingly, he was feeling a sense of release from his hatred of Freda. He had cherished the hatred, he thought, but he was letting it slip away unnoticed and uncared for.

"That sounds just like him," he said. "The whole thing sounds like him. I never could believe that he was capable of falling in love with anything more animate than a statue, and now you've explained everything." Suddenly he leaned forward and asked sharply, urgently, "Do you love Ballard?"

"Yes." The answer was quick and direct. "That's what I wanted to tell you. And he loves me—not the way Oliver did, the way you did, I mean. And, Tommy, I'm going to tell you something. I wouldn't say it to anybody else, but I must to you. Oliver knows, of course. Morton and I are just alike. He went to Groton and Harvard and had tutors and trips abroad, but underneath he's just like me. We're both from across the tracks." She laughed at Tommy's start of surprise. "Oh, yes, we are. We both know all the tricks and we show them off for people, but alone we're ourselves." She leaned forward, a little smile twitching at her lips. "Tommy, I'll tell you something that'll make you sick. You gave me cotton sheets and I thought they were wonderful. Oliver gave me linen sheets and I loved them so I thought I could eat them. But"—she paused and giggled like a child—"Morton gives me *satin* sheets!"

"Satin!" cried Tommy, all rural New England in his voice.

"Yes, satin," she repeated, openly delighted with the effect she had produced. "Satin, and he likes them just as much as I do. And he bought me a negligee with more lace and feathers on it than anything you ever saw, and I have mules with feathers on them too." Her cheeks grew pinker and her eyes seemed to grow bluer as she smiled. "Sometimes when nobody's around I put on an evening dress I've got. Oh, you would hate it. It hasn't any back and not much front, and it's satin too—pink satin. Then Morton puts all the family jewels on me—*all* of them, the diamonds and emeralds and sapphires and pearls, all of them at once. I just blaze. You would throw a fit if you could see me, and Oliver would faint. But nobody sees me. Just Morton and me; that's all. I'm just right for other people, but alone we're nice and common."

"And that's all he asks?" said Tommy wonderingly. "Isn't that being a model all over again—different from the kind Oliver wanted, but just a model, all the same?"

She shook her head in the old negative gesture that he remembered so well. She always seemed like a little girl when she moved her head with slow definiteness from side to side. "No. We're happy together. There's lots of things we like to do together. Besides, I run his house, remember, and entertain for him—and I know how to do it now, Tommy." She hesitated and then spoke with deep seriousness. "There's one thing that matters a lot to Morton, and that's the family. He wants children—and he's going to have them, all he wants. I'm—I'm—well, in six months now."

Tommy looked at her a long time without saying anything. She had turned his feeling toward her upside down so quickly that he found it difficult to put his new attitude into words. And another emotion clouded his mind, an emotion strong in its newness, stronger in its memories. The loveliest woman . . . He blinked his eyes, tried to bring his mind into control.

"Freda," he said at last, his voice deep and warm, "you did me a great kindness in coming. I know that you came for the sake of your pride, but you've done a lot for mine too. I'm too confused right now to explain; besides, it doesn't matter. All that matters is that you cleaned all the bitterness out of me. And I think I admire you more than I ever have. I'll have to think it out, but somehow I know right now that you've done the brave and honest thing every time. I'm glad you're happy. I'm surprised, awfully surprised, but—"

His telephone rang. "Yes?" he said.

It was Mae Vadney. "If you're free, Mr. Jonathon would like to see you in his office. It's rather important."

"Right away," he assured her and turned to Freda.

"I'm sorry," he explained, "but I have to turn into a business man again."

She stood up and held out her hand. "It was—oh, well, you know how I feel, I think. I told Morton I was coming and why. If we happen to meet, Tommy, can't we be friends?"

He pressed her hand and looked long into her eyes. "Freda," he said, "you can always, always count on one thing: we *are* friends."

## CHAPTER IV

THAT night Tommy did not find his apartment empty; it was filled with the company of his thoughts. Amazing Freda! And amazing Oliver! How easily he could imagine those two standing before *The Birth of Venus*. He could hear Oliver asking—oh, ever so gently, "Now, my dear, what do you find interesting in that picture?" And ten to one Freda answered, "The funny feet." Well, thought Tommy, they were funny feet, but Oliver would ignore them. Or, more likely, he said, "Keep them a secret, Freda; keep them a secret. When some one says Botticelli, you say line. His line is wonderful. Remember that—Botticelli's wonderful line." And probably Freda frowned in her earnest way and murmured over and over again, "Botticelli's wonderful line, Botticelli's wonderful line."

If Oliver had done his job as well as Tommy suspected he had, Freda responded to key words as automatically and accurately as an electrically controlled robot. But the chances were that she understood more and appreciated more than Oliver ever gave her credit for. Oliver's standards were fit only for Oliver, and that morning's interview had taught Tommy that Freda's mind was far from as simple as he had always believed it. He had never dreamed that she had a sense of humor, an understanding of the ridiculous. Why, she had fun in her, a world of fun. "Oliver and I just got her ready for Ballard, that's all," he thought grumblingly.

That dressing up business . . . Oliver went a whole lot too far if he made her think she really liked to dress like that and that mess of jewels. She always liked quiet clothes, and jewels didn't mean half as much to her as linen napkins and silk underwear. No, that dressing up was just a performance—a rebellion from too much Oliver. . . . He supposed Ballard was probably rebelling from an Oliver-like family. Or, what was even more likely, Oliver had put Ballard up to the whole business because he thought Freda would enjoy it. Well, she did enjoy it; so the reason didn't make any difference at all.

But what a story Freda's life made! It was really wonderful. Why, she had been brought up like a gypsy, dragged around by that drunken father of hers, but she'd wanted something, wanted it hard; and in spite of hell and high water, she'd got it. It seemed as if she had gone steadily toward it guided only by some kind of instinct like a cat finding its way home. Nothing had stopped her, not poverty, nor dirt, nor even hunger. He didn't believe she had ever known what she wanted; he doubted that even now she could formulate in words the yearning that had driven her ever forward, but she had had some kind of guiding star that she had followed straight to her goal.

Her life was polarized. Maybe that was the wrong way to put it, but he knew exactly what he meant. Her life had always been polarized; she didn't need ambition or religion or even acquisitiveness as a guide. She had instinctive direction, a subconscious purpose that led her on to the something that constituted happiness for her. He believed that she was really happy and that she would be happy. She had lost fear and found humor. Surely that indicated happiness if anything did.

And he was glad—completely, surprisingly glad. Oliver's careful training hadn't touched her sweetness; wealth hadn't affected her honesty. She was the old Freda—free at last. How lovely she was, lovelier than ever. He ran his fingers through his hair and twisted a little as memories rose to tease him. The loveliest thing in the world. . . . Even today there in the office, even while he was listening with all his might, even when he thought he hated her, he'd been conscious every minute of her loveliness. Why, she could take him like that—any time she wanted to. . . .

He slapped the arm of his chair. That kind of thinking wouldn't do. The first thing— No, he mustn't think that way. Forget that! Where was he, anyhow? He'd been getting somewhere, getting at something important—important to him . . . There'd been a word. . . . He must think about that, that word . . . What was it? The word that'd popped into his head about Freda? Magnetism? No—no, polarization. That was it; he'd thought of Freda's life as polarized.

And his wasn't. That was the trouble. Anyhow, it didn't seem polarized. He didn't know where he was going. It was something to make a man crawl, that talk with Freda. Here he was with a better mind than hers, a thousand times better background, a million times the opportunities—he'd had everything, and the best he could do was chase his tail in a crazy circle, while Freda went straight toward what she wanted. Seven years of college—four at Dartmouth and three at Harvard—hadn't even taught him what to want. Though he'd thought in those days that he knew, he'd be damned now if he could even remember what it was. He'd seen himself trailing clouds of glory, a kind of social and professional comet blazing across the American sky while the populace stared awe-struck up at him. At twenty he had seen life always as a movement, an ever going forward, an attainment of one shining goal that immediately became a stepping-stone to one more shining. And now?

The buzzer sounded. Startled, he looked around blankly, incapable for a moment of translating the sound into a fact. Then, as understanding came back to him, he picked up the receiver of the house telephone and said, "Yes?"

"It's Charlie Lovett," a voice explained, "and Craig. All right if we come up?"

"You bet. Glad to see you."

A few minutes later there was a knock at the door. He

opened it and said, "Come on in. I'll have the drinks ready in a minute."

Craig Sherman laughed. "You're clairvoyant, Tommy. How'd you know we were dry?"

Tommy took their topcoats and threw them over a chair. "How do I know you're breathing?" he retorted. "Pay day for you is three days off; you ring my bell. Q.E.D. A child of six would know."

"Well," said Charlie, "we always knew your power of logic made you what you are today." He followed Tommy into the kitchen and explained while Tommy collected the essentials for highballs. "We were over at the club bulling with a gang. Of course, we got on the depression, and, of course, it turned into the usual knock-down fight. Remember how Nat Warren was all for Roosevelt two years ago? Well, he's turned Communist and he won't give Roosevelt credit for anything. I said he'd have to admit it was damned good not to see breadlines any more, and, by jingo, I'd touched a match to a powder keg. He let go on economic planning and governmental control and the abolition of poverty and the distribution of wealth until I was plumb cock-eyed. I think the guy's got something on the ball all right, but he's so damned dogmatic you want to contradict everything he says. Here, let me carry the siphon."

They returned to the living-room, prepared their drinks, and relaxed comfortably into the big chairs.

"I know how you feel about Nat Warren," Tommy said. "He'd get anybody's back up, especially when we all know his old man's a banker. You can't help feeling he's dishing up caviar for Nat with his right hand while he holds out an idealistic tract in his left to the starving proletariat. I suppose you made a speech, Charlie."

Charlie grinned. "Not this time. Doc Chambers did the honors. He blew the bugle and waved the flag. He was all but singing the 'Star-Spangled Banner,' and Nat was all ready with the 'Internationale.' It was swell for an hour or two, but they got to yelling at each other; so Craig and I set out for a walk—and our noses knew. They brought us right to this damned good rye."

Craig Sherman sat up suddenly. He was a slender, nervous young man with curly black hair and snapping black eyes. Smaller than he liked to be, he was inclined to strut a little, moving his shoulders aggressively from side to side when he walked, and often stating his opinions so emphatically that he sounded defiant. At the moment, however, he was all male curiosity.

"Say," he began, "I've been wanting to ask you something. This morning I saw a girl go into your office—absolutely the —well, I don't seem to be able to produce the poetry; but, honestly, Tom, I've never seen anything like her. Laugh if you want to, but she reminded me of sunshine and daffodils. And class, too—worlds of it. Is she a client?"

"No," said Tommy. "She's just some one I know."

"Well, who is she? Don't be so damned secretive."

"She's Morton Ballard's wife."

"She is? I didn't know they were friends of yours."

"They're not."

"Mystery," said Craig, turning to Charlie Lovett. "Beautiful blonde visits office of Thomas Beamish Gray for reasons undisclosed. Not a client, not a friend. Mystery, say I."

Tommy had no great objection to telling Craig who his visitor was, but he knew that a full disclosure would be embarrassing, and so he temporized.

"I happened to bump into Mrs. Ballard the other night in the Waldorf and she thought she'd said the wrong thing at the wrong time; so she dropped in to explain. That's all there is to it," he said casually.

"Mysteriouser and mysteriouser," insisted Craig. "Casual acquaintances don't drop into an attorney's office to apologize for chance remarks. They send a note on crested notepaper. Come on, Tommy. Give us the low-down."

"Very well," said Tommy, his voice even and quiet.

"Mrs. Ballard is not exactly a casual acquaintance—and I didn't say she was. Hardly that. Five years ago she was my wife."

"Oh!" Craig lowered his glass. His eyes and mouth opened, and a hot flush colored his face. "I'm sorry—honest, old man—I swear," he stuttered.

Tommy smiled. "It's all right, Craig. Don't apologize. It was all natural enough, and I don't mind. You're wondering, I suppose, how I ever let anything so lovely get away from me. I was wondering the same thing when you buzzed. Well, it wasn't my fault or hers either; it was just one of those things. To tell you the truth, I've been thinking all evening about her—I don't mean romantically. I haven't been mooning or suffering regrets or anything like that. It's just that she's had a hard row to hoe, but in spite of everything she's managed to find meaning in life, real significance, and I was thinking about the way she had done it."

Craig's face had resumed its normal color and he was sipping his drink again. Feeling that his guest was probably at ease once more, Tommy slid away from the subject.

"That's something I've been thinking a lot about recently," he went on, "—the significance of life, I mean. I don't know whether that kind of thinking is juvenile or not, but I don't think it hurts a man to check up on himself once in a while—ask himself, I mean, if he's going where he meant to, and if he is, if it's the right place. Though that really isn't what I was getting at. Actually, I was wondering about the meaning of life itself. People obviously find different reasons for living. It's easy enough to see what the significance is for some people, what gives life real meaning for them. I think I know what it is for you, Craig."

"What?" Craig demanded. "I know, but what do you think?"

"I think you want to be a great trial lawyer, a composite Webster, Choate, and Untermyer. I don't think you like the work in our office, and I think that you're going to get out of it just as soon as you find an opening that will lead into a courtroom."

"Check," admitted Craig. "Handling the details of estates isn't my idea of the law. No, by God, I want some fight in my work—and when I get the fight, I'll feel plenty of significance, all right. What's significant for you, Charlie? You like mortgages."

Charlie rumpled his red hair, scratched his nose, and considered. "I don't know what you mean by significance," he said at last.

"Well, put it this way," Tommy said. "What gives your life continuity? All our lives are broken into bits of experiences. Well, Craig's are all pulled together by ambition, if you know what I mean. Lots of people's are. Some people find the continuity through a never-ending desire for wealth or power. You aren't like that; at least, I don't think you are. You take life pretty easily, but anybody can see it has meaning for you. We're wondering what it is. What gives it its meaning?"

"Oh, that! That's simple," said Charlie placidly, no longer needing to consider. "My religion does that."

Craig sat erect with a sudden jerk of his body. "Honest, Charlie," he said aggressively, "you gripe me every time you say anything like that. You're intelligent. You've got brains. You know something. You didn't make Phi Bete and the Law Review on nothing." He got up and strode to the table. "I've got to have another drink. It makes my gizzard dry to hear a man like you talk medieval mush."

"I don't know why you always get so worked up about it," Charlie remarked reasonably. "You don't have to eat the mush."

Craig squirted soda water angrily into his glass. "Hell, it makes me gag just the same. I don't have to eat kidneys, either, to get sick. The smell's enough. I wouldn't give a damn if I didn't respect your intelligence, but I do. Start you on any line of argument and you'll follow it no matter where it goes. You'll accept your conclusions no matter what they do to you. Except when they happen to touch your religion. Then you snap them off cold and stop thinking. I don't see how in hell you do it or why in hell you do it." He drank deeply and glowered at Charlie over the rim of his glass. "My God, Lovett," he added with angry bluntness, "you won't even argue with *me* about it."

Charlie waited for him to sit down again and then asked with the utmost good humor, "Why should I argue with you or anybody else? I'd be arguing with my happiness. I'm happy in the Church. Wouldn't I be a fool to talk myself out of it?"

"No!" Craig exploded the denial, and Tommy held up his hand.

"Shut up, Craig," he commanded, "and give Charlie a chance. You're going off half-cocked. I want to know why Charlie's religion makes him happy."

"I didn't say it made me happy," Charlie contradicted. "I said it gave meaning to my life—and if I left it, I wouldn't have happiness. I suppose it's like this, Tommy: the Church gives me all the answers. They were given to me when I was a child, and they're a part of me. I'm not full of doubts and fears like unbelievers; I know. Or, as we say, I have faith. I was taught to believe, and I do believe. That faith is always operating in me and guiding me. It gives me standards and direction. When—"

"Standards!" cried Craig, incapable of remaining silent longer. "Standards! Hooey! You Catholics make me sick. *You* make me sick. You think fornication's a sin, and I don't think it's a sin—but you've committed adultery from the Battery to the Bronx. You go around to some priest in a cage and say, 'Pretty please, Father, I'm sorry; I won't do it again,' and he gives you a little penance, and you do your little penance, and he says, 'My son, you're now as pure as the driven snow;' so you start whoring from scratch again. Standards, blah!"

Charlie laughed. "Ain't he eloquent?" he asked Tommy. "No, Craig, you're such a sanctified Joseph you can't understand. You're so pure that you can't get past fornication to religion. You miss all the essentials. You always do; that's why I shut you up. You're always wanting to talk about such non-essentials as holy relics, for instance. You're always wanting to know whether I believe Mark Twain really saw two complete skeletons of John the Baptist or not, and whether I think the barrels of nails from the true cross in Italy really were in the cross, and whether those footprints in the chapel of Quo Vadis were made in marble, or whatever it is, by Jesus Himself. Believe me, I'm sorry you ever saw Italy.

"Well, my pugnacious little atheistical friend, what do things like that matter? Do you honestly think my God hangs on the identity of a nail? Do you really believe that my faith would be touched, shaken the least bit, if every holy relic were proved a fake? You're an atheist because you can't get past mundane things like nails and blocks of marble."

He paused and his blue eyes grew dreamy. "No, no," he continued softly, "such things don't matter. Even priests don't matter. They're just the servants of God, and only God matters. And arguments about God don't matter either. If you have faith, if you believe in Him, He is—and when you know that, you've got the truth that sets you free."

"But how do you *know?*" Craig asked insistently, but more gently than Tommy would have believed possible.

The dreaminess in Charlie's eyes deepened and a little smile touched his lips. "I know," he said softly. "Oh, I know."

Craig threw up his hands. "Yes, like hell you know! You know the way the ancients knew the world was flat. You—"

But Tommy intervened. "Stop it, Craig," he said sharply. "I can't follow Charlie. I admit that, but you're acting like a jealous kid. Do you know that? You haven't Charlie's faith, and so you want to spoil it."

"I don't!" Craig denied hotly. "It's just that I'm fond of the bastard and I want to respect him. I'm rooming with him. I roomed with him in college and law school, and I've been trying to understand his damned religion ever since I've met him—and that's as far as I ever get." He whirled on Charlie. "Yeah, and you're always looking down your nose at me," he cried, his voice harsh with emotion. "You've got the crust to pity me."

"Yes," said Charlie, "in a way I suppose I do pity you. You're always so worked up. You're always banging your little head against the hard wall of your own ignorance and agnosticism. You've made a religion of ambition. You're trying to inflate yourself into your god because you can't find any other. You suffer with doubts because you haven't any faith. You try to answer eternal mysteries with scientific negations, and so you can't explain anything so you're satisfied. Of course I pity you. We've been friends a long time, and nobody likes to see his friends suffer. Listen, Craig: do you know why you call me a fornicator? Wait," he urged as Craig prepared to speak; "don't say anything yet. You know well enough it's one-tenth standards and nine-tenths envy. Well, all right; fornication's a dirty word, but I'll admit it if you want me to. And you say the priest makes me pure so I can fornicate again. It isn't as simple as that, old man, and you know it isn't. And just because I don't talk about it isn't any sign I haven't a consciousness of sin. But I don't suffer the way you do because I know where I can find peace."

"But how *can* you find peace that way?" wailed Craig. "I don't see how any intelligent man can find peace that way."

"By faith."

Craig snapped his fingers and opened his hand in a gesture of futility and defeat. "The same old circle! Can you see any sense in it, Tom?"

"Well," said Tommy thoughtfully, "it makes Charlie happy and so it's got all the sense in the world for him. You and I are different; that's all. I think I'm temperamentally incapable of that kind of faith, but," he added in a flash of sudden understanding, "I think you might make an awfully good Catholic, Craig."

Craig swore long and blasphemously while Charlie laughed. "I've told him that lots of times," he explained to Tommy, "and it always sets him off like this. Let's leave the poor guy alone. Are you going to Cambridge for the Dartmouth game?"

From then on the talk switched from one inconsequential subject to another. Tommy enjoyed the visit, but he wasn't sorry when Craig and Charlie left. He was interested in what Charlie had said. It blended so completely with his thoughts about Freda. In some incomprehensible way those two, so completely different, were attaining somewhat the same ends by means as utterly dissimilar as any one could conceive of. And Craig, too, was going to find that same end probably through another means—if he didn't suddenly surrender to the mysticism that he was fighting so bitterly.

"Well," he thought wearily, "it's bedtime—and none of it applies to me. I suppose it did six or seven years ago, but not now. It's awfully interesting, but I seem to be entirely outside all of it." Was he weaker, he wondered, than Craig and Charlie, shallower, or was he just a little more mature? After all, he was several years older than they were, and he had done a lot more living. Yet he envied them. He lifted his arms and yawned mightily. "I've lost Freda and I've never had God." What now? Then he saw his reflection in the mirror staring blindly at him, and he grinned at it. "Boy," he said, addressing his mirrored self, "you're turning adolescent again."

# CHAPTER V

## I

THE next day was a busy one, and Tommy's mind was fully occupied with legal matters until four o'clock. Finally the job on hand was done. He leaned back in his desk chair and stretched. "Phew, what a day!" Well, a few fast games of squash would take the kinks out of him and set him up again. The sooner Fred Homans phoned, the better. He was eager to get on the court.

The door opened softly and Mae Vadney's head appeared. "Busy?" she asked.

"Just done. Come on in. What's on your mind?"

"Oh, I just need a signature and you're the only partner left in the place." She came to his desk and laid a paper on it. "Just scribble Thomas B. Gray right here and I'll leave you in peace."

Tommy wrote his name and then looked up at her smilingly. "You see my faith in you, Miss—'scuse it, please—Mae. For all I know I'm signing away my fortune and my life."

"It's only—" she began, but Tommy interrupted with a laugh.

"What do I care? I'm tired, and I know it's all right if you say so. It must feel pretty good, Mae, to know that everybody in this office has perfect faith in you."

"Well, it does," she confessed. "I get pretty cross sometimes, and sometimes I hate all of you—or I like to think I do. Then I take it out on poor Mr. Jonathon. I tell him all men are too careless to live, but he just laughs at me. You are careless, though, every one of you."

"I suppose we are, but we wouldn't be if we didn't have

75

some one like you to depend on. You're terribly necessary. You know that, of course."

"Of course I know it! How do you suppose—?" She snapped off her question and eyed him shrewdly. "What's on your mind? I'm not going to let any conscienceless lawyer lead me into a trap; I've been around lawyers too long."

"There's no trap, Mae," he assured her. "It's just that you work terribly hard and we get all the credit—most of the money, too. I was just wondering if you thought it was worth while."

She looked toward the chair beside his desk and then shook her head. "No, I haven't time to sit down. Don't you suppose I've wondered about that a thousand times? I never saw the inside of a law school, but I know more about a lot of things than any man in this office—and I've got a better mind for details than the whole kit and caboodle of you put together. Of course, I know that. But—oh, well, I'm too busy most of the time to do much thinking, and I'm too tired, too. Anyway," she added, putting up her hands to the big knot of hair at the nape of her neck, "it's nice to be necessary." She pulled out a hairpin, reinserted it, pulled out another and poked around with it until she found the spot where it would do the most good. "I'm happier than most old maids."

Tommy wanted to ask her if she found the office a satisfactory substitute for husband and children, but he lacked the courage. Most of the time Mae did seem happy. She scolded everybody, but it was affectionate scolding. What was her life away from the office? He supposed Mr. Jonathon knew; probably Mr. Frederick did, too, but in the years he had known her it had never occurred to him before that she didn't cease to exist when she closed the office door behind her. Did she go to a little apartment somewhere and feel lonely the way he did? Or did she go to the movies and suffer raptures over a handsome shadow? There must be something in her life besides endless work.

"What are you thinking?" Mae demanded.

"I was thinking about you," he said carefully. "I was thinking that I've been letting an opportunity slip by me. You're pretty wonderful, you know, and it's just dawned on me— well, that I need a woman like you in my life. Will you have dinner with me some night?" He grinned up at her. "I mean will you let me dress up in my soup and fish and trail humbly after you into the Sert Room?"

Mae leaned forward and patted his cheek. "You're a darling. I'm not lonesome. I have a niece who lives with me."

"Who's talking about being lonesome? I'm the one who's lonesome. How about it?"

"You lonesome!" scoffed Mae. "You and your poker games and deb parties and a harem of girl friends. Lonesome, my eye! Spend your money on a pretty girl. You won't want to waste an evening on me. You get enough of me in the office."

"But I don't," Tommy insisted. "You stick your long nose in the door a couple of times a day and snarl at me, but we never get a chance to talk. Come on, Mae, be a sport and break bread with me. Honestly, I'll be grateful."

"Well, if I'm not getting a thrill!" cried Mae. "I half believe you mean it! Well, sir, I'll just take you up on that, and I warn you right now that I dote on guinea hen. When'll it be?"

They agreed on a date just as the telephone rang. It was Fred Homans calling. "I'm ready when you are," he said.

"O.K.," said Tommy. "I'll meet you at the club just as soon as I can get there."

II

That evening Tommy looked over his long list of engagements. He was overdoing it, he decided. He hadn't read a book since he had returned from his vacation, and there were at least a dozen new books that he wanted to read. And he was accepting invitations that he didn't really want to accept. Anything to avoid an evening alone.

That was no go. He was running away from himself, running away from the world; and he knew that there was something unthinking, almost frantic, about his meaningless efforts to escape something undefined and unnamed.

"If I keep this up," he thought irritably, "I'll be something a psychiatrist will find interesting." He read the *Times* conscientiously every morning, the *Sun* every evening, but he knew that he was reading them with the top of his mind. The world was simmering; dangerous little geysers were bursting forth, here, there, everywhere. Hitler pointed a menacing finger, and rumbles of defiance and fear followed. England was speaking sharply to Mussolini, and Mussolini was thumbing his nose at England. Spain was in a ferment. Something was going to happen there. Stalin was building airplanes by the thousands and training flyers apparently by the tens of thousands. England was frankly getting ready for rearmament, and France seemed to be already armed. Japan and China . . . Japan and Russia . . . Germany and Russia . . . Germany and Austria . . . Italy and Ethiopia . . . And money in every country about as stable as a ball of mercury on an oscillating board.

What did he think about it all? He hardly knew. Good luck and his father's foresight were bringing him safe through the depression, but no one was safe in a world so terrified, so downright hysterical. And if the worst was over, as it apparently was, there were still those millions lacking work—and those millions were listening to demagogues. Fire-eaters mounted soap boxes and screamed defiance of the government; Father Coughlin bellowed dubious economics into a microphone; book reviewers judged even romantic novels by economic standards equally dubious; brain trusters went to Washington, bided their little while, were busted and disappeared; Roosevelt smiled, something went wrong and somebody else took the rap, and Roosevelt leaned toward the radio, said, "My friends," and charmed unknown millions into believing in him by the sheer magic of his voice.

The bankers, now that their banks were safe once more in spite of them, were growing cocky again and demanding power as if they had it by divine right; the great industrialists no longer rushed to Washington and pleaded for remedies and aid. Once more the wheels were turning, and they wanted the power curbed that had started the wheels. Labor was beginning to stir. There was a strike here, a strike there. Would there be a surplus of goods? If there was, what would the government do about it? What should it do about surpluses? Should it do anything? Were depressions the result of economic cycles, or were they the result of man's stupidity and greed? Was economic planning a necessity? What about it? What did he think?

The truth was, he knew, that he had been refusing to think. He had not thought, really thought, since he had come to New York; instead, he had evaded thought as carefully and completely as he could. He had a deck of ideas from which he dealt whenever necessity required, but he had not shredded those ideas into their various strands, examined them, evaluated them. He owned, he thought, a logical mind, and he despised people who did not estimate their premises before they spoke; but his power of analysis was growing rusty from disuse. He found careful, disinterested thought a genuine effort.

Even the depression had touched his purse far more than it had his mind. During the worst days Mrs. Frederick Winchester had run a soup kitchen to which he had contributed heavily. He had given more to the Community Chest than his income warranted, and nine times out of ten he had succumbed to the pleas of beggars. And relatives whom he hardly knew popped up and asked for aid that he could not refuse. At the end of each year he found that he had spent every cent of his income and salary, most of it on others.

But the giving of money, he knew well enough, was something largely apart from himself. After all, he had been denied nothing that he really wanted, and so he did not have even the satisfaction of feeling generous. Whenever possible he had escaped the problems and ugliness and horror of the depression in work and pleasure—and he knew that Polly had been especially precious to him because she had made his escape almost complete. It was a tremendously interesting, fascinating, terrible world he was living in; but he was observing it rather than experiencing it. Most people, he suspected, either weren't aware of it or escaped from it whenever possible. To nine out of ten the great problems were significant only so long as their stomachs were empty. After a month of good feeding, most of them did more thinking about their desire for a new car than they did about anything else. He didn't even have a car to think about. He could buy one if he wanted it, but he didn't want one in New York City.

Well, that indifference and selfishness were to be expected of uneducated, stupid people. After all, possessions were about all most them got out of life, and the possessions were visible evidence of progress. To people like that a new car meant a lot; it was a symbol.

But he didn't believe he was that kind of person. He thought he was intelligent, and he certainly had been given the opportunities of an education. And the other men in the office had the interest he lacked. Mr. Jonathon and Mr. Frederick were conservative to their toes, but they had watched the rise and fall of the NRA with passionate absorption. To his surprise, they had found virtues in it, though from the first they had insisted that it was unconstitutional. Those men, both well into their sixties, were absorbed in the day-by-day changes in the state of the nation. They followed the discussions in Congress far more eagerly than most of the club lounge orators followed them. They were alive to the world; and being alive to it, they were an integral part of it.

So was Martin Tucker, though he looked so dry and academic. He was a bitter man, apparently cold and disillusioned, but somewhere in him a spark of hope still glowed. The Russian experiment fascinated him. "It's the most important human experiment," he said, "since the American constitution was written."

Teddy Winchester, only a few months out of the Columbia Law School, was full to bursting with Utopian ideas; Craig Sherman was sardonically contemptuous of every politician's good faith, but alive to their every move; and even good-natured Charlie Lovett would burst into a flame of excitement whenever Communism or Fascism was mentioned.

Tommy alone remained cold. He was interested, but unmoved. His mind stirred, but not his emotions. The others felt a part of the world they discussed so hotly, but he did not. Yet he once had. In college he had cared passionately about economic and governmental problems. He had been a red-hot liberal in those days, and he thought he was still a liberal—but all the fire of battle had died in him.

The things he had once cared about! How he had dreamed! If only he could care about anything now the way he had once cared about being a mile runner. His father had been a great track man, and he had dreamed about being one, too. He had abstained from cigarettes, liquor, and women for the sake of that dream. Nights he had lain in bed and run imaginary races—even when he was twenty years old he had done that. "Down on your marks, get set—" the crack of the pistol. They were off. That famous man from California had the pole. He held the meet record. Lord, what a pace he was setting! But, take your time, Gray; take your time. There're four laps and this is only the first; take your time. Relax. That's it. Remember what coach told you. Relax. There, a Princeton jersey was ahead now. Well, he wouldn't last. He never did. The first lap . . . Feeling fine. Legs felt good. Plenty of wind. The second lap. In fourth place now. The pace was fast, but not too fast. Stay where you are. Let the other fellows break the wind. The third lap. Beginning to feel it. Never mind; remember the others are feeling it too. The man ahead falls back. In third place now. All right. Just hold it. The pistol. The last lap. Stretch out. Stretch out. The California man breaks ahead, five yards, ten yards. A Harvard man holds two yards ahead of him. Somebody passes. Hold it. Hold it. They reach the curve and the other fellow falls back. Stretch out. Stretch out. Stretch. . . . I'm gaining. I'm— Everything now. Everything! And then the blinding, gasping, agonizing effort, forcing dead legs on, on, passing something, knowing that something was ahead, fighting toward it, fighting, fighting, fighting —falling into somebody's arms.

"You won! You won, Tommy! You beat him at the tape! You won!" Friends holding him up, pounding his back, hugging him. "You won!" And then the voice of the announcer: "The mile race. Won by Thomas Gray of Dartmouth." A pause while the Dartmouth cheering section roars applause. "In four minutes, seven and seven-tenths seconds, breaking the record."

Oh, how many, many times he had dreamed that dream— and he had never broken 4:23 in his life. Yet the dream, all the effort, even the failure itself had been worth while. Why, that dream and the vague possibility of its fulfilment had made him tingle. And all the lost ideals were worth while, too. Strange, it was hard to remember what they were, but they were all twisted around dreams of greatness that went beyond winning races. Sometimes in spring up in Hanover he had sneaked off for long walks by himself. He had avoided the Outing Club trails lest he meet somebody. He wanted no company but his thoughts. Trudging over the hills, he analyzed himself and his fellows. Some of them he admired, and some of them he rather despised; and in those days he had known so certainly just why this one was the right kind and that one the wrong. About many things he was confused, uncertain, but about his standards he was very sure.

Now he was no longer sure. It wasn't so much that he had broken faith with himself as that people did not fit so definitely into pigeon-holes as they had nine or ten years before. How neatly he would have classified Polly Beeman, and how wrong he would have been! In those days a professional politician was a crook to him, and he never could have understood that sometimes crooked politicians ran a government more efficiently than honest reformers did. Well, he still couldn't understand that to his complete satisfaction. He knew it was a fact, but to accept the fact as a working principle meant that he must lower his opinion of mankind rather more than he wanted to. Skepticism was all right; so, he supposed, was cynicism, but he was damned if he wanted to be a pessimist.

His telephone rang.

"Hello," he said.

"This is Fred—Fred Homans, Tommy. I'm getting up a crowd to go to Cambridge for the Dartmouth game. Want to go along?"

"Thanks, Fred, but I can't make it. But I'm on for the Yale game if the gang's going."

"Sure we are."

"Well, count me in. Six clients and two broken legs couldn't keep me away from a Yale game. You're always sure something's going to happen."

"Yeah," said Fred, who had gone to Princeton, "except that Dartmouth will win."

"We'll break that hoodoo someday, and that thirty-three to thirty-three game was worth a couple of hoodoos."

"I'll say it was. O.K., then; I'll fix it up. Squash tomorrow?"

"You bet. Thanks for calling."

The conversation had broken his mood. He was sorry because he felt in a confused way that he had been working toward some kind of decision. He had to do something. It was stupid to let his life slip by without reason or meaning to it. He wanted to *feel*. He wanted to work for something or somebody; he wanted to have ambition again.

What, he wondered, was ambition, anyway? How many people really had it once they had reached maturity? Not many, he was sure. Oh, well, it didn't make much difference so long as they wanted something hard—and someway, somehow, he was going to want something. He had to break through the emptiness and vague meaninglessness of his existence to significance. He'd be damned if he would go on sitting around mooning like a rattlebrained kid. He was a partner in a distinguished law firm; he was supposed to be grown up.

It was really preposterous that a man with his gift for pleasure should have his feeling of emptiness. Nobody had better times than he had, and most people with his capacity for pleasure and his opportunities for it would feel that they had attained happiness. Broadway was jammed with people who didn't seem to ask for anything more than a succession of good times.

But his pleasures were isolated. He did not look forward to them or back on them. He met them, enjoyed them—and then they ceased. One couldn't forever run from poker game to squash court, from concert hall to dinner party, from theater to ballroom, from country club to the Metropolitan. And one couldn't satisfy sexual hunger, either, with casual goodnight kisses with girls one didn't care about or with a night now and then with some one like Harriet Carrington, about whom he cared even less. Somehow, he had to get a fresh start, a new approach.

Thirsty, he went to the kitchen for a drink of water. Ah, a note from Maribelle. What was it now?

"Dere Mr. Gray," Maribelle had written, "you forgot to leve my munney and I needs it awful bad because my husband up and died on me and the undertaker man wont do no waiting at all. I knows you forgot but I needs it, the funneral cost a awful lot Mr. Gray but it was turribel swell and Augustus made a wunnerful korpis. He wore yore blue suit with the dubble brest, I bet you never thot it was agoing into a grave afore you did but you wooda been proud of it on Augustus honest, hopeing you are the same, Maribelle."

Tommy chuckled and then grew sober. Poor Maribelle. She was probably fond of her Augustus for all his "settin'."

He counted out the money he owed her and placed it in the glass on the ice-box; then, moved to generosity by pity, he added a five-dollar bill, picked up the pencil and wrote:

"Dear Maribelle: I'm sorry about the money, and I'm very sorry to learn about your loss. You must be very lonesome. The extra five dollars is to help you pay the undertaker. Please accept it with my sympathy."

Maribelle's note, he found, had cleared his mind, and before he went to bed he came to a decision: he would go to Hanover for a day or two. Next week-end? No, not a weekend at all. Either there would be crowds in town for a football game or most of the boys would be away for one. He wanted to be there when the college atmosphere was normal; he wanted to get back into it again. He wanted to step back nine years and take a look at himself. There was nothing that absolutely demanded his presence in the office for a couple of days. Yes, that was what he would do. He couldn't get any perspective in New York, and he hadn't been back to Dartmouth for eight years. The sudden, complete change of atmosphere ought to shake him out of himself, make it possible perhaps for him to break the circle of his thoughts and straighten it out into a line that pointed somewhere.

The next evening he went to the ice-box to leave a note for Maribelle to tell her that he was going out of town. A note from her was waiting for him.

"Dere Mr. Gray, I guess you no I wasent hinting for no munney and so ive taken the munney, you is the kinnest gennelmum I works for and I sure does thank you. No sir I aint lonesome none because my brudder Charlie that uster take care of yore furnus is living with me now and he sets jes as good as Augustus uster, I allus seems to have a settin man round, Maribelle."

# CHAPTER VI

## I

TOMMY'S first reaction to Hanover was altogether different from what he had anticipated. Even his reaction to White River Junction was unexpected. When he left the train there, the gritty bleakness of the railroad yards struck him as if he had never experienced it before. He knew, of course, that the station had always been dirty and ugly, but he had no memory of such shanty-like ugliness and grime. Why, the station seemed even smaller as well as dirtier. Surely, it must be. Then he remembered that there had been a fire, which, unfortunately, had been extinguished before it had completed its divinely appointed task.

The Junction actually depressed him, but almost immediately he remembered a story current at Dartmouth in his student days, and he smiled. The incident was supposed to have taken place before his time. Perhaps it was apocryphal, but it sounded real enough. It seemed that an English instructor decided to fill an hour by reading themes to his class that he had not previously read to himself. Suddenly, to the wild glee of the listening freshmen and to his own consternation, he heard himself reading a student's placid assertion that he had seen a certain professor, whom he named, in White River Junction in a "house of ill fame."

An hour later Hanover rang with the story, and the professor was alternating angry denials with insistent demands that the lying freshman be immediately dismissed from college. The freshman was utterly bewildered. He said he didn't know what all the excitement was about—and he hadn't lied.

He *had* seen the professor. But what of it? What was the matter with being in the station at the Junc?

Well, reflected Tommy, as he made his way across the tracks, the freshman had certainly used his words accurately enough even if he had been too innocent to understand what they connoted. At Dartmouth the Junc Station had furnished material for a thousand scathing quips, and the memory of the story made him eager to get to Hanover. It brought the college back to him with a rush. It reminded him how close-knit the college community was, what a unit it was—as different from New York with its scattered, constantly changing, constantly disintegrating groups as it was possible for a place to be. He hurried to the bus. It would be good to get there.

But at first it wasn't good. He suffered an immediate let-down. Several students were passing the Inn as he entered it. He knew none of them. His time had passed. He was a stranger.

Within an hour, however, he felt a lightening of his spirit. Boys were kicking a football on the campus; the clock in Dartmouth Hall struck four; somebody yelled to somebody else, "Come on and get a coke," and the other fellow yelled back, "Can't. I've got to go down to the gym"; students passed, students and students and students, some of them sober with thought, some of them laughing, all of them casually dressed, all of them young. The rains had held off and the hills still retained much of their incredible autumn brilliance. The air sparkled, coldly crisp. Somebody cried gleefully, "Was that exam a pipe? Boy!" He was back. This was Dartmouth.

Slowly he walked under the great elms. He hesitated before the administration building. The president was coming down the steps. Tommy half turned, then moved on. "He won't remember me," he thought regretfully.

"Oh, Gray!"

He turned. The president was smiling at him. "It is Tommy Gray, isn't it?"

Tommy glowed. This was wonderful. Imagine the Prex remembering him after all these years.

"Yes, sir," he said, grasping the proffered hand; "I'm Gray, but I didn't think you would know me."

"Of course I remember you," the president said, his brown eyes smiling. "Do you want to know why?"

Tommy grinned and shook his head. "No, I don't. I know what it is. You remember the day I fell across the track ten yards from the finish and three men piled on me. That's it, isn't it?"

"Well, yes—that and other things. How long are you going to be here?"

"I think I'll go back tomorrow. I've just come up for a day or two for a little visit. The place seems so familiar, but I miss the little white church. The new library is grand, of course, but I can't imagine Dartmouth without the little white church. I felt sick when it burned."

"We all did." The president held out his hand. "I'm sorry I have an engagement, and I mean that honestly. I should like to have a real talk with you, but I'm a little late now. Tonight I have to go to Boston, but the next time you come please look me up. I'll see to it that we have time for a talk."

Tommy thanked him, shook hands, and walked on feeling warm with gratitude and pleasure. He felt as if he had got his identity back. It was something to be remembered by the president of the college after all these years. The little mark he had made on the Dartmouth slate hadn't yet been quite erased. He turned, passed Sanborn House. Two men were standing by the steps. He remembered both of them well, though the smaller one hadn't worn that little imperial beard in his day.

The other man was taller, blue-eyed. He certainly hadn't changed much. His hair was white now, but it had been so fair that the whiteness didn't make him look older. Tommy had had a course with him. What was it? Chaucer? Yes—of course, that was it.

"Tommy Gray," the blue-eyed professor said, holding out his hand. "What are you doing up here? Somebody told me you were getting rich out of the law in New York."

Tommy flushed like an undergraduate. "Why, mostly I'm being terribly surprised. I didn't expect any one to know me."

"Why not?" asked the smaller man. "You haven't changed. Do you think I could read forty or fifty thousand words of yours and forget you?"

"I thought you could, but I'm awfully glad you haven't."

The professors were in no hurry. Nobody seemed to be in a hurry, and later Tommy knew that at least half of his initial depression had been due to the sudden slowing of the tempo of life, to the quiet, the serenity. The whole atmosphere had seemed unnatural. He had remembered college as an exciting experience; now he knew that the peaks of excitement had been well spaced and that the valleys between had been broad, filled with classes, study, sport, movies, and endless discussions. He strolled across the campus with the professors, caught a football that happened to come his way, threw it back to a smiling boy who shouted, "Thanks a lot." He left the professors at the bookstore, promised to call on them both in Sanborn House next day, and returned to the Inn.

He no longer wanted to walk. The nervous impulse that had made movement a necessity an hour before was gone. Now filled with contentment, he wanted to relax and savor it to the full. He found an empty chair on the Inn porch, lifted his heels to the porch railing, lighted a cigarette, and leaned back. Lord, it was good to be here!

He wasn't thinking. He didn't even want to think. In a little while the evening cold would drive him indoors, but the twilight haze made his college beautiful and he didn't want to miss a moment of it.

People passed: housewives going to or from the shops, students hurrying to a preposterously early dinner, professors on their way home or to a store, townspeople, and even tourists seeking the last glorious moments of a New England autumn. But Tommy paid no attention. Finally some one spoke.

"Pardon me. Aren't you Tommy Gray?"

A slender, rather unkempt-looking man was facing him. Tommy blinked. A vague thought had been drifting through his mind, and for a moment it clung. Then recognition came.

"Mr. Kingston!" he cried. In jumping to his feet and leaning forward, he bumped his knees against the porch railing, but he paid no heed; he was glad to see this man. "It's good to see you."

Kingston had been his instructor in freshman English, and a friendship had been begun that had lasted during Tommy's four years at Dartmouth. Kingston had been very kind to him, and he repeated how happy he was to see him.

"I like to hear that," Kingston said frankly. "We must have a talk. How long are you going to be here? Can you come to dinner tomorrow night? I know my wife has an engagement tonight or I'd ask you to come along with me now."

"I expect to leave sometime tomorrow," Tommy explained. "But why can't you have dinner here at the Inn with me tonight? I was planning to go to the Nugget just to see if the fellows still threw peanuts, but I'd a thousand times rather talk to you."

"Well, I'll put your mind at rest; they still throw them. I caught one in the ear night before last. Why, yes, I can have dinner with you. I'd like to. I'll have to go home first, but I'll be back by the time the doors are opened." He held out his hand. "It's mighty good to see you."

II

Darkness was coming and with it the cold. Tommy secured his key at the desk and went upstairs to his room. He had better than an hour to wait for Kingston, and, finding himself quite inexplicably weary, he took off his shoes and stretched out on the bed. The quiet! He'd forgotten the quiet of Hanover. The toot of an automobile horn, a boy's voice now and then—and then the quiet again.

In his college days the quiet had seemed natural to him, though he hadn't recognized it as quiet. He had never really known anything else except at rare intervals. Andover had been quiet too, and the little western Massachusetts town where he had lived his boyhood days had been even quieter. The stillness brought peace and memories. He thought of his mother out in California. Then quickly he put her out of his mind and concentrated on his father. He wished he could remember his father better. There were memories that were so vivid, so heartbreakingly real that they almost brought tears, but those were memories only of especially happy moments in a child's life. He could see his father only through a boy's eyes, and he wanted to see him through his own, a man's.

Tommy had had a happy boyhood until he was twelve. His father, also Thomas Beamish Gray, had been a lawyer who had gone to Harvard and the Harvard Law School and then returned to practice his profession in his home town. A long line of Grays had slowly and carefully accumulated money and goods, each adding his share, each passing a larger total on to his successor. Tommy's father never lived in but one house, the house he was born in, a big, white colonial building with a fanlight over the door. The lawns stretched fifty yards down a gentle slope to the elm-shaded street. Tommy was born in that house too, but now a cousin lived there. Thomas Gray, Senior, was dead, and without him the house held memories that his son wanted to forget.

Tommy's father had died in France of influenza in 1918. Tommy would never forget the day the telegram came. His mother had promptly had hysterics, and it wasn't until his twenty-first birthday that Tommy understood why her screams had angered him. He had no desire to protect her, to weep with her, only a wild need to escape, to be by himself. He fled to the snowy hills and fought his way through drifts as if at the end of a hidden trail he would find understanding; but it was all futile striving. He could not realize that he would see his father no more, that they never would go fishing together again, play catch again in the twilight, skate in January, fly kites in March. His father was dead in France and his mother would hang a flag with a star on it out of the window. She would wear black and look proud and sad. She would; he knew she would. For the first time he realized clearly that he hated his mother, and he didn't know why.

A week later Mr. Burton called him into the bank and handed him a letter. "Your father was going to war, Tommy," he said gently, "and, of course, he knew he might not come back; so he left everything in order. In his will he instructed me to give this letter to you, and there is another one you're to have when you're twenty-one. I don't want you to read this one until you're alone."

He talked a long time, but Tommy only half understood much of what he said. He did understand that he was to go to Phillips Andover Academy in another year, then choose his own college and his own profession. He was told something about a trust fund that was to be his when he was twenty-three, and something about interest that was to be used in the meantime for education and travel. Mr. Burton and the bank were executors. He didn't know what executors were, but somehow he gained the idea that Mr. Burton had just as much to say about him as his mother had. He was glad of that. He liked Mr. Burton.

It was a long letter that his father had written him, so understanding and tender that he wept over it time and time again. Parts of it became part of his consciousness. "You and your mother never have seemed to understand each other, my boy. I think I know what the difficulty is, but I can't explain to you now; you're too young. It's a lot to ask patience of a boy your age. I know that, but I do ask it. And it's almost cruel to say this, but I must say it. I have no choice. I feel quite sure that your mother will marry again. I hope she will. Remember that, Tommy; I hope she will. So try not to be resentful. Be generous."

And later in the letter: "It is cruel for you to lose a father just when puberty is so near. That's when a boy needs a father most, and I hope you find somebody to take my place. You've never been one to confide in people, though, and I doubt if you will; so I must try to guess what advice you will need in the next few years. The worst of it is, Tommy, I don't know what advice to give you. I wish I were wiser, but all I have to go on is my own mistakes.

"I'm glad now that I've answered all your questions and that we had those good talks. About facts you know everything there is any need to know, but it's ideals I ought to talk about and I don't know what to say. You're an intense boy, and if you're like me, you'll be a passionate one. In a way I'm glad of that. I pity people who lack passion. And never be ashamed of your own. I can say that much to you positively. Never be ashamed of your passion. It's wholesome and normal. I know I ought to tell you to be chaste always, but I know what happens sometimes. I know what happened to me. How I wish you were a couple of years older. You would understand so much better what I'm trying to say. I can only hope you'll read this letter when you are older.

"If you're the normal boy I'm sure you are, temptation may be very strong and very sudden. That's what happened to me before I was sixteen. The girl was older and lots wiser than I was. Well, I didn't care after that—and that's where I made my mistake. I suffered for it, too. I think there's safety in chastity, Tommy, but remember that you have to have

standards whether you are chaste or not. The standards are
a lot more important than the chastity. That, at least, is
what I think. Don't do anything you think is cheap. I can't
tell you how much I hate to admit to you that I have done
things I thought were cheap, but I have and I don't want you
to suffer my shame and my regrets. It's terribly important
that you should respect yourself."

Tommy tried hard to be kind to his mother, but her
parade of her sorrow angered and repelled him. He was a
New England Yankee by training and inheritance, and his
sorrow was secret, something that he could share with no
one. His mother luxuriated in emotion, rolled in it like the
family pussy in a bed of catnip, gloried in the dramatic opportunities her widowhood brought with it. And deep, deep
down in him Tommy knew that her sorrow wasn't real, that
her tears were just a performance. He was glad when the day
came to go to Andover. He kissed her good-bye dutifully,
let her weep over him, and then went away without once
looking back.

A year later she married Melville Clarke, a handsome
actor. He was a year or two younger than she was and had
been twice divorced. Tommy never learned where or how
they met. He didn't care about anything so long as he didn't
have to be with them, and it was many years before he even
suspected that he might have been unjust to Clarke. He
took an immediate and abiding dislike to the man and spent
as little time in his company as possible. The evasion was
easy. Clarke, of course, insisted on living in New York, and
his wife was delighted to leave behind the town she had
always loathed. Tommy spent as many Christmas vacations
with schoolmates as invitations provided; and so long as he
was in preparatory school, he spent his summer vacations in
camps. The year that he entered Dartmouth, Clarke got his
chance in Hollywood. Tommy had seen his mother only
once since. Occasionally he saw Clarke on the screen, nowadays only in bit parts. Usually some one was with Tommy,

but he never revealed to his companion that they were looking at a likeness of his stepfather.

When he was eighteen, Mr. Burton explained his father's
will to him. Later, after he had studied law, he realized how
carefully security for him had been planned. Probably by
cajolery, perhaps even by duplicity, Thomas Gray had succeeded in getting his wife's signature on papers that took all
control of the estate out of her hands. There was a trust fund
for her, another for Tommy. Tommy's share of the estate
became his when he reached his twenty-third birthday, but
her share was in trust for her lifetime, and it was to revert to
Tommy at her death. Each of them had a few thousand a
year. Some of the money had been invested in real estate,
but Thomas Gray had been careful to invest nearly all the
remainder in Liberty Bonds before he sailed for France.

Tommy spent four of his five college vacations traveling
in Europe and South America. Once he went to California.
That was after Burton had sent him the letter his father
had written as his twenty-first birthday present.

"Dear Tommy," it read: "It doesn't seem possible that
you will be a man grown when you read these words and
that I shall have been long years in my grave. Well, be sure
of this, my son: if there is any life after death, my spirit will
be with you. I've never dared tell you what you've meant to
me. I don't dare tell you now. But when you were born, I
thought life might be worth living—and it was.

"Your mother didn't want you. She didn't want any children. She was terrified, and I'm cruel enough to believe that
it was the possible loss of her figure that terrified her most.
Therefore you might as well know that you were entirely
an accident, and if various medicines had been as effective
as she hoped they would be, you wouldn't have been at all.
Probably I sound bitter, but I've never quite got over the
arguments your mother and I had in those days. She bore
you, it is true, but I suffered something worse than labor
pains for nine long months and for months thereafter.

"I think I've started quite the wrong way, because I'm writing this letter hoping that it will help you to understand your mother. Perhaps when you have read it, you'll understand me and yourself a little better too. I'm taking it for granted that she has married again and that you don't like her new husband. You wouldn't, partly because he has taken my place, but mainly, I think, because you're like me: you aren't likely to take to the kind of man your mother admires.

"And that's the first thing for you to understand, Tommy. I've been a terrible disappointment to your mother. You see, she was a beauty. (To me she still is a beauty.) And so she had lots of chances, but they were the wrong kind. Her family, as you know, is rather poor, and so she didn't meet the kind of men generally that she wanted to marry. That, remember, is really something to her credit. Then quite by accident I met her at a college dance. She had been brought by a fellow who lived near her in Roxbury. I fell in love with her at first sight.

"I honestly believe she was in love with me, too, and I suppose I seemed pretty glamorous. When she saw our house, it was wonderful to her—and so was my car and your grandfather's horses.

"I don't think she was really happy for six months. She hated the conventions of a small town, and she couldn't understand me. She was ashamed of her own family, though I never knew why, and thought we were ashamed of her. In her own way she suffered, I feel sure. And I don't suppose I've always been kind. I know I practically forced motherhood on her when she hated the thought of it. I wouldn't let her wear the kind of clothes she wanted to wear, and I walked out over and over again and killed the emotional scenes that were the breath of life to her. I think she might have loved me if I could have shouted at her now and then.

"Well, Tommy, she's put up with fifteen years of unhappiness with me. Remember that. Why didn't we part? You won't understand this; so just accept it. I've never stopped loving her. For no reason I can understand she is the one woman in the world for me. And if you grow bitter sometimes, remember that she was loyal to me long after she had quit loving me, that she suffered me without complaint in your presence, and that she did her conscientious best for you. She would have done better if you had given her a real chance, but from babyhood it was to me that you turned always. You and I understood each other. You and she never did. That must have been bitter for her.

"So now, Tommy, if she has found happiness with another man, don't be censorious; be glad. You'll never understand her. I know that. Be kind to her. You're twenty-one now (how incredible that seems!) and you promise to be a good-looking man. (I'm confusing my tenses. I can't separate the present when I'm writing from the future when you'll be reading. I should have said, of course. 'You promis*ed* to be a good-looking man.') Good looks mean a lot to her. She'll love going to expensive places to dine with you and excursions of that sort. She suffered at the hands of her husband; I hope she can find some happiness in her son."

So that summer Tommy went to California, but he and his mother were strangers who could never become friends. Her talk was all of clothes, parties, and motion-picture stars. She was a walking, talking directory of Hollywood; and she spoke of every picture in which Melville Clarke had two scenes as if he were the only person who drew audiences to see it. Obviously she was happy with Clarke, though how any woman could endure the man's vanity, his posturings, and continuous self-glorification, Tommy could not understand. He and Clarke were born to be courteous strangers at the very best; and to him, his mother was Clarke's wife, nothing more. Try as he would, and he honestly did try, he could feel no kinship with her.

Thereafter he dutifully wrote to her at long intervals, sent her birthday and Christmas presents, and she responded in kind. But she did not need him and made no pretense of needing him. His father's letter had reached him years too late. No effort could attain the end the letter asked for.

As he waited for Kingston, Tommy thought back through the years. Yes, he had needed his father, needed him badly always. Mr. Burton had been kind; so had the masters at Andover. And perhaps the track coach had done as much as anybody with his constant, "Take it easy, Tommy; take it easy. Remember that you're only a kid. Don't try so hard. You'll burn yourself out. It's a long pull to be a great miler. You can't be a record-breaker tomorrow or the day after tomorrow. Milers develop late, but they don't develop at all if they try too hard. You're always trying too hard. You take everything too seriously. Relax, kid; run easily and you'll get there faster."

Well, decided Tommy, he hadn't done so badly for a fellow who'd practically been an orphan. He'd kept a lot straighter than most. Even when he was thirteen he'd known what his father had meant by needing his own respect. He had needed it then; he had always needed it. He supposed some people called it pride. He didn't know; but whatever it was, it had kept him from excesses. There had been some pretty bad times now and then, moments when he had hated himself, but even in such a moment he had known that the lapse was only temporary, that he would fight his way back to his own standard. An Andover master had told him once that he was a walking relic of all his Puritan ancestors. The master had been teasing, but there had been truth in the gentle jibe.

Tommy stretched on the bed and spread his arms wide. Puritan ancestors, he decided comfortably, were a pretty darn good thing for a fatherless boy to have.

# CHAPTER VII

DINNER with Kingston was pleasant. He had much to tell Tommy about the changes in the college, about what had been done and about what the administration hoped to do. People came into the dining-room whom Tommy recognized. He asked Kingston about them; he asked him about everybody who came to mind. He felt an eagerness to learn everything he could about Dartmouth College. During a momentary break in the conversation he remembered that he came to Hanover to step back in time, not to catch up with it; but his curiosity was in full flood and swept unresisted over his original intention.

After dinner he and Kingston passed into the neighboring lounge.

"Shall we sit here?" Tommy asked. "Or would you like to go up to my room?"

"I like it here," said Kingston. "There won't be anybody much around, and it's very comfortable."

Tommy agreed, and they selected two big, overstuffed chairs in a corner. Across the room a college boy was talking with his father and mother. People crossed the lounge on their way from the dining-room to the lobby. For half an hour there was talk and movement; then the quiet was almost complete. Kingston and Tommy had the lounge to themselves.

"I'd forgotten," said Tommy, "how lovely Hanover is. I'd forgotten particularly how restful and quiet it is. Somehow only the exciting moments had stuck in my memory. Right now I envy you. Life must be very pleasant up here."

"It is," Kingston said placidly, "if you like to teach and if

you like college boys. I happen to, and so I'm more contented than some of my colleagues. Some of them miss the
excitement of a city, you know, and a few of them don't
really care very much about teaching; they're interested
mainly in research. We don't have many intellectual moles,
though. For an undergradute college we have our share of
scholars, I think, but we don't have much patience with men
who slight the students. Most of us take teaching seriously;
and if you do, this is a grand place to work and live."

"But isn't it an awful grind?" Tommy asked. "I've seen
your desk simply stacked with themes, and most of them
must be dull. How do you stand marking misplaced commas
and dangling participles year after year?"

"The themes aren't dull if you're interested in the fellows
who wrote them—and I am. Sometimes, of course, I bellyache
with the best of them, but you'd be surprised at how often
I'm really eager to get at a batch of themes, especially if they
show a reaction to a class discussion. No, Tommy, I don't
find my work a grind most of the time. Usually I'm keen
about it. And it's different from most work. You think it's
just repetition, but it isn't. I go over the same material year
after year; that's true—but I go over it with different students. Every year a college is rejuvenated. It is always young.
The students always run largely to type, of course, as all
humanity does, but within the type they are infinitely varied.
And I like them. Probably I'm a little sentimental about
them. I'm enormously pleased when an old grad looks me
up. I hope you would have."

Tommy shook his head and grinned shamefacedly. "I
doubt it," he confessed. "I wanted to, all right, but I'd have
been afraid you might have forgotten me."

Kingston laughed. "I know how you feel. We never quite
get over our fear of our old teachers. I don't know why, but
we don't. I remember once being in Cambridge. I wanted
terribly to see Dean Briggs, but I was afraid I might intrude
or that he wouldn't remember me. Then he stopped me in

the Yard. I was pleased to my toes and terribly ashamed."

"That's exactly the way I felt this afternoon when you spoke to me," Tommy said. "But I want to ask you something. Do you do any scholarly work—any writing, I mean?"

"Very little. I dig up something interesting now and then and write it up for a learned journal, and I've edited a couple of books. Why do you ask?"

"Well, I'm wondering what you're working for. That's pretty personal, but I came up here to find out if I could what I was working for. I have a right to feel that I've done well, but I don't. A couple of months ago I was made a member of the firm, and it's a firm anybody would be proud of. I've got what I wanted, and now I don't see just what I'm getting out of it—outside of more money, of course. Now, the amount of money a professor can get is pretty strictly limited, and at best it isn't much. I know you work hard— probably harder than I do, and there must be something besides money that you're working for. You could make more money doing something else. You have the friendship of the students, I know, but a lot of them must disappoint you—and you must give up a lot, too, that you must want."

Kingston nodded thoughtfully, and then smiled at Tommy, his dark eyes twinkling behind his glasses. "In other words," he asked, "where is my ambition?"

"Oh, I didn't mean—"

"No; you just implied. Never mind; it's quite all right. Have you ever asked yourself just what ambition means to most people?"

"Well," said Tommy, "I've asked myself what it means to me, and I haven't found an answer."

"You don't want to be Dartmouth's second Daniel Webster?"

"No. I know I don't want to be that. I don't quite know why not, either; but I think I have an aversion to any kind of public demonstrativeness. At any rate, I know I have no desire to go into public life."

Kingston studied him. "Perhaps," he remarked shrewdly, "that's why you aren't sure where you're going."

"I'm afraid I don't understand. One can get somewhere privately, surely."

"We were talking about ambition," said Kingston, "and an ambitious man doesn't want to go anywhere privately. It's his privacy he objects to. He wants to be known, to be admired, to have wealth or power or both. Ambition means that a man wants to stand out, and he can't stand out without being noticed—and if he did stand out without being noticed, he would feel that he had failed. Do you know, I think perhaps you are too well balanced to need ambition. Ambition, you know, is so often a compensation for something lacking."

"Perhaps," Tommy admitted, "but surely that is only a small part of the explanation. Certainly it doesn't explain the great majority of ambitionless people, and that's most of the people."

"Is it? I doubt that. I think most people want to stand out for some reason or other, but most of them want to stand out in their own very tiny worlds. But, never mind; we won't argue about that. You asked me what I got out of my ambitionless life."

"I didn't say that. I asked—"

"I know," interrupted Kingston, "but that was in your mind. Well, everything you said about my teaching was entirely true, and I think that down in your heart you still have a little of the common contempt for people who bury themselves in the academic life. You feel that they are escaping life rather than living it. Some remnant of Browning's philosophy must have stuck with you from your classes with me."

"Browning? You mean the success in failure philosophy you used to talk about?"

"Yes—and I'm still talking about it. You feel with him that it is better to aim for a million and miss it than try for a hundred and get it—and you think I'm trying for about fifty. Well, I'm not. But I'm a teacher, you see—and a teacher aims for others, not for himself. Oh, of course, I want to be the teacher of my dreams and all that sort of thing, but the dream merely raises my standard for inspiring the students."

"That means, doesn't it," interjected Tommy, "that you're sinking your personality in others?"

"No! It means that I'm trying to inspire others *through* my mind and personality, which is something that makes all the difference between living in my work and merely earning a living from it. Of course, there are disappointments. I always rather shrink when the alumni come back for reunion. It's a shock to see most of them ten years later. It's the exceptional undergraduate who doesn't have something fine in him, some ambition or idealism that makes him worth while; but most men of thirty or forty have lost the idealism. It's nearly always a shock to me to meet alumni I haven't seen for ten years. A fellow graduates young and slim and hard; he comes back soft—soft all through. Oh, not all of them, of course. You haven't, for example. You look much the same as you did when you were a senior, and I think you *are* much the same."

"I'm afraid I am," said Tommy ruefully. "I've been wondering if I weren't suffering from a second adolescence."

"I doubt it. Your doubts and confusions mean to me that you are still growing, that you haven't given up. If that means immaturity, I think you're lucky. Do you know what most people mean when they say they're mature?" He didn't give Tommy a chance to answer; he answered his own question. "They mean that they've succeeded in justifying their own incompetence and failures and prejudices to themselves. It means that they are smug, completely satisfied with the dogmas they call their ideas. Remember, Tommy, 'adolescent' comes from *olescere,* meaning to grow, and that 'mature' comes from *maturus,* meaning full-grown or ripe. Well, there's no growth after full growth, and there's nothing but

rot after ripeness. A man at your age ought to be intellectually still adolescent. If he isn't, he's already ready for the
dustbin."

Tommy thought that over. If Kingston was right, there
was consolation and encouragement in what he said, but he
wasn't sure Kingston was right.

"Most men," he said dubiously, "seem a good deal more
assured than I feel."

"Most men," said Kingston sharply, "are assured because
they aren't trying for much. Most of them aren't trying for
much besides physical pleasure. They wouldn't admit it, but
actually their only ambition is for money, and their only
use for the money is to buy better seats at more night clubs,
and to buy more liquor and more women."

That statement Tommy refused to believe. "I don't think
that's true of most of the men I see," he objected, "—around
the Harvard Club, for instance. A few of them are like that,
but they're the exceptions."

"You don't see many of the failures around the New York
Harvard Club." Kingston pointed his pipe at Tommy for
emphasis. "Most college men fail. Most people fail. You're
a success, and probably most of your friends and acquaintances are successes, too. But at Reunion I see scores of men
who aren't successes, and their failure sticks out all over
them. I don't mean they've failed to make money. I'm too
academic to make money a standard. I mean they've failed
to find a purpose in life, any significance in it. Their intellectual vitality is all gone and—probably I'll seem sentimental when I say their dreams are gone too. That to me is
when a man fails—when he has lost his dreams."

Tommy wanted to say that he was a total failure by Kingston's definition, but he found the confession impossible. It
would demand an explanation that would reveal more than
he was capable of revealing to any one. And so instead of
saying anything, he lighted a cigarette and waited for Kingston to continue.

"That's why the life up here suits me to perfection," Kingston explained. "I work with people whose dreams are terribly real to them. Most of them are almost frighteningly alive. And my colleagues are alive, too, though the students don't know it. They are intellectually alive, I mean. Some of those who are dullest in the classroom are tremendously stimulating out of it. They just don't know how to talk to students. And I'm part of a community. I have roots. I live in beautiful surroundings. My children are growing up in the finest kind of atmosphere. I rub hard against my fellows. Sometimes, I'll admit, the rubbing chafes horribly. There's another side to academic life, but I escape it pretty well. And the students are always there to make the chafing worth while. Why, Gray, I can't tell you the satisfaction I experience when one of my students goes out and justifies my faith in him. I have a kind of success by proxy. I know I didn't create the success, but I helped—and once in a while one of my former students goes out of his way to let me know I helped. That means more than I know how to tell you."

"I suppose," said Tommy thoughtfully, "that there must be enormous satisfaction in helping others to live a full life, but we can't all have that kind of work. For that matter, not many people are fitted for it—and lots of people who try it out of the kindness of their hearts merely ball things up and get in the way. Certainly, my work isn't like that. It has a small human side, but it's mostly technical. I can't pretend to get your kind of satisfaction out of it."

"Well, what matter?" asked Kingston. "You like it, don't you?"

"Oh, yes, very much, but after what you've said it seems pretty selfish."

Kingston smiled. "We all have our doubts occasionally."

"You mean," Tommy asked slowly, "that all of us wonder sometimes if our work is worth doing—that everybody feels once in a while that life is hollow?"

"Of course. All intelligent people feel that way now and

then. Probably it's their livers. I don't know. But, anyway, it's mostly foolish doubt, I think, because any work is important if it doesn't do anything more for us than earn us a living. And if we do the work well, it's important to others, too. It's bound to be. No work exists independent of humanity."

Tommy began to discuss his work as an attorney, not because he particularly wanted to, but because he had talked around the questions in his mind as long as he could. Much as he liked Kingston, he could not really confide in him; and he couldn't get closer to the vital questions without revealing far more than he was willing, or temperamentally able, to reveal. And the solution Kingston had found for himself, he felt sure, was no solution for him. A year later he found significance in Kingston's remarks that he missed entirely at the moment. Now it seemed to him that an all-absorbing interest in other people no doubt made Kingston the stimulating teacher he was, but Tommy did not believe that he could acquire that interest. He didn't want to be a teacher. Kingston was valuable. Tommy prized him. Undoubtedly scores of his former students prized him as highly; but the qualities that made him so valuable were qualities that Tommy lacked, and he wasn't sure that he even wanted them. As men they could touch hands, like each other, come close to understanding each other, but Tommy did not believe Kingston could really understand the tangle of problems that were making his life a meaningless snarl. Kingston would speculate interestingly about those problems, but the speculations couldn't possibly be personal enough to offer a solution. That, Tommy began to feel sure, he would have to find for himself.

# CHAPTER VIII

TOMMY relaxed comfortably on his way back to New York. He stared out of the window at the loveliness of the Connecticut Valley and let his thoughts drift around his visit to Hanover. Given confidence by Kingston's pleasure in seeing him, he had called on several of his former professors and found a hearty welcome waiting. A clerk in a drugstore called him by name; so had a barber. The visit had done him a lot of good. He had enjoyed every minute of it. . . .

But he hadn't done what he had meant to do. He hadn't thought about his undergraduate ambitions and yearnings. He hadn't stepped back in time; indeed, he had never been more intensely his own age. Dartmouth had not revived his youth in him; it had made him, instead, sharply aware of his maturity. He wondered if he would have enjoyed a discussion, an old-fashioned bull session, with a group of students. He doubted it. They all looked so damned young. And he knew that they would have said things that would have made him feel shopworn and grimy. They would have made him feel disillusioned, unduly sophisticated. Not that plenty of undergraduates didn't think their sophistication was complete. Any undergraduate who had done away with his chastity thought his sophistication was equal to any one's. As if a night with a woman really stripped away your illusions. . . . It taught you something about yourself, perhaps, but that was all. No, he was glad he hadn't had anything to do with the students. If he had had, he would have felt older than ever, and that was the last thing he wanted.

Funny, his talks with the professors hadn't made him feel young. He had felt some of the gawkiness of his undergraduate days, but nothing more. The changes in the professors had made him almost uncomfortably aware of the passage of time. They looked older. He knew that he must look older, too. Well, he was—and he had to look at life from the point of view of a man. It was silly to think he could go back and look at it from the point of view of a boy. One never could go back. The last nine years had done things to him, and Thomas Gray attorney was a very different person from Tommy Gray of Dartmouth. He hadn't even gone into his fraternity. He remembered too well how hollow the welcome to old grads was . . .

No, he had to accept his maturity. What was it Kingston had said? There was nothing but rot after ripeness? Yes, but that was more of a wise-crack than anything else. It sounded wise, but he didn't believe it was. A man could be ripe a long time without rotting. And a man could grow, too, without remaining green all his life.

But Kingston was no fool, far from it. He was glad they'd had that talk. It had done something for him. The whole visit had. Once he'd really thought it out—

"Is this seat taken?"

He was startled. Subconsciously he had known that the train was in the Springfield station, but his thoughts had absorbed him so completely that he had been unaware of the movements in the car.

He looked up. "Good Lord," he thought. "Good Lord!"

The woman looking down at him must be, he decided, as tall as he was, and he stood only a fraction of an inch under six feet. She had the warmest color in her cheeks he had ever seen; her large eyes were black and very brilliant; her mouth suggested decision and strength.

"No," he replied, picking up a magazine from the other half of the seat; "no, it's not taken."

Then, before he could rise to help, she picked up a heavy-appearing suitcase and tossed it to the rack. With a quick movement, she pulled off a little reddish felt hat and tossed it after the suitcase. Next she slipped out of a severely tailored topcoat, folded it, and set it beside her hat.

"What a woman!" Tommy thought. At the moment he hardly knew whether she was beautiful or not; he could not form immediately an estimate of one so large and vivid. She wore a black woolen skirt and a rust-colored pull-on sweater. Her shoulders were magnificent, her body Amazonian. Her straight, lustrous black hair was cut almost as short as a man's, parted on the side and swept back in a shining wing. Tommy tried not to stare, but it was hard to look away; she was such a lot of woman.

"Would you like to sit by the window?" he asked. "The view is beautiful."

"No, thanks," she replied, and he was caught by the beauty of her voice. It was a rich contralto, dark and velvety. "For the present I've had my fill of views."

He looked at her inquiringly and she explained, "I've been up in the Berkshires painting, and right now I feel saturated with color. I have a stack of canvases tied together back in the baggage car."

Tommy wanted to make her talk so that he could listen to the music of her voice, and so he said, "I envy you. I've been up to Hanover, and the colors were marvelous. Of course, they're past their prime, but I'd have given a lot to have been able to paint them."

"I like them best when they're faded a little," the big woman said, "and there's a blue smoky haze at this time of year that does things to them." For the first time she looked at him directly. "Do you know about painting?" she demanded, and Tommy thought he detected a challenge in her voice.

He smiled at her. "It depends on what you mean. I've been through all the great galleries in Europe a good many times. One of the masters at prep school got me interested

in painting when I was about sixteen, and I've never lost
the interest. I know all the galleries in this country, too,
especially those in New York. I really like pictures, but I
can't say I know anything about painting—about the
technique, I mean."

"Technique!" She sniffed. "I'm fed up with technique.
What good does that do you? I've got all the technique in the
world, and I'll probably burn all the damn daubing I've
been doing. Technique isn't worth a hoot." Her black eyes
flashed and she glowered at Tommy. "What do you want to
know about technique for?"

"I don't," Tommy said, smiling at her indignation. "My
interest in it is pretty slight. I'm one of those people who
don't know much about painting, but I know what I like.
Once in a while I think I know why."

She turned squarely in her seat and looked him over. Her
scrutiny was stern and totally without embarrassment. Suddenly she smiled, and Tommy reduced her age from thirty-
five to thirty.

"You sound intelligent," she said, "and you look intelligent. Want to talk?"

"Haven't I been doing my best to make you?" He grinned
because her bluntness left him on the defensive.

"You look about fifteen when you grin like that." Her
comment was as impersonal as if he were a statue. "You drop
years with a thud." She held out her big, strong hand. "My
name is Mary Carter, and if you aren't in advertising, don't
pretend you've heard of it because you damn well know you
haven't."

"I haven't," Tommy confessed, gripping her hand in return for her firm grip. "I'm Thomas Gray, and I'm not in
advertising; I'm an attorney."

"Except for your mouth, you don't look old enough.
When you smile you look like a kid; but until you do, your
mouth gives you away. How old are you?"

"Twenty-nine." Tommy wondered what she would ask

next, but he didn't much care; this magnificently big woman was beautiful, and she was a person. He wanted to know her.

She didn't ask anything. Instead she studied him for a minute or two. Then she said thoughtfully, "I'd rather like to paint you. Your face is interesting. Your hair is a good brown, and it catches the light. There's something candid about your eyes that's interesting. They're what make you look so young. They have a kind of trustful, questioning look. Your nose? Nostrils a little thin, suggest passion. And then I'd paint your mouth—pain, restraint, too damned reticent, a little tight—contrast with your eyes. Boy's eyes, man's mouth." She seemed to become aware of him as a person and smiled at him. "Your eyes mean you stick out your chin, and your mouth means you can take it but it hurts like hell."

Tommy blushed a little and managed a small smile in response. Inwardly, he squirmed. This Mary Carter was altogether too observant and too shrewd.

"You must be a good painter," he said because he didn't know what else to say. "You see a lot."

"I'm a lousy painter. I told you that, didn't I?"

"No; you said you had all the technique in the world."

"I have, but any damned fool knows technique doesn't make a painter—or he ought to, anyway. I'm a commercial artist and a good one. I can paint an apple so you'll think you can eat it off the canvas, and you'll want to, too. I can paint a woman so you'll know how much the silk in her dress cost by the yard, and I can paint a dog so that his whiskers will wiggle. And so I make a good living, but I don't fool myself; I can't paint a picture. I've been up in the Berkshires trying, and I've had a swell time, too; but I've painted only what I saw. I haven't painted what I felt. That's something different."

Mary Carter interested Tommy enormously, but he hardly knew how to meet her frankness. A line of poetry came providentially to his aid, and he recited softly:

" 'Still what an arm! and I could alter it.
But all the play, the insight and the stretch—
Out of me! out of me!' "

"So you know Browning. I used to read that poem to my
kid brother. Well, that gives the idea perfectly, but Browning did del Sarto dirt. He was a painter. Just the same,
Browning knew what he was talking about. I could paint
you, for example—good color, good likeness, everything, but
I know damn well I'd miss the thing that makes you an individual. I always do. I'd paint a likeness, not you. I'd never
get what I think about you in the picture. See what I mean?"

"Yes, I see." But personal discussions with strangers embarrassed Tommy and he was afraid that she might analyze
him again; so he switched the conversation to modern methods of painting and held her to the subject until the train
pulled into the New Haven station. Then she said unexpectedly:

"I hate this joint."

"New Haven? Why, I've always liked it. I don't know anything I like better than the Green with its three old
churches."

"I don't mean New Haven. It's all right, I guess. I've never
seen it. I meant Yale. I have a kid brother who graduated a
year ago, and what it did to him! I was responsible, too, and
I kick my behind every time I think of it."

Puzzled, Tommy looked at her questioningly. She saw his
confusion and frowned.

"I sound cracked, don't I?" she said, a note of bitterness
bringing sharpness into her rich voice. "Well, I shouldn't
be surprised if I am. You see, I'm the duck that adopted a
chick and kicked it into the water. It's like this: We're from
Ohio, and our folks died ten years ago, and so I had Bill—
my brother, I mean—on my hands. He was a swell kid, and
I was nuts about him, just plain nuts. Well, I was already
earning good money even if I was only twenty-three, and I

could take care of him. He's ten years younger than I am, and I didn't think anything was too good for him. Besides, he was gifted as hell. He could make words sing.

"So know-it-all big sister sent him to Yale. Of course, he had to be ready just when the depression got to going good and all the advertisers were laying off. But I managed it. I had the devil's own time, but I pulled him through and gave him a summer in Europe in the bargain.

"And did Bill like college! He ate it up. Made his letter and a swank club and everything. Used to spend his vacations out on Long Island and up at Bar Harbor. He didn't touch me for that; he was invited. He was a success, you see. Too damn much of a success! He didn't see writing in a garret or working for a publisher when he got out. My God, no! The depression didn't mean anything to him. He'd made contacts in college. You know, contacts! He got him a job with a broker, and now he goes to deb parties and hangs around the Yale Club bar. He'll marry a rich girl and be a well-kept louse."

Again Tommy struggled for the right thing to say even while feeling uncomfortably sure that there could be no right thing. "You're an artist," he began tentatively, "and so writing probably means more to you than it ever meant to your brother. I've been told that the creative faculty often dies with adolescence. I know it did with me. I couldn't write the stories now that I wrote in college to save my life. Probably your brother's gone into business because he instinctively knows that's where he belongs."

She looked out of the window and then turned to him. Her mouth was set, her eyes stern. "Ever love anybody?" she demanded pugnaciously.

"Yes."

"Know what it is to have him turn into a skunk?"

"Well—yes, in a way. I thought that for a time, but I was wrong."

"Maybe you can guess, then. I told you I'd never been to

New Haven. Didn't that strike you as funny? Remember,
I was footing the bills. Can you guess why I never went?"

"No. No, I can't."

"I wasn't invited."

Something turned over in Tommy. He felt sick. With the
unnatural speed that is common on ships and not uncom-
mon on trains, he and Mary Carter had skipped past the
preliminaries of acquaintance and arrived at an intimacy
that was as real as it was probably temporary. He had known
that sudden intimacy on trains and ships before. It was due,
he supposed, partly to the unaccustomed environment, the
strange and isolated world in which one was moving, and
partly, too, to the fact that subconsciously one expected the
intimacy to end when one left that world. He wasn't particularly surprised, therefore, by Mary's frankness, but the
revelation was too intimate; it upset him, almost repelled
him. He didn't want to know what this big, handsome
woman had suffered, and he was ashamed of himself for
not wanting to know. The revelation embarrassed him, and
he resented the embarrassment.

When he said nothing, she continued, her rich voice dry
with bitterness. "He was ashamed of me, you know. I wasn't
any more outspoken, I'll bet, than his deb friends; but I'd
never been a deb—and I'm so goddamn big. He was afraid
I'd do the wrong thing in his swell club and around some
of his swell friends. And I'm not invited now. I see him
once in a blue moon. He comes down to the studio and we
have a fight. He knows what I think of his friends, and he
sneers at mine. Well, he doesn't get any more checks out
of me, and he can rot before he'll get one. Let's talk about
something else. I'm sorry I shot my mouth off."

Thankfully Tommy agreed, and they made idle conversation until the train flashed past 135th Street. Then he
asked if he might come to her studio and see her pictures.

"No," she said bluntly. "Now, get me right; I like you.
You're all right. But I've quit fooling myself about people

like you. I've tried being friends with your kind before, and it's no go. I live down in the Village, and a lot of nuts hang around the studio. Some of them are talented, and some of them are just nuts. But you're so normal and wholesome you'd make me hate the lot of them, and I don't want to hate them. They're my kind."

"Oh, come now," Tommy objected; "you're exaggerating. I'm not creative; I admit it, but I am appreciative. Isn't that enough?"

"No, it isn't. Listen." She swung around and faced him. "A person has to make adjustments. I've made mine. I may not be a good artist, but I'm an artist. So are my friends. Do you know what that means? It means we're all freaks by your standards. Somebody said some time or other that art was a diseased growth, and he was right as rain. All kinds of art come from overexposed nerves. Life hits artists too hard. If they aren't warped to begin with, it warps 'em. Can you understand that? Well, we don't like to think we're warped. We don't want to feel queer. So we herd together because we understand each other's queernesses. You're normal as sunshine, and you'd light up all our crazy twists until we'd hate each other."

"I think you're cock-eyed," Tommy remarked comfortably. "You make me sound like a prig, and you talk as if you were a circus freak. You know, don't you, that you're the handsomest woman that ever escaped the Follies?"

"Man o' War escaped the Follies, too," she replied caustically.

Tommy laughed. "I suppose you'd like to be cute and kittenish, but nobody else wants you that way, you can be sure." He grinned his most boyish grin. "I'm going to call."

"I'll kick you downstairs."

"Try it."

She looked at him, and her great eyes were so soft and dark that the smile faded from Tommy's lips. When she spoke, her voice was deeper even than usual, vibrant with appeal. "Honest, I'd rather you wouldn't."

"You mean that?"

"Yes. Yes, I mean it."

Tommy could do nothing but accept the situation, but he was genuinely sorry. He was fascinated by Mary Carter, by her beauty, her honesty, her individuality.

When they reached Grand Central Station, she permitted Tommy to accompany her to the taxi stand. They shook hands. She got into the taxi, and he stepped back. Then she beckoned to him.

"Come if you want to," she said softly, and even in the dim light Tommy could see that her cheeks were flaming.

"Well, I'll be damned," he whispered; "I will be damned."

# CHAPTER IX

## I

THE day after Tommy's return to New York, his telephone rang.

"This is Gene Cantwell," a voice said. "How are you, Tommy?"

Tommy looked as if he were smelling something that not only smelled bad but that he had smelled often before. There was a look of patient disgust on his face, a weariness with something that had to be endured. He had known Gene Cantwell at Andover, and for no reason that he understood he had been Gene's hero. Year after year the boy had trailed after him, grateful for the slightest sign of attention. Tommy hadn't let him know that he was going to Dartmouth until Gene had said that his application for Cornell had been accepted. Then he breathed a sigh of relief and fondly believed that he was rid of Gene forever.

It was only a few months, however, after he came into the offices of Winchester, Winchester, and Tucker that he met Gene on lower Broadway. There was an immediate invitation to dinner, tonight, tomorrow night—any night. Tommy could not escape. Once that painfully tiresome evening was over, he swore that he would never spend another hour with Gene Cantwell. There never was, he thought, a man so pompous, so dull, so insensitive, so smug. Gene's talk was all about Gene, about Gene's collection of toy soldiers, Gene's boat, Gene's country home, Gene's business, Gene, Gene, Gene, *ad nauseam*. If he hadn't inherited money, he would probably have been a country grocer, but a lucky grandfather and a provident father had left him the means necessary to support an expensive, overdecorated Park Avenue apartment and an expensive, stupid wife.

Fortunately for Tommy, his paths and Gene's seldom crossed. Miles separated their offices, they did not belong to the same clubs, and they associated with few of the same people. Therefore he had to evade Gene only when Gene telephoned.

Now once more Gene was calling. Tommy sighed and prepared to evade a new and pressing invitation.

"I'm well enough," he said in response to Gene's question, "but I'm all-fired busy. I've been out of town, and now I have to catch up. What's on your mind?"

"Norma and I want you for an evening. We've given up sending you invitations for big parties. We know you don't like them; so this is just an evening with us—dinner and then the theater if you want to go. If you don't, we'll just sit and talk."

"What night?"

"Wednesday of this week, Tuesday or Friday of next. Norma's going to France the week after that and I'm going to join her in November. We're going to winter on the Riviera."

"Thank God," Tommy thought. This was going to be simpler than he had dared hope.

"Wait a minute," he said. "Let me look at my calendar." He let his watch tick off thirty seconds and then added, "No can do, Gene. I have to go to Scarsdale Wednesday night; next Tuesday I'm going to the Thiesel party, and the Friday after I have tickets for the fight. I'm taking a girl; so I can't get out of it. Thank your wife for me, won't you?"

For several minutes Gene urged that an engagement be broken, but Tommy assured him earnestly that he couldn't possibly break these engagements. Eventually Gene accepted defeat, promising to call Tommy immediately on his return from Europe.

Tommy replaced the instrument in its cradle and leaned

back in his chair. He felt tired. Telling social lies was not easy for him, though the first two engagements had been real enough. He must make a note to ask somebody to go to the fight. The chances were more than good that Gene would go himself, and if he did, he would search Madison Square Garden for Tommy.

Well, Tommy thought, that was one good thing about New York—the ease with which one could escape people one didn't like. In a town of even a hundred thousand people he would be seeing Gene Cantwell constantly; the evasion would be impossible. There were bores and spongers everywhere, but in New York one could usually slip away from them if they didn't work in the same office. He met them in his clubs, said a polite word, pleaded an engagement, and fled. Pretty largely he went where he wanted to go, associated with the people he enjoyed knowing. New York's size, distances, mobs, were sometimes depressing, but they left a man freer than he could be anywhere else in the world.

II

Tommy had meant to call on Mary Carter very soon after his return from Hanover, but for several weeks he was busy and she slipped from his mind. He did, however, mention her once to Fred Homans while they were dressing after playing squash.

"Mary Carter?" said Fred. "Sure I know her. Everybody in advertising knows her. She's one of the best."

"You mean as an artist?"

"Sure, and as a business woman, too. Mary's got brains. She understands what you want, and she gives it to you. She'd make a swell advertising man. Got ideas, you know. And she knows how to do business. No feminine lures or any of that tripe. Knows what she wants. Makes you come through—and sticks to her end of the bargain. Mary's all right. When'd you meet her?"

"On the train coming back from Hanover. I thought she was quite a person."

Fred chuckled. "All of a hundred and sixty pounds of person, I'd say. But, man, isn't she an eyeful?"

Tommy agreed and made a mental note to telephone Mary soon, but engagements piled up on him and he forgot. Everybody he knew was back in town, and he knew a great many people. Besides, he received many invitations from people he did not know. He was that most sought after of all people in New York, an eligible bachelor.

Sometimes he was amused by the flood of invitations that began to pour in on him every autumn. He knew exactly why most of them came, and he found little for satisfaction in the reason. He had Dartmouth and Harvard degrees; he belonged to a good fraternity and acceptable clubs; he was connected with a firm of attorneys whose senior members were in the Social Register; and, presumably, he had some money. If his manners had been bad and his appearance unpleasing, he would have received a large proportion of the invitations just the same. From his college days he had been on the lists for débutante parties, and so the invitations were largely impersonal. As he once put it, he was on the Social Sucker lists.

The débutante parties no longer interested him, and in the previous year he had not attended a single one. This year a famous rich girl was making her début. He thought he might go to her party; it promised to be a good show. The remaining invitations he tossed without an instant's regret or hesitation into his waste-basket. There were many other invitations, however, to be considered, to parties before and after football games, to the theater, to small dances, and to dinner. He accepted enough of them to fill his evenings. In the past he had always kept at least one evening a week free, but now, even while contemptuous of the cowardice that made him do it, he stuffed his calendar. Once he had learned to live without Polly, he promised himself, he would keep evenings for himself again. Until then, though, it was better not to be much alone.

November passed. He had Thanksgiving dinner with the Frederick Winchesters in their home in Bronxville. He had gone to New Haven for the Yale-Dartmouth game and seen Dartmouth defeated once again. Craig Sherman, who was from Yale, had taken ten dollars of his money with loud cries of triumph, and Charlie Lovett took ten more, though he assured Tommy that he took them only out of loyalty to his *alma* academic *mater*. He had gone with them after the game to Charlie's college club. It had been a good day.

There had been lots of good days in the office and out of it, too many good days. Early in December Tommy realized that he was getting tired, that he needed more sleep and more genuine relaxation, more time to himself, more time for thought. He had eluded thought until it began to seem attractive again, even necessary. "Thought," he decided, smiling to himself at the strained simile, "is a lot like a girl. If you run away from it long enough, the first thing you know you find yourself running toward it. I'll be dating Harriet again the first thing I know." But he didn't date Harriet. Another girl, maybe, but not Harriet Carrington. This time, he assured himself, he had learned his lesson. Besides, for the moment he was tired of girls, tired of dinners, expensive glamour, casual conversation. "I'd like," he thought, "a long evening in a smoky room with a gang of good guys." He did some telephoning, left a note for Maribelle. He had his gang; Maribelle would see to it that they ate and drank well.

III

A few days later he finished a conference with Nicholas Tyckman in his office. It was five o'clock. They leaned back in their chairs, grinned wearily at each other, and relaxed.

"That's all, I think," said Tommy.

"So far as I know," agreed Tyckman. "I wonder at you.

My aunt's gift for tangling her affairs evidently didn't desert her even in death. How you've ever straightened out the mess, I don't know, but you seem to have done it."

"Only the broad outlines," confessed Tommy, laughing. "The details are another matter. But I don't think there's anything more we can do today."

Tyckman stood up. "I should say not. I'm dizzy. Come on over to the Yale Club with me and have a drink. I need one, and you must need it worse."

Tommy accepted the invitation without argument. He liked Tyckman, though the aunt's estate was their only connection. Tommy rarely entered the top social stratum where Tyckman moved by right of wealth and ancestry, but he had found the man pleasant and without condescension.

The Yale bar was crowded, but they managed to get their drinks and to back off into an open space. Tommy noticed a young man standing with a group a few feet away. He was talking, and the others were listening, interrupting occasionally with shouts of laughter.

The young man was so handsome that he would have stood out in any company. He was tall, an inch or two over six feet, and a good tailor had done credit to a remarkably well-proportioned body. Tommy thought he had never seen more splendid shoulders. For that matter, everything about the young man was splendid. He was far handsomer than a movie star and without most movie stars' suggestion of perfumed prettiness. If there had been a wave in his shining black hair or color in his cheeks, he would have lost something of his masculine vigor; but the glossy hair was quite straight and his cheeks an even warm olive. His straight nose was big enough to give character to his face; his eyes were blue-gray, and his teeth dazzlingly white. When he smiled, his whole face seemed to be alight with happiness and humor. Charm radiated from him.

"Do you know that fine-looking chap over there with the million-dollar smile?" Tommy asked Tyckman. "I'm sure

I've never met him, but there's something familiar about him. I suppose I've noticed him in a crowd somewhere. Once seen, he's not likely to be forgotten."

Tyckman followed Tommy's glance and said, "Oh, you mean young Carter. No, you can't forget him. He's the handsomest man in the Club and one of the most popular, too. Graduated a year or two ago, I believe, and is with somebody or other downtown—a broker, I think. Everybody likes him. You can't help it. He's on his way."

Carter? That explained it. Mary's brother. Of course. He was the man, Tommy thought, that Mary ought to have been.

"I've never seen him before," Tommy explained, "but I've met his sister. That's the reason I thought I'd seen him; the resemblance is remarkable."

Tyckman lifted his blonde eyebrows. "She must be something to see, then."

"Believe me, she is."

Just then, the story over, the group broke up, and young Carter approached Tyckman and Tommy.

"How do you do, Mr. Tyckman," he said, a pleasant hint of deference in his voice. Tyckman was forty.

"Hello, Carter. This is Thomas Gray. He's just been telling me he knows your sister."

Bill Carter held out his hand to Tommy and looked at him in surprise.

"Mary? I never expect to see any of her friends uptown."

The tone was light, casual, but its very lightness irritated Tommy. Remembering what Mary had said about her brother, he thought it implied condescension; and Bill Carter, even though he might be the Club's pet and Society's darling, was in no position to condescend to Mary.

"Why not?" he asked briefly.

"Oh, you don't look like a Villager."

"I'm not one. But one doesn't have to be a Villager to

know your sister and admire her. Or," he added with a little bite in his tone, "does one?"

Confused, young Carter glanced at Tyckman. Obviously he didn't know what to make of this man Gray. If Nicholas Tyckman sponsored him, he must be a little better than all right. Tyckman was a famous snob, and everybody knew that he didn't drink with his inferiors.

Tyckman was watching him, and so he turned to Tommy. "Oh, of course not, Mr. Gray," he said, smiling a little to hide his embarrassment. "It's just that I can't stomach most of Mary's friends. She's always surrounded with a bunch of short-haired women and long-haired men. Her studio's a regular Midway, it's so infested with freaks."

Tommy ignored the explanation. "Miss Carter," he explained to Tyckman, "is an artist, and Fred Homans tells me she's a remarkably good one. I haven't seen any of her work myself, but I can't imagine her doing anything fussy or clumsy."

"You can bet she doesn't," said Bill. "She knows her stuff, but, just the same, she does have the damnedest friends."

"What's the matter with them?" Tyckman asked suddenly.

"Oh, you know what you find down in the Village—fifth-rate writers and tenth-rate artists, most of 'em—and nine-tenths of them queer as hell. I don't know how Mary puts up with them."

Tyckman was frowning, and Tommy watched him with sharp interest. He knew the man's reputation for snobbery, and he suspected that it was about to be revealed.

"You don't expect artists to behave like brokers, do you?" Tyckman asked, a challenge in his heavy voice. Then before Bill had a chance to answer, he asked another question, brutal in its demand: "Is your sister a freak, too?"

Bill flushed, and Tommy took pity on him. "Miss Carter," he said quickly, "is a remarkable person. She is talented, of course, and she has brains. That ought to be enough, but it isn't. Do you remember Dolores in the Follies years ago?"

"Do I?" said Tyckman. "Well, rather!"

"Well, I was only a kid when I saw her, but she was the kind you never forget. Miss Carter comes mighty near to being her equal."

Bill Carter was smiling, and Tommy couldn't tell whether he was smiling because he was pleased or because he was trying to mask embarrassment.

Tyckman turned to Bill. "Why, then," he demanded, "do you keep her hidden? She must be something to be proud of."

With an adroitness that Tommy was forced to admire Bill turned Tyckman's heavy verbal saber aside. "Try to get Mary uptown!" He laughed lightly at the idea. "If I asked her to go to a cocktail party, she'd blast me out of the studio. She has less use for my crowd than I have for hers, and she has lots of words to tell me what she thinks."

Tommy laughed. "She has the words, all right," he confessed and glanced at his watch. "I've got a dinner engagement and a crowd coming up later. I've got to be going." Then to Tyckman he added, "We'll want to get together again sometime next week. I'll let you know."

"Fine. Whenever you say. Good-bye."

Five minutes later Tommy was in a telephone booth calling Mary Carter. He was heartily ashamed of himself. He ought to have called her long before.

When she answered, he said, "This is Thomas Gray—the man on the train, you know."

"I haven't forgotten. What brought me to your mind all of a sudden?"

"You're putting me on a spot with that question, but I'm going to be honest and take the consequences. I've been busy as the devil since I got back, because I was a fool and accepted a lot of invitations I didn't care anything about. Now I've canceled about half of them and I can look around me again."

"Is that what brought me to mind?"

Tommy laughed. "Back I go on the spot, don't I? No; it wasn't that. It's something else. By accident, I've just met your brother."

"Bill?"

"Yes."

"Your breath must smell of Yale Club liquor."

"It does. But let that pass. Could I call tomorrow night?"

The silence following his request lasted so long that he said, "Hello. Hello."

"Hello," she replied. "I'm here. I'm thinking. Anyway, I'm trying to. You know, I think it would be a damn dumb thing for you to call."

"I'd like to argue that out in person instead of over the telephone."

"Well, come if you want to—but you won't enjoy yourself. People are always barging in here, and you won't like 'em."

"My tastes are more catholic than you think they are."

"Like fun! Wait a minute! What's that Dartmouth song I've heard? Oh, yes, I know. 'With the granite of New Hampshire in our muscles and our brains.' That's you to a T."

She was laughing and Tommy laughed with her. Somehow she seemed different talking into a telephone from what she had on the train. She must be a very complex person. He began to look forward to his call with unexpected eagerness.

IV

Tommy had five guests that evening. He had planned on only four, but Mr. Tucker had remarked during the day that his wife had gone on a cruise to Bermuda. Tommy had immediately felt sorry for him. He always felt sorry for Tucker when Mrs. Tucker was mentioned.

"She's going for her health," Tucker had explained. And

Tommy had thought, "And it won't be her fault if she doesn't begin taking the tonic the first night out."

He remembered something Craig Sherman had once said to him and Charlie Lovett: "If you ask me, and I take it you do, Evelyn Tucker's a trifle nympho—if you know what I mean, and you damn well do know. Every time Tucker takes me to his place for dinner, she makes me so damned conscious I'm male I don't know where to look."

Tommy had suffered Craig's experience more than once. Mrs. Tucker was ten years her husband's junior. In a full-blown, large-breasted, flamboyant way she was handsome; but her smiles at younger men were too eager, her eyes too bright when they were present. And she was what Tommy called a toucher. At the dinner table, her foot happened to touch his; her hand happened to touch his; and with each accidental touch there was a smile.

She sang rather prettily, and on one occasion—just one— he offered to accompany her. Later, he wondered how he managed to read the notes and to play them. Apparently she became shortsighted, for she leaned forward, far forward, to see the music; and in leaning, her breast pressed hard and often against his shoulder. Martin Tucker sat, watched, and listened. He must know what she was doing, Tommy thought unhappily. Tucker was far too shrewd and too observant not to know.

He was a scholarly man, usually dry in his manner, often sardonic. Yet, Tommy thought, he might enjoy an evening with younger men. At any rate, it would take his mind off of what his wife was probably doing. It wouldn't hurt to ask him, anyway.

"I've got four fellows coming in this evening," he said. "I don't think you know any of them except Craig Sherman. Fred Homans, who's a couple of years older than I am, is coming. He's in advertising. And Walter Newton. He's with the Steplanders downtown. He went to Cornell, but I knew him in law school. And Stephen Austin. He was—"

"The man who wrote *Sere and Yellow?*" Tucker broke in.

"Yes. It's his first novel. It got good reviews, but it isn't selling."

"I've read it. It's a good book. How old is he?"

"My age. He was in my class at Dartmouth."

"I'd like to know him. It's a good book."

"Well, that's what I have in mind. The fellows are coming around tonight. The idea is supposed to be poker, but they're a great gang for talking. I wondered if you would like to come, too."

When Tucker smiled, his lined face seemed to crack. His head was bald, his forehead very broad, his eyes small and sharp under overhanging dark eyebrows. His broad forehead and big nose made his thin face seem very narrow, and his thin mouth looked bitter. He was the keenest lawyer in the place, the most scholarly and the shrewdest. He was so observant and so sensitive to facial expressions that he often seemed clairvoyant. Tommy sometimes wondered why he had come into a firm with the two Winchesters and spent his talents on law largely concerned with estates. He would have been brilliant and devastating in a courtroom. Like all the people in the office, Tommy respected the man and was a little afraid of him.

Now, suddenly and unexpectedly, the harsh lines in Tucker's face broke into a smile surprisingly warm. "I'd like very much to come," he said with a frank pleasure as surprising as his smile. "I haven't had an evening like that in years. It was kind of you to think of me."

Tommy assured him of his own pleasure, but inwardly he wondered how Tucker would fit into the group. Both Fred Homans and Craig Sherman were great story-tellers, and their stories usually had a Rabelaisian vigor that Tucker might find a little strong. Walter Newton was conventional enough, but Steve Austin was openly, often belligerently, a Communist. Tucker knew a vast amount about Russia. He and Steve might clash. Worse, Steve was an avowed pacifist, and Tucker had been an infantry major in the World War. Tommy wondered if he hadn't made a mistake. Before the evening was over, he discovered that four years of association with Martin Tucker in a law office had hardly served as an introduction to the man.

Tucker arrived later than the others, and Craig was matching Fred story for story when Tucker appeared. He acknowledged the introductions to the three men he had not met before and then said, "I heard laughter when I was in the hall. If I'm stopping good stories, I'm leaving now."

Craig looked startled. Tell a smutty story to Tucker? Catch him!

But Fred Homans did not work for Winchester, Winchester, Tucker, and Gray; so he shared none of Craig's timidity. He had had a story on the tip of his tongue when Tucker had arrived, and it slipped off with glib ease. High as long-hung meat, it demanded a strong stomach. Both Craig and Tommy glanced uneasily at Tucker. He sipped the drink Tommy had given him, eyed Homans from under his brows, and waited for the point. It came—so unexpected that it was like an explosion. In spite of his concern, Tommy was surprised into laughing. When he had gained a measure of control, he turned to see how his eldest guest was taking the joke. It was a laugh bomb, all right, but it gave off a lot of smell.

Tucker was roaring, but his reaction wasn't as startling as Craig's. That young man was staring at Tucker as if he had seen a miracle. He had felt the bite of Tucker's sarcasm more than once. Now he was seeing something, hearing it, but he didn't believe it.

Afraid that Tucker might notice Craig's amazement, Tommy sought to attract attention to himself as soon as the laughter had subsided.

"You know," he said, "I'm fascinated by the psychology of dirty stories. It goes without saying that at least ninety percent of the really good stories are dirty. To get a really comic shock, you have to use sex. I've often wondered why."

"So have I," said Stephen Austin. "It's something a writer has to count on, though God knows I'm no comic writer. Just the same, that sex shock is something every serious writer uses because it's a part of life. I don't mean he uses it necessarily to shock his readers. Not that at all, but he has to recognize its effect on his characters."

Tucker nodded his head and pressed his lips tight together before speaking. "Yes," he said; "you're right, and I thought you used it admirably in *Sere and Yellow*. You mean John's reaction, don't you, to the girl's naive statement about the rutting bitch?"

"Now, that was neat," thought Tommy, noting Austin's pleased smile. "He gave Steve a nice compliment without making him self-conscious."

Walter Newton, who usually said little, spoke up before Austin could reply. "There's a perfect example," he said. "Just those words, 'rutting bitch,' give me a shock—and I haven't an idea why. They're perfectly good words, but both of them have connotations for me that sort of make me squirm. You couldn't do it with words that didn't suggest sex. There aren't any other words that'll do it."

"Right," said Craig, gathering courage from Tucker's apparent mellowness. "And the only theory I've heard is cockeyed. A psychology professor in college said the shock was due to repression. He said that people who lived a perfectly natural sex life didn't get a kick out of sex stories. Why, I know a man—"

"I know Fred," Tommy broke in, laughing.

Fred Homans joined in the laughter that burst around him, and his pale skin flushed. "All right," he said when the laughter subsided, "all right; I admit it. I live a perfectly natural sex life, and nobody gets a bigger kick out of a good dirty story than I do. Why? Hell, I don't know."

"I think I do," Tucker said quietly. "Maybe I'm wrong,

but I have a theory that'll hold some water at least. I agree
with Sherman that the psychologist is wrong about repres-
sions, though I think the shock is very often so great to re-
pressed people that they can't see the humor. Indeed, they
are often nauseated by stories that are howlingly funny to
the rest of us.

"No, it isn't that. Sex is like God. We don't understand
it. It's mystery; it's life. We can swear only two ways, you
know: by God and by sex. Did you ever think of that?
We can be obscene and profane; we can't be anything
else—I mean anything else objectionable. Or, put it this
way: We can't be anything else that will bring a strong
shock. We can offend other ways, but we can't really shock
without being either profane or obscene."

"You're right," Austin agreed thoughtfully. "I never
thought of it before, but you are certainly right. And pro-
fanity has largely passed out of existence because so many
people have done away with God. When I was a child, 'by
God' was a terrible thing to say. So was 'Christ' or 'Jesus.'
You don't find Dickens or Thackeray using words like that.
I don't suppose they dared write them or a publisher print
them. Now you hear girls saying 'Christ' as casually as they
say 'darling' or 'damn.' "

"Yes," said Tucker, " 'damn' and 'hell' used to be associated with religion, with God, and so they were strong
words, even terrifying words to lots of people. Now they're
just rather mild expletives. Tommy, could I have another
drink?"

"Indeed you can. Rye again?"

"Yes, thanks." He held out his glass to Tommy and turned
to Austin. "Don't you agree with me?"

"Yes, but your explanation doesn't seem quite complete.
We've done away with most of the sex tabus, too, but ob-
scenity remains. Publishers will print almost any word now,
I'll admit, but the words still seem dirty."

Tucker waited until Tommy had filled his glass and handed it to him; then he explained. "But, you see, we can't do away with sex. It's always there with all its terrible power. As I said, it's life; it's the eternal mystery. We may laugh at it, abuse it, try to analyze it in the laboratory, but it always escapes analysis. It's something beyond us; it's the eternal hunger, the basic hunger. Flesh meets flesh—and a new life appears. Why, when you come to think of it, it's so inconceivable, really, that's it's a marvel man ever connected the cause with the result. We don't know why a life appears as a result of that meeting. We know the process only, not the fundamental reason. It's the greatest of all miracles. That's the reason, I think, it forms the basis for most great tragedies and the funniest stories. It has the greatest power to shake us to tears or laughter because it *is* the greatest, the most inexplicable power."

There were half a dozen comments Tommy wanted to make, several questions he wanted to ask, but a cross-current swept the conversation away from him. Stephen Austin was reminded of something, Walter Newton of something else. And that something reminded Craig, brave at last, of a story he wanted to tell. The talk whirled around, serious for fifteen minutes, frivolous for thirty. Two hours later, when all of Maribelle's excellent sandwiches had been eaten and many drinks had washed them down, the conversation made a wide loop and circled back to its starting-point. Fred told a story of a childhood experience when a small friend had wet his pants in Sunday-school. Everybody laughed, and Craig said:

"There you are, just what we were talking about a while back. I suppose that's funny to us because we all went to Sunday-school and took it seriously. I don't suppose it would be funny to us now. We'd just want to take care of the kid."

"I suppose the Sunday-school teacher felt that way, too,"

Tommy said, "though if she was like some of the old girls, she probably felt that there was some sacrilege in it. People felt that way about churches twenty-five years ago."

"Some still do." Craig turned to Tommy. "Look at Charlie. Remember how he sounded off here one night? But most people our age don't. I'll admit that. We had God when we were kids, and I'll be damned if I know where we lost Him."

Tucker put down his glass. "You never had Him, Sherman, the way my generation did. We're the ones who lost Him; you've never really had Him. That's why you don't know where or how the losing took place. My generation knows."

"I don't understand, sir," Craig said.

"I'm ten, fifteen, twenty years older than you men. I was twenty-five years old in 1917—about your age, Sherman. You were just a baby. You don't remember the war. We lived it."

"I remember it," Homans said. "I was only ten or twelve when we got into it, but I got a great kick out of the soldiers and marching and flags. All of us kids did."

"Yes, a great kick. So did we." Tucker cradled his cheek in the palm of his hand. He seemed to be talking half to himself. "A great kick. It was an adventure to most of us, the adventure of a lifetime. We were full of idealism, though; we were going to make the world safe for democracy."

He looked up, dropped his hands, and his small eyes blazed. "We were cheated. Oh, I know you've heard that before. Probably you're sick of hearing it, but you wouldn't be if you could understand."

"Yes," said Tommy, "we've heard it before, of course, but that doesn't mean we wouldn't like to hear your side of it."

Walter Newton stirred in his chair. "I'd like to very much, sir. You see, they're getting ready to make soldiers out of us, and I'd like to hear about what happened to you."

"It isn't what happened to me that matters," Tucker explained. "Personal experiences aren't important. It's what happened to all of us. You see, it was the cheating that killed God for us—the whole, horrible, obscene mess. You don't know. You can't remember. But we weren't idiots. We heard the ministers praying for victory, praying for the destruction of our enemies. What bloodthirsty, pious devils they turned out to be! In the name of Jesus Christ, the Prince of Peace, they prayed that the Germans might be destroyed. And the German ministers prayed in the name of Jesus Christ that we might be destroyed. It made a lot of us sick because we believed that Jesus Christ was the Prince of Peace, and we loved Him because He was. Do you see? We believed in the Allies' cause, mind you. We didn't know anything about the causes of the war yet; we weren't disillusioned yet. We were just chock full of propaganda. But we were sickened when ministers of the gospel stood in the pulpit and screamed for vengeance. We weren't ready for hate and bloodthirstiness in church. We still had God. We could still be shocked.

"I know it's an old, old platitude to say that the Christian religion has never been given a chance. It hasn't, of course, but we didn't understand that then. We didn't realize that the only god we had was the old Jehovah of the Old Testament—the god of vengeance, I mean. We thought we'd been worshiping a god of love, but the instant the little veneer of our civilization was scraped off, the truth broke out—and we didn't want any part of it.

"Then there was the war itself. Well, never mind that. I couldn't make it real to you. For no reason I can understand men are about war something the way women are about childbirth. It's something indescribable, but once it's over, the agony seems to be forgotten. Women welcome the next child, and men make ready for the next war. Why, God knows; I don't. It doesn't seem possible; it's beyond human understanding that any one who had anything to do with that hideous, that utterly futile slaughter could ever even imagine another one. Imagine it? Well, you all know what's happening. How can they do it? I don't know, but if you can get your mind around this, maybe you can understand: I saw a man killed at three minutes of eleven the morning the Armistice was signed. Thousands of men were killed that morning. Thousands! Yet everybody knew the Armistice was to take place at eleven. Did the guns stop? Oh, no; the game had to be played until that last, sixtieth second.

"And when the guns stopped? What then? Did the English soldiers hate the German soldiers? They'd hated each other for years, killed each other by the million—but at the stroke of eleven they quit hating. They literally quit by the clock. If you can get your mind around anything like that, you can understand why another war is on the way. I've been trying to get my mind around it for sixteen or seventeen years, and I haven't succeeded yet."

He threw up his arm and dropped it to his chair in a weak, futile gesture. "Then we came home," he went on bitterly, "to find that we'd been cheated from first to last —to find that our noble cause at best was half a lie. And ten days after the Armistice was signed we weren't heroes any more; we were just a damned nuisance. Prohibition had been slipped over on us just as the war had been. Our women were wearing skirts up to their knees or above them and raising hell. We went for the adventure. I'll admit that. But we went with illusions too, and when we came back we weren't ready for a world without illusions. But the Jazz Age was on. It wasn't eat, drink, and be merry because tomorrow we die. No, that was war and understandable. No; no, this was to hell with illusions, with decency, with standards because what in hell is the difference?

"That's the world you younger men have inherited. The depression has taught us something—manners for one thing. There's nothing like poverty to teach manners, but otherwise the disillusionment has only been deepened. We haven't any faith, any direction. When I was growing up, we thought we knew what we were living for, and so life had meaning. We had a god, and man needs a god. Only very unusual people can really live at peace in agnosticism, and there aren't many unusual people. Death is always waiting, and almost no one can find meaning in life without some feeling, some assurance through faith that there is some meaning. We have to have standards; we have to have faith in our leaders—and my generation left mighty little to yours. I sometimes wonder what men your age find in life."

"We always have our egos," said Austin softly. "I suppose we have substituted them for faith."

"That," said Tucker, "reminds me of a line in a book called *Queed* that was popular years ago. A girl said something like this: 'The trouble with you, Mr. Queed, is that your cosmos is all ego.' You don't think that applies, do you?"

"I think," Tommy said, "life would mean a lot more to most of us if it did apply."

"Yes," Tucker agreed; "yes, I suppose it would."

# CHAPTER X

## I

THE next morning Tucker came into Tommy's office. "I want to thank you for a very pleasant evening," he said. For some reason his face seemed more heavily lined than ever; his little eyes looked very tired.

"Oh," exclaimed Tommy, "you made the evening."

"It's kind of you to say that. I've rather regretted talking so much."

"Regretted! Why, Steve and Fred hung around for an hour after you left. Craig was there for a while, too. They all said you'd made it the best evening they could remember. Steve is very anxious to know you better, and I think you might like him."

"I'm sure I would. Couldn't you and he have dinner with me some night while Mrs. Tucker is away? Come out to the house, and we can have a long evening together."

"That would be fine, and I know Steve will be delighted. Besides, he needs a good dinner."

Tucker frowned. "Is he having a hard time of it?"

"Awful. He says the depression has wiped out writing as a profession, and I guess it pretty nearly has. He managed fairly well up to '30 selling a story now and then. Then the advertisers quit, and, of course, the magazines stopped buying. There just wasn't anything he could do about it. Now he's writing for the pulps, and he finds it mighty hard going. He hasn't the knack, he says, and he has to work harder to write a bad story than he does to write a good one. I think he manages to sell a story or two a month for a cent or two a word. That just about keeps him alive."

"And *Sere and Yellow* is a failure, you say?"

"Yes. He got a two-hundred-dollar advance on it. He says he'll feel lucky if he gets five hundred out of it altogether."

Tucker shook his head at the pitiful smallness of the sum. Then his eyes lighted. "How many people can you send copies to?" he asked.

Tommy smiled. "I've already sent out fifteen, and *Sere and Yellow* is going to be the Christmas present I send to everybody else."

"I can probably send out twenty," Tucker said thoughtfully. "I'll speak to Jonathon and Frederick. A book like that oughtn't to die unread, and Austin deserves encouragement. I think I can drum up a good bit of trade. But don't say anything about it to him," he commanded, his voice sharp with insistence.

"I won't. When would you like to have us for dinner?"

"Arrange a date with Austin and let me know."

When Tucker left the office, Tommy leaned back in his chair. What a lot of knowing that man would take! "I wonder," he thought, "what he was like twenty years ago. He must have been as idealistic as all get out—probably is yet, though he wouldn't admit it. . . ." What was that story he'd heard when he first came into the office? Somebody had told him something—something about Tucker and a girl. He'd been engaged. No, that wasn't it. Ah, now he remembered. Tucker had made one of those last-minute war marriages. He'd sailed for France a day or two after the wedding. Then when he came back he was served with divorce papers or something of the sort when he got off the boat. No wonder he was bitter . . . It must have taken him a long time to get over that girl, because he'd been married to Evelyn only about ten years. And look at her, cheating on him every chance she got. No children, either . . . Tommy had never thought of it before, but he'd bet Tucker would like children. "I guess," he decided, "he feels cheated out of about everything. Well, who wouldn't?"

II

Tommy's taxi swung through Washington Square and stopped before a studio building. "Here you are, Mister," the driver said.

Tommy paid the fare and looked up. The building was tall and modern. "Hm," he thought, "she must make plenty to afford a studio here."

The studio quite lived up to his expectations. It was a large room with an enormous window in the north wall. There was a model's stand, a canvas on an easel; otherwise there was nothing to suggest a workroom. Tommy had subconsciously expected disorder, dust, and confusion. Instead he found a well-swept rug on the floor, ash-trays that had been emptied and washed, and furniture as bright as if Maribelle herself had polished it. The pillows on the big couch lacked the cast-iron perfection of form that Maribelle strove for and unfortunately attained, and the magazines on a table did not overlap each other with geometrical precision; but the studio was as neat as his own apartment without his apartment's emptiness of personality.

Mary was even more of a surprise than the studio itself. Since he had last seen her wearing a sweater and woolen skirt, he had, man-like, supposed that she would be wearing if not the same costume, something similar. Instead, she wore a gray silk dress with a dull red collar and belt. It did something to her, made her seem younger, disconcertingly more feminine.

She held out her hand and smiled. "You look a little confused. What's the matter?"

Tommy shook hands, surrendered his hat and coat to her. "It's you and the studio. You know how you form impressions. Half the time there's no sense in them, but you form them, just the same. I think I expected an artistic mess—and there isn't any."

"I don't like messes," Mary said. "I suppose you expected to see long-haired poets lolling on the floor eating hashish."

"Well, hardly that—but, well, I don't know." He grinned at her because he felt unsure. "I think we'll have to start all over. You look quite different from what you did on the train. I feel as if I'd just met you."

"Embarrassed?"

The grin broadened. "A little."

"Well, so am I—embarrassed as the devil. I've kicked myself a dozen times for sounding off to you the way I did—and you look different too, older or something. Let's have a drink. Maybe that'll help."

Tommy glanced around the studio. "I'd rather look at the pictures, if you don't mind. Are these yours?" he asked, motioning toward the walls.

"No. None of them are mine. Some of them are good. Take a look."

They went from picture to picture, making appropriate and somewhat formal comments. The strain did not lessen. Instead, Tommy grew increasingly uncomfortable. He was achingly aware of Mary as a woman, and he had not expected to be. He tried hard to think of the pictures instead of Mary. He stopped before the easel.

"That's yours, I suppose?"

"Of course. It's a job."

Tommy studied the picture. A slender girl was half sitting, half reclining on something that so far was barely indicated. He imagined that it was a hill-top. Her thin cotton dress was pressed against her body as if by a breeze, and her long golden hair streamed behind her. The blue eyes were vague with dreaminess.

"For an ad?"

"Yes."

Suddenly Mary laughed. "You ought to see the wench that's posing for it. She's a little slut, and her eyes look like calculating machines. I tried and tried, but it was no go. Finally I copied the eyes from a photograph of a little boy. That, Mr. Thomas Gray, is commercial art."

"Well," said Tommy, "not everybody could do it, at that. What's this picture for?"

"A life insurance ad. It's supposed to make fathers go dewy-eyed with tenderness, so soft that they'll run, not walk, to the nearest salesman. Think it'll do the work?"

Tommy wanted to say, "What does it matter? You're beautiful," but he was afraid to make even a slight advance. He knew with absolute sureness that he was in that studio on probation and that he had to be a very good boy indeed if he wanted to stay there.

"It might," he said. "Anyhow, it's certainly as skilful as I expected. Won't you let me see your Berkshire pictures?"

"I wrecked all but four. They made me sick."

"Well, let me see the others, please. I really want very much to see them."

"O.K. Have it your way. Sit down and I'll show them." Suddenly she whirled and said fiercely, "No pretty compliments! You be honest—" Her black eyes flashed and she lifted her hand significantly. Tommy suspected that she might actually strike him if he insulted her with false admiration.

"I'll be honest, don't worry," he said, dropping into a chair and stretching out his legs. "Just remember I'm no critic and don't mind anything I say."

Mary went into another room and returned with the canvases. She removed the picture of the dreamy girl from the easel and set a picture of a brilliant hillside in its place. Tommy studied it. Though he was not aware of the change, his interest relaxed him. His embarrassment faded and so did his desire to make love to Mary. The picture held his attention.

He took his time about making a judgment. Finally he said, "I like it. You're a better painter than you said you were. I expected something neat and tight—nothing so free and impressionistic. I like that picture, but I don't want to live with it."

"Why not?" she demanded, her eyes shining with interest.

"I don't know. It's good painting—first-class painting, I think; but—well, I don't know. I'm that way about lots of pictures. I'd like to live with Rembrandt's *Old Lady Paring Her Nails,* but I don't want to live with his *Syndics.* Do you know what I mean?"

"Of course," she said tersely and removed the picture from the easel. Tommy's reaction to the second picture was the same as to the first; it was the same to the third, but the fourth made him sit up. It was smaller than the others, less ambitious. It showed a bit of a hillside, a sweep of sky. There was a green tree, a sumac bush, its red faded until it was almost rusty.

"That, I think," he said, his admiration in his voice, "is a picture. That does something to me." He looked up at her and smiled. "There's New England in autumn in that picture—all of it. There's the color and the softness and the sadness. You may not think you're an artist, but I do. No second-rater could do that."

Mary looked at the picture for a full minute before she looked at Tommy. Her eyes were so soft that he thought there might be tears in them.

Her deep voice had an organ's richness when she spoke. "It's the best picture I ever painted—and you saw." Suddenly she threw off her emotion. "We've got to have a drink! You've got taste. I'm glad I let you come. We'll have to celebrate."

The last thread of tension snapped. Tommy knew that he had passed a test, and he was glad. Mary was herself again, not the Mary he had met on the train—there was something different, something new and elusive—but she was as obviously at ease as she was obviously delighted.

"I didn't want to show you my pictures," she explained when she had brought the drinks and given him his. "I was afraid to. When an artist shows his picture, he shows his soul—and he doesn't like to do that to any one he isn't sure of. I supposed you had an academic interest in painting, but that's a long way from enough."

"I know," said Tommy; "it's different from law. My work is outside of me; yours is you."

"That's saying it. But let's leave me and my pictures alone. Tell me about Bill. How did you happen to meet him?"

"Why, I was having a drink with Nicholas Tyckman in the Yale Club bar and he introduced us. We just talked a minute."

"Do you know Tyckman?" she demanded with surprising eagerness.

"Only in a business way. We're handling his aunt's estate. Why?"

"He's a collector, you know, and he has a John Van Eyck that I'd give a lot to see. What's he like?"

"To tell you the truth, I don't know. Of course, the Tyck-mans have been here since New York was a trading-post. He's the ninth or tenth Nicholas, and he's supposed to be an awful snob. I've found him pleasant. He's a big man—a good six-three, I'd say. It was before my day, of course, but I know he was All America—full-back, I think. Let's see . . . He's blond, sort of a big Viking. Everything about him's big. His features are big; his hands are big; and so's his voice. I don't think he does anything but handle the Tyckman estate, but that's job enough for any man. I don't know what he's like socially. He breathes somewhere in the upper stratosphere, and I don't."

"How does he happen to know Bill, then? My guess is Bill hasn't got much beyond the new riches."

"I think they're just Yale Club acquaintances," Tommy explained. "Everybody knows who your brother is around there, I imagine. He's so handsome he's bound to be noticed."

Mary lit a cigarette, puffed at it until it was well alight,

and then asked with a casualness that seemed hardly real,
"He is a beautiful animal, isn't he? A regular collar ad . . ."
She paused and her face softened. "When he was sixteen, he
was the handsomest, sweetest kid that ever drew breath.
There never was anything like him. I—oh hell, what's the
difference? You know how I feel. I'm sorry I told you about
him, and I wouldn't have if I'd ever expected to see you
again. But I did; so that's that. Bill's turned into a louse, and
I might as well make my mind up to it. Only I can't."

"Are you sure?" Tommy asked. "Aren't you judging him
pretty severely just because he isn't what you wanted him to
be? He's young. You can't tell how he'll turn out." Having
met Bill Carter, Tommy only half believed what he was
saying. Apparently, Bill was ashamed of his sister: and if he
was, he was worse than a prig; he was a fool. Just the same,
Tommy knew that he would have liked Bill Carter instantly
if he hadn't been forewarned about him.

Mary jammed her cigarette into an ash-tray and ground it
viciously. "No," she contradicted, lifting her voice. "No, I'm
not doing that. He's got a job and he's making some money—
not much, of course, but enough to live on. He's lucky as hell
if he only knew it, but he doesn't. He's got half an eye on
sister all the time. His clothes! Don't I know what they cost?
My God, his tailor bill his senior year! I damn near passed
out when he sent it on—and this studio looked like a bar-
racks, there were so many poor devils sleeping here. I
couldn't get a commission for more than a tenth my price,
and if the landlord hadn't been the whitest man in the world,
I'd have had to give up the studio.

"Well, I sold my last two bonds—and got fifty for them. I
paid his damned tailor's bill. But do you think he's paying it
now? Don't fool yourself. He's in debt. I know he must be.
You can't dress like Bill on what he's making. He goes to
swank parties five or six nights a week. What's his laundry
bill come to?"

"Twenty a month. Thirty maybe."

"Yes, and I'll bet he owes three or four months right now. He's hinted. He hints every time I see him. But I won't give him another cent." She brought her fist down on the arm of her chair. "I damn well won't!"

"You would be a fool if you did," said Tommy. "You'd just be hurting him. I expect you've been too good to him all along."

"I expect I have. I know part of the fault is mine. But when I think how I—oh, never mind. Somebody will always take care of him." There was a knock at the door. "Damn! I knew some fool would come in—and it's too early for Hollis." As she moved toward the door, she explained over her shoulder. "I'll tell you about Hollis later. I'm expecting her." She opened the door and said to some one in the hall, "What's eating you, brother? You look sick or cock-eyed or something."

She stepped back, and a little, bedraggled youth entered the room. His face was thin and white. Even his lips were almost white. The collar of his shirt was frayed and dirty; his pale brown hair needed cutting and combing. But there was some kind of power in his big nose and a fever in his brown eyes that caught Tommy's attention and held it.

"This funny little thing," said Mary, towering over the poor fellow, "is Verne Ticknor." Tommy stood up to acknowledge the introduction. "And this is Mr. Gray, Mr. Thomas Gray. Tommy, I suppose, to his friends, but we haven't got that far yet. Verne," she explained to Tommy, "is a poet. He looks hungry, and he is hungry." She gazed down at little Ticknor and demanded fiercely, "Aren't you?"

Ticknor touched Tommy's hand weakly and said in a strangely soft voice, "Don't be cruel, Mary."

"Cruel? Don't be a sensitive damn fool, Verne. Hunger knows no manners. Story come back again?"

He nodded and whispered, "Yes."

"Well, don't bawl about it. Better writers than you are getting their stories back these days. The magazines are just beginning to buy. If my bourgeois advertising agencies weren't beginning to feed them, I wouldn't be able to feed you. Come on out to the kitchen. Or go on out. Eat what you want—and don't eat your pride with it. You know you're welcome."

Ticknor faded like a wraith through a door. Tommy and Mary sat down again.

"He starves," she explained, "until he can't stand it, and it's dangerous to starve people like him. They spit fire when they're hungry." She looked toward the door and lowered her voice. "He'll make you sick, but there's a lot of starving people who might make you sick."

"Yes," said Tommy sharply, "and a lot of well-fed people, too. One of my best friends happens to be a hard-up writer. Please don't judge me until you have reason to."

Mary smiled broadly. "Atta boy! You can get mad, can't you? Swell! Well, probably your friend is a good writer."

"He is. He's Stephen Austin. He wrote *Sere and Yellow.* Have you read it?"

"No, but I will if you say it's good. But Verne, you see, isn't a good writer. Anyway, I don't think he is. And he tries to sell Left Wing stories and poetry to capitalist magazines, and he thinks they're vicious because they won't buy propaganda written to destroy them. Verne is very, very queer. Sometimes he seems pitiful to me, and sometimes he seems like a snake some one's stepped on. He's too weak to strike, but, God above, how he can hiss!"

Tommy said that Austin was a Communist too, but that he divorced political theory from literature. He was trying to explain Austin's point of view when Verne Ticknor reappeared. His pallor was less evident and his eyes looked less feverish. He threw himself down on the big couch and accepted a cigarette from Mary.

Suddenly he spoke to Tommy. "You look like a Republican."

Tommy's laughter broke from him spontaneously. The

fellow was so little and his malice so open, so deliberately provocative, that he couldn't help laughing. Ticknor's eyes flamed and his thin cheeks reddened.

"You laugh from a full belly," he said, loading his voice with scorn. "There's caviar and chicken à la Maryland in your pampered pot."

"Don't be murderous, Verne, on my food," Mary admonished him. "Don't snarl at my guest just because your pride is hurt. It isn't his fault, you know." Her words were sharp, but her voice was gentle. This, thought Tommy, was a third Mary. What was the woman really like, anyhow?

"Damn bourgeois food!" cried Ticknor. "You sold your cowardly little soul to get it turning out saccharine tripe for lying advertisers. You painted lies just to keep your belly full."

"And yours, remember," said Mary placidly. "Well, Verne, you ungrateful little asp, I don't know anything about Mr. Gray's politics, and I don't care anything about them. This is my studio, and we'll leave them alone. See? Now if you've got a poem to recite, recite it. We'll listen and maybe we'll like it. But you mind your manners or we shan't listen at all."

In a gesture of weakly futile rage, Ticknor threw the stub of his cigarette on the rug. Mary picked it up, crushed it in a tray, and then in one stride she was at the couch. Leaning over, she gripped Ticknor's thin shoulders, lifted him to a sitting position, and shook him until his teeth chattered. Then without a word she dropped him and returned to her chair.

To Tommy's goggle-eyed amazement, Ticknor smiled, and his eyes shone with pleasure as he rubbed his shoulders.

"Mary, darling," he said in a high, fluty voice, "you're so impulsive."

"If you throw things on my rug, you'll find out how impulsive I can be. I've told you before that this isn't a joint. I'll stand you, Verne, as long as you stick to the rules. If you

don't, I'll kick your little behind until you can't sit for a
week."

"I'd like that," said Verne, stretching luxuriously. "I'd
love it. Give me another cigarette, darling, and I'll make you
do it."

Through the haze of his own disgust Tommy saw Mary's.
She was controlling a repulsion as strong as his own. To what
lengths, he wondered, did she carry her pity? How could she
endure this twisted, diseased, ungrateful little—little . . .

His search for an epithet was lost in Mary's reply. "Verne,"
she said, her contralto voice deeper even than usual, "I draw
a line. You've reached it." Her dark eyes looked into Ticknor's. He squirmed and muttered, "Sorry, Mary."

"All right. Forget it. Now if you want to recite the poem,
recite it."

Ticknor leaned on his elbow; his eyes kindled; his free
hand stretched toward them, trembled. The flutey quality
was gone from his voice.

> "There's a sickle coming,
>   Sweeping through the sky.
>   The fat bond-holders cannot hear it.
>   The smug bankers cannot see it.
>   But it gleams in the sunlight. . . .
>   Hark, how it shrieks,
>   Swung by the hand of God!
>   Please, God, let it strike soon."

His voice broke on the last line; his eyes filled with tears.
With total unexpectedness, he jumped to his feet and rushed
out of the studio, slamming the door after him. There was a
clatter of his feet on the stairs. Then silence.

Mary and Tommy looked at each other. She shook her
head. "That might seem like immortal poetry to us if we
were starving," she said softly, "and he was starving when he
wrote it."

Tommy nodded in agreement. "Yes," he said. "I understand. And yesterday there were millions hungry enough to think it was immortal poetry, and tomorrow there may be millions hungry enough again. Right now it doesn't look like it, but it didn't look like it in '29 either. There's a lot of difference between Austin's Communism and Ticknor's. Austin thinks, but Ticknor feels. He hates. He *is* like a wounded snake, isn't he?"

Mary stood up and moved to the window. For a time she stared out at the night; then she turned and asked, "Why shouldn't he be? He was given brains enough to know he's a freak. Of course, he hated you. You're everything he'd give his soul to be, but he wouldn't admit it if you burnt him with fire. He can't strike God for what's been done to him. He'll do what anybody else would do: he'll strike what he can."

Tommy hesitated to speak, but the silence lasted too long. "You have great understanding," he said gently, "and great pity."

She lifted her hand and then let it drop to her side. Again she looked out at the night, and Tommy thought she asked, "Why not?"

"Why not?" What did she mean? Surely she wasn't— She couldn't be. . . . He remembered how she had blushed when she said for him to call if he wanted to. No, that was insane. . . . But what in the devil? An artist, she must know what a magnificent creature she was. She must know. Otherwise she couldn't dress to such advantage. She knew how to set herself off. At first he had thought her close-cropped hair a mannish affectation. Now he knew better. A pug on that head? It would be ridiculous, and so would a cluster of curls. No, she knew exactly what she was doing. Then, what in hell?

His meditations were broken by the sound of the buzzer. Mary turned. "The janitor must have shut the front door," she said and walked across the room. She pressed a button. "That's probably Hollis."

"A girl?"

"Yes. Oh, I meant to tell you about her. Now there isn't time. But I'll tell you this much: she isn't like Verne. You can relax. Hollis is as wholesome as hominy."

She opened the door and waited. Somewhere down the corridor a sweet, clear voice cried, "Hello, Mary!"

"Hello, Hollis. My, it's good to see you again."

"Oooh, Mary, I've got such news!"

Tommy saw a girl, who seemed almost childishly small, put her arms around Mary. She laughed. "You're such a lot for me to hug."

Mary's laugh was like music. Without warning, she lifted the girl six inches from the floor and swung her into the room.

"Mr. Gray," she said, "this happy mite is Hollis Graham. Hollis, this is Mr. Thomas Gray, attorney at law and a judge of good pictures. He likes mine."

Hollis wriggled and laughed. "Juno," she commanded, "let me down. I can't acknowledge an introduction to an attorney at law from up here. Let me down! I'll call you names!"

"I'll let it go at Juno," said Mary. She casually lowered Hollis's feet to the floor and watched while her embarrassed guests shook hands.

"I'm very glad to meet you, Miss Graham," Tommy said, hardly knowing what else to say.

"And I'm glad to meet you, though an attorney is the last thing I ever expected to meet here. The depression must be over."

"Don't crack wise, little one," Mary ordered dryly. "Take off your hat and coat, park where you will, and tell us the good news." She turned to Tommy and explained, "Hollis is a musician, a professional musician—a musician with a public, what's more. I don't believe Kreisler has a larger public."

She was joking, Tommy knew. The coat that Hollis Graham was throwing over a chair was cheap even to his eye, and badly worn. Even the little felt hat looked old. The girl was poor.

Hollis ran her hands through the mass of soft curls that hung almost to her shoulders. Her hair was light brown, and Tommy would have sworn that the curls were God-given. They had none of the ordered, rigid quality that marked even the most expensive curls produced by a permanent-wave machine. Her features were small, prettily formed, her eyes blue. Probably her lips were reddened with rouge, but her cheeks were free of it. Beside Mary she looked pallid, frail and insignificant, though she wasn't quite as small as Tommy had first thought. She was at least an inch or two over five feet.

"Yes, indeed," she said; "but you don't know the half of it, Mary, not the quarter, nor the eighth. I'm leaving my public."

"You're what?"

"Leaving them flat—like that." She spread her little hands, palms downward. "I couldn't tell you over the phone. I just had to see your face."

"Well, let's all sit down," Mary said. "A shock's coming. We'd better be set for it."

She and Tommy returned to their chairs; Hollis sat on the edge of the couch and looked up at Mary. She began to speak, hesitated, and turned to Tommy.

"My public," she explained to him, "is in Woolworth's. I sit and play sheet music all day. You know."

He smiled. "Well, you can be sure of having a public, anyway."

"You have no idea! Well, today I came back from lunch and nobody was around. Sometimes that happens. For hours there will be a crowd, and then everybody disappears—from the music counter, I mean. Have I set the stage?"

"You haven't," Mary replied, "but we'll take the stage for granted. Lift the curtain."

"Oh, it's already up. Down left I'm sitting just strumming,

you know, and then I began to play some of Schumann's 'Carnaval.' Dear me, I've mixed up my tenses. Well, let 'em go . . . I forgot a passage and so I switched to Debussy. I'd forgotten all about my job, and I was having a perfectly lovely time all by myself."

"You're really a trained musician, then?" Tommy asked.

"No—not really. I studied the violin and piano for years, but most of the time I had second-rate teachers. That's all I deserved, because I've got only a second- or third-rate talent. The fiddle's really my instrument. I majored in music at Vassar, and I didn't aspire to anything more than a high school job, but you can imagine the chance I had of getting one two years ago."

Tommy nodded. "Yes, I can imagine. Several men I know took a year or two of graduate work just because they couldn't find jobs."

"That's what I wanted to do, but I couldn't scrape up the money for the tuition. I was so anxious to get a job that I didn't apply for a scholarship until it was too late. Luckily, I can play jazz."

"But, Hollis," Mary objected, "don't get historical. Forget the past now. What's the big news?"

"Well, where was I? Oh, yes, playing Debussy . . . Oh, Mary, it was perfect—a real Cinderella story. Somebody spoke, and what do you suppose he said? In Woolworth's! He said, 'I beg your pardon, but can you play any Scriabine?' In Woolworth's! I just stared at him for a minute and then I asked him what he wanted me to play. He said he just wanted to know. Then he began to talk about music and asked me a lot of questions. He's about fifty, with gray hair and glasses and a mustache. He told me later he'd come in to buy a pencil. On such things do the fate of nations depend. Don't glare at me, Mary. I won't keep you in suspense much longer.

"He turned out to be the manager of Sturmen's Fifth Avenue store—the music publishers, you know. And they needed a salesman, somebody who knew about music. Most of their customers are real musicians, you know, and he offered me the job on the spot. Double the money, Mary!" Too happy to remember the stranger in the room, she jumped up and began to dance, singing, "Double the money! Double the money!"

Mary clapped her hands, cried, "Hurrah for you!" Then she leaped to her feet, caught Hollis's flying hands, pumped them up and down. "It's grand! It's wonderful!" She and Hollis smiled happily at each other. Mary laughed, tilted back her head and sang, "Happy days are here again."

She could sing magnificently. Her big contralto filled the studio, made it ring. Hollis joined in with her little high soprano.

Tommy had felt uncomfortable, an intruder. He had no place in this happiness, but it was so complete, so free, that it caught him up. Though still a little self-conscious, he began to sing. Mary smiled her approval, disengaged a hand from Hollis's and held it out to him. Laughing, he shook his head. He'd feel like a fool. Mary wrinkled her nose at him, took Hollis's hand again, and whirled her around the studio while the three of them sang at the top of their lungs.

"Hey," cried Mary, turning to Tommy when they had finished the chorus, "you've got a good voice."

"You've got a wonderful voice!" he retorted.

"Fiddlesticks!"

"Won't somebody please say," Hollis pleaded, panting, "that I've got some kind of voice? Small but true; something like that, you know?"

"You sing like a good fiddler," said Mary. "I feel like music. I want to sing. If I only had a piano."

"I've got one," Tommy said.

"Can you play it?"

"Yes."

"Let's go up to your place, then, and sing." She looked at him, her great dark eyes shining. "Can't we?"

"Can't we? Of course we can. That's what I meant. But we need a tenor. Who's a tenor?

"Tenor, tenor," chanted Mary. "Who's got a tenor?"

"I know!" cried Tommy. "Steve Austin! Come on. We'll pick him up on the way."

Something had died in him and something had been born. He hadn't felt like this in years. Some confining reticence had been stripped away, something tight and stifling. And he felt free and glad and eager. Sing? That's what he wanted to do—sing and sing and sing. And laugh. For no reason he was laughing as he helped the girls into their coats, laughing as he jerked on his own, laughing as they ran down the stairs.

He hailed a taxi, gave the driver Austin's address, and dropped into the seat between Hollis and Mary. Hollis bent forward and studied the picture of the driver that the law requires to be placed in every New York City taxicab.

"His name's Aaron Pogor-nor-sel-ski," she whispered, "and he looks dangerous."

"They always do," said Mary. "Happy days are here again," she hummed.

"Happy days are here again," hummed Tommy. Mary hummed. Hollis hummed.

Aaron Pogornorselski swung his cab through the Square and lifted his voice, loud and clear. "Happy days are here again," he sang.

"He's a tenor!" Hollis screamed excitedly. "A tenor!"

"Hey, driver!" Tommy shouted. "Hold on a minute! Altogether now!"

Through the arch sped the taxi, into Fifth Avenue. A pedestrian stopped, listened. "That," he said to himself, "is a pretty damned good quartet."


### III

Three hours later Tommy lay in bed, his head cradled in the palms of his hands, his eyes wide open in the darkness.

His body relaxed gratefully, but his mind was bubbling with thoughts.

What an evening! Why, he hadn't had such a good time since—since . . . Since Freda? No; they'd never had times like that. Lots of good times, yes—but different, quieter, more, more . . . What was the word? Careful? Yes, that was it. They'd always been careful. He didn't let go easily, and Freda had always been afraid. He hadn't known that then, but he did now. Probably she and Ballard had really good times. He'd bet they did. Well, the more power to them. Freda had earned the right to laugh . . .

There'd been good times with Polly, too, but not like this. Tonight—why, tonight he'd felt really *young,* young the way he had in college. It'd been a real song fest, a real letting-go.

And how old Steve had loosened up! "I'll bet," he thought, "he hasn't let go like that for five years. It must've done him a world of good." Clearly in the darkness he saw Steve's amazement when he had rushed into the dingy little hall bedroom. Remembering, he chuckled.

"Come on, Steve," he had cried. "We need a tenor."

Steve had turned from his writing and frowned. "Tenor? Listen, Gray, I'm experiencing a moment in literature. There's a bandit at the bottom of a canyon with the sheriff and his posse riding along the rim. I can't leave them there. The suspense will kill them. Besides, I need the money."

But Tommy had been too exhilarated for argument. He would listen to no No's. They needed a tenor. Steve had to come.

When had they begun using first names? Tommy couldn't remember. Sometime or other the Misses and Misters had disappeared, and it was Steve and Tommy and Mary and Hollis. Of course, they'd called Steve Caruso because his voice broke into a thin falsetto whenever he had to sing higher than F sharp. What was it Steve called Mary? Oh, yes, Brünnehilde . . . Then for half an hour Steve had been

Siegfried. They'd acted like a lot of crazy kids, but it was a hell of a lot of fun.

Glorious voice Mary had. Beside her, Hollis looked like a robin and sounded like a linnet. She could play the piano, though. She had sat with him on the bench and the two of them had gone jazz mad. Regular Harlem stuff . . . He wished some of the highbrow critics could have seen the author of *Sere and Yellow* strutting his stuff. He'd forgotten what fun Steve could be. Why, he remembered back in Hanover—where was it, anyway? Oh, yes, that blond fellow's room in Hitchcock. Steve had put on a show all by himself. He'd had a drink or two and let go. The show had had a name and everything. "The Bride's Dilemma or Should I Tell?" That was it . . . Tommy smiled at the memory. They had rolled on the floor laughing.

Steve and Hollis certainly got together in a hurry. You'd think they'd known each other for years . . . Steve had a girl somewhere, though, didn't he? Or did he? One never knew about Steve. He talked a lot, but he didn't tell anything. Maybe he had a dozen girls and maybe he'd never had one. It didn't seem possible, but you couldn't tell . . . Hollis had a kind of wistful charm. She wasn't thrilling like Mary, but she knew music, and—well, he didn't know, but he liked her.

Sometime during the evening he had learned her story. She came from Iowa, and her father was a mathematics teacher in a country high school. He had gone to the State university, but his sister had gone to Vassar and he had been determined that Hollis should go there, too. Then the depression had hit them.

"It was actually cheaper for me to stay in college," Hollis said, "than go home. I had a scholarship and I managed to get a job. I could just about pay my own way. Dad's salary was cut and cut and cut, and he had to take care of his mother and sister. Grandma owned a farm. It was leased, you know, and she and Aunt Edith lived on the rent. You can imagine what happened. They couldn't even pay the taxes. There wasn't anything any one could do; they had to come live with Dad and Mother. And there we were. When I graduated there wasn't any sense in going back to Iowa. There wasn't any sense in going anywhere. I came to New York because it was near and because I knew a couple of girls I could stay with."

She laughed. "It was really awfully funny—anyway, it seems funny now. They had two rooms in a basement in the Village. We didn't like each other at all after a month. We just couldn't abide each other, but there never was a mean word spoken. We didn't dare say boo. You see, one of us always had a job, but only one. There wasn't a single week when two of us had jobs at the same time. Just as sure as I got something, a bank would close and Ethel's boss would close down—or if Ethel got a job, Sue would lose hers. We were absolutely necessary to each other and so we were perfect little ladies every single minute.

"Then a few months ago we discovered that we all had jobs at once. You ought to have seen the fur fly. Maybe it was just relief. I don't know, but all three of us let loose and said all the things we'd thought and hadn't dared to say. We got out of that basement as if it was haunted. Each of us got a room to herself. We've made up since, of course, and Ethel and Sue are back together again. I had dinner with them tonight. That's why I was late getting to Mary's—but I'm glad I'm alone."

She had a little room, it seemed, in a run-down brownstone house far uptown on the edge of Harlem. The room was dark and the neighborhood a little frightening, but for the present she was satisfied. She had talked a lot about Mary, Tommy remembered. The grandest woman in the world, she said.

Well, she was right at that. There was something magnificent about Mary, something grand and noble—and it wasn't just because she was big, either. She oughtn't to be living alone, not a woman like her. She ought to be mothering sons, big, lusty fellows . . . She'd make a wonderful mother—a wonderful wife, too . . . She'd give everything when she gave, her body, her heart, everything. . . .

Drowsiness dimmed his mind. "I'll have to get them together again soon," he promised himself, rousing a little to catch at the wisp of thought before sinking into slumber. "It was grand . . . grand evening. . . ."

# CHAPTER XI

## I

THE next morning he promised himself again that he
would collect the same group for another evening soon,
but New York defeated his intention. That day he sent Mary
a copy of *Sere and Yellow* and wrote on the fly-leaf, "To
commemorate a joyous evening," and two days later he received from her a note of gratitude. Twice in December he
tried to call her by telephone, but received no answer. He
and Steve went to Westchester for dinner with Tucker and
assured each other that the quartet must sing soon again and
often thereafter. But Steve's shabby rooming-house boasted
no telephone; and without Mary, Tommy had no way of
getting in touch with Hollis. He had taken her home that
evening, but he had made no note of her address. Besides,
she had said something about moving as soon as she began
work at her new job.

New York, he reflected irritably, scattered people like a
high wind. Outside of his clubs, he rarely saw by accident
any one he knew. One always had to telephone or write to
make an engagement, and usually chance meetings provided
the best times. But there was Mary away down in the Village;
he was in the middle of Manhattan far over on the East Side;
Hollis was clear out to hell and gone; and Steve thirty blocks
in the other direction. A group was hardly formed before the
city smashed it. Down in the Village, of course, certain
groups ate in certain restaurants regularly, just as uptown
certain groups drank regularly in certain fashionable bars;
but the restaurants, after all, were really the Villagers' clubs.
During the day those groups were as widely dispersed, he

imagined, as he and his friends were. Perhaps they did meet more casually than uptown people did, wander in and out of each other's rooms and apartments more generally; but if the Village did succeed in imitating community life, it did it by intention, not by normal accident, and it did it by resisting the intrusion of thousands upon thousands of Italians who were outside the community. Besides, what was the use of thinking of Greenwich Village? It was the last place in the world that he wanted to live.

Even in Boston, he knew, there was no such dispersion as there was in New York. In his Harvard days, he was always seeing friends and acquaintances in the Common or on Tremont Street. If he went tea dancing at the Copley Plaza, he saw people he knew; and if he went down to Dirgan-Park's for a steak and cornbread, he almost certainly saw people he knew, too. Boston spread far and wide, but it had a center, the core of a community. So had Paris. And so had London. Of course, in Los Angeles one expected to motor thirty miles to see anybody, but who wanted to live in Los Angeles? He smiled at his own irritation and confessed that about a million people seemed to find Los Angeles endurable, but he certainly wasn't one of them.

No, New York was *sui generis,* bigger, richer, harder, more complex, more conglomerate than any other city in the world. London for all its Sohos, Cheapsides, and Limehouses was English—but New York? What was it? It was everything; it was the world pressed, twisted, squeezed into an unnatural, tortured microcosm. No wonder no novelist had ever succeeded in getting it between covers. It was impossible for a writer to fix attention on more than one of its thousands of groups at a time, and the thousands of groups were always operating, touching, separating, conflicting. They broke up, blended, assembled into new groups. New York was a prism in motion, its colors ever changing. How could a writer describe it? One might as well try to describe a scrambled spectrum.

Time and again Tommy had found himself part of a group only to discover in a few months that the group had disappeared. Some of his friends lived in Manhattan; two or three on Long Island, a good many in various Westchester towns, and still others in New Jersey. His bachelor friends seemed to be contented enough in Manhattan so long as they were bachelors; but if marriage did not drive them to the suburbs, the first baby always did. Then they were seldom in the clubs, except perhaps for lunch. Greetings became casual. In a little while there was nothing to talk about. "Why don't you come out to see us, Tommy? We want you, you know, old man, and it isn't a bad trip—only forty-five minutes by train, and we'll meet you." Tommy always promised to come, always meant to; but the invitations were seldom for a definite date, and one does not travel forty-five minutes or more on impulse to make a call.

And so, though the intention was firmly fixed, Tommy did not succeed in getting his quartet together again for a long time. Christmas and its festivities arrived. Because he was always afraid of loneliness during the Christmas season, he accepted enough invitations to keep him almost sternly occupied. Wealthy friends invited him for Christmas Day to their Long Island estate. There was a large crowd, much liquor, wild gaiety. For no reason that he could understand, he was achingly lonely.

The January weather did its worst. Blizzard succeeded blizzard. The gutters were piled high with filthy snow; the streets were treacherous. Horses slipped and fell and lay waiting with fatalistic patience to be hauled upright. They tried when they were told to try, and slipped despairingly prone again. Taxis slued wildly and their drivers cursed. The wind shrieked through the canyons that New York called streets, making eyes water and faces ache. Beggars moaned piteously, and only the most tender-hearted could bring themselves to pause long enough to find a coin. Like ants fleeing the stream from a garden hose, Manhattan dwellers fled into the man-made anthills they called home. Tommy did likewise. His particular cell seemed very empty, isolated from all other cells, utterly alone.

II

Tommy went to the Longstruthers' dance because he was lonely and blue. His acquaintance with Charles Longstruther and his third wife was of the slightest, and he had no idea why he had been invited. Probably, he decided, because the stag line hadn't promised to be long enough.

Charles and Marcia Longstruther belonged to the group that kept the gossip columnists in copy. Life to them seemed to be the Ritz or Colony for lunch, "No. 21" at five o'clock for cocktails, some other bar or fashionable restaurant for dinner, a first night, and the night club of the moment. Members of that group seemed always to be "Renovating," "merging," or "phffting." And once in great while a couple surprised themselves and all their acquaintances by "blessed-eventing." The men were perfectly tailored, barbered, manicured, and massaged; the women were so completely the products of couturiers, modistes, and Charles of this or Emile of that, that they hardly seemed real. Most of them drank incredible quantities of cocktails, and they gossiped about each other's doings and misdoings with all the gusto and malice of the Ladies' Aid Society of Little Four Corners.

Tommy knew well enough what the dance would be like —a combination made at tremendous expense of a country picnic, a taxi dance-hall, and a vaudeville show. Instead of deviled eggs and lemon pop, there would be champagne and caviar canapés; instead of many tickets to dance there would be only one; and instead of vaudeville acts performed in a setting where they were most effective, there would be vaudeville acts performed in a setting where they would be most ineffective. People would smoke too much, drink too much, and scream too much. Oh well, he told himself, what the hell? He might have a halfway good time. Anyway, it would be better than sitting in his apartment slumping down into stupid and entirely unreasonable blues.

The music and champagne proved good, and by one o'clock he found himself dancing with a good deal more verve and pleasure than he had hoped for. Nevertheless, he planned to slip away soon. He had had just about enough.

Then Kay Stilton beckoned to him from over her partner's shoulder, and he obligingly cut in. He had met her half a dozen times in the past few years, but he knew her best by reputation. Less than thirty, she was supposed to have attained a brilliant sophistication that was the envy of all the younger women in her group. There were always rumors that she was going to Hollywood, that she was going to Reno, that she was going to write a book. As a matter of fact, a year before she had gone to Reno and divorced her wealthy husband. Tommy had not seen her or heard of her since.

He said something of the sort and she explained, "I've been back only a couple of weeks. I spent six months in Hollywood, you know, three more in Mexico, and the rest of the time abroad. You're looking bonny. How's that? I was in Edinburgh three days."

Tommy leaned back a little to smile at her. "That's remarkable. Do you speak Spanish, too?"

"No nice words. Let's dance in no language."

No language? Tommy smiled to himself. Her body was speaking a language no man could fail to understand. It was a language that asked questions, and his own body automatically made the answers.

There was a pause in the music. She looked up at him, smiled almost wearily, and asked in a soft, drowsy voice, "You collect etchings, don't you?"

"Yes—and I show them, too."

"I'm crazy about etchings."

"Shall we go look at them?"

"Pretty please."

Tommy watched Kay Stilton make up her lips in his dresser mirror. She was very careful, very exact. It was fascinating to see how deftly she restored to herself her glazed perfection. The curls had already been attended to, the mascara on her lashes, the rouge on her cheeks. Now she was applying the finishing touches, and apparently she had forgotten he existed.

She looked at him in the mirror and surprised him by asking his image, "You don't want to go back, do you?"

"Oh, no," he said, "but I'll see you home."

"Home?" She turned and looked at him in surprise. "The party's good for hours yet. But there's no need for you to go with me. As a matter of fact, I'd rather you wouldn't. Just call a taxi, that's all."

"But didn't you say just a few minutes ago," Tommy asked, "that you were fed up with the party?"

"I am, but I'm going back, just the same. It's sad to leave you, but I must."

"It is sad, but there'll be another time, I hope."

"Another time?" She looked at him and smiled. "Oh, no. I never try to improve on a pleasant memory. Now I must be going. My husband will be waiting."

"Your *husband?*"

"But yes, my husband. I always like to go home with him."

The worst of it was, Tommy thought later, she knew perfectly how completely she had shocked and repelled him; and he suspected that she got some kind of perverted satisfaction out of her knowledge. Apparently she had been married again somewhere, and undoubtedly she would be divorced again sometime. What did it matter? All that mattered was that she had left him with a foul taste in his mouth. She had given him satisfaction, taken satisfaction from him, and then deliberately, coldly, maliciously robbed him of his. Once more his senses had deceived him into an hour of passion. With almost painful sureness he knew there would be a week of regret.

"I'll be a fool," he told himself severely, "if I let myself get low on account of this. I didn't know she had a husband, and I didn't know what she was like. There's no sense in trying to fool myself into thinking I can go without women all the time. I know damn well I can't. She was willing. Besides, she started it; I didn't. And what difference does it make, anyway? Of course, if I'd known . . ."

His thought trailed off. He wasn't getting anywhere. Somehow one couldn't argue away disgust; one couldn't analyze regret out of existence. And it was always like this. There was always something to make him wish he hadn't, something that made the memory ugly. If it had been some other girl, it would have been something else. There was always something grimy about taking a girl you didn't care anything about. Some men would rather have it that way. . . . Off with the old; on with the new. . . .

Not him. No; no, he wasn't made that way. How many times he'd tried to be, and how many times he'd failed! And when he reasoned about it, he reasoned like a sixteen-year-old boy. At his age there should be no need to reason. But at his age a man who'd been married couldn't turn into a monk, either.

"I'm made wrong," he thought miserably, "or society is. I've got to have a wife, and there isn't a woman on God's green earth I'd dare to marry. Besides, there isn't any woman I want to marry." He prepared to go to bed. "What's the difference? Tomorrow I'll be going through the motions of living again, and by day after tomorrow maybe half the time I'll think I really am."

III

Early in February Nicholas Tyckman was again in Tommy's office. After long discussion another troublesome detail of the aunt's estate was taken care of, and they leaned back in their chairs.

"You know," said Tyckman, "I haven't been in the Yale

Club since that day I was there with you—not until yesterday, that is. I saw young Carter again, and that reminded me
of what you said about his sister. I was interested. I thought
his attitude was very odd—or, rather, he seemed a little embarrassed, a little—I hardly know how to put it—a little unsure? Something like that, anyway. Certainly not natural."

"Well," said Tommy, "I don't know." He reflected that
Bill Carter's relations with his sister were none of Tyckman's
business—or of his, for that matter. "I don't know Carter.
You heard everything I ever said to him. I've called on Mary
Carter, though, and I admire her enormously. She's an artist,
as I think I told you. A good one, too, if I'm any judge. I
don't know whether she exhibits or not. I doubt it, though;
she doesn't think well enough of her work."

"How does she sell it, then?"

"Oh, she earns her living as a commercial artist, and I'm
sure she does very well. I suspect she feeds about half the
down-and-outers in the Village; and I suspect, too, that
they're the ones her brother's objecting to. I saw her feed
one myself that I half wanted to put my foot on. In her way
she's as stunning as Bill Carter, and she has a beautiful contralto voice. Brains, too. I assure you Mary Carter's worth
knowing."

"Sounds like it. I'm interested in art, you know, and I'd
like to know her if she's really good. But didn't her brother
say she wouldn't come uptown?"

Tommy smiled. "I told her you'd introduced me to
brother Bill, and she said she'd give anything to see a picture
you own—a John Van Eyck, I think it was."

"Oh, so she's heard about my Van Eyck! Well, if that's a
lure, let's use it."

Tommy considered the idea. He didn't know whether he
liked it or not. Tyckman was Tyckman, and Mary was Mary;
their worlds were far apart. Tyckman was famous for his
rigid social standards, and his mother was even more famous
for standards even more rigid; Mary fed Verne Ticknors and

his like. Tommy didn't care how much Mary might shock
Tyckman, but he had no intention of putting Mary in a
position where Tyckman might snub her.

He was too tired to think up a tactful evasion. So he said
frankly:

"To be quite honest, Mr. Tyckman, I doubt if you and
Miss Carter would get along. I'm not implying criticism of
you, but she's a Villager and—"

"I'm a snob," Tyckman broke in.

Tommy was so startled by having the thought spoken that
he had had no intention of speaking, that he could only
gasp and hunt for a denial.

Tyckman smiled at his confusion. "Listen, Gray," he said;
"I know exactly what you've heard about me and what you're
thinking. I presume I'm a snob, but definitions differ. Consider my position. I was born where I am. I had nothing to
do with it. I think you're intelligent enough to recognize
that my position brings certain penalties with it. People
want to know me—not because I'm me, mind you, but because I can do something for them socially. Maybe they're
nice people otherwise, but I don't get a chance to see their
nice side. I see them only when they're sucking up to me.

"That's been going on since I was a kid. When I was
younger, I let myself be used a few times—and then found
out that I'd been used. I didn't like it. I made up my mind
it wouldn't happen again, and it hasn't—not to my knowledge, anyway. Probably I've cut some people I'd like to
know. I can't help that. I had to escape hundreds I didn't
want to know. I've liked working with you because I soon
saw you didn't give one small-sized damn about knowing me."

"That's not so," Tommy contradicted quickly.

"All right. I'm glad to hear it. But you didn't give a damn
about my being Nicholas Tyckman."

"That's true. It would be all the same to me if you were
Nicholas Murphy or Nicholas Ginsberg." He grinned imp-

ishly. "I'm not prejudiced—not even against the aristocracy."

Tyckman threw back his big head and roared. "That's good," he gasped. "That's damned good. I must tell Mother. She'll love it."

"Your mother?" Tommy asked, astounded.

"Certainly. You think she'd be offended? Not Mother. She may be a Bourbon, but she's a realist, too. She respects a good poke in the nose. If you'd been toadied to as much as she has, you would, too."

He paused, gazed thoughtfully at the window, and then went on, his voice heavy and serious: "No, Gray, I'm not a snob in the sense you thought I was. Circumstances force me to stick pretty much to my own crowd, but I go out of it when I get a free chance. Now, quit being a careful lawyer for a minute and tell me honestly why you don't think Miss Carter and I will get along."

"Very well," said Tommy, "I'll tell you exactly what I think. You've got to understand first that Mary Carter is a very big woman—almost as tall as I am. She's magnificently built and carries her height perfectly. I don't pretend to understand her, but I have a hunch she's sensitive about her size. Anyway, when I first met her she seemed to go out of her way to be blunt and mannish. Maybe I'm wrong, but I'll bet she always does that with strangers. And she uses any language she wants to."

Tyckman's blond eyebrows went up and he smiled broadly. "You think she'll shock me?" He chuckled. "I have six nieces. I probably meet as many débutantes as you do. Now, honestly, Gray, do you think any Village artist could even startle me? I'll stack my youngest niece's language against the most eloquent truck driver in town."

Tommy threw up his hands. "You really want to meet Mary Carter, don't you?"

"I do. Maybe it's because you said she looked like Dolores, and I was mad about her. Maybe it's because she's an artist, and painting is my greatest interest. Maybe . . . But I think it's mainly the way Bill Carter acted. I'm not subtle. My worst enemy wouldn't call me that, but once in a while I try to think—and he made me think. If she's what you say she is, I can't understand him. I don't know him well, but I've always liked him a good deal. Just the same, if I do understand him and if his sister is what you say she is, he ought to have his tail kicked."

"Well, maybe," said Tommy, "but I don't know enough to judge. Would you like me to take you to call on Miss Carter?"

"I'd be grateful if you would. Or maybe she'd like it better if we used the Van Eyck as an excuse for you to bring her to my place. I think from what you say that she'd like it best if you just put it up to her."

"I think so too. If I can get in touch with her, I'll let you know tomorrow."

"Fine. And remember, please, that I'm not trying to escape a call. In a way, I'd prefer it because I'd like to see her work. But don't consider my wishes. Whatever Miss Carter wants will be entirely satisfactory to me."

## IV

Tommy telephoned to Mary that evening and found himself unexpectedly moved by the sound of her rich voice.

"I called you twice in December," he said, "but got no answer. I wanted to get our quartet together again."

"Oh, I'm sorry; that was such a grand evening. I slipped out of town a couple of times for a day or two to paint some clean snow. You must have called me then."

"Probably. Tell me, do you still want to see Nicholas Tyckman's Van Eyck?"

"Do I! They say it's a treasure."

"Well, I can manage it."

"You can!"

"Yes. You see, Tyckman is often in my office. I told him

about your painting, and I said you were anxious to see his
Van Eyck. He seemed delighted and said to bring you along.
He said he'd like to call and see your work, but I knew how
you felt about showing it to strangers; so he said to arrange
it anyway you liked best."

"Well, if that isn't a surprise! I knew he was a collector,
but I didn't think he'd speak socially to any one less than
Marin."

"That's what I thought, but he really isn't like his reputation. I think you'll like him. I do. Would you rather he'd
call?"

"No-o-o; no, I don't think so. That would make it social,
wouldn't it? And we won't want to know each other. Can't
I just rush in and look at his pictures and rush out again?"

Tommy chuckled. "I don't know how many butlers will
be in the way, but I'll be glad to run interference for you.
How about tomorrow or the day after?"

"Fix it to suit Mr. Tyckman. I can always drop my brushes
and go."

When Tommy suggested to Tyckman that he bring Mary
the next afternoon, Tyckman was immediately agreeable.

"How about a little after five?" he asked. "I have a dinner
engagement at eight, but I'll be free until seven-thirty."

"I'm sure that will be fine."

Mary was ready and waiting when Tommy called for
her. He stared without shame. She was wearing a black
dress made of very light-weight wool. The collar, belt, and
sleeves were heavily embroidered in coarse woolen thread,
red, green, yellow, and blue. Her felt hat was black, too,
with a red buckle placed in exactly the right spot.

"I'm not one to comment on women's clothes," he said,
"but yours are so stunning that I can't help it. They suit you
perfectly. You must have a wonderful dressmaker."

Her color deepened and her dark eyes shone. "I have," she
acknowledged, smiling. "The woman is an artist."

"She is. You're right."

Mary laughed. "Well, that was one way of making you admit it."

"You don't mean—?"

"I do, indeed. I've always made my own clothes. I can't go into a shop and buy a stylish stout, you know. Women with my shoulders usually have stomachs sticking out to here." She laced her fingers together and held her arms as far as possible from her body. "Or if they're as tall as I am, they're slats the rest of the way. So I roll my own. Besides, it's lots cheaper, and I like to sew." She handed him a black fur coat. "This goes back to '29 when I could afford furs."

Tommy held her coat for her and found himself fighting a sudden, unexpected desire to embrace her. Instead, he said, "You're quite a woman, you know."

"Five-feet-ten in my bare number eight tootsies." There was more than a hint of bitterness in her voice, Tommy thought, but when she turned to him she was smiling. "Let's go," she said, "and crash the Four Hundred." Then she laughed softly. "If Bill could only see me now!"

v

Tommy, having been in penthouses before, found Tyckman's drawing-room no less magnificent than he had expected. The room, he estimated, was fifty or sixty feet long, with an enormous fireplace at either end. The walls were broken by windows that ran almost from ceiling to floor, but now they were hidden by brown velvet curtains. There was a picture over each fireplace, two or three on the paneled walls. Somewhere Tyckman must have a gallery to house his collection.

Tyckman met them at the door of the living-room.

"It's very kind of you to come, Miss Carter," he said in acknowledging Tommy's introduction. "I wanted to call, but Mr. Gray said flatly that you preferred seeing my pictures to seeing me."

When she replied, Tommy noticed that her rich speaking voice surprised Tyckman. His blue eyes opened a little wider, and his right hand touched his small blond mustache.

"If Tommy said that," Mary observed, "he's a lot poorer lawyer than I think he is. Tommy's nothing if not cagy."

Tyckman smiled. "Well, his caginess is saving me money. Now I want to present you to my mother."

Tommy had not noticed the elderly woman sitting on a davenport at the far end of the room. His mother, no less! Tyckman was certainly doing the thing up right. He had brought her here to make something plain to him and to Mary. Well, Tommy liked the man for it.

Mrs. Tyckman was unexpectedly large. Smaller than Mary, perhaps, but big, very big; and age had brought more weight than she probably liked. She wore no hat, and her white hair, carefully waved, fitted her head like a crown. Her eyes were a faded blue, her nose uneven and craggy, and her mouth, big though it was, looked too small to hold her big teeth.

She held out her hand to Mary. "Miss Carter," she said, "you're the only tall woman I've ever envied. I've always fallen over my height. You carry yours."

Mary made Tommy proud. Women, he reflected, were wonderful. If she felt any embarrassment, she gave not a sign. She seemed just as much at ease with the great Mrs. Tyckman as she was with Verne Ticknor.

"I don't know how I look," she said, "but I feel like an overloaded truck out of control."

Mrs. Tyckman laughed with delight. "My dear, don't I know!"

She turned to Tommy.

"Mr. Gray, Nick tells me you called us a lot of snobs."

"Oh, no!" Tommy protested, horrified. He turned to Tyckman. "Surely—"

"Don't deny it," the old lady interrupted. "Why should

you? We are. We're the worst snobs in America. Do you know why?"

Bewildered, Tommy could only shake his head. He felt exactly as he had when he was ten and his teacher had said, "Thomas, bound Colorado," and he couldn't.

"We're better than other people," Mrs. Tyckman explained, gazing sternly up at him. "We're much better than other people, Mr. Gray—but not because we think we are. We're forced to be better because *other people* think we are. The aristocrats don't make themselves; the sycophants make them. Look at Eleanor Roosevelt. She's a marvelous woman. She's always been marvelous. But what do people say about her?" She answered her own question after snapping her big teeth together for emphasis. "They say she's democratic. Do you know what that implies?"

"That she's stepping down?"

"Exactly. She's got the courage to be just herself, but nobody can believe that. They didn't say Mrs. Coolidge was democratic. They said she was sweet. She was, too, but you can see the difference."

"Yes, I can see," said Tommy. "But, Mrs. Tyckman, I'd really like to explain—"

"You needn't," she interrupted, smiling suddenly. "I understand. I understood all along. But now Nick wants to show you his pictures and the gadgets he's so proud of. Take a look and then we'll have some tea. I'm going to sit here and look at Miss Carter and thank God for the first time in my life that I'm not cute."

Mary looked down at her, then up at Tyckman, who was smiling contentedly. "If Tommy weren't such a runt," she said, "I'd feel something less than outsize myself for once." She laughed softly and turned to Tyckman. "Did you build this skating rink just so you could move without knocking down the vases?"

"No, I built it for my pictures, and I *did* build it. The Tyckman estate owns the building."

"But where are the pictures?" Tommy demanded. "Surely there are more."

"Oh, many more—a great many more."

"Now Nick's happy," said his mother. "You've asked just the right question. All right, Nicky; turn on your magic. I'm beginning to want tea."

Tyckman smiled, looking as pleased and expectant, Tommy thought, as a youngster with a secret.

"One minute," he said and walked rapidly the length of the room. At the door he stood well away from the wall and extended his arm. "I have nothing up my sleeve," he called. At the distance Mary and Tommy were not quite sure what he was doing, but Tommy suspected that he was pressing a button.

Every panel in the room swung slowly outward, turned, swung into position—and the drawing-room had become a picture gallery.

Grinning, watching for them to show surprise, Tyckman strode back to them. "Magic!" he cried.

"It *is* magic," said Mary. "How is it done?"

"I like pictures, but I don't like to live in a room cluttered with them—but I like to live with them, if you get what I mean. And I don't like a gallery. It's too much like the Metropolitan. So I thought out this scheme. I can have my cake, you see, and eat it too. The pictures are hung on the reverse side of the panels. All I have to do is touch a button and I can look at them any time I want to. Then I touch another button and I have a drawing-room again. Nice?"

"Very nice," said Mary so dryly that Tommy glanced at her. He had an idea that she wasn't impressed with the millionaire's plaything. By Jove, she wasn't impressed at all—not by the enormous room, not by Nicholas Tyckman, and not by Nicholas Tyckman's famous mother. That's why she was so at ease. If Tyckman's pictures were good, she would be impressed, not otherwise.

The pictures were good. Some of them were indubitable masterpieces, and Mary admired them so profoundly that Tyckman glowed. Then she paused before a small portrait. Presumably it was of a woman, but the distortion was almost painful and the eyes seemed mendaciously misplaced. It was the kind of picture talented small boys drew on the blackboard and labeled "Teacher." To Tommy the color was raw and harsh, the caricature carried to brutality.

Mary looked at the picture, then at Tyckman. She turned to Tommy.

"Like it?"

"No."

"Neither does Mr. Tyckman."

"What!" Tyckman exclaimed. "Why, that's—"

"Yes, I know. It's a Matisse, and you paid thousands and thousands for it. But you don't like it. It hasn't any place here."

Tommy could not tell whether she was scorning the picture or Tyckman; but whichever it was, or if it was both, she was making no effort to conceal her scorn.

Tyckman flushed and objected vigorously. "But, Miss Carter, how can you say that? How can you tell?"

"Do you like your other pictures?"

"Of course. Why, of course, I like them."

"Then you don't like this Matisse."

Tyckman was struggling with his good breeding, and so Tommy tried to save the situation with: "But, Mary, people's tastes are catholic. I don't like the picture and maybe you don't, but that's no sign Mr. Tyckman doesn't."

"The counsel for the defense enters an objection," Mary retorted, openly sarcastic. "Can the tact, Tommy. I like the picture a damn sight better than you do—and better than Mr. Tyckman does, too. That picture's so clever it's a wonder it doesn't leap out of the frame and turn handsprings. I couldn't paint anything like it to save my neck. I've tried. I know. So I can appreciate the cleverness. But Mr. Tyckman can't. He doesn't like cleverness. He suspects cleverness is a little vulgar."

Tyckman was red to his yellow hair. Mary was stepping hard on his most sensitive corn, and she seemed to be doing it deliberately.

"But—but, Miss Carter," he protested. "You surely aren't implying—"

"That you bought it just because it's a Matisse? Of course I am."

"And, what's more, you're right!"

The three of them whirled. None of them had heard Mrs. Tyckman approach over the heavy rug.

"You're absolutely right, Miss Carter," she went on, "and I'm glad you've got the courage to say it. Most people just say the pat thing. That picture makes me sick. Oh, don't lift your eyebrows, Nick. You can't crush *me* with a Tyckman stare. I've lived down stares from dozens of Tyckmans. I know I don't know anything about art, and I know my taste is bad, but I know a lot about you—and I know you don't like that picture. It isn't a picture, anyway; it's a contortion. It reminds me of a nasty little boy pulling his mouth out to his ears, sticking out his tongue, and crossing his eyes. I beat you more than once when you were a boy for doing that, and I'd like to beat you now for doing it by proxy. Tell me honestly now: what does that thing remind you of?"

Suddenly Tyckman surrendered. He stepped to the panel, lifted the picture from its hook, and set it on the floor with the face toward the wall. When he faced them again, he was smiling. "Girls," he said good-naturedly, "you win. How about tea, Mother?"

"There's the man for you," Mrs. Tyckman said to Mary. "Trying to distract our attention. That picture made you just plain mad, didn't it?"

"The picture didn't. To tell you the truth, it fascinates me. But it made me mad to see it here. I reached it full of respect for your son's taste—for the honesty of his taste, I mean. I don't think much of his Ziem, and I don't like the Paul Potter at all; but, then, I've never seen a Potter I did like. But that doesn't matter. I was sure Mr. Tyckman bought them because *he* liked them. Then I run smack into the Matisse. It has just about as much place in this room as a dirty postcard would have." She smiled at Tyckman. "You should have shown it to me first. Then I might have remembered my manners."

Tommy was startled by the sincerity in Tyckman's heavy voice when he said, "Miss Carter, please believe I'm glad you said exactly what you did. I had it coming to me, and you've given me a kind of faith in my taste I think I lacked before. Now let's have tea—and no evasion this time."

Tommy and Mary stayed half an hour longer. When they rose to leave, Mrs. Tyckman said, "I'd like to know you young people. Will you come to see me?"

Before Tommy could reply, Mary said flatly, "Not me."

Even Mrs. Tyckman was momentarily disconcerted, but nothing could disturb her social balance for more than a brief moment. She studied Mary and smiled a little.

"That's false pride, isn't it?" she asked. "I think you like me."

Mary's rich color deepened. "I do like you. I think you're grand. And I wasn't rude out of false pride, and I'm afraid I was very rude. It isn't that, Mrs. Tyckman; it's that it's just foolish for a person like me to mess up her life trying to mix with people like you. Surely you can see that."

"That's what you said to me, Mary," Tommy said. "You said you didn't want to know me. We haven't got along so badly."

"Yes, we do get along badly. And if I'd never met you I wouldn't be all hot and bothered at this minute. We don't get along at all. Your damned tact makes me sick. Well, thank heaven, Mrs. Tyckman doesn't need tact. She can take it. You don't belong in my life for one reason, and she doesn't belong in it for another. You walk right spang in the

middle of the road. I walk on one side, and you," turning
to address Mrs. Tyckman directly, "walk on the other. Isn't
that true?"

"It's quite true, my dear. I know exactly what you mean.
But I like you very much. I don't meet many people like
you." She leaned back against the davenport and showed
her big teeth in a smile. "If you won't come to see me, I shall
have to come see you. And I shall. I'm older than I admit,
but I get around."

Mary was so completely nonplused that Tommy chuckled
audibly. "What's the matter with you?" she demanded furi-
ously.

"Oh," he jibed, "I'm just being tactful, that's all. Well,
Mrs. Tyckman, you've given me great pleasure. You've done
something I can't do—shaken Miss Carter." He bowed to her,
held out his hand to Tyckman.

He was still chuckling as he and Mary rode down Park
Avenue in a taxi.

"I don't blame you," Mary said amiably. "I got what was
coming to me; but you know very well that Mrs. Tyckman
would complicate my life horribly. I do like her, and I'd
give a lot to paint her. Just the same, I haven't a scrap of
interest in what she stands for."

"I know. Neither have I, and I suspect she doesn't have
too much. Well, Mary, maybe she won't call."

Neither said anything for a dozen blocks. Then Mary
spoke.

"Nicholas Tyckman surprised me," she said.

"Why? You like him, don't you? I told you he was all
right."

"Yes, I like him, but I expected something different. My
acquaintance with the aristocracy is limited to this afternoon, but I never dreamed he would be what he is."

"What do you mean?" Tommy asked. "What is he?"

"Aren't you the thick-head? Why, Tommy, he really *is* an
aristocrat."

# CHAPTER XII

## I

FOR a week there had been something strange about Tommy's apartment. At first he had been merely conscious of a difference. Then he noticed that a magazine was lying on the piano. He had left it there the night before. Two or three days later he became aware of the general disorder. The rooms were dusty; the air seemed stale; his bed was badly made; there was lint on the floors; the wastebasket was full; the wash-basin was greasy.

He looked around and rubbed his cheek. "Well, what in the world," he wondered, "has got into Maribelle? She's been here, all right. That ash-tray's been emptied." He walked into the bedroom. The sheets had been full of folds and wrinkles the night before. Suspicious, he threw back the covers and found that the folds and wrinkles had multiplied. With the sudden surge of energy that anger brings, he tore off the covers and sheets and made the bed up properly.

The labor did away with his irritation. "She's probably sick," he decided, "and is doing the best she can." He thought of giving the apartment a good cleaning. No, that wouldn't do. Anybody with Maribelle's standards had pride in her work. If she came in the next day and found everything in order, she would feel reproved; and surely she deserved no reproof after her years of perfect service. He could endure the dirt a few days more.

Anyway, he told himself, he wouldn't have been so irritated if he hadn't been all ready to be irritated. Seeing Robert Constant had upset him, though why he should care what Constant did, said, or became, he did not know. They were the most casual of acquaintances, and since Constant was perfectly satisfied with himself, why should he care?

At Mr. Jonathon's request Tommy had joined a small club two years before after a wait of more than a year for admittance. "The Hinton," Mr. Jonathon had explained, "is a dull place to visit, but its very dullness gives it respectability. It has standing, and more than one man has gone from the Hinton to the Union League. It will help the firm to have you a member, and I'll be glad to see that your name is properly presented."

Tommy had, of course, agreed, and after his election to the Hinton, he dropped in once in a great while for the sake of appearances. The membership was almost exclusively professional. Attorneys made up the majority, and Tommy found most of them almost unpleasantly staid and dignified. The club, however, subscribed to a great many foreign magazines, and he made them the reason for his infrequent visits.

That afternoon he had been in the library reading *Punch* when Robert Constant entered. Constant was close to fifty, and ten years before he had been considered one of the most brilliant lawyers in New York City. Then in '29 he had gone into the stock market and sold short at the right moment daringly and most successfully. By the time the bottom had been reached, he was several times a millionaire.

Then he retired. He said he was going to enjoy life from then on, and apparently he was enjoying it. Overnight, it seemed, he turned from a legal grub into a Broadway butterfly. Somewhere he had a wife, but she was never seen. Instead, he appeared with a succession of beautiful girls, who clung to his arm and worked hard in public, and almost certainly in private, for another square-cut emerald.

Constant's hair was entirely white, with the cold whiteness that shows only when bluing has been added to the rinsing water; and his skin had that curious softness and pretty pinkness that comes from daily massages with lotions and creams. He let it be known that he changed all his linen at least twice a day, sometimes more often; and his shirts always had a starched cleanliness that reminded Tommy of a woman he had known as a child. His grandmother had said that she was "nasty clean." Constant's cleanliness was always noticeable; it forced itself more on one's attention than dirty linen or rumpled trousers could have—and because Constant was always aware of the cleanliness and obviously proud of it, it was offensive. His hair, his face, his clothes, his stick, were all matters of great importance to him. Tommy wondered if anything else was.

Constant entered the library, looked around, and spotted Tommy.

"Ah, Gray," he said. "How are you? Have a drink?"

"No, thank you—not now. Feeling well?"

"Oh, I'm in perfect shape. I always am. I spend an hour in a gymnasium every afternoon, and I have a masseur work on me every day, too." He touched his stomach. "Nice and flat, you see." Then his soft cheeks melted into folds and his blue eyes grew sly. "The girls like flatness there, and one must please the girls—eh, Gray?"

"Oh, yes, indeed."

"I'm calling for the loveliest of girls in an hour. Lovely, lovely, lovely. . . . We're due at Jack and Charlie's. Then—" and he was off with a long dissertation on bars, hotels, theaters, night clubs, and parties. Tommy listened and wondered as he listened. Was it possible that a brilliant mind could disintegrate so rapidly, that a man of real accomplishments could find complete satisfaction in a merry-go-round of trivial pleasures? Could a really intelligent man completely discard his mind and devote his entire attention to his body? Apparently Constant had done just that and was proud of his success. To Tommy he seemed like a superbly embalmed walking, talking corpse. The man was dead and didn't know it. Underneath that expensively preserved exterior he was decaying. Worst of all, he was ridiculous, a drawing out of *Esquire*.

As soon as Tommy decently could, he made an excuse and left the club. Dinner had been lonely, and he returned to his apartment feeling morose and a little unclean after his talk with Constant. The dirty apartment under the circumstances had been a little too much. It was with a real effort that he restrained himself from going at it with mop, dustcloth, and broom. He might have swept Constant out of his mind along with the dust and lint from the apartment; but he could not bring himself to a reproof of Maribelle even by inference.

Two evenings later there was no improvement, but he left the money as usual for her on the ice-box. The instant he entered the apartment the following evening he knew that there was a change even before he switched on the light. The very air smelled different, cleaner, fresher.

The place gleamed. Once more the pillows were plumped to perfection, the magazines overlapping neatly, the furniture polished, the floors immaculate. He examined the bedroom. It, too, was in perfect condition, and one glance at the bed was enough to tell him that the sheets were tight, the covers firmly tucked in. The bathroom was speckless. How about the kitchen?

It, too, had been scrubbed until it looked as antiseptic as an operating-room, but Tommy hardly noticed. The money was still in the glass on the ice-box. That was funny. . . . Had Maribelle's black head cracked?

There was a note on the pad. He picked it up and read:

"Dere Mr. Gray, Ime so mad Ime goin to brake sombuddys neck and I dont mene maybe neether, when I come in this morning and seen the filf you been livin in I was so mad I kinder got sick to my stummick. That Charlies going to wish hed never been born thats what hes going to wish you beleve me Mr. Gray, Ile lern him how to trete nice gennelmums. Cause hes so filfy ant no reesin you got a be filfy to, I bin havin the flu and I sent that good fer nuttin Charlie to do my work. I ant takin the munney cause I dont want no munney for havin filf round yore pahtment, you dont owe me nuttin Mr. Gray. Thank you kinley, Maribelle."

Tommy left the money where it was and scribbled a note: "Dear Maribelle, I'm sorry you were ill, and if I had known you were, I should gladly have taken care of the apartment myself. It wouldn't kill me, you know. Hereafter if you aren't well, don't bother to send Charlie. Just let me know and I'll take care of things. Take the money, please. Your sickness wasn't your fault and neither was Charlie's carelessness. T. Gray."

He returned to the living-room feeling curiously relieved and happy. He did not trouble to find the reason for the lightening of his spirit. Subconsciously he knew that he had needed his faith in the black girl he had never seen. In her own way she held to a standard of perfection, strove for it and attained it day after day, beyond any one he had ever known. Her habit of cleaning all the personality out of a place had amused him sometimes, irritated him sometimes; but when Charlie had impinged his slovenly personality on the apartment, Tommy hadn't liked it—and he had actually missed the emptiness that Maribelle had always managed to leave behind her.

Pleasantly relaxed, he thought again of Robert Constant. Strange, how he had associated Constant's offensively evident cleanliness with Charlie's inescapable dirtiness. The comparison that was forming in his mind seemed impossible, but the apparent absurdity fascinated him. Under Charlie's dirty black skin and Constant's pretty pink skin there was the same kind of spiritual flabbiness, the same kind of deadness. Charlie never had had the brains or ambition to make an effort; from birth he was damned to be what he was, and he was incapable of anything more than instinctive movements toward physical contentment. But Constant, probably driven by his environment and need, had made a brilliant effort. Then the moment he had attained security, he had begun to rot. "I'd like to know," Tommy thought, "about his background. He'd rather have the admiration of bar-flies and Broadway hams than the respect of the people in the Hinton. Apparently his backbone was made entirely out of his need to earn a living. I suppose the psychiatrists would say he had an inferiority complex. Maybe . . . But I wonder if anybody might not slump that way without the need to work for something." The thought made him uneasy. *He* didn't really need to work.

Then he thought of Maribelle and smiled. No, lots of people weren't like that. Maribelle's pride didn't come from a need to earn her living. It was a part of her, part of her perfection. He felt grateful to her at that moment for just existing. She might be an invisible jinnee, but he needed his faith in her. If he ever lost it, he would lose something that he valued dearly.

II

One evening early in March Mary telephoned.

"I had to tell you right away, Tommy," she said. "I'm so flabbergasted."

"What happened?"

"They called!"

"Who called? Eleanor and Franklin?"

"Pretty nearly. Nicholas Tyckman and his mother."

Tommy laughed. "I wish I'd been there. I'd give a lot to have seen your face when they showed up. Did you say, 'Scat!'?"

"I did not! I was a perfect lady, a regular little love. But that's not all, Tommy. Honestly, it was like a play—and an awfully bad play, it was so impossible."

"And you're being a playwright, aren't you? Working up suspense and everything. Come on, tell me all about it—or do you want me to jump in a taxi and come down?"

"No, don't come; a gang of people you wouldn't like are coming in later. I'll tell you about it now. Well, everything was going just beautifully. Mr. Tyckman had admired my pictures like a gentleman, and his mother embarrassed him terribly by going ga-ga over a just too darling baby I'm painting for a breakfast food ad. And I served tea. I was being such a lady, curling my little finger all around my cup and everything when who do you suppose busted in?"

"I've had my three tries," Tommy said, "and I give up."

"Verne Ticknor!"

"What!"

"Yes, Verne—hissing on all six cylinders. Of course, he knew who the Tyckmans were, and he saw Russian red in a minute. He was going to tell them just what the social revolution was going to do to the likes of them when Mrs. Tyckman hauled out her lorgnette. It's a tremendous thing. She could have brained Verne with it, and I hoped she would."

"But she didn't, I suppose," Tommy said regretfully.

"She did better. She looked at him through it. I wouldn't have believed it could be done—but she just looked, and she looked him clean out of the studio. Honestly, you could see her thinking, 'What an interesting, slimy little slug you are,' and Verne couldn't take it. He just plain ran."

Tommy laughed and then said, "He deserved it, of course, but I can't help feeling sorry for him. She had power and position back of her stare, and he didn't have a thing in the world back of him."

"Well, I felt sorry for him later, but at the moment I could have killed him. I hate to admit something, Tommy, but I suppose I'll have to. Mrs. Tyckman licked me. I promised to go see her sometime."

"It won't hurt you—and you can take Ticknor along to preserve your self-respect."

"Will you go to hell?"

"You're going—and you know it. And you've been sniffing at Brother Bill."

"I'm still sniffing. Thank God, there's my buzzer. Now I can say good-bye to you."

"Good-bye, Lady Mary."

"Oh, you—!" And then her receiver clicked on its hook.

At first Tommy was honestly amused, but a little thought erased the smile that was playing around his lips. This wasn't so simple as it looked. Mary was getting into something, and he didn't blame her for being upset. And all just because she had happened to sit beside him on a train. . . . "Springfield to New York and points beyond." Where were those points? What were they? He wondered. . . .

And what was he going to do about Mary? So far, so good —but how far would it be good? Not much farther, probably, not very much farther . . . No use fooling himself; he wasn't going to be able to keep up a pretense of casual friendship much longer. When he'd held her coat for her that day an almost overwhelming desire to embrace her had swept over him. Lord, but she was a magnificent creature! . . .

But what could he do about it? He didn't really know what she was like. How old had she said she was? Thirty-three? Yes, that was it. Thirty-three, an artist living alone down there . . . It didn't seem possible she'd held off all the men, but somehow he'd offer odds she had. She had her defenses up all the time. That casual "we're just a couple of good fellows together" manner was a defense; he knew damn well it was. Her pretense of masculinity was a defense. Hell, she was woman to her toes; he could feel it.

Was he in love with her? No, of course not. Maybe he'd like to be, but he wasn't. Just the same . . . Just the same, sometimes when he was with her he felt— He didn't finish the thought because it wasn't a thought he liked. She hadn't given him the slightest hint that he had any right to think that way.

Yet in spite of his intention, he went on thinking. Could he say anything to her? She wouldn't get angry. She was too understanding for that—but, but if she said No, they couldn't go on being friends any longer. He didn't want to give her up, certainly not just on a chance . . . He enjoyed being with her too much, liked her too much, admired her too much. She wouldn't be angry; no—but she wasn't like Polly. There was a big difference somewhere. Besides, Polly had made it clear enough beforehand . . .

Mary hadn't made anything clear, and she wouldn't, either. She liked him. He was sure of that, but that didn't mean anything. . . . How she seemed to glow! She had such strength, such vitality—such, such warmth. A wonderful woman! Wonderful!

"Oh, hell," he cried aloud, "what's the use of thinking about it?"

### III

Tommy paused. The floods of people on Fifth Avenue swirled around him. He took a step, paused again. Surely he heard somebody calling.

"Tommy! Tommy Gray! Over here! Tommy, over here in the car."

He turned and saw her. Freda was leaning out of the window of a limousine and waving to him. He made his way through the people across the walk.

She held out her hand. "How I screamed!" she said, laughing. "I thought you'd never hear."

There was a big, ruddy man sitting beside her.

"You met Morton before, Tommy," she said. "You remember?"

"Oh, yes, of course. How do you do, Mr. Ballard."

Ballard smiled and held out his hand past Freda. "I'm glad to see you, Mr. Gray. I hope it won't sound—well, you know what I mean—embarrassing, I guess, when I say I feel I know you. Freda talks about you so much."

Tommy gripped his hand. "No, Mr. Ballard, I'm not embarrassed. I'm just glad. I'm glad Freda wants to talk about me and that you're willing for her to. And I'm glad to see you looking so well, Freda." He addressed Ballard again. "I have never seen her so beautiful."

Freda laughed happily. "I feel mountainous—honestly; but it'll be any day now. Then I'll look like a dishrag. Most women do after the baby is born."

"You won't," said Tommy. "I hope everything goes just as easily as anything."

"Oh, it will. I'm a peasant, Tommy, and we peasant women don't think anything of having a baby. But Morton's got some nerves. I've engaged a doctor for him and a couple of nurses."

She turned to laugh at her husband, who grinned affectionately at her in return. "Don't you believe it." Then he looked at Tommy. "I wish we could know each other. I wish you could come to our house and be friends."

"Oh, so do I!" cried Freda. "Honestly, Tommy!"

Tommy shook his head slowly in denial. "I wish so, too. It makes me happy to see Freda here so happy. I've been happy about you, Freda, ever since you were brave enough to come to my office. But you know how people would talk. Your friends don't know about me, do they?"

"No," admitted Freda. "Just Oliver."

"That's what I mean. People are what they are, and it's so easy to spoil happiness even when your intentions are the best. We found that out, Freda. I don't want to spoil yours now. I think we might manage it if people would let us, but they wouldn't. We'll meet sometimes. I think we'd better let it go at that."

"Yes," Ballard agreed, "I suppose you're right, but I'd like to know you, and Freda's so fond of you. It seems a dirty shame."

"It's worse than that," said Freda. "But you do like us, don't you, Tommy?"

"You know I do." He held out his hand. "I've got to go along. I have a luncheon engagement with a client, and I don't want to be late. Good luck, Freda. Good-bye, Mr. Ballard."

For a block he moved blindly among the passing people.

It'd been a shock—and talking quietly like that with his emotions roiling and boiling, what an effort it'd been! She'd never been so beautiful, never! She was—what was it somebody had said? Craig? Yes; that was it . . . daffodils and sunshine.

Did Ballard really think that he could be around Freda and not care? If he did, he was crazy. Why, one evening . . . It was getting late. He forced himself to walk faster, but his knees still felt weak.

## IV

It was the in-between season; spring was coming, but winter hadn't yet departed. There was still slush, but no clean snow; there was sunlight, but little warmth. Tempers shortened, and people went about their work with sluggish determination. They withdrew, finding more satisfaction in nursing their discontent than in sharing it with others.

Tommy was declining invitations almost automatically. He hated his aloneness, feared it, but he found people a strain; and parties demanded a forcing of gaiety that left him tired and dispirited. And talk always seemed nowadays to swing to politics.

The talk wearied him in its pointlessness. Many's the time he had heard husbands say that women were incapable of dealing in generalizations because they immediately applied every generalization to themselves. Well, maybe that was true; he didn't know, but he did know that when men discussed politics they did exactly the same thing. If a banker had the floor, sooner or later he always said, "Now, take banking—" and went on from there. If the speaker was a merchant, he said, "Take my business, for example—" and on he went, proving to his complete satisfaction that the low tariff on a single article of merchandise was the cause of the depression.

Nobody seemed to be able to think in terms of the whole country; nobody apparently was capable of attaining broad conclusions that were possible only when the problems were studied from a disinterested point of view; and everybody seemed to base arguments on premises that were guesswork at best. He listened for hours to a group discussing money. Two of the men were bankers, three were lawyers, one a college professor, and one was a doctor. Half of them were positive that Roosevelt had saved the country when he took it off the gold standard; the other half were equally positive that he had merely prolonged the depression and confused America's relations with foreign countries. All of them were amazingly sure of themselves. Tommy had studied money in college and he had studied it since; yet it remained to him only a vague and confusing problem.

The next day he retailed the arguments to Frederick Winchester. Mr. Frederick was a quiet, shy man who left as many contacts with outsiders as possible to his colleagues. Plump, round-faced, and bald, he offered the world a blank stare and a formal manner. Tommy knew, however, that he was a student and that money was his hobby.

He leaned back in his chair and laced his fingers over his stomach. "Well, Tommy," he said in his gentle way when the last contradictory argument had been stated, "I don't know. I've been studying money for more than forty years. I've discussed it with many bankers here and with the so-called experts in Washington—and I don't know. Doctors know, and English professors, and grocery-store philosophers, and men who review popular novels; they all know, but I admit I don't. The effect of going off the gold standard is plain enough, of course, so far as international trade is concerned. There can't be any argument about that. But when it comes to this country—I just don't know. I suspect that to most people a dollar has been a dollar all along no matter what the Treasury called it. It's easy to speculate and produce arguments pro and con, but I suspect that any effect on the people themselves was psychological, not real. But I don't know." He smiled shyly. "The only people who seem to know are the ones who haven't bothered to study the problem. It's simple to them because they don't even see the complexities. A little ignorance gives a man a lot of confidence."

Tommy thought he was right, but, then, Mr. Frederick was usually right. Tommy knew that if he asked him about the coming campaign he would get no such positive answer as he could get in any club discussion in the city. Mr. Frederick didn't find all good in one party or the other, and he didn't think of national economic problems in terms of his own income. Tommy found them hard to think about in terms of anything. He felt outside of them. People were talking about Landon of Kansas, and some of them were saying that the man hadn't had enough experience in government to make a satisfactory President.

Tommy wondered if any experience was needed. He wondered if people who governed didn't make their work seem infinitely more complex and difficult than it actually was. What experience in government had Washington, Jefferson, Hamilton, and Franklin had? Yet they managed to found a new nation under apparently insuperable difficulties, set it firmly on its recalcitrant feet, and govern it in spite of fanatical opposition and ever-threatening treachery.

Look at Lenin and Trotsky. They hadn't been even ward heelers. They had been propagandists kicked about from one country to another. Then one day they found themselves the rulers of Russia, a country smashed by war, a revolution, and a counter-revolution. There was no money, no unity; and they had no experience to fall back on. But out of the terrible confusion they had created a new type of government and made it function. Trotsky had been everything except a general. He had written pamphlets and pressed pants, but he had attended no war college; yet he produced the mighty Red army in a country sick to death of armies.

There was Mussolini, an editor. Who taught him to rule? Where was his experience? You might hate him, loathe his methods, fear his objectives; but you had to admit that he

ruled and ruled effectively. And the same was true of Hitler.
What would a house-painter know of government, of the
intricate problems of currency, of foreign relations, of in-
ternal politics and policies? You might not like anything
about Hitler from his Napoleonic forelock to his comic
opera posturings, but the fact remained that he was govern-
ing Germany, and, so far as Germany itself was concerned, doing a job of it.

Roosevelt had done this, that, and the other thing; he had
formed one alphabetical organization after another. Good?
Some of them almost certainly. Others? Tommy didn't know.
But he felt sure that Roosevelt's first "fireside talk" had done
more to start the people toward economic recovery than all
the scores of acts he had rushed through a terrified Congress. They had listened to that beautiful, friendly voice
coming from their radios. They had heard, "My friends,"
and listened; and as they listened, they relaxed. They had
faith—and faith, he felt sure, sometimes moved economic
mountains far more quickly and effectively than even hundreds of acts of Congress could. Fear, uncertainty died. Recovery was then possible—and nothing was possible so long
as panic ruled.

So Tommy wondered—and then wondered if he was right.
The worst of it was that he didn't care very much whether
he was right or not. His interest was academic, impersonal.
He had the disinterested attitude that he sought in others;
but he recognized that his altogether admirable disinterest-
edness lost much of its value through the coldness of thought
that made it possible. If his conclusions were wrong, he
would like to have them set right; but the corrections would
neither sadden nor gladden him.

He wasn't like Steve Austin, who had embraced Communism with a deep, idealistic passion. No, he was more like
Tucker, who had studied Communism far more carefully
than Steve ever had—and then discarded it.

"A tremendously interesting experiment," Tommy had

heard Tucker say to Steve when they dined at Tucker's home. "The greatest experiment in government, I believe, since the founding of the United States. And what's more, it's working—in Russia. But it isn't working, I suspect, because there is any magic in the formula, but because Russia is a dictatorship. One might as well admire Fascism because it's working in Italy and Germany under dictators. Lenin was certainly a great genius, and in his own strange way Stalin seems to be a genius too. But Lenin was a dictator, and so is Stalin. It would take just one normal dictator crook to wreck the whole machine, and an ideal government must be crook-proof. Our democracy comes a lot closer to being that than Russian Communism does."

"But, Mr. Tucker," Steve had objected, "you'll have to admit that Communism has checks against the exploitation of the masses. It does take care of the people. The kind of depression we're having isn't possible under Communism. Even a political crook couldn't cause it, not so long as the Socialist form of government remained. Isn't that true? And isn't that enough to make it worth while?"

"Perhaps it's true, though I doubt it," Tucker replied. "When nature goes on a rampage with floods, crop failures, dust storms and so on, no government can stop famine. But let's suppose it is true. How is literature doing in Russia?"

"I know what you mean," Steve said, "and please don't bring up the Left Wing critics either. I think they're just as silly as you do—half-baked economists, most of them, and bad critics, too, because they measure everything by the same scale. But isn't feeding people, caring for them, more important than literature?"

"And freedom of speech and individual initiative?"

"But that's the dictatorship, not the Communism."

Tucker had smiled in his dry way and said, "I haven't managed to divorce the two yet, and neither has Russia."

Well, it had all been very interesting to Tommy, but he had felt quite outside the discussion. He felt sure that he knew more about international law, political theory, and economics than Steve knew; but Steve cared, and he didn't. To Steve, Communism was a living issue; it stirred his emotions, gave meaning and significance to his life. But Tommy could no more grow passionate over Communism, pro or con, than he could over the Republican party.

Damn it, he couldn't grow passionate over anything. And he was too young to meet life with merely a detached kind of skepticism. It was ridiculous for a man of his education and background not to care deeply about what was being done to his community and to his country. He took it for granted that Tammany was fundamentally an evil organization, but he also took it for granted that something like Tammany was inevitable. He had no desire to go out and fight against the evil, to destroy it. Desire? "Hell," he thought, "I'm worse than Robert Constant. He wants something, anyway, if it's only to look like a poster and parade around with show girls. Men like me are useless. Well, men like him are, too, I suppose, but he's having a good time, at least—or thinks he is. I'm not even thinking I am." No; men like him were merely born to grow, eat, sleep, procreate their kind, and die. What was the point to it?

He had no meaning to life as life had no meaning to him. He enjoyed this pleasure and that, but he enjoyed them in a vacuum. Nothing lasted; nothing meant anything.

His pessimism and moroseness disgusted him. "It's just the rotten weather," he told himself, trying to lift his spirits a notch. "Spring'll be here before long. A few rounds of golf will set me up—and if I break eighty, I'll think life's wonderful. I'm like a kid in the dumps. I can't see that there'll ever be a sunny tomorrow. . . ."

## v

Mae Vadney was out of the office for two days. Tommy asked Mr. Jonathon if she was ill.

"Yes," he replied, "but nothing serious. She telephoned in and I expect her back tomorrow."

When she returned, Tommy thought she looked as if she were still ill. Days passed, and she looked no better. He teased her a bit but could not rouse her to one of her sharp retorts.

One afternoon he met her in the reception-room, put his arm around her waist and drew her into his office.

"Now, Mae," he said, "I want to know what's the matter with you. I've asked you three times if you were sick, and three times you've said No. All right, then; you aren't sick. But something's wrong, and you know we're friends. We are, aren't we?"

She looked up at him and her eyes filled with tears. Then suddenly, to his horror, her head was against his shoulder and she was sobbing hysterically.

He didn't know what to do. He thought of calling one of the other secretaries, but somehow he knew with absolute certainty that Mae would not want the girls to know that she was crying. "If Mr. Jonathon would only come in," he thought wildly, but no one opened the door. Frightened, he did the only thing he could do; he patted her back awkwardly and said, "There, there, Mae; hang on. It'll be all right. There, there."

He could have kicked himself for his own inadequacy. He heard himself repeating, "There, there. There, there, Mae," and stopped abruptly. "Damn it," he thought, "I sound as if I were trying to quiet a horse."

Mae's sobs eventually ceased. She found a handkerchief, dried her eyes, blew her nose with angry vigor, sniffed jerkily, blew her nose again, and then looked up at him.

"I'm sorry," she said huskily. "I never thought I'd do anything like that."

"Forget it. There's nothing like a good cry for cleaning out the system. Come on, Mae; sit down and get it off your

chest. Maybe we can do something about it. What am I here
for?"

He was so relieved to have her in control of herself again
that he felt enormously cheerful and ready to conquer
any difficulties. Anything to keep her from feeling like
that. . . .

Mae sat down in the chair by his desk, cleaned her glasses,
fiddled with her handkerchief and waited for him to sit
down. Then she looked at him uncertainly.

"I think I'll tell you," she said at last. "I can't tell the
others. They'd be kind but they wouldn't understand; I
know they wouldn't. But maybe you will. You'll try to,
won't you?"

"Of course I'll try. And I bet I do understand. Try me,
anyhow."

He was so earnest and boyish that she managed a little
smile.

"You're awfully kind . . . Well," she began, "this—oh, I
don't know how to start."

"Don't start. Just tell it."

"You remember my niece? You met her that night you
took me to dinner."

"Yes, I remember her. Why?"

Mae leaned forward and said urgently, "Tell me what you
thought of her. Tell me your honest opinion."

Tommy considered, seeking a kindly method of telling a
harsh truth. "Well, honestly, Mae," he said at last, "I don't
know. I didn't say ten words to her. I thought she was rather
pretty—but, well—well, let's put it this way: she didn't look
the way I'd expect your niece to look."

"What do you mean?"

"She was dressed quietly enough and all that, but—oh, I
might as well say it, I suppose. I had a feeling she was kind
of common."

"Common? What do you mean by common?" She pressed

her arm on the desk and bent closer to him while she studied him unblinkingly through her glasses.

Tommy squirmed and then came out with it: "Well, I thought she was what the fellows call easy. If I saw her on the street, I'd think I could pick her up without any trouble."

Mae fell back in her chair as if all her strength had suddenly left her. She looked at Tommy and her lips quivered. She pressed them together, obviously fought for control and won it.

"You'll understand," she said finally. "I'll tell you about it. Bessie—that was her name, Bessie Beeson; she was my sister's girl—well, Bessie came to live with me three years ago after her mother died. Her father was no good, and he ran away years ago.

"She was eighteen then, and I didn't know what to do with her. She wasn't very bright; she wasn't bright at all. I think maybe she was actually feeble-minded. She couldn't get a job, of course, in times like these, and so I had her take care of the apartment. I taught her to sew and knit to pass the time because she never read anything. And I took her to movies, and she met young people at the church. She was sullen a good deal of the time, but I didn't think much about it."

She paused, began a sentence, paused again. "It's hard to tell it, you see, because it all came on me so suddenly. I got home a couple of weeks ago to find her terribly sick. I called a doctor. He sent for an ambulance and had her taken to a hospital. Then he—he told me she'd had—she'd had—" The poor woman faltered in her shame and distress and then bravely brought out the word: "—she'd had an abortion."

Once the word had been spoken, she took courage and told the remainder of the story rapidly. "She was able to talk only a little while, but she told me all I needed to know. She's been spending her afternoons on the streets, and she's been using my apartment—for that. I ought to have known! More than once I thought she had a lot more money than I'd given her. And I didn't trust her. I never trusted her." She lifted her hand, let it drop to her lap. "She died," she concluded, her voice bleak and despairing.

"Oh, Mae," Tommy said, feeling sick with sympathy, "I am so sorry." What a terrible experience for a Victorian like Mae to endure! She had nothing with which to meet an experience like that, no background, no modern hardness or cynicism. "You must have had an awful time of it. Didn't you have anybody to go to? Anybody to help you?"

"No. There wasn't anybody I could tell."

"You could have told me. You know that now. I'm sorry you had to suffer so terribly, but it's just as well—better, perhaps—that she died. If she was that kind, there wasn't a thing in the world you could have done about it. Some day you would have found out, and then what could you have done?"

"I don't know." Mae looked at her lap, lifted her glasses to touch her eyes with her handkerchief; but when she looked at Tommy her eyes were already bright with new tears. "I don't know," she repeated, "but I was happier while I had her. She was some one to care about—to go home to. Now—" her voice broke dangerously—"now there just doesn't seem to be anything—not anything. . . ."

Tommy bent forward, took her hand and held it in both of his. "I know, Mae," he said softly; "I know what that lonesome feeling is. But we can do something about it. I know we can."

The tears began to stream down Mae's face. Tommy got up and went to a window. Behind him he could hear Mae sobbing softly, and he kept his gaze fastened on the traffic far below.

Something had to be done! The poor old girl. What a shock she'd had finding out she'd been taking care of a feeble-minded tart! It'd be a shock to anybody. But she was so damned lonesome she missed even the tart. She ought to have somebody with her, some friend or something. . . . There were lots of nice girls who would love to live with her. Yes, but if they were nice enough for Mae they'd be nice enough for some man, too—and they'd get married and go off and leave her and she'd have the same thing over again. A woman like her ought to have a kid to love. A kid? A kid!

He whirled. "Mae!" he cried, his face breaking into a delighted smile. "Mae, I've got it!"

"Got what?" she asked. She had taken off her glasses, and she blinked at him myopically. "What do you mean?"

He strode back to his chair, sat down, and leaned far toward her in his excitement. His eyes were shining, and again he took her hand. "Listen, I know just the thing. The world's full of homeless kids. They're lonesome, and they need somebody like you. That's what you need—a kid, somebody really worth coming home to. You can adopt one."

Mae polished her glasses with her handkerchief, put them back on, and looked at him. Then she smiled with weary despair at his enthusiasm. "But, Mr. Gray, I can't keep a child in an apartment. I've got to work. Who's going to take care of it while I'm away?"

"I didn't say a baby. I don't mean a baby." Tommy did some rapid calculating. Mae must be fifty. In ten years, fifteen years . . . Sure, that was it! "You want a kid about ten—a boy."

"A boy?" she repeated, startled.

"A boy—and I mean a boy. Boys can take care of themselves, and you don't worry about them the way you do about girls. Now, Mae, you listen to grandpa. You want a boy about ten years old. He'll be old enough then for you to know what you're getting, but he'll be young enough to need you for years and years. And he'll be in school all day while you're working."

She shook her head. "I don't get home until five-thirty. He wouldn't be in school that long, and I wouldn't want a boy playing in the streets. It's not fair. I don't think they'd let me have a boy if I couldn't do better for him than that."

Her objections were sound enough, but Tommy liked his idea and refused to give it up. "Well, then," he said firmly, "move out to the suburbs. There's nothing to stop you, is there?"

"No-o," she confessed doubtfully.

"All right. You move out to Long Island or to Jersey. You get a little house. You go to work and the kid goes to school. When he comes home, he plays or rakes the lawn or what have you. Then you come home—and there he is, waiting. Why not?"

Mae didn't answer. She was looking out of the window, her eyes cloudy with thought. When she turned to him again, some of the strain was gone from her face. "I have a friend in East Orange," she said thoughtfully. "She has an eight-room house, and three years ago they made the upstairs into an apartment because they were so hard up. It's been rented, but I think it's empty now. She has a little boy and she's very kind. She'd look after . . ." Her voice trailed off as plans formed in her mind.

Tommy grinned at her. "If that isn't perfect! You wouldn't have anything to worry about, and the kid would have somebody to keep an eye on him after school and during vacations. And wouldn't you like living out there with gardens and trees better than living in an apartment?"

"Would I? It'd be heaven! Oh, do you think I could do it? Do you really think I could?"

"Why not? You go around to the societies and orphanages till you find just the boy you want—and there you are. You try each other out and then you take out papers. Of course, they'll investigate you, but a little perjury from Winchester, Winchester, Tucker, and Gray will endow you with the necessary virtues. It's all as easy as that, Mae."

"But," she objected, "I have my job. I can't be running off to societies and orphanages."

"Can't you?" Tommy waved his hand in what he hoped

was a lordly manner. "Can't you? What am I a partner for? If I say to Mr. Jonathon, 'The Vadney and I have business hither and yon. I'm taking your secretary; you can have mine,' what do you suppose he'll say? He'll smile and say, 'Tommy, you're up to some devilment. I don't trust you, but I trust Mae. God bless you, my children.' "

"Oh, I'd tell Mr. Jonathon!" Mae exclaimed.

"Of course. And we'll start out right away."

"You mean you'll go with me? You'll help me?"

Tommy was feeling good, full of bounce and eagerness. He leaned far back in his chair, drew his eyebrows together in a tremendous frown, and demanded with comically exaggerated importance, "Do you suppose, Miss Vadney, that out of your experience with the noble and virtuous men in this office, I would permit you to select a boy to share your heart and home? What do you know about boys? Can you spin a top? Can you shoot marbles? Have you ever gone in swimming stark as the day you were born? Have you ever been an Indian? Come, come now, woman; don't be absurd. No woman understands a man—and this is a man child you're going to adopt. I shall accompany you and question the candidates severely about their ability to throw an in-shoot. You can't have a son who can't throw an in-shoot. At least, he will have to want to throw one. Yes, indeed, I shall accompany you. Nobody is going to be selected for the sake of his starry eyes or golden curls. My—er, imprimatur will be necessary."

Mae's eyes were shining now and her face was tremulous with smiles. She stood up. Suddenly she bent forward, whispered, "You're a darling," kissed his cheek and fled. She ought to have paused for at least one look, because Tommy's face was crimson.

## VI

For the next three weeks Tommy spent every spare daylight hour with Mae Vadney; and every time they visited

an organization for homeless children, he thanked heaven
that he had not let Mae come alone. She saw dozens of boys
she wanted to adopt, and she could not understand Tommy's insistence on care and deliberation.

"But what difference does a boy's background make?" she
asked impatiently. "Boys from the finest families go wrong."

"I know; I know, Mae. All we can do is reduce the chances
as much as possible. Take that handsome kid you were so
crazy about today. He's a winner, I'll admit it—and I don't
care any more about his illegitimacy than you do; but his
mother was a tramp and nobody knows anything about his
father. And the kid tried to sell himself. He's too slick for a
ten-year-old. No, we'll go slowly. Besides, you haven't sub-
leased your apartment yet, have you?"

"Yes, I have," she retorted pertly, "and I'm going to move
out to East Orange this week-end."

"Good! It's better for you to be settled before we select a
boy. Now have patience. This is important. We can't take
any chances we can avoid."

They were in the second week of the search when he
paused one day before a Fifth Avenue shop. Blankly he
stared at the shop window. His mind at the moment was full
of Mae's problem and he hardly knew why he had paused.
Something had attracted his attention, interrupted his train
of thought. Oh yes, the Ravel piece. He and Craig Sherman
had gone to a piano concert at Town Hall the week before,
and the pianist had played something he had liked. He'd
meant to get the music right away. What was the thing
called? He couldn't remember. But it was by Ravel. He was
sure of that, and he could whistle the main theme. Maybe
the salesman would know.

He realized then what had stopped him before that particular shop. It was a music store. He turned in and sat down
at the counter. The clerks all seemed to be busy. What was
that piece called? He ought to have made a note of it. . . .

"Yes?" a voice said. "Is there something . . . ?"

Tommy looked up. Why, he knew this girl. Somewhere . . . He'd met her somewhere. Why . . .

"Why, Mr. Gray!" she exclaimed. "For a minute I didn't
know you."

Then he remembered. "Hollis Graham!" He held out his
hand impulsively. "I'm glad to see you again. I tried a couple
of times to get our quartet together again, but Mary was out
of town and I wasn't sure where you lived."

She was smiling. Funny, he hadn't thought of her as exceptionally attractive, but she was. He'd never seen prettier
hair, and her eyes were beautiful. There must be some gray
in them because they lacked the crystalline quality he usually
disliked in blue eyes; and they were so direct in their gaze, so
alive. That smile, too; it couldn't be sweeter. Wonder why
she'd seemed sort of drab and colorless. . . . Mary, probably. Mary was so gorgeous she'd make almost any other girl
look insignificant.

"I've moved," said Hollis. She was living now, she explained, at a girls' club in the Fifties. "I couldn't stand that
place any longer," she concluded. "It was a question of new
clothes or of being scared to death every time I went home,
and so I let the clothes go for a while."

Tommy looked her over and grinned. "You fudged a
little, didn't you? That dress never survived the depression."

Hollis placed both hands on the counter and leaned
toward him. What pretty little hands! He'd noticed them
when they were playing the piano together. So little and
soft-looking and so strong—nobody would ever guess they
were so strong.

"Two and a half in a bargain basement," she whispered,
her eyes bright with amusement and pride. "I spent two evenings making it over. Don't tell anybody."

"I won't. It looks like money to me."

She stood erect again and laughed softly. "That's the idea.
It's supposed to look like money. It looked like two and a

half when I bought it, though. I didn't leave much but the blue silk. There was a five-cent gold buckle and glass beads. I ripped off everything and made the white collar and cuffs; and if I do say it, and I admit I certainly shouldn't, I did a good job." She laughed. "You didn't come in to discuss my clothes. What did you come for—'Red Sails in the Sunset'?"

"Lord, no! If I hear that once more, I'll—" He let the threat remain unspoken. "No, this is what I want," and he whistled softly.

Hollis listened, her head slightly tilted, her lips puckered. "Oh, yes!" she exclaimed suddenly. "Ravel. I know. Wait a minute." She turned to the shelves, pulled out one box after another, finally found the right one, and returned to Tommy with a folio of music in her hand. Tommy opened it, glanced at the notes, said, "Yes, that's it. I want it," and handed it back to her.

Once the music had been rolled in a sheet of paper and Tommy had given Hollis the necessary money, there seemed to be nothing more to say; yet he found himself entirely unwilling to leave.

"Listen," he said, "I'll make one more try to get the quartet together again. You're living only a few blocks from me now, and I can drop in any time for you. I'll phone to Mary and barge around to Steve's place in a few days. Would you like that?"

"I'd love it. I had the best time that evening I've ever had in New York."

"I may not be able to manage it right away," he explained. "It's hard to get people together in this town, and I'm awfully busy right now. I'm helping a friend find a boy to adopt, and it's a slow business. I can't always figure when I'll be free, but would it be all right if I just dropped into the club some evening and picked you up for dinner?"

"Of course it would be all right—but—well, that is, it would be if we went to some place modest. I haven't any clothes yet. You wouldn't mind?"

"Mind? Why should I mind? Besides, that dress you have on is good enough for any place."

Tommy meant what he said. He thought the blue dress with its white collar and cuffs exceptionally attractive.

But Hollis shook her head. "No, it isn't. Besides, my coat is disgraceful. It'll have to be some quiet little restaurant."

"We'll go to a one-arm lunch if you want to." He stood up and held out his hand. "I'm awfully glad I ran into you this way. Don't be surprised to see me popping in any time."

She placed her hand in his. "I won't be surprised. I'll be glad."

He liked the way she said that—no flirtatiousness, no coyness, just a direct statement of what he believed, and hoped, was a fact. He had every intention of calling on her before the week was out, but two unexpected engagements spoiled his plan. For another week his free time was taken up with Mae's problem, and then he was called to California. Hollis Graham slipped from his mind.

## VII

At last in a New Jersey orphanage Tommy saw the boy who seemed to be the one he had been seeking.

"We'd better find a youngster in New Jersey if we can," he had explained to Mae. "Now that you're a resident of Jersey, it may simplify the legal problem."

Tommy asked her what she thought of the boy with the brown hair and blue eyes.

Mae studied him. "He looks something like me," she said at last. "My hair used to be that color. Do you see a resemblance, too?"

"Yes." He smiled at her teasingly. "That's why I like his looks, of course."

They talked with the boy, with the superintendent. Robert Corbin was the boy's name. He was ten years old, Protestant, legitimate, and he had been an orphan for five years. He had been born in Bennington, Vermont, and came from New England stock. His mother had died at his birth; and when his father died five years later, a spinster aunt in Newark had taken him. At her death two years before, he had been accepted into the orphanage.

"Robert is a good boy," the superintendent said. "He deserves a home. We've placed a score of less worthy boys since he has been here, but he keeps in the background and people don't notice him. Besides, he isn't as good-looking as some of the boys."

Tommy chuckled softly and glanced at Mae, his eyes alight with mischief. She wrinkled her nose and pinched his arm in retaliation.

"Well, I like his looks," Tommy said, "and I like his background, and I especially like the way he looks right into your eyes when he talks to you. But I don't think Miss Vadney ought to be hasty. It isn't fair to her or to Robert. Suppose she calls again soon and has another talk with him?"

The superintendent agreed heartily, and they departed. Three days later Mae told Tommy that she had had two more visits with Robert Corbin and that he was the only boy she wanted and, furthermore, she was going to have him no matter what Mr. Thomas Beamish Gray said. "I'm free, white, and a whole lot over twenty-one," she told him defiantly, "and there's nothing you can do about it. We like each other. So there!"

"So what?" said Tommy. "We'll see. Now, Miss Proud and Independent, I have work to do, and certainly you have. Vamoose!"

Half an hour later he was on his way to New Jersey and the orphanage. He felt responsible. He mustn't let Mae take a single chance he could eliminate for her.

The superintendent permitted him to see Robert alone. Tommy talked to him about Vermont, about his aunt, his life in the orphanage, games—anything to draw the boy out;

and the more Robert talked, the better Tommy liked him. This, he decided, was what boys would call a good kid. To his mind such a recommendation was perfect.

"Did Miss Vadney tell you what she wanted?" he asked.

"Yes, sir. She said she wants me to come live with her."

"You'd like that?"

The child's eyes shone. "Oh, yes!" he breathed hopefully.

Tommy considered a moment and then decided to have his say. "Listen, Robert," he began, "I want to tell you about Miss Vadney. She's very lonely, you know, and she wants very much to have you with her. She'll love you very hard and do everything she possibly can for you. Do you know what that means?"

The boy stared earnestly into Tommy's eyes and answered, "It means I'd have to be awful good, don't it?"

"Not necessarily. She doesn't want an angel. But it means you would have to be awfully kind. She would love you a lot; and when you love a boy, he can make you terribly unhappy if he isn't kind. Do you understand that?"

"Yes. I can understand that easy."

"That's good. She'll be a little afraid of you, Robert, because she hasn't been around boys. She'll want to kiss you goodnight, but she won't be sure you'll want her to."

"I'll kiss her hard. Honest, I think she's awfully nice—the nicest lady I ever saw. You'll let me go live with her, won't you?"

Tommy patted his knee. "That's all I wanted to be sure of, Robert. I wanted to be sure you *wanted* to live with Miss Vadney. I didn't want her to take a boy who was just looking for a home."

"I want *her!*"

"You're going to have her."

Tommy visited a five-and-ten-cent store before returning to the office. Once there, he went to Mae's little office and dropped a bag of marbles on her desk.

Surprised, she looked up. "What are these things for?"

"For Robert Corbin Vadney, of course." Then he fled. He didn't want to see Mae's tears.

His secretary stopped him as he stepped into the reception-room. "I've been looking for you, Mr. Gray," she said. "There's a telegram."

"Thanks." He took the telegram, went to his own office and opened it. Then he lifted the telephone. "Ethel," he said, "will you call the Newark airport? I've got to go to California."

# CHAPTER XIII

## I

THE telegram had been from Melville Clarke, Tommy's stepfather. Unduly long, hysterical, it had seemed to Tommy exactly the kind of telegram a ham actor would write. Clarke always irritated him; and while he made preparations to be away from New York for a week or more, he was more aware of the irritation than of any other emotion.

He held a brief conference with Mr. Jonathon, made the necessary explanations, called his secretary and gave her a list of names. "Please telephone to these people and break my engagements with them," he said. "I have been called to California." To his colleagues he had to explain details of his work that could not wait for his return, and he had to get to his apartment, pack a suitcase, and leave a note for Maribelle.

Eventually everything that had to be attended to was attended to, and he found himself in the plane. He was breathless and tired, but the need to hurry still excited his nerves. When the plane rose, he leaned back in his seat and tried to relax. Flying was no new experience for him, and for the moment he had no desire to view the scene that was dropping away from the plane so rapidly.

Then for the first time the contents of the telegram began to have some meaning. His mother was dying, Clarke had wired; she could not live more than a day or two longer. Cancer . . . She had never even hinted at it in any of her infrequent letters. She must have a kind of courage that he had never suspected.

He knew that he ought to feel distressed, sorrowful, but

the obligation refused to evoke the emotion. His mother
was a stranger to him. He had seen her only once in many
years, and he had not missed her. If she had missed him, she
had given no hint. The boyish hate that had burned in him
at the time of his father's death had long since died away,
and nothing whatever had taken its place.

As he had sometimes before, he wondered how she had
ever met Clarke. Probably on a visit to Boston. But how?
Her relatives and friends were the last in the world to associate with actors. Yet somehow she had met him. Like Freda,
she had made a good marriage with a Thomas Gray and endured it. Endured it? Yes, probably. . . . She must have
been very unhappy in that little New England town. Strange,
he had never realized that before, though his father had made
it plain enough in his letter. One always seemed to realize
things too late. Hollywood with its glamour and theatrical-
ism was the kind of place she loved—and she had got there.
He felt a moment's honest respect for her, admiration for
the instinct that had guided her eventually to happiness. It
was a kind of happiness that he could not understand, but it
was the kind she wanted. Clarke was the kind she wanted,
too. Well, she had been happy. He was glad of that, but he
could not pretend he would miss a mother he had never
really had.

"Mae," he thought, "will be more of a mother to that
strange kid in a week than Mother ever was to me. She'll
love him to death. He's a good kid, too." It made him feel
good to think of Mae and her Robert. Come to think of it,
he had been feeling good for the past three weeks. None of
that depressed feeling—no bogging down with loneliness.

Good deeds, he reflected, were certainly their own re-
ward, and then smiled at his sentimentality. Never mind;
they were. Look at him—low as hell; then he'd got interested
in pulling Mae out of a hole and his imaginary troubles had
disappeared as if by magic. He hadn't been thinking about
himself at all. What's more, he hadn't been in a fret about

some Harriet Carrington or Kay Stilton either, which was all to the good.

Maybe that's what he ought to do, get interested in boys' clubs or something like that. He considered the idea, gave it up. You couldn't take up a job like that just to escape yourself. If you gave anything worth while to it and got anything worth while out of it, you took the job because you wanted it, because you felt an honest desire for it; you didn't just use it to escape from your problems. If anything was true, it was true that negative efforts never produced positive results.

Mae was going to be happy, and the kid was going to be happy. There was no doubt in his mind. But he didn't want to adopt a boy. "Not by a damn sight; I want one of my own." This was a crazy life he was living. Say what you would, it was a crazy life. For a normal man anything outside of marriage was abnormal. Continence made sex almost repellently important. Man mated instinctively like a bird, built a nest, raised a family. A man without a woman was only going through the motions of living, and a man with a temporary mistress was only putting off the day when he would begin to live. Even if she was as grand as Polly, she was only an interlude, an escape. But how about a man, though, like Robert Constant? To a man like him a succession of mistresses was a purpose, a goal. "He's just bucking up his own ego," Tommy thought scornfully. "He's trying to convince everybody on Broadway that he's as potent as Casanova."

Well, to hell with Constant. He wished Constant wouldn't keep forming in his mind like a horrible portent. Things were bad enough as they were. Here he was, thirty in a few weeks, single, lonely, bitter half the time, and with no one to blame for his bitterness. Once he had blamed Freda, but he could blame her no longer.

And there wasn't any one he wanted to marry. Mary Carter? He didn't know. . . . She was a grand woman, but she was so damned big. And—well, a woman like her made a swell friend, but he was a conventional soul and she wasn't. His half-year with Freda had taught him that a man's pride in his wife was as precious to him as his pride in himself. Mary said and did things that amused him now, but a lot of them wouldn't amuse him if she were his wife. He wouldn't like them, and he would despise himself for not liking them. Besides, the chances were that Mary wouldn't have him. . . .

There were other girls, lots of them—some of them pretty, some of them talented, but they all said "damn" and "darling" and all of them seemed to have been stamped from the same die. They were good to play around with, dance with, kiss goodnight, but there wasn't one he wanted to live with for the rest of his life.

"Here," he admonished himself, "this won't do. Thinking like this is dangerous." More than one man had leaped into marriage just because he was lonely—and then discovered that he was lonelier than ever. What's more, he knew that he was afraid of marriage. Look at what had happened to his father. God, it must have been hell living all those years with a woman who didn't love him, loving her and wanting her all the time. Worse hell than living alone . . . Losing Freda had been worse hell than living alone. Nothing could be worse than that. "I couldn't go through with that again. Anything would be better . . ."

## II

Tommy stepped out of the airplane at Glendale and looked around. Melville Clarke was nowhere in sight. "Probably at the hospital," Tommy thought. "I'll take a taxi and go to the house. Somebody there will know what to do." It was a little let-down not to be met. He had telegraphed that he would be on that plane.

A young man approached and asked hesitantly, "I beg your pardon. Are you Thomas Gray?"

"Yes—yes, I'm Thomas Gray."

"I'm Fred Norton. I'm a neighbor—of your mother's, I mean."

"Oh, I see," said Tommy. "It's kind of you to meet me."

"Mr. Clarke's waiting in the car for you. I offered to find you for him if I could."

Clarke was here—not at the hospital. He looked at Norton. "You mean—?" he asked, unwilling to finish the question.

Norton nodded. "Yes, early this morning. I'm sorry, Mr. Gray."

Tommy thanked him and followed him to the car. Clarke was in the rear seat sobbing heavily. "Acting as usual," Tommy thought contemptuously and then instantly hated himself for the thought. His mother had been Melville Clarke's wife for almost seventeen years. Apparently they had been devoted to each other. It was just possible that Clarke's sorrow was real.

In the days that followed he could never quite decide whether it was real or not. Regardless of how uncharitable his judgment might be, he felt positive that Clarke actually enjoyed the funeral. There was, to Tommy's surprise and somewhat to his consternation, a large crowd at the church. To him, the funeral was an agony, not because he sorrowed but because there was a public parade of sorrow. He could not understand how any one could weep before others, and here were scores of people weeping. Clarke wept—what was the word? Bravely? Yes, that was it. That was the part he was playing—the utterly bereaved husband broken with sorrow, but determined to bear his sorrow bravely—and too hopelessly sorrowful to succeed.

Yet the next morning when he and Clarke sat down together for a final talk, he had to admit that the man's face was ravaged. He might act in public, but in private he really suffered. For the first time, Tommy felt a liking for Clarke and honest sympathy for him.

"I'm sorry to rush this, Mr. Clarke," he said gently, "but I have to go to San Francisco for the firm and then get back to New York. I left at an inconvenient time. If it isn't too much for you, I'd like to straighten out the financial matters."

"I understand, Tommy," Clarke said. "You needn't explain. Your mother and I—well, we were happy together, and I didn't know until recently about her sickness. She kept it quiet. It was her breast, you know, and she was afraid of an operation. She couldn't bear to be disfigured. It was a shock—and—and she suffered so—"

"Don't," Tommy interrupted. "Don't think about it. Don't talk about it. You will make yourself more wretched and you're already worn out. Try to think of something else if you can. Tell me about the financial situation. Keep your mind on that."

"The financial situation?" Clarke looked blank as if the words had no meaning for him. Then light came into his eyes. "The financial situation? Oh, yes. Your mother didn't leave a will. I have always understood her money reverted to you."

"Only the trust fund. That comes to me, yes; but didn't she have anything else?"

"This house and everything in it. You see, Tommy, when we first came out here, I had a good contract. I made all we needed and a lot more. We spent it. We were both like that, but she didn't spend any of the income. That accumulated. Then I grew older." His lips twisted in a sardonic smile. "I grew older and I didn't get good contracts. For a while I didn't get anything—only a bit now and then. Now I'm growing old enough to be a type and things are a little better."

"I'm glad of that," Tommy said and was a little startled by the sincerity in his own voice. He really was glad. "But you were going to explain about the house."

"Oh yes. Well, the income had accumulated for nearly ten years; so your mother decided to build a house and furnish it. It's in her name. I haven't any rights in it."

"Under California law you have, I think, but it doesn't

matter about the law. Mother would want you to have it, and so do I. I want you to have everything except the trust fund itself—any money in her account, her jewels, and so on. She did have jewels, didn't she?"

"Yes, but, Tommy, I didn't expect—"

"Never mind. I know you didn't. If Mother had left a will, she would have left everything to you—and that would have been only right. I'm not being generous. The trust fund will double my invested income, and I make all I need, anyway. Did she have many jewels?"

"A good many. Your father gave her some, you know, and I gave her a good many more. Wouldn't you like to have those your father gave her?"

"No. Yes—one thing, her engagement ring. Father told me once that that had been my great-grandmother's and my grandmother's too. I'd like to have that, but I'm sure there's nothing else."

"Of course, my boy—anything you say. You're being very generous; you're giving me security."

Tommy smiled. Why, he almost liked the man. "Let's just let it go, shall we? Tell me your attorney's name. I'll go down and see him and have the necessary papers drawn. I'll sign anything I need to sign. Then he can take care of everything for you."

### III

The next day Tommy flew to San Francisco. When he had told Mr. Jonathon that he was leaving for California and why, he added, "If there's anything you'd like me to take care of out there, of course I'd be glad to do it."

"But at a time like this, Tommy—"

"Mr. Jonathon, my mother and I are practically strangers. It's a long story, too long to tell now; besides, it doesn't matter to you. I'm going because I think I ought to go, but you must understand that the circumstances aren't the usual ones at all. It will shock you to hear me say it, but there are many people who mean more to me than my mother does. I hardly know her. So I'd rather nothing was said around the office; and if there is anything you'd like to have me do, I'd be glad to do it."

Understanding as always, Mr. Jonathon accepted Tommy's explanation without comment. "Yes," he said, "it happens there is. Somebody ought to see Powers in San Francisco. It can be done by mail and telephone, but you could save us a lot of time and trouble. I'll have Mae get the papers together. You've corresponded with Powers, haven't you?"

"About the Chisman estate? Oh yes. I can take care of that."

Powers, who had been apprised by wire of his arrival, met him at the airport. He was an exceptionally jovial-looking man with black hair, blue Irish eyes, and rosy cheeks. Probably forty or more, he did not look within ten years of his age.

"I'm glad to see you, Mr. Gray," he said, shaking hands cordially. "I'll admit I'd be glad to see anybody from your firm right now. There's a tangle or two that really needs talking over, though I think we can straighten it out in an hour or two. Then if you like, I'll show you the city."

"I've been here before," Tommy explained, "and done a tourist's duty; but I would like to get a ground view of the bridges. They're going to be tremendous, aren't they?"

Powers smiled. "Bigger and better, you know, in the California way. Well, you'll see them. You can't help it." He drove his car rapidly up a steep hill, over the crest, down the hill, up another one. "If you don't want to sight-see, how about coming home with me tonight? I live in San Rafael over in Marin County. You'll get a grand view of the bridges from the water and my house is better than a hotel." He grinned. "It's better even than a San Francisco hotel."

Tommy had liked Powers at sight and accepted the invitation without a pretense of argument. Californians, he had heard, were given to sudden hospitality. They took the stranger in immediately; then later, if they found they did not like him, they kicked him out. In Tommy's town people looked the stranger over until they were very sure they liked him. Then they opened their homes and their hearts to him, comfortable in the knowledge that he would abuse neither their affection nor their hospitality.

The ride across the Bay was very beautiful, Tommy thought and said; and Powers, true Californian that he was, agreed with him with unashamed pride. He seemed to feel that he had part ownership in the beauty surrounding them; he even seemed to feel that he had a part ownership in the partly built bridges. He did not brag, but Tommy could feel the man's deep satisfaction in his surroundings and his strange eagerness to share that satisfaction.

To Tommy's surprise, he felt almost at home in San Rafael. It had something of the umbrageousness of a New England town, the quiet and serenity. And there was an unexpected atmosphere of dignity and age. Southern California, for all its cultivated gardens, was backed by treeless hills; there was a desert-like emptiness that seemed almost as far away from San Rafael as New York itself.

Powers' home proved to be a long, low brown shingled house. Half of it was covered with rose vines, the other half with purple wistaria and star clematis, both now in full bloom. Behind the house stood several great oaks; before it swept a wide lawn shaded with maples.

"This makes me almost homesick," Tommy said. "It reminds me of New England. If that was a white clapboarded house, I'd probably break down and bawl."

"I love it," Powers said frankly. "I've lived here all my life. That's why, I suppose. It's home. As soon as you've met my wife and had a wash-up, I want to show you my garden." He smiled. "I'm like all gardening maniacs. I'll rope a stranger in on any pretext or none and make him admire every square inch and every bud and blossom. We're like that. And of course," he added, as a big collie came racing down the walk, "my dog has to be admired. Here you are, Laddie, old boy."

Mrs. Powers was not home. "She go see Missy Kane," the Chinese house boy explained. He smiled, showing his white teeth, and laughed softly. "New baby. Missy Janet go, too."

"Well, they'll be home soon," said Powers. "They don't let visitors croon very long nowadays over new babies. Mr. Gray is going to wash up, Wong. Then we're going out into the garden. Highball, Gray. Rye?"

"Yes, thanks."

"Have them ready when we come in, will you. Wong?"

"Okey kay."

Tommy hardly listened later while Powers took him slowly from one end of the garden to the other. There was talk of ageratum and calceolaria, of cineraria and clarkia, but the words meant nothing to Tommy. He knew a carnation from a rose, but there his knowledge of flowers ended.

"There's nothing like a garden," said Powers, straightening up after having carefully eliminated a snail. "Sometimes I come home after a hard day all tied up in knots. I come out here and work, and by dinner time there isn't a knot left in me. I don't know why it is, but I think it's impossible to work with flowers and be strained or nervous. The people who work with them all the time never are. I've noticed that for years. I don't believe there's any group of people in the world as nerveless as nurserymen. They always have time, and they're always generous. They just can't resist throwing in a few extra plants."

Tommy listened politely, but he wasn't interested in nurserymen or gardens. He was interested in Powers, though. This was a happy man. You could feel his happiness, and Mrs. Powers was happy, too. She was a quiet woman, obviously proud of her husband. Both of them were devoted to Janet, the seventeen-year-old daughter.

There was an atmosphere of serenity and contentment in the house that was almost entirely new to Tommy. He had

friends whom he believed to be happily married, but he had
none he could think of who seemed so completely at home in
their happiness, so alive to it and yet so relaxed in it. Powers
loved his wife and daughter, his garden and his dog, his city
and his state, probably his country too. He was rooted in his
community, rooted in his family—and the roots were love.
It was good to be in this man's home, but he wished he
weren't there. Envy ate at his pleasure.

He returned to San Francisco the next morning with Powers. They still had a little work before them, but it was soon
taken care of. Powers asked, "How long are you staying?"

"I'll leave tonight if I can get accommodations on the
plane."

"What are you doing this afternoon?"

"I think I'll go over to Berkeley. There's a man I knew in
college teaching at the University. We were pretty good
friends and we correspond once in a while. I ought to look
him up while I'm here. I'll telephone and make a date."

He lunched with Powers and then said a genuinely regret-
ful good-bye. He liked Powers. He hadn't met any one in
years, it seemed, whom he had liked so much and with whom
he had felt so immediately at ease.

Powers had told him that he was seeing Northern California at its best, and he believed it as he strolled across the
University of California campus. The hills were still richly
green and the flowers were everywhere. As he approached
the Life Science Building, where Cameron had said over the
telephone he would wait for him, he paused to admire the
grove of towering eucalyptus trees. "Beautiful," he thought,
"really beautiful. Elms are softer, but these are beautiful."
A border of bright calceolaria attracted his attention. He
had seen the same flowers in Powers' garden, but he hadn't
paid any attention to the name. "Probably," he thought,
"they have them back East, too; I just haven't noticed. Well,
I bet Cal doesn't know any more about them than I do. He'd

just want to get a flower under a microscope. I'm not that bad, anyway."

He found Calvin Cameron busy in his office among microscopes, retorts, and test tubes. He had belonged to Tommy's fraternity at Dartmouth, and most of the brothers had considered him definitely unfraternal. He had been an irritable youth, a hard student who scorned the student gaieties and the student gods. Now he was a doctor of philosophy and an assistant professor.

His black hair had thinned since Tommy had last seen him, and deep lines had cut their way from his nostrils to the corners of his mouth; but his black eyes had their old glitter, and his tongue retained its bite.

He welcomed Tommy warmly and then said, "Let's get out of here. Some damned student will be breaking in asking fool questions or trying to polish an apple."

"That means sucking up for a grade, doesn't it?"

"Yes, and it's a major student activity. Come on up to the house."

"You sound as if you hated the students."

"Of course I hate them. A lot of lumps, if you ask me."

"Well," said Tommy, "I saw a good many of them while I was crossing the campus, and I thought they were the handsomest lot of young people I'd ever seen. What girls! Man, how do you do any work with so many beauties around?"

Cameron held open the office door. "Come on and don't talk like a sophomore. They're good-looking, all right, but they aren't students." At Tommy's look of doubt, he explained, "Oh, they're quite as good probably as you'll get anywhere. The California schools are good; so the level of mediocrity is fairly high, but like undergraduates the country over they aren't interested in education. Teaching's a futile business at best."

"I was talking to Kingston up at Hanover a few months ago and he said just the opposite."

"Well, Kingston's got a great heart and all that sort of thing. He's a sentimentalist. You have to be to get worked up over teaching. I can't. I want to be left alone with my research, and teaching interferes. We go this way. I live up in North Berkeley."

Cameron's house was white stucco with a red tiled roof, small but clean and cool. He was proud of it, but, unlike Powers, he tried to hide his pride. He even tried to be casual about his wife, who, to Tommy's amazement, turned out to be an exceptionally pretty girl in her early twenties. Her bright fair hair was bobbed, her lips heavily rouged, her fingernails brilliantly varnished. She was wearing a thin jersey and shorts.

"I've been working in the garden," she explained. "Cal saw one weed, two slugs, and an aphis this morning, and I had to get rid of them before he came home. If there had been two weeds or three slugs, he would have cut classes and spent the day chasing the slugs up into the hills."

"Don't listen to Beth," Cameron said, trying to restrain his shamed smile. "She hasn't learned respect for her elders and betters. Get into some clothes, Beth, and give us tea. Tommy's a New Englander and you shock him."

Tommy denied the possibility and permitted Cameron to lead him into the garden while Mrs. Cameron changed into a dress. "Where did you two meet?" he asked.

Cameron looked at him and drew down the corners of his mouth. "I hate to tell you. You look and act like a kid, and I know what you'll do. Well, go ahead, damn you, and do it. Beth was one of my students."

Tommy did it; he roared while Cameron stood by and looked his disgust. Five minutes later, however, he seemed a different man. He moved from plant to plant and talked. For a second time within twenty-four hours Tommy was asked to admire flowers that meant nothing to him. Once more he heard explanations of calliopsis and campanula, delphiniums and digitalis, lupine and lobelia.

"Do you do your own work?" Tommy asked because he could think of nothing even remotely intelligent to say.

"Oh yes! Beth helps, of course. But there's no fun in gardening if you don't do your own work, and I tell you, Tom, you don't know what fun is until you have a garden. I began because Beth wanted one, and I'll have to admit I wasn't any too pleasant about it, either. Then in spite of myself I got interested. First, it was the lawn. I had New England ideas about lawns, and mine had California ideas about weeds. It was a knock-down fight, but look," he said, waving a proud hand; "New England won. Then the roses and vines began to interest me. They grew so fast and bloomed so profusely, and when things grow, they catch your eye. Before long I was comparing notes with the neighbors and exchanging slips. Then I began to play with dahlias. They grow beautifully here. There's enough fog, you know. You can do almost anything with them by crossing. Then it was other plants—and now you see me, a real gardening nut."

"I see you are," said Tommy, "and somehow it's all out of character. I see what I see, but, just the same, I can't imagine you digging in a garden."

"Oh, yes, I dig; indeed, I dig." Then Cameron added a sentence that came back to Tommy months later while he was walking alone in the New Hampshire hills.

Cameron said, "A man needs to get his hands into the dirt."

# CHAPTER XIV

## I

WHEN Tommy reached New York he felt as if he were being awakened from a pleasant dream by a slap in the face with a wet towel. One day he was in Berkeley. The sun was warm, the grass gleaming green, the flowers profusely in bloom. Bare-headed girls were shooting with bows and arrows at big targets on the California campus, boys and girls in brief shorts were playing tennis, hundreds of students were lolling in the sunshine, sprawled on the lawns. The next day he was in New York. The soggy, blackish-gray clouds seemed to rest on the towers, the icy rain slanted between them, and pedestrians shied away from the danger of one umbrella only to meet the same danger from another. The city was dark and bleak, and there was no perfume of flowers. Instead, the damp air held the exhaust fumes close to earth. Never had they seemed so acrid, so poisonous, so inescapable.

Man's inventiveness, Tommy reflected, had far outstripped man's adaptability. One's emotions couldn't keep pace with modern speed. If he had remained in New York he would have accepted the rain as a normal part of the season; but yesterday he had been in what now seemed Paradise, and so the dank day blanketed his spirits and crushed them. "We move too fast," he complained to himself. "We pay proudly to have our bodies hurtled through space at an inconceivable rate, and then we suffer while we try to adjust ourselves far faster than we are able."

Fortunately he met a stacked desk. His colleagues were

waiting with questions that only he could answer. He was forced to think about his work, not about himself; and work, he decided at five o'clock that afternoon, was the best cure in the world for the blues. "Now I've got to fill the evening or I'll have the blues again."

It isn't easy, however, to make last-minute engagements in New York. Since the people are usually widely separated, they must plan ahead if they would meet each other. It was male company Tommy sought. He was too tired, he thought, to entertain a girl. But his telephone calls to men brought only, "Sorry, old man, but I'm all dated up. How about next week?"

Well, then, it would have to be a girl. But who? He thought of half a dozen and rejected each almost with distaste. All of them would want to go to noisy, gay places, and he wanted no noise and not much gaiety.

Mary Carter? Why hadn't he thought of her in the first place? He'd rather see her by far than any of the girls he had been considering or any of the men he had called. Eagerly he reached for the telephone. Mary answered, and he asked to see her with almost plaintive eagerness.

"Of course, I'd like to see you," she said. "It's been a long time since I have. Come on down and have dinner with me."

"Oh, I don't want to bother you. Why don't you go somewhere for dinner with me?"

"Because I've got a great big T-bone steak waiting to be broiled, and, brother, I can broil a steak. Baked potatoes, tomato salad with a dash of alligator pear to give the plutocratic touch, green peas, fruit, crackers and cheese, and coffee. How does that strike you?"

"Like nectar, ambrosia, and heavenly honey. You've saved my life, Mary. I've been in homes recently. I hated the thought of a restaurant."

It seemed to him that he had never been so grateful for an invitation. He had been afraid of dining alone, afraid of the cold impersonality of a restaurant, and most afraid of the emptiness of his apartment. Mary was wonderful, and it was going to be wonderful, wonderful to see her.

He wasn't surprised by her housewifely accomplishments. She could no longer surprise him. Apparently she could do anything and do it perfectly. The steak was broiled to tender lusciousness; the salad was an artist's composition of gray-green avocado, rich red tomato, and the crisp green of lettuce; the little rolls were warm; there were daffodils on the table, green candles—and behind their light the studio was deep in shadows. Tommy relaxed and ate with a gusto that made Mary smile with pride.

Later she permitted him to help with the dishes. Then he sprawled in a chair, puffed at a cigarette, and said with quiet sincerity, "You don't know what you've done for me, Mary. I've been rushing around California, dashing back and forth across the continent. Terribly busy, you know, and I suppose it was the let-down, but I was ready for an attack of black glooms. Now I feel utterly at peace."

"You sound," Mary said, "as if I'd found the way to your heart by the immemorial route."

"That dinner would find the way to any man's heart. You're a very wonderful woman, you know, Mary."

She smiled at him maternally. "Yes, I can cook. Lots of women can."

"I didn't mean that." He gazed dreamily at the smoke curling up from his cigarette. "No, I didn't mean that. I didn't even mean you were remarkably gifted, though you are. You're a better artist than you admit, and you've got a magnificent voice, you know. If it had ever been trained, you could have been a singer. Real contraltos are rare. And you have brains—lots of them. But I didn't mean things like that. It's your honesty, I'm thinking about, and your generosity. I think you have a great heart."

The warm color in her cheeks deepened, and her dark eyes grew very soft. "That's sweet of you, Tommy, to say that. I don't really believe you, but I love to hear you say it."

"But I do mean it, Mary, and you know I'm a hard-headed Yankee. I think twice before I let myself think as much of anybody as I do of you."

She looked at him, looked down. "Are you thinking now?" she asked, her voice low and husky.

Tommy didn't know, and he didn't care to know. He seemed to be drifting in a dream of peace that glowed from the big, beautiful woman opposite him. Everything seemed calm and tender, infinitely restful. The world was far away.

"No; no, I'm not thinking now," he replied, looking at her affectionately. "I'm feeling something I haven't felt in a long, long time. I wasn't sure I was ever going to feel it again."

Mary said nothing. She rested her cheek on the palm of her hand and stared somberly at the floor. Outside the noises of the city murmured, rose to a roar, murmured again. The rain dashed against the great north window; a taxi hooted somewhere far away; somewhere in another studio there was music that came to them faintly. The silence lengthened, filled the studio, and Tommy sank down into it, letting his thoughts drift in a vague, unmeaning stream through his mind.

Finally Mary spoke. "Tommy. . . ."

He looked at her. "Yes?"

"What do you feel? I want to know what you meant when you said you were feeling something you hadn't felt in a long time."

"Peace, Mary. Peace with you. . . ."

"Do you know why? I'm wondering . . . I'm curious."

He roused himself then, sat straighter in his chair, and the dreaminess faded from his voice. "Because you're wonderful. You give so much and ask so little, it seems as if there must be peace with you. Because maybe I'm falling in love with you."

"Oh, don't!" Her rich voice throbbed in a cry.

"Don't!" he repeated, opening his eyes in surprise. "Why not, Mary?"

"Because you mustn't. Because we'd both be unhappy. I've been afraid of this; I've been afraid right from the first." She leaned forward and spoke rapidly. "Listen, Tommy, I want to be friends with you—and we mustn't fall in love. I like you—oh, more than you know. And you attract me, too. I'll admit it—but don't ever kiss me; please don't ever do that. I'm afraid of you that way; I've always been afraid right from that first day on the train."

"I want to," said Tommy with a sudden, unexpected surge of passion that shook him. "I want to like hell."

"I know, but you mustn't. You really mustn't. I'm older than you, Tommy, too much older, and we're different. We couldn't be happily married. You know that as well as I do, and we don't know each other well enough, anyway. And the other thing—" She shook her head. "That isn't for me, Tommy. I wouldn't dare. It would break my heart."

"You mean," he asked, too confused and shaken to analyze her words, "you'd be ashamed?"

"Maybe. I guess I would. I don't know. But I'd love you and I'd know it would have to end. I couldn't stand that." She paused and then added softly, "Tommy, I'm going to tell you something. I've—I've never let myself love a man because, because I'd love so hard he could kill me. I'd have to be sure of him; you don't know how sure. I'm—well, I'm made that way. I'd—"

"Yes, I know," Tommy interrupted because he could not bear to have her reveal herself more; "I know, Mary. You would. I can understand. I'm as selfish and as predatory as the next man, but I couldn't hurt you—not after what you've said. In the back of my mind I'd hoped. I admit it, but I know you're right. Friendship isn't easy for a man and woman like you and me, but we can try." He smiled. "I hate like hell to say it, but I will: I'll lay off. You can bank on it."

Her eyes were dangerously bright, but she smiled. "I know I can. Well, that's out of the way, thank God. Now let's talk about something else. Tell me about California."

Fortunately, a few minutes later a friend of Mary's knocked at the door. Within half an hour two more friends appeared. The studio rang with talk and laughter. The strain was gone and with it the need to make conversation.

When he was alone in his own apartment, however, Tommy knew that the strain would come again. Once he had said what he had said, and once Mary had said what she had said, the old relationship became impossible. Those words might never again be mentioned, but they would never be forgotten. When a man and woman had confessed passion for each other, the passion had escaped the fetters of silence; it was harder to control.

"I'll have to be careful as hell," Tommy thought, "and that's going to spoil everything." He didn't want to be careful; yet he knew that Mary had spoken the truth. They weren't in love.

Strange, how he had always known what she was like behind her pose of masculinity. He'd always known it was a shield, and he'd always known, too, that he could knock it down when he would. Well, she'd put him on his honor, and she had a right to do it. The first move had been his. He couldn't even say that she had tempted him.

Funny, when he thought of Mary and her fear of love, her passion that she controlled so relentlessly, he kept thinking of Kingston up at Dartmouth. What in the world could be the connection? Something Kingston had said last fall? No; they hadn't talked about love. That was one thing they hadn't even mentioned. It was something that went far back—back to his undergraduate days. There was a classroom in it somewhere. A poem? Maybe. Browning? He wondered . . . Kingston had made Browning very real, but this had nothing to do with a success in failure philosophy. Just the same, it was Browning. It was a line—a line that somehow fitted Mary. It said what he was trying to say about her. What was it, anyway? *Andrea del Sarto?* No. He'd thought of that because Mary was a painter. And it wasn't *Fra Lippo Lippi* either. *Confessions?* No. *Saul?* Yes, by damn, that was it. It was *Saul.*

He went to his bookshelves, found a copy of Browning, and leafed rapidly through the poems. Ah, here it was. What a devil of a long affair it was, too. Pretty dull, a lot of it, he remembered. Here was something good, though:

Oh, our manhood's prime vigour! no spirit feels waste,
Not a muscle is stopped in its playing, nor sinew unbraced.
Oh, the wild joys of living! the leaping from rock up to rock—
The strong rending of boughs from the fir-tree—the cool silver
    shock
Of the plunge in a pool's living water,—the hunt of the bear,
And the sultriness showing the lion is couched in his lair.

He read on through the famous ninth stanza with its immortal apostrophe to physical joys. Yes, it was beautiful, he thought, and all true enough—but, just the same, life had to mean something more or it didn't mean anything. Or did we just fool ourselves into thinking we had to have something more because we liked to think we were civilized, and we knew damn well we weren't? Get a man sexually aroused and his civilization disappeared fast enough. Or did it? Maybe, but it certainly came back—it did to him, at least, and spoiled the memory of *that* physical joy. Weren't people often happier, he wondered, when they sloughed off remorse and didn't even try to be civilized? He didn't know. It would take a bit of thinking. . . .

But this stanza wasn't what he had been looking for. It was something else. What was it? Oh, yes, Mary. He'd been looking for a line that fitted her. It was here somewhere, he was sure.

Ah, here it was. Queer, how he had needed those few words. Browning hadn't meant them the way he meant them, either, but they were the right words, just the same: "Behold! I could love if I durst!" Yes, that was it; that was Mary: "Behold! I could love if I durst!"

" 'If I durst'—'If I durst. . . .' " What a crime it was, how absolutely pitiful—to be made like that, rich with a power to love and afraid of it. That was terrible. It was tragic.

He turned toward his bedroom. He ought to have been in bed an hour ago. " 'I could love if I durst!' " He hoped the line wasn't going to run through his head the night long, but once you had realized something like that, it wasn't easy to get rid of it. Besides, he didn't want to think about fear of love. It brought back memories that gave reason to the fear. Love could hurt. Didn't he know it? Hard as he had wanted Mary for a while that evening, there had been actual relief when she had told him that marriage for them was impossible. He might have slipped into a proposal. It would have been easy. . . . Too dangerously easy. " 'I could love if I durst—if I durst. . . .' "

II

Tommy was so busy in the office for the first week after his return that he had no time to get a satisfactory report from Mae Vadney about young Robert. Eventually, however, everything that needed his immediate attention had received it, and he went into her office.

She looked up from her typewriter. "What do you want?"

"To talk. Very busy?"

"No. I'm just pretending to be. I always pretend when a partner comes in. Sit down and tell me all."

Tommy dropped into a chair. "I want to hear all there is to hear about Robert. Or do you call him Bobby?"

"Bobby. He likes that, and so do I." She spoke so smugly that Tommy laughed.

"You certainly sound pleased with yourself. Well, I don't blame you. Tell me all about him. Has he started school? Is he getting along with the other kids?"

"Yes, he's started school. He's in the fifth grade, and he's smart too. And I think he's getting along with the other children all right, though he did have a fight yesterday. I came home to find him with a black eye and a split lip." Mae mentioned the wounds with an air that suggested that Bobby deserved a Carnegie medal.

"A fight already! How come?"

"There's a boy lives about a block from us—a mean, nasty boy about twelve years old. He said—oh, I guess I'll have to explain first. You see, I told Bobby to say his name was Vadney—Robert Corbin Vadney, because I'm going to adopt him just as soon as they'll let me and I thought he'd better use the name right to start with. So he did. And he calls me Mother. I explained that Aunt would be better because—well, because of everything, mothers being married and all that. But he said," she explained, lifting her head proudly, "that he didn't care; I seemed like a mother and so he was going to call me Mother, and he does."

"Good for him!" exclaimed Tommy. "Did that bring on the fight?"

"In a way. Of course, the neighbors don't know much about us yet, but children find things out. He said I was his mother, and they knew I was *Miss* Vadney. And this Herbert knows too much. He told Bobby I wasn't his mother. Bobby said I was. He said I wasn't, and Bobby kept saying I was. Then he said Bobby must be a—a—"

"Bastard?" Tommy suggested helpfully.

Mae blushed. "Yes, that's what the nasty little thing said. So Bobby licked him."

"Licked a twelve-year-old?"

"Yes; he licked him good. Bobby said so, and Jimmy downstairs said so, too."

"And what did you do, Mae, when you found out about it? Scold him good for fighting and send him to bed without any supper?"

"I did not! You bet I didn't. I made it just as clear to him as I could that he was perfectly legitimate, and I washed him up and told him I was proud of him. So there!"

Tommy held out his hand. "Shake, Mae. You're going to make a good father."

His praise made Mae radiant, and she immediately launched into a long story about everything Bobby had done and she had done. There was much to tell, and she kept what she considered the best for the last. When she had told Mr. Jonathon that she had selected a boy, he had handed her a check and said, "Use this, Mae, to buy the boy new clothes. He'll want to get rid of everything he wore in the orphanage." Wasn't that just like Mr. Jonathon, so generous and understanding? But everybody in the office had been wonderful. All the girls were coming over to see her, and they'd never done anything like that before—and Bobby would be overloaded with presents if she'd let people give all the things they wanted to. But the biggest surprise was Mr. Sherman. Why, she never would have dreamed. Never . . . She was so pleased about Mr. Jonathon's check that she'd told everybody, and Mr. Sherman had said:

"Now, listen here, Miss Vadney, don't you go dressing that boy up all pretty in Eton collars and Windsor ties. The kids will guy the life out of him if you do. What are you going to get him?"

Well, Mae hadn't known. She made a timid suggestion and Mr. Sherman just hooted at her. He was awfully superior, Mae said, but men were like that with women, especially young men. Anyhow, he had finally declared that as one man to another he felt he owed it to Bobby to see that he got what he called he-clothes. He announced that he would oversee the shopping himself. What's more, he had, and he and Bobby had got along just wonderfully. And when the shopping was over, Mr. Sherman had taken them to the Radio City Music Hall and then bought a ball and mitt for Bobby. What did Tommy think of that?

Tommy thought Craig had acted admirably, and said so.

But when he returned to his own office, he felt cheated. He would have liked to have done that shopping himself. They might have waited until he got back. What did Craig mean horning in like that? Who'd thought of the kid, anyway? Found him and everything?

"Hell," he thought, exasperated with his childish jealousy, "I'm acting like a kid myself." Just the same, he still felt cheated.

### III

There are occasional days in April when spring forces itself on the attention of New Yorkers. It drifts down between the skyscrapers, gently forces aside the gasoline fumes, clears the air, sparkles. People grow less rude, jostle each other with less animosity, even occasionally apologize with a smile. They notice that the grass in Bryant Park has a touch of green and lift their eyes to the sky beyond the Library.

It was on such a day that Tommy was striding down Fifth Avenue to keep an appointment at the Harvard Club with Fred Homans. Suddenly he stopped, snapped his fingers, and dashed recklessly across the street. "Damn my forgetfulness," he thought irritably. "She'll think I'm all kinds of a liar." He did not pause to wonder why Hollis Graham had appeared in his mind from nowhere.

She was behind the counter when he entered the music store, recognized him immediately, and smiled a welcome.

"I'm ashamed of myself," he began breathlessly. "You must think I'm a liar or something worse."

"No I don't. I just thought—"

"That I'm one of those. I don't blame you. But I'm not really. The fact is I was called to California that very day or a day or two later. I forget now. Anyway, it was soon after I'd seen you. I was gone a week, and when I got back I was up to my ears in work. I'm awfully sorry."

Hollis waved her little hand and flicked her forefinger.

"It's forgotten—like that. Besides, I thought you'd turn up sometime, and you have."

"You're a sport. When can we have dinner?"

"When would you like to have dinner?"

"Tonight?"

"I can't. Mr. Austin is coming around."

"Steve?"

"Yes. We often Dutch treat each other. I have to thank you for meeting him. I think he's grand."

"You bet he is—one of the best. Tell me, what are you doing later?"

Hollis laughed. "Steve and I never do anything later. We can't afford to. We go back to the club and talk, or he goes home and works. Why?"

"Well, it just occurred to me that you and he might come up to my place, and maybe we could get hold of Mary. Then we'd have our quartet again."

"Oh, I'd like that. I'll tell you what. Steve and I will eat down in the Village and then we'll collect Mary if she isn't busy and bring her along. Steve and I will come, anyway."

"Swell!" He held out his hand. "I've got to hurry. Be seeing you."

IV

At eight-thirty that evening Hollis and Mary and Steve arrived in a storm of arguments. Mary didn't even acknowledge Tommy's hello; instead, she walked backward into the room and continued berating Steve.

"You're a stupid, fat-headed male!" she cried angrily. "You've got a lot of false pride and no sense. Besides, I hailed that taxi; you didn't."

"Well," said Steve, advancing into the room, "I can afford it and I'm paying."

"Like hell you can afford it, and like hell you're paying!"

Hollis trailed after them. Tommy looked at her questioningly. She cocked an amused eyebrow, lifted a hand, opened

it, closed it, let it drop. The gesture was completely expres-
sive. It said as plainly as words: "They're both temperamen-
tal; they're both cock-eyed; they're having a wonderful time
fighting; and there's not a thing in the world we can do
about it."

"You're crazy in the head!" Steve retorted. "And don't
think you can bully me. I say I can afford it."

"I say you can't. I make more in a week than you do in a
year. I'd walk before I'd let you pay."

"You didn't walk, and I paid. So what?"

"So you're going to take this money or I'll stuff it down
your throat. I won't be gypped like that."

"Here! Here!" cried Tommy. "Shut up. What's the fight
about anyway?"

Mary and Steve began to talk wildly at him together and
he shouted at them to be quiet. "Let Hollis tell me," he ordered. "She's still sane."

"Well," she said, "Mary called a taxi down in the Square,
and Steve paid before she could. Now they're both mad. Me,
I'm not saying a word. I'm just taking the ride—and thank
you, pretty please, everybody."

"The little squirt thinks he's smart because he put something over on me, and I'm not going to let him get away
with it," Mary declared hotly. "I'm not taking any taxi rides
off of impoverished po—po—what do you call 'em?—poetas-
ters?"

Steve pushed her nose impudently with the tip of his
forefinger. "I'm not a poetaster and I'm not impoverished.
Can't a man celebrate?"

"Celebrate what?" Tommy asked while Mary rubbed her
nose indignantly.

"You tell 'em, Steve," said Hollis. "And, Mary, you be
good. Stop glaring at Steve, and leave your nose alone. You
can't massage it back in joint. I let the great man treat me
to a four-bit dinner."

"Yes, and you're going to let me treat you to a taxi ride,

Carter, old kid, old kid," said Steve, threatening her nose
again. "Because I'm celebratin', see? If I can't take a taxi
up to this jernt, who can? I'm a financial success. See?"

Tommy ordered Steve to spill it, whatever it was, and
Steve eagerly spilled.

"It's like this," he explained; "I've just got my spring
royalties. I'd have been tickled to death with two hundred
and fifty. I knew *Sere and Yellow* had picked up some, but
that meant two-fifty to me. And I got seven hundred and
thirty-eight dollars and sixty-three cents! In one wad!"

"You did!" shouted Mary. "Tommy, bring out the drinks!
We celebrate!" She grabbed Steve's hand, shook it vigorously, and begged his pardon with wild enthusiasm. Steve
laughed happily, reached up with a sudden movement,
caught her head with both hands, pulled it down a little
while he lifted on his toes and kissed her. "Oh, the impudence," Mary cried, "the lovely, lovely impudence! Drinks,
Tommy!"

Tommy added his congratulations and smiled at a secret
he knew. This was Martin Tucker's work, and it showed
what one man could do. Tommy had no idea how many
copies of *Sere and Yellow* Tucker had bought, but he knew
that the number was fairly large and that Tucker had
shipped the books far and wide. "Start ripples," he had explained. "People don't know about the book. Call it to the
attention of one, and he calls it to the attention of another."
He had enlisted Mrs. Frederick Winchester's aid. She was an
important person in women's clubs, and Tommy knew that
on one occasion she had reviewed *Sere and Yellow* before a
thousand women. He did a little mental arithmetic. About
three thousand copies of the book had been sold. Tucker
must have been directly or indirectly responsible for a lot of
them.

He produced the drinks Mary demanded and they all
toasted Steve until he was red with pleasure and embarrassment. Eventually he called a halt. "I'm toasted inside and

out," he said, "and I'm beginning to burn. Let's have music."

Then for the first time Tommy noticed a violin case and asked about it. "We made Hollis bring her fiddle," Mary explained. "You can play for her."

There was no quartet singing that night. Once Hollis had drawn her bow across the strings, Tommy wanted no popular music. This girl could play. After a Chopin nocturne he told her so.

"Just competently," she said; "that's all. And to be a good violinist one has to be very good. There's no in-between. I'm good enough to teach or play for us, but I'm no artist and I know it."

"I didn't say you were a great violinist," Tommy explained. "I know you don't even pretend to be one. But you have a lovely tone, and you know what the music means. More Chopin?"

"Let's go deeper. Beethoven?"

"Oh, grand!"

They forgot Steve and Mary, forgot everything but the music and each other. An understanding existed between them; there was a flow of emotion that blended with the music. There was an exaltation in playing together, a kind of spiritual rapture. An hour passed, another hour. They played on. Tommy opened a book of Bach fugues, and Hollis lowered her bow.

"Not tonight, I think," she said softly. "We should have begun with Bach. All of a sudden I'm tired."

Tommy turned on the bench. "It's been wonderful. I'd forgotten how much—" Then he remembered Steve and Mary and broke his sentence off in the middle. He looked at them and smiled. "I'm sorry. I've been having such a glorious time that I honestly forgot all about you."

"I've been having a glorious time, too," said Mary, "and I'm glad you forgot me. I could just listen."

"Yes," said Steve; "that's it. We were alone."

# CHAPTER XV

## I

MAE VADNEY timidly invited Tommy to dinner. He accepted with such prompt and obvious pleasure that she was startled. Somehow she hadn't thought that Mr. Gray with all his fine Park Avenue friends would want to come over to East Orange . . . Of course, he was awfully kind and thoughtful, and he'd been wonderful about Bobby. She'd never be able to thank him enough for that, but there was a big difference between being kind to a secretary and being her guest. Yet he had accepted her invitation, and he couldn't have seemed more pleased if it had come from Mrs. Astor. You couldn't tell about Mr. Gray. He kept things back. She'd heard that he'd been married, and you'd never guess it. . . .

She was startled a second time when Tommy appeared at her little flat in East Orange bearing an enormous box of flowers.

"I hope you like it," he said. "I told the florist to make it look like spring."

Mae opened the box and pushed back layers of tissue-paper. "Oh, he did!" she cried. "He did. They're beautiful. Bobby, look! Delphiniums and snapdragons and jonquils and tulips and—and this white flower that smells so sweet. What is it?"

"Freesias," said Bobby casually.

Both Tommy and Mae stared at him. "Well, how in the world," demanded Tommy, "did you know? I've never even heard of them."

"Everybody had a little garden all his own at the home,"

Bobby explained. "It was fun, and I had freesias in mine—jonquils too."

Mae fluttered around the living-room hunting vases and chattering excitedly. Bobby showed Tommy his ball and mitt and talked about Craig Sherman. Mr. Sherman said this and Mr. Sherman said that. Mr. Sherman could throw a swell drop. Mr. Sherman had been short-stop on the Yale team. Mr. Sherman had a sweater with a Y on it. Mr. Sherman was the best marble shooter he'd ever seen. Mr. Sherman was going to take him to Coney Island this summer. Until Mae sent Bobby to bed he talked about Craig Sherman.

Tommy wanted to tell him that he had a sweater with a D on it and that he'd shoot marbles for keeps with Craig Sherman any day in the week, but he refused to permit himself to talk like a small boy even if he persisted in feeling like one. It was evident that Craig had made several visits to East Orange, and quite unreasonably Tommy resented the place Craig had won in Bobby's heart. He recognized that Craig's kindness deserved admiration, but it was a let-down to have to take second place before he had even had a chance to try for first. He and Bobby got along pleasantly, but Craig was Bobby's god; and it never occurred to him to hide his worship.

It was actually a relief to learn a few days later that Craig's visits to East Orange hadn't been entirely unselfish. Tommy hardly knew why he resented so keenly Craig's intimate position in Mae's household. It wasn't that he was himself especially fond of Bobby. He liked the boy, but he had had no desire to father him until Craig had taken the opportunity out of his hands. He resented his own resentment so strongly that he sought the cause for it until he found one that satisfied him. Helping Mae had filled a gaping hole in his life. He had felt useful and necessary, and now she no longer needed him. The hole gaped once more. Out of the bigness of his heart, Craig had slipped into his place.

He had known for a long time that Craig was hunting a berth with another firm. Now he had found it and offered his resignation to Winchester, Winchester, Tucker, and Gray. With its acceptance, he announced that he was going to get married. "We're going to live in East Orange," he told Tommy, "not far from Miss Vadney and Bobby. We've been over lots of times house hunting. I'll bet Bobby never breathed a word about Jane."

"He didn't. Did he know about her?"

"Of course he did. Why, he's met her half a dozen times, but I swore him to secrecy—blood from my finger touching blood from his, you know—and I knew he'd never let out a hint. He's a great kid. I'm nuts about him."

Charlie Lovett was in Tommy's office with Craig, and he said, "You're nuts all the way through. Didn't Mr. Frederick say he wanted to see you?"

"Hell, yes!" and Craig departed in a rush.

Charlie smiled and shook his head. "I'll be glad when he's married. It's been like living with a madman; but I'll miss him like the devil, just the same."

"I suppose you will, all right. You've roomed together so long. I bet a nickel, Charlie, you get married yourself before long. It works that way."

Charlie did not smile. Instead, his blue eyes grew very serious and his lips tightened.

"Are you very busy?" he asked. "Got a little time to spare?"

"Of course."

Charlie sat down. He looked out of the window, caught his lower lip between his teeth, and pounded the palm of his left hand lightly with his fist. Then he turned to Tommy and said softly:

"I am married."

Tommy's head snapped back. "What!" he cried. "You're married?"

"Yes. Of course, it's a secret. I'm telling you because I know you'll keep it dark—and I've got to have advice. You keep your head."

"Doesn't Craig know?"

"No. I think the world and everything of him; but he'd get all worked up, and I couldn't stand that just now."

"But you're still rooming with him, aren't you?"

"Yes. Don't look so bewildered. It's simple enough. You see, Craig thinks I go helling around from one end of the city to the other, but for more than a year there's been only one girl. I can trust you, I know, and I'm going to tell you all about it."

He paused, breathed deeply, and then explained: "Her name's Clara Easton and she lives with her father and mother on the Drive. They've got a good deal of money—not millions but plenty. I don't understand them at all. They barge around to night clubs and all that sort of thing and let Clara do what she damn pleases. She's twenty-one now and she's just been killing time since she got out of boarding-school.

"She's an awfully good-looking kid, honest as the devil, too. When I first met her, she was just another girl to me. I played up to her, of course, and pretty soon I knew she was falling. I'm no skunk, Tom, but lots of girls from homes like hers don't think anything of a night with a man, and I never supposed she did. Well, I was the first man—and that kind of floored me."

"I should think it might," said Tommy. "But if you honestly thought—"

"I did, but that didn't alter the fact one bit; and once I began to use my head I knew she—well, she cared everything for me. I didn't know what to do. I hadn't meant to seduce her, but that was what I'd done, just the same. I'd never dreamed she wasn't just as wise as I was. And I wasn't in love with her. Besides, she's a Protestant, and I—"

"Yes," Tommy interrupted. "I can understand how that might stop you. But you say you are married?"

"That comes later. You've got to understand that Clara never made any demands. She never put any blame on me, and she never asked a damn thing of me—but once we'd started, we kept on. Well, a couple of months ago she told me she was going to have a baby. We'd been careful—but, oh hell, accidents will happen."

He paused and looked out of the window again. His eyes were dull with worry, and his slender face seemed taut and drawn. Tommy was bewildered. He had always considered Charlie a casual Lothario who took what he could get where he could get it and suffered no compunctions later. More than once he had envied Charlie his carefree philanderings. Now it was evident enough that Charlie was quite as capable of remorse as he was himself.

Charlie interrupted his reflections with a sigh.

"I'm not telling this well," he said, once more facing Tommy; "but it's damned hard to tell. You see, she offered to have an abortion and that made me just plain sick. Maybe it's my religion—it's partly that, I guess—but it was Clara, too; I just couldn't stand for that. I felt—I can't tell you how I felt. She was such a sport, you know. She didn't consider herself at all. It was what I wanted that mattered. Her folks had shipped her off to school while they played around and then let her go hang, and in spite of everything she was so damned decent she'd kept herself straight—and I knew as well as I've ever known anything that I got her because she loved me. Tommy, I swear I could have broken my own neck, I hated myself so hard."

"Don't talk about that, Charlie. It doesn't do any good. I can imagine how you felt. You're decent; you would."

"Well, I didn't feel even a little bit decent; I tell you that. I felt like a skunk, but I made up my mind I needn't be a skunk all my life. I told Clara we were going over to Jersey and get married. She actually fought me about it. She said she wasn't going to rope me into a marriage I didn't want. And then suddenly I realized I did want it. Isn't it funny that I hadn't known all along? But I hadn't; I'd never even guessed. But I knew then. I knew I wanted to marry her more than anything else in the world. I had a hard time making her believe I was telling the truth, but finally I won out. It would take six Shakespeares to tell my relief."

"But what's the trouble, then?" Tommy asked, frowning in his confusion. "Why keep it secret? The sooner it's known, the better it seems to me."

"Because her folks are raising hell; that's why. They want an annulment or an abortion or anything. God, they're brutal about it. They like me all right. It isn't that, but they won't stand to have Clara married to a Catholic. They're as prejudiced as Hitler. I want a religious ceremony. I've got to have that, of course. I don't feel really married now. Clara's willing, but they've suddenly remembered they're parents, and they're pretty nearly driving Clara crazy. Me, too, for that matter."

Tommy's lips drew together and his brown eyes grew hard. "You say Clara's willing to go through a religious ceremony?"

"Yes. She'll do anything I want."

"She just has to promise that your children will be raised in the Church, doesn't she?"

"That's really all, and she's willing to do that, too. Her folks have never given her any religion, and she's willing to give mine a chance. It's the children business that gags her parents, Mr. Easton especially. You'd think she was promising to drown them."

"Never mind that. She's twenty-one?"

"Yes."

"Then I think you're a pair of damn fools."

The assertion was made with such cold emphasis that Charlie stared at him and said nothing.

"What does somebody's prejudice matter?" Tommy demanded. "The baby matters. That's what matters. And you and your Clara matter. To hell with prejudices. Go hunt up a priest and marry Clara. Let her folks howl. What good'll it do them?"

"You mean tell them after it's all over?"

"Of course! You're so all-fired ashamed of yourself and so chuck ablock with honorable intentions that you can't think straight; and Clara is probably so unhappy she can't think at all. There's no better answer to an argument than a *fait accompli*. Isn't that the trick rulers pull every time they get in a tight place? Watch Mussolini. And Hitler'd be licked without it. He sends his troops into the Rhineland and then just sits tight. Well, you get married and sit tight. Then you *are* married—and your in-laws can accept it and sulk or accept it and smile. There isn't any other choice."

Charlie's face was radiant. "You're right, Tommy! You're dead right." He held out his hand. "I always knew you were a damn good friend, and you're a hell of a good lawyer too."

## II

Two days later Charlie told Tommy that Clara was willing to go through with the secret marriage, and a week later he swung into Tommy's office, all smiles.

"I can tell from that homely mug of yours," said Tommy, "that the deed is done."

"And how! Boy, you ought to have seen the fireworks when we broke the news. Pa Easton threatened to have the law on me and shoot me dead and disembowel me on the living-room rug; and Ma Easton—well, Ma tried to work up a nice case of hysterics, but Pa was hollering so loud nobody would pay any attention to her. Clara and I just plunked ourselves down comfortable on the *fait accompli* and watched the show. Honest, Tommy, I've never had a softer seat; and Clara, so help me, was as placid as Jim Farley when

he knows he's got the votes. Once we'd gone through with
the ceremony, she wasn't afraid of anybody. When her father got tired of yelling, she said just as quietly as you please,
'Charlie and I are going to a hotel. Then we're going to hunt
an apartment out in Westchester somewhere. We'll be glad
to see you. Now I'll pack my clothes.'

"Tommy, you ought to have seen them. Wham! she'd hit
'em smack on the button. Honest, I could see them reel.
Then they were all over her, calling her their little girl and
kissing her and loving her nearly to death. Mrs. Easton
kissed me and the old man damn near wrung my hand off,
and—" the gaiety faded from his face—"and I don't know
how to thank you, old man. You're the greatest little fixer
in the world."

"Yes," thought Tommy morosely, "I'm a great little fixer
all right—for everybody but myself."


### III

It was only a week later that Fred Homans asked him to
be his best man.

"You, too!" Tommy exclaimed.

"What do you mean, me too?"

"Every man in New York I know seems to be getting
married. I'm going to see if I can't get a price on etchings if
I buy them in dozen lots." He held out his hand. "You know
you have my congratulations, Fred, and, of course, I'll be
glad to hold you up during the ceremony."

He listened patiently while Fred told him the story of the
romance, listened to the plans for a home on Long Island,
"only forty-five minutes into town and a couple of miles
from her folks and ten miles from mine. You'll have to come
out and stay with us week-ends, Tommy."

Tommy promised, but he knew that the week-ends would
probably never materialize. Only one thing was sure: there
would be no more squash. There were other men, of course,

who would be glad to play with him, but he and Fred were evenly matched and they had played together for two years. One didn't give up a long-standing, pleasant association without a sigh and a feeling of loss.

It seemed to Tommy at first that an overwhelming number of his friends were getting married all at once, but a few minutes' thought made him realize that three was a very small number, indeed. He knew a great many people, and no spring and summer passed without several times three invitations to weddings. Most of his friends were between twenty-five and thirty-five. He should have taken the weddings for granted, but the weakening of a single tie of friendship seemed serious. Other people's weddings made him feel too much alone.

In May, Steve Austin called one evening to say good-bye. "It has just dawned on me," he said, "that I'm the well-known double-plated jackass. I came to New York in the first place to be near the editors, to get acquainted with them, I mean. And here I've stayed, though I've been acquainted a long time. I've lived in that dirty little room, roasted in summer and frozen in winter, and I've eaten in one-armed lunches until my stomach sits up and begs for mercy if I even pass one of the places. I've got a little money now and I want to write another book. I don't need to swelter in New York. I'm going back to my old home town in New Hampshire—Laconia, and I'm going to swim and walk through the woods and eat home-cooked food and relax into a human being again. And I'll write better; I know I will."

Steve was going, too, and probably if his next book was a success, he would marry Hollis. They were together a lot, and they seemed to think everything of each other. Certainly he was pretty sure of her, for he said, "Go around and see Hollis once in a while, won't you? She likes you, and she doesn't know many people in New York she does like. I think she's lonesome most of the time."

Tommy promised, but he felt depressed. He was losing four of his best friends. It was stupid to say that he wasn't losing them; he was. Of course, he would see Charlie in the office as usual, but Charlie would dash away from the office the minute he was free to get home to his wife and baby. Fred would be rushing out to Long Island, Craig to New Jersey—and, besides, Craig's office would be downtown; he probably wouldn't see him more than once in six months. And Steve would be up at Laconia. Oh, they would write to each other now and then, but what was a letter?

He called on Mary the following evening and found her surrounded by suitcases and canvases.

"I was going to telephone to you tomorrow the first thing," she said. "I'm leaving town."

Tommy threw up his hands. "You, too!"

"What's the matter? I know Steve's going. Who else?"

"Everybody else. Everybody I know is getting married or leaving town or something. I know it always happens at this time of year, but it's just too damn much. I got three invitations to weddings in this morning's mail. Three! Don't tell me you're going for good."

He sounded so tragic that she laughed. "No, just until September or October." She kicked a suitcase out of the way, picked a dress off a chair and threw it on the couch, sat down, and explained: "I'm going to see if I'm a painter or just a hack. I've done pretty well in the last year and I can afford to take a few months off. Bill's clean off my hands, and I'm free to do what I please. Next fall I'll exhibit and see what comes of it."

"Where are you going?"

"Here and there in Maine—Bluehill first. I'll try it a while and then go some place else. What are you looking so glum about?"

"I'm going to miss you like hell," he said flatly. "I think you're doing just exactly the right thing, but, God, how I'm going to miss you!"

IV

The next day he marched into Sturmen's Fifth Avenue shop, strode to where Hollis was standing, placed both hands on the counter, leaned far forward, and demanded, "Are you leaving town?"

She touched the counter with her finger-tips and looked unsmilingly into his eyes.

"I am not."

"Are you getting married? Don't blush or evade or tell me it's none of my business. *Are* you getting married?"

"I am not."

"Will you take pity on the lonesomest man in New York?"

"I will not."

Tommy was looking his sternest, and Hollis smiled serenely at him. He slapped a hand on the counter and asked in his best courtroom manner: "Have you, Hollis Graham, or have you not a heart? Answer yes or no."

"Well, that depends on—"

"Yes or no!"

"Yes!"

"Aha! In one breath you say you have a heart; in the next you say you won't take pity on the lonesomest man in town. There's perjury somewhere."

"You've got your breaths mixed up," Hollis admonished him sweetly. "I breathed about the heart second."

Tommy laughed and sat down on the stool. "So you did. Have you heard about Mary and Steve?"

"Yes, and I don't know what I'm going to do without them. They're pretty nearly my New York world. That's why I won't take pity on the lonesomest man. I'm far and away the lonesomest girl and I'm looking for pity myself."

"Well, let's pity each other—together. Let's go on a bust tonight, and I mean a bust. Dinner, show, night-club—shoot the works. Let's dance on our broken hearts, smile bravely at each other through our tears."

"Tear laughs out of throbbing throats while the fiddles sob?"

"Yes, and sob secretly ourselves."

"It sounds like an orgy," said Hollis, smiling gaily, "and I dote on an orgy. You left out drowning our sorrows in liquor. Mine will drown quickly, I'm afraid. Two sips and two sniffs and I'm woozy."

"Lucky girl. I'm afraid I'll have to drink for hours to do the job. It's a date, then? And don't tell me you haven't the clothes. What do clothes matter to breaking hearts?"

"Listen," said Hollis, leaning forward and speaking softly, "I'll tell you a secret: I've got the clothes. I'll let you guess what the dress cost when you see it, and I've got a new spring coat, too—the biggest bargain, I'll bet, in New York. Indeed, it's a date. I'd just love a bust. I'll feel like Cinderella."

"I bet you look like her, too," and Tommy meant exactly what he said. For the dozenth time he wondered why he had thought Hollis just another girl the first time he met her. Her slim little figure was lovely in its grace, and in her face there was such sweetness and humor that she would have been pretty even if her skin hadn't been satin smooth and her features delicately formed. "She takes a lot of knowing," Tommy thought admiringly. "She's got brains or Steve wouldn't have bothered with her, and she's got taste, too. Anyhow, she doesn't paint her nails—thank God."

## v

There are those who maintain that New York City is the most delightful summer resort in the world, but Thomas Gray was not one of those. He thought New York City in summer bad at its best, intolerable at its worst. He was sensitive to smells, and when on humid days the moisture in the air lay like a blanket on the city's odors and held them close to earth, he felt smothered, sometimes nauseated. The beaches were always crowded, and all the bathers seemed to have figures lumpily molded out of soft suet and voices mercilessly forged out of ringing brass. The air in the subways was like rancid soup, and most of the people one saw on the streets seemed to be going down for the third time and not caring.

He hated New York in summer, but he told the partners that he would be glad to delay his vacation until autumn. Mr. Jonathon, who had to take tender care of his health, was planning to spend the entire summer at Seal Harbor. Tucker was going to Europe and trying hard to pretend that he wanted to go.

He fooled nobody. From Mr. Jonathon down to Ethel, the telephone girl, it was quietly assumed that it was Mrs. Tucker who wanted to go. Evelyn Tucker often came to the office, and even the youngest office boy told his friends that "that Mrs. Tucker was sure on the make." Where she went, Martin Tucker went, too, if he possibly could. Tommy felt achingly sorry for him. It must be ghastly trying to chaperon your own wife while pretending not to see what was evident to every one. Worst of all, Tucker was far too shrewd not to know that it was evident to every one. Well, the strain showed in his eyes and his mouth, but Tommy knew that all the devils in hell could not burn a confession of his knowledge from Tucker.

Mr. Frederick would spend the summer as usual at his home in Westchester County. He couldn't leave his garden, but he would come into the office only on the cooler days. One of the partners had to be there every day, and as the youngest, Tommy could only make the offer to be the one and make it as gladly as he knew how.

It promised to be a bad summer. It was easy enough to fill the week-ends by accepting invitations to Long Island and Connecticut; and if no desirable invitation came, Mr. Frederick's door was always wide open to him. It was possible to leave the office early many afternoons for a swim or golf, but the evenings in the city would be deadly. Time and time again as June got hotter and the city emptier of people he knew, Tommy thanked God for Hollis Graham. He could drop into the girls' club where she lived and be almost sure of finding her there. Sometimes they sought the coolness of an air-conditioned theater; sometimes they took bus rides; sometimes they walked on Riverside Drive or in Central Park; and often they sat in the roof garden that the club provided and tried not to hear what other couples uncomfortably close were saying.

As the summer wore on, Tommy depended more and more on Hollis, grew more and more disturbed about her. She made the relationship as easy and simple as possible, but to him it became increasingly a strain. Sometimes he wondered if she were really indifferent to him, since he could detect no sign of strain in her whatever.

At first she had demurred when he suggested going some place that promised to be expensive. He merely insisted a few times, and then he said, "Please, Hollis, don't argue. I can afford the money without a thought. You're so used to counting pennies that you can't realize I don't have to. I'm not even being generous, because there's no sacrifice. Steve was far more generous when he treated you to that four-bit dinner. And I enjoy it. Don't let false pride or needless consideration stand in the way of my pleasure. I'm asking *you* to be generous."

She looked at him, studied him. "All right," she said. "I shan't say anything again. I'll just believe you're telling the truth."

He found her a conundrum, most fascinating because she was impossible to solve. Her manner was always gentle, delicately feminine; yet she was as independent as Mary Carter herself. She was never pugnacious, she rarely argued, but he found himself giving in to her time and time again when he had had no intention of giving in. Why, he did not know. It took him months to discover the key to her character; it eluded him through its very obviousness. Girls, he believed, were by nature actors. By instinct, they played a part, and they changed it more or less with every man they met. He had learned to watch for evidences of play-acting, and he could find none in Hollis. Apparently she had simplified her philosophy of life until she dared to say what she meant.

Dubious, he asked her once if she never evaded.

"Not nearly as much as I used to," she replied. "I think coquetry is innate in girls. It is in me, anyhow. But it's a weapon I was never very skilful with. It always backfired, and instead of slaying my man with it, I burned my fingers. So I just gave up. I decided I didn't want to be clever or cute, and I didn't much like men who wanted me to be. Mostly nowadays I either say what I think or keep my mouth shut. It makes life much simpler."

Perhaps. . . . He didn't know. He wondered if she was keeping her mouth shut when she accepted his pretense of unemotional companionship as if it were the most natural thing in the world. It wasn't natural; it was so unnatural that at times it seemed as if he could no longer maintain it. But he did not dare to make a move. He was not afraid of offending Hollis. She might even accept his desire to kiss her as a compliment, but he knew that once he kissed her, the pretense was gone; and without that, the companionship ended. Either they parted or they became lovers, and he dared not take a chance of losing her.

There was a strain now in his relationship with Mary, but that could be borne because Mary did not stir him as Hollis did; but if he ever declared a passion for Hollis, the strain would be unbearable. With her, he felt that he had to have all or nothing. Nothing? No, that wasn't right. He had her friendship. He couldn't lose that, and if he said a single word, he might.

He grew careful and timid. If Hollis noticed, she gave no sign. They talked often about music, went to several summer concerts, but she never suggested that they go to his apartment and play duets. She must wonder, he thought, why he never suggested it. For a time he wondered himself. Hollis wouldn't be the first girl who had visited his apartment alone, and some of those girls had walked out of it unkissed.

But Hollis? No; no, he didn't dare. It would be impossible to sit there playing the piano when he wouldn't be conscious of a thing in the world but her. He had always felt that he could control himself if he wanted to, but with Hollis he was afraid to put himself to the test.

Hollis never pretended that no man had made love to her. She told him that she had been engaged.

"It happened when I was a freshman in college," she said. "I went home for my first vacation. I suppose Vassar gave me glamour because Dick suddenly found me wonderful. He was the best-looking boy in town, and I suppose most of us had been in love with him at one time or other. Besides, he had the sweetest manner imaginable. I was simply in heaven when he asked me to marry him, and I wore his little diamond all through college. By the time I was a junior, I was dubious; and when I was a senior I was sickeningly sure. I still thought he was charming, but I knew I wasn't in the least in love with him. Outside of the old home town, we didn't have a single thing in common.

"I sent back the ring and made the depression an excuse. I said times were too hard for him to take on the burden of a wife. I was being disingenuous, of course, but I had the comfort of knowing that he would know I was. Dick's no fool. You know, I almost fell in love with him all over again when his answer came. He's a born courtier. He said just the right things so flatteringly and heart-brokenly that I felt precious beyond all women. But I noticed that he didn't argue. He seemed, you know, to be too humble to argue. Well, his humility kept me from asking for the ring back." She paused to laugh softly. "Two months later I was mighty glad I hadn't. I got an invitation to his wedding."

Hollis, he told himself, had been kissed and she wouldn't

be shocked at the idea that she be kissed again. Besides, girls
took kisses so casually these days. But he didn't want Hollis
to take his kisses casually. That was the devil of it. They
wouldn't be casual. And then, besides, there was Steve. . . .

But one night he did kiss her, and he was as surprised by
his act as she was. They had been walking on the Drive, but
the night was so humid that even the slowest movement was
tiring. They sat down on the lawn and talked idly. The
fleet was in the river, and they watched the brilliant signals
from the ships flashing and sparkling. It grew late. Light after light disappeared on the New Jersey shore; the sailors
with their girls departed. An occasional couple passed on the
walk below, and up above them the automobile tires whispered endlessly.

"We must go," Hollis said wearily. "Work tomorrow."

Tommy stood up, bent, placed his hand under Hollis's
arm and helped her to her feet. His hand clung to her arm.
He forgot all his arguments with himself, all his fears. Without warning, his emotion took control; he drew Hollis to
him and pressed his lips hard against hers. She did not struggle; she made no move at all.

At last his mind began to function and he loosened his
arms, then dropped them weakly to his sides.

"I'm sorry, Hollis," he said in a husky whisper. "I don't
know what—"

He broke off. She wasn't looking at him. Her hands were
laced together and her head was bent.

Fear swept over him. "Please," he whispered; "oh, please
understand."

She looked up then. "Why, Tommy, of course I understand. It wouldn't matter; I mean I—I wouldn't mind if—if
—oh, Tommy, I wanted you to and now I'm afraid. I'm so
sorry."

For a moment her words bewildered Tommy. She was
afraid? Sorry? Why be sorry if she wanted him to? Then he
remembered.

"You mean Steve, don't you?"

"Steve?" She looked up at him in empty wonderment and repeated blankly, "Steve?"

"Aren't—aren't you and he—I mean—"

"Engaged?" Her surprise broke the strain. "Steve and I?"

"I'd thought—I'd supposed—" Tommy was stuttering pitifully. A relief, a gladness that he feared was making him tingle. There was too much emotion, too many kinds of emotion all at once. He was afraid of the conflicting emotions, and most of all he was afraid of himself.

"Oh, no. Why, never for a moment . . . Why, Tommy, didn't you know Steve's been engaged for years to a girl in Hanover—some professor's daughter?"

"No. No, I didn't know. Steve doesn't tell things like that."

"He told me right away, and I was glad he did. We managed a real Platonic friendship for a few months, and I thought you and I were going to, too. Steve was wonderful to me, and I'll never be able to tell you what you've meant to me this summer. But we can't kiss and be friends, Tommy. I know we can't. That's why I'm sorry—and that's the only reason."

Tommy wanted to cry, "To hell with Platonic friendship!" and take her in his arms again. He had no fear that she would resist, but he had a deep fear that he might never see her again. He gazed down on her, thought rapidly, and came to a decision. He could not lose this girl from his life. If she was as wise and kind as he thought she was, she would understand what he had to tell her.

"Let's find a bench, Hollis, and talk," he said. "If we sit here, a cop will come along and interrupt. It'll be so hot in your room you won't sleep, anyway, and this is important."

She assented without argument, and once they had found a bench in a shadow, she sat down beside him and waited.

"I'm going to come clean," Tommy began. "And that's hard for me. I don't know why, but I don't like to talk about myself—about things that really matter, I mean. I don't think I've even told you I've been married."

"I knew. Steve told me," she said gently.

"Oh! I hadn't thought of that. He knew, of course. But you don't know the details, and I want you to know them." Then carefully, gravely he told her about Freda. "It was nobody's fault, you see," he concluded, "but it did something to me. I know that. It isn't that I'm still in love with Freda. I can't see her without being moved; she's so beautiful, you know—but I don't really miss her. We never really grew together. But when I think of my marriage, I think of my father's. It was worse than mine.

"I think I'm afraid. I tell myself that my fear is silly. Freda had the courage to try again and make a go of it; and what she can do, I ought to be able to do. I talk to myself that way all the time, but it doesn't seem to do much good. I'm timid with girls who attract me. That's why I've been so timid with you. And, Hollis, I'm afraid of my loneliness. I oughtn't to be lonely. There's no reason for it—but I am; I'm lonely as hell."

"I know what you mean," said Hollis. "Don't I know! You're afraid you'll get married just to escape your loneliness. There's a man at the store who likes me. He's nice. I like him. I haven't let him ask me to marry him; I haven't even let him call but two or three times because I'm afraid of my loneliness. I don't know what I'd have done if you hadn't broken my loneliness for me."

Tommy looked at her with wide eyes. Somehow he'd never thought of other men, but of course there would be; there was bound to be. . . .

"You mean," he asked fearfully, "that you don't know whether you love him or not?"

"I know I don't. That's why I've been afraid. It's so easy

to convince yourself you're in love if you're lonely enough. I've been so grateful to you. You've made me sure about him. Just the same, I know what you're talking about; I know how you feel.

"And I'm so glad you've explained. Why, Tommy, don't you suppose I've wondered about you all summer long? I've wondered and wondered. I've asked myself if you were just killing time or if you really liked me. I wondered why you never made a move toward kissing me. Any girl would wonder. And then I wondered what I would do if you asked me to marry you. Any girl would ask herself that too. Then it was the same thing all over again; I was scared to death of my loneliness. Why, I've been so scared I haven't been able to think about you—as you, I mean. Then I was afraid you would kiss me and spoil our good times, and I couldn't bear to have anything happen to them. I knew if you ever did, we'd have to start all over. And now you don't know how to start. That's it, isn't it?"

"Yes, that's it—and it's wonderful of you to understand and make it so easy for me. I don't know whether I'm in love with you or not, Hollis—and that's the honest truth. I want to be with you. I keep planning to see you. I—I'm so hungry for you—" He broke off and looked away. "You see," he said at last, his voice rough and uneven, "I can't think."

Hollis touched his arm and said gently, "Don't try to now, Tommy. There's no need. You see, I'm not sure, either. I know you could make me think I love you, but I'd rather you wouldn't. I think maybe you could sweep me clean off my feet. I don't know, but please don't try. I'm old-fashioned, Tommy, in lots of ways. I come from old-fashioned people. I couldn't have an affair. I mean I couldn't be happy about it. You see, I never could make my parents understand; and even if they never knew anything about it, I'd always be trying to make them understand in my mind. I'd always be trying to justify myself to them and to myself, too. You wouldn't insult me at all if you asked me to live

with you, because I know you care for me, but I hope you'll
never ask me."

Tommy took her hand in his and held it tight. "I never
thought of that, Hollis. I give you my word. It isn't because
I've never had such an affair, because I have. I was happy in
a way, and there's nobody I respect more than I do that girl.
Can you understand that?"

"Yes, I can understand it perfectly. You were really fond
of each other, and she was honest."

"That's it exactly. There was never anybody more honest.
Not even you, Hollis, and I know now that you're as honest
as honest can be. But I didn't think of you that way. I feel
altogether different about you. It's so much deeper, so much
stronger. She never wanted to marry me, and she knew I
didn't want to marry her. There wasn't any confusion at all.
But you—you're different. You could tempt me into an affair without trying. You could make me marry you if you
wanted to. When I kissed you . . . You could take control
of me."

Hollis shivered and said pleadingly, "Don't talk that way.
Please, please don't talk that way. You make me feel dangerous to you. It's an awful feeling."

"I didn't mean it like that." He paused and then asked
humbly, "Hollis, do you suppose we can go on being friends
for a while? I mean do you think we can go on being honest
with each other? I've got a lot to think about. I haven't told
you all of it yet, but I will. I mustn't tonight. It's too late.
But I've got to do something about my life. It's got away
from me. I'm missing it. I've known that for a long time. I
need to be married. I want to be married, but I know that
marriage won't solve my problem. It will for a while, maybe,
but I'm old enough to know that it'll come back. I didn't
think so when I was twenty-five. Now I'm thirty, and I know
I must think. I want you to help me. Is it asking too much?"

"It isn't asking anything, and all I ask is for you to go on
being honest with me."

She lifted her eyes bravely to his, but even in the dim light Tommy could see that something was wrong. She looked so little and tired—and she looked afraid.

## VI

The next evening Tommy waited in the lounge of the girls' club. He fiddled with his straw hat, walked up and down, caught the clerk in the office watching him, sat down hastily, immediately forgot the clerk, got up and began walking again. Hollis would be there any minute and he was afraid to see her.

He had never wanted so much to see a girl and at the same time feared so much to see her since his junior year in college. Then on a moonlit Saturday night in Northampton he had proposed to a pretty Smith junior. She promised him her answer the next morning, and he had waited in that dormitory living-room for what had seemed time interminable. Saturday night he had pleaded for her love; Sunday morning he was terrified lest he might get it.

What would Hollis say? How would she look? Could they ever be natural together again? Damn it, he had spoiled everything. Why couldn't he have hung on? He had hung on for more than three months; then suddenly—! And he was just as confused as he had been before. More confused! Thirty years old and with no more sense than he'd had at twenty.

"Tommy."

He whirled. Hollis was coming toward him with her hand out. Was she awfully pale or did he just imagine it? He knew that he wasn't imagining the weakness in his knees. That was insistently real.

He took her hand in his, felt his face burn, gulped, and then came out with it: "Hollis," he said, "I feel like a man that's been in an automobile accident. If he doesn't get into a car and drive right away, he'll never dare drive again. I came tonight because I was afraid to come."

Hollis smiled weakly and nodded her head. "I could have been downstairs five minutes ago, but I couldn't get up my courage. Now I feel—well, kind of relieved."

Relieved? Yes, that was it; he was relieved. He wasn't really frightened any longer. The worst was over.

"You know," he said, "that automobile stuff wasn't as pat as an experience I once had myself. Once when I was a kid I almost drowned. One of the big fellows told me to go right back into the water. I howled. I was never going into the water again. He was a smart fellow. He picked me up and threw me in. I don't know why I didn't die of fright, but I didn't; I swam—and suddenly I wasn't scared any more. Understand?"

"Indeed I understand. I don't know why not, but I don't feel scared either." Her blue eyes shone. "Why, Tommy, I honestly think we can manage it. I honestly do."

"So do I. There may be moments, but now that we've survived one, we'll manage the others. We can manage anything. Come on; let's go up to the roof garden. There's a world of things I want to tell you, and I'm going out of town tomorrow for the week-end. I promised and I've got to go, but I want to tell you everything first."

The need to unburden himself to Hollis was so imperative that he did not pause to wonder why there was a need. It was simply necessary to him that she understand Thomas Gray. He began with his childhood, told her about his father, his mother, and about his father's letters. He evaded nothing. There seemed to be no need to evade. Occasionally she helped him with a comment or a question, but mostly she merely looked at him intently and listened. At last he came to his loneliness in recent years, to the feeling of emptiness, the lack of any significance in his life.

"I can't understand it at all," he said. "There's no sense in it. But you can understand now, can't you, why I said last night that marriage would be only a temporary solution?"

"Yes," she answered; "yes, I can understand, and I think you're right. A man has to have some purpose beyond marriage. I can't solve that for you, Tommy. Maybe I'll get an idea, but I doubt it. I think it's something that nobody can solve for you, but somehow I feel sure you will solve it yourself. I think you think so."

"For the first time I do. I don't know why, but I do. You've given me some kind of new confidence. Anyway, you've made me hopeful."

Hollis looked past him toward the city's towers. When she brought her gaze back to him, she seemed to have lost something of her naturalness, her ease. When she spoke her voice was blurred. "Tommy," she began hesitantly, "I—I want to say something now. When you asked me last night to go on trying to be friends, I was frightened; I—I felt sure one of us was going to be terribly hurt. I still think so, but now I don't care. You've given me your confidence, you see."

"I told you things, Hollis, that I've never breathed to another person. There's never been another person I could talk to the way I can to you. You believe that, don't you?"

"Yes—and now I don't care. If I'm the one who's hurt, it'll be worth while. I'll be glad I knew you, no matter what happens."

## CHAPTER XVI

### I

$M$ARY CARTER returned to town in September and telephoned to Tommy. "I want to see you," she said, "and I want you to see my paintings. When can you come?"

Tommy considered. He had an engagement with Hollis, but he could break it. She would understand. Bless her heart, she always understood. Besides, he had seen her the night before. His relationship with her was turning into something entirely new in his experience. It was so quiet, so peaceful—and so breathless. There was no longer a strain of which he was aware, only a kind of bright expectancy.

"I can come tonight," he told Mary. "How's that?"

"That's noble of you. You don't know how glad I'll be."

When Tommy replaced the telephone in its cradle, he leaned back in his chair and gazed blankly at the ceiling. Why would she be so glad? She'd sounded excited—as if seeing him would be something tremendously extra special. Or was that just her exuberant way of talking? He hoped so. He wanted to slip back into calm friendship with Mary. Anything else would disturb the perfection of his relationship with Hollis, and he would permit nothing, no one—not even Mary—to do that.

There was nothing emotional about her welcome that evening, but she seemed curiously excited. No, that wasn't the word. What was it? *Exaltée?* Yes, that was it. High. . . .

She had never looked handsomer, he thought, never seemed so vital. She gave him a rapid résumé of her summer. She had spent a week here, two weeks there, a few days the other place. "I even went high-hat," she said, "and lolled a couple of weeks away at Bar Harbor. You ought to have seen *me* wallowing in luxury." And everywhere she had painted. Just wait, he would see.

"Why wait?" Tommy asked. "I'm here. The pictures are here, aren't they? Let's see 'em."

Mary stood up. "You know," she confessed, "I'm downright scared to show them to you. I respect your opinion a lot; you know that. You've got an eye, and you've got taste. Oh, well, if your opinion didn't matter to me, I wouldn't be scared. But don't take pity on me. You'll be honest? You promise?"

Tommy's right forefinger slashed diagonals across his chest. "Cross my heart," he swore. "Come on; don't teeter like a timid deb. You're an artist; show your pictures."

Mary thumbed her nose at him, turned, picked up a canvas and placed it on the easel. She looked at it, then at him, and waited.

Tommy studied the picture. "It's good," he said at last. "You know it's good. I like it almost as well as the little Berkshire scene you did last fall."

That was tempered praise, but it seemed to satisfy Mary. She showed another picture, another, and another. Tommy liked them with increasing enthusiasm. Then she produced a portrait of an old Maine fisherman with a net over his knees.

Tommy studied it a long time. Finally he lifted his eyes to hers. "So many Maine fishermen have been painted with nets over their knees," he said. "You set yourself a hard task —but, Mary, I think Winslow Homer himself would have been willing to sign that canvas."

"*Tommy!*"

"Yes, I mean it. I'm only an amateur critic, of course, but really fine things proclaim their fineness even to an amateur —and there has to be real fineness to make a trite subject distinguished. Your others are good paintings. All of them have quality, I think, but this is something more. You knew it was, didn't you?"

"I hoped it was," she admitted shyly. And then, obviously nervous, actually timid, she said, "There's one more."

Tommy waited. All of the usual sureness of her movements had vanished. She had difficulty placing the portrait against the wall, more difficulty in substituting the last picture for it on the easel.

Tommy looked at it a long time before saying anything. It was a small seascape showing a bit of cove with the sun-lighted surf breaking against a rock.

"What is it called?" he asked without looking at her. His eyes never left the picture itself.

*"The Tide Comes In."*

Still Tommy looked at the picture. "It's sold," he said softly. "Hang it if you want to when you have your show, but mark it sold. It's mine."

"But, Tommy—"

Then finally he lifted his eyes to Mary. "Yes," he insisted, "it's mine. My first Carter, and Carter's finest." He stood up and held out his hand. "Mary, I think you're a damn fine artist. I'm proud of you."

He could feel her hand trembling when it touched his, and her great dark eyes were brilliant with unshed tears.

"Oh, damn you!" she cried suddenly. "I'm going to bawl!" She dropped his hand, rushed into another room, and slammed the door behind her.

Tommy chuckled softly to himself, lighted a cigarette and sat down to enjoy the picture. He wished Hollis were here. She would like it. Vaguely he wondered why Mary hadn't thought to ask Hollis, too. They were such good friends. . . .

In five minutes Mary returned, dabbing a bit at her eyes with her handkerchief, and smiling shamefacedly.

"I'm sorry, Tommy," she apologized, sitting down in a chair opposite him. "It was just a little too much. You see— well, somehow I'd felt I'd done good work, especially those two pictures. And I *do* respect your taste. You aren't bothered by theories and schools the way the professional critics are, but you've got the background and a real love for good painting. Nick raved, but I was afraid—"

"Nick?" Tommy interrupted. "Who's Nick?"

Mary's face flamed, and her attempt to cover up the slip was pitifully inept. "Mr. Tyckman," she said, clearing her throat and dropping her handkerchief. She bent, picked it up, and added, "Nicholas Tyckman, you know."

"Yes, I know. I know. Oh, yes, Mary, I know. Nicholas Tyckman, his name is." His voice was heavy with hints and accusations. "Oh, of course I know. You just happened to see him, I suppose, and so you begin to drop things and turn as red as a turkey's wattle and—"

"I did not, Tommy Gray! You're a liar."

"Says you!" mocked Tommy. "All right, Mary, come clean. Spill it."

Impossible as it seemed, Mary's color deepened, and she gave Tommy a single glance so blazingly baleful that he laughed.

"Shut up!" she ordered wildly. "You shut up. How can I talk with you braying like a cock-eyed jackass?"

Tommy shouted, and there was nothing she could do but wait and writhe until his laughter ceased. Then she said with quiet ferocity, "Do I talk or do you go on cackling?"

Tommy gulped and controlled his yearning for more laughter. "You talk. I'm sorry, Mary, but you did look funny. I know now what 'impotent rage' means."

She smiled at him then. "I felt like all hell in eruption. I still do." She waved her arms and sighed, "I'm so hot."

"Don't discuss your temperature, please. Tell me about Tyckman."

"I was going to tell you. Don't think you've discovered something all by your little self. That's one reason I got you down here tonight—that and to see the pictures. You've guessed it already, haven't you?"

"Don't tell me you're engaged?"

Once more Mary's cheeks burned, and her head sank in a gesture of assent.

Tommy whooped, leaped from his chair, and grabbed her hand. He was astonished, delighted, and completely confused. The violence of his enthusiasm paradoxically restored Mary's self-control. She told him to quit acting like a kid with a new bicycle and to sit down.

"But, Mary," he insisted, "I'm so glad! Honestly, you don't know how glad I am. But I'm nearly busting with curiosity. I didn't know you were even seeing Tyckman."

"Why should you?" she demanded pertly. "And I suppose you feel like Cupid because you introduced us. All right, feel like Cupid; and if you get too smart I'll have Nick hold you while I paddle your rosy little bottom."

Tommy sprawled in his chair, laughed tauntingly, and said, "It would take the two of you, all right. Now, come on, Mary, tell me all about it."

"Well," she began, "in a way Mrs. Tyckman had more to do with it than I had. After she'd called on me I was ashamed not to go see her. Nick was there and brought me home. He came a number of times after that, and several times he took me to his mother's place. I liked them from the first. You know that—and Mrs. Tyckman and I hit it off perfectly. Nick wanted me to go to the galleries with him, and of course I loved that.

"Then he trailed me around more or less all summer. He asked me a month ago to marry him, and I said No quick. Well, we fought it out all over the State of Maine. Finally Mrs. Tyckman took a hand. She made me come visit her for two weeks, and then she and I had it out. It was catch-as-catch-can with no holds barred—just two big husky gals in a knock-down fight. She asked me if I liked Nick. I said Yes and dared her to make anything of that. She wanted to know how much, and you know how she is; she wouldn't let up until I'd admitted it was an awful lot. She had a toe-hold or a strangle-hold then, or whatever you call it, and went to work. She wanted to know what I was afraid of, and I came right out with it. I told her it was idiotic for a Greenwich Villager to marry a Tyckman. I told her I wasn't made for society and that I didn't want any part of society; and I said I'd said what I wanted to all my life and that I was going right on saying it and that I'd be damned if I'd turn into a tea-drinking hypocrite for ten Nick Tyckmans, no matter how crazy I was about the whole ten."

She paused and smiled in reminiscence. "Well, Tommy, you didn't laugh any harder a while ago than she did. I got so mad I actually swore at her, and then she laughed harder than ever. She's a great old girl! Finally she quieted down and then she said, 'My dear, there are just two kinds of people who can afford to be as honest as you and I are—people with your talent and people with my position. Marry Nick and you'll have both. Then you'll be able to spit in anybody's eye.'"

Tommy laughed. "That sounds just like her, and it's a whale of an argument, too."

"It was too much for me. Besides—well, Tommy," she added softly, "Nick was too much for me. I can't tell you—"

"Don't try to. I'm glad you gave in. I think you're marrying just the right man, and you'll find that Mrs. Tyckman is right: as Nick's wife you can go right on being yourself. Has it been announced?"

"No. It's a dead secret yet, but it's coming out in a couple of weeks. I haven't told a soul but you, but you were really responsible for the whole thing—and I thought you ought to know before the others."

"But your brother? Surely you've told him?"

"Bill?" The happiness faded from her eyes. "No," she said bitterly, "I haven't told Bill. And that's the thing that makes me wish Nick were anything in the world but a Tyckman. Bill will be so damned disgustingly pleased." Her voice grew mannered in heavy contempt. " 'My brother-in-law Nicholas Tyckman, you know.' How Bill will eat it up!"

"You're pretty hard on him, Mary."

"If you knew what he could have been, you wouldn't say that. God gave him everything but guts. No, I haven't told Bill—and I don't give a small-sized damn how he finds it out or when he finds it out. He'll be so tickled he won't care either."

II

It happened that Tommy had seen Bill Carter once that summer at a country club dance. Carter had apparently not remembered him, and so Tommy had not spoken.

But two weeks after his conversation with Mary he saw her brother again, and this time they spoke. It was Saturday morning, and Tommy was on his way to Long Island to a house party. It had begun, he believed, on Thursday or Friday, but he had had neither the opportunity nor the desire to leave the city sooner. The days were often pleasantly cool again, and he had so many plans for going somewhere or for doing something with Hollis that even the most promising week-end seemed an unwelcome interruption. He liked the Tomlinsons, however, and they had often been kind to him. He felt that it would be rude to decline an invitation that had been generously given.

The train was still in the station when somebody asked, "Is this seat taken?"

Tommy looked up and said, "No, Mr. Carter, it isn't."

Bill's handsome face frankly showed his surprise. "I'm sorry," he began, "but—"

"But you don't remember me? I don't wonder. Nicholas Tyckman introduced us months ago in the Yale Club, and I remembered you because you look so much like your sister."

Bill placed a suitcase in the rack and sat down. "I remember now, but I don't remember your name."

"Gray—Thomas Gray."

"I promise to remember it the next time," said Bill, holding out his hand.

They shook hands and Tommy thought, "He's got a remarkably pleasant manner. If Mary hadn't told me . . ."

Bill interrupted his thoughts with, "I remember now that you said you knew Mary."

"Yes, and the first thing she ever said to me was, 'Is this seat taken?' It was at Springfield and she was coming back from the Berkshires. Going somewhere for the week-end?"

"The Tomlinsons'." Bill's voice sounded weary.

"Why, so am I. You don't sound very enthusiastic."

"I'm not. I've week-ended all summer, and if I don't get out into the woods with a gang of fellows before long I'll begin to feel like a gigolo." He seemed displeased with himself, almost bitter.

Tommy glanced at him in surprise. "I'm sorry," he said, "but I don't get you. Why accept if you don't want to come?"

They were rumbling through the tunnel, and Bill leaned closer to make himself heard. "Business. I go because I meet people."

He settled back and waited until the train broke into the sunshine and the echoing rumble ceased. Then he explained: "It's like this. I'm downtown in a broker's office, and the more people like the Tomlinsons I know, the better. You can see that?"

"Oh, yes. Of course."

"So I go. I like some of it, though parties aren't really my dish. If they'd let me play tennis and swim and talk to people I like, I'd enjoy the whole thing; but, you see, I can't get away with that. I'm not invited because I'm a pal, as you are probably. Not by a damn sight. I'm invited because the girls want a lot of single men around, and I'm a single man. I have to earn my welcome."

Tommy knew that there was a great deal of truth in what Bill said, but he was surprised to hear him say it. Climbers and social-bootlickers never admitted that there was any string tied to invitations they were fortunate enough to receive. Bill seemed out of character—out of the character, at least, that Mary had attributed to him.

"You're just fed up," Tommy remarked, more for conversation's sake than for any desire to draw Bill out. "It isn't so bad."

"No?" Bill's eyebrows went up. "Well, maybe you know how to escape. I don't. I have to dance four hours after I'm sick of dancing, and I have to take one girl after another outside and do my stuff. 'Oh, Bill,' he mimicked, 'I'm so hot. Let's go out and cool off.' That's my cue. Oh, hell," he broke off suddenly and looked sharply at Tommy, "you know how it is."

Tommy knew. He had made obligatory love to a great many girls between dances; but, then, he wasn't the handsomest man in the Yale Club and Bill Carter was.

He grinned at the younger man. "I know, but the burden hasn't been unbearably heavy. You have to pay, I suppose, for being exceptionally good-looking."

"Good-looking!" Bill spat the words out. Again he mimicked, " 'Oh, Bill darling, you're the best-looking thing. How do you keep out of Hollywood?' Hell, I—"

He forgot a half-formed word and swung in his seat toward Tommy. "I don't know why I'm talking to you this way. I've never talked to a stranger like this in my life. You must think I'm an emotional damn fool."

"No," said Tommy, "I don't think anything of the sort. I think you're surprisingly like your sister in some ways. But don't stop, please. It's just occurred to me that a man as handsome as you must have his difficulties. I'm honestly interested."

"Difficulties?" Bill laughed and relaxed. "All right, Mr. Gray, I'll get it off my chest. Don't expect me to go coy on you, though, and pretend I don't know I look like a collar ad. It's one of my liabilities I have to take into account."

"Liability?"

"Of course it's a liability. It's all right to be good-looking like you. That helps. But when your mug looks like mine, it hurts. In the first place, people take it for granted that you're crazy about your mug—and if you aren't damned careful, you are. Why, a month or so ago I must have eaten something that disagreed with me, and one morning when I was shaving I noticed a couple of little pimples. Well, I was bending forward examining them in the mirror the way you will, you know, when I happened to notice the expression on my face. I looked like a mother who's just discovered her baby's cross-eyed. I give you my word I was so disgusted with myself I damn near puked in the basin."

Tommy laughed so heartily that Bill grinned and laughed a little with him. "I know it's funny," he said when Tommy's laugh had quieted to a lingering smile, "but there you are, just the same. And people are always suspicious of very good-looking men. They expect you to expect something for nothing. The men are suspicious, I mean. I can feel that suspicion nearly every time I'm introduced to a man, and I don't pretend to be psychic either.

"But the women! I'm as normal as the next man and maybe no better, but I'm choosy, too, and I want to do my own picking. I get so sick of having to play up at these house parties and of putting the damper on at just the right moment that I feel half-kept even while I'm running away from some girl like a scared rabbit." He turned and studied Tommy frankly. "You're no collar ad, I'll admit, but you're a lot better-looking than most men. You must have had the experience a hundred times yourself."

Tommy nodded. "Of course," he said quietly. "Girls on the make are pretty damned embarrassing sometimes, and there are a lot of them. It's your misfortune, it seems to me, not to be fat-headed. If you were, you'd take all the adoration as your right. Unfortunately, you don't seem to be fat-headed and apparently you don't believe in picking all the rosebuds that come your way."

Bill smiled and recited softly:

"Gather ye rosebuds while ye may,
    Old time is still a-flying;
And this same flower that smiles today
    Tomorrow will be dying.

"That's a swell poem. I've always been nuts about it, but it's about marrying, Mr. Gray, not about necking debs. Remember?

"Then be not coy, but use your time,
    And while ye may, go marry:
For having lost but once your prime
    You may forever tarry."

"Yes," said Tommy, "I remember." Remember? He wished he could forget. Besides, he didn't want advice, poetic or otherwise, just now. Not yet . . . He was drifting, but he felt that the drift was toward a harbor. At any rate, it was good to rest from a futile struggle for a while. Pretty soon he would have to think again, but he wasn't quite ready yet. Someday he would find a starting-place; then he would begin to think.

He turned. Bill had spoken.

"I think the next station's ours," he said.

III

The house party was large and Tommy hardly so much as saw Bill Carter again until the next morning, and he had no opportunity to think about him. There was a dance Saturday night. How long it lasted, Tommy did not know, for at one o'clock he slipped away and went to bed. He was tired, and, unlike Bill, he had the comfortable knowledge that he had been invited for himself; so he felt no responsibility to pay with his presence for his entertainment.

Sunday morning there was no one around when he went for his dip in the surf. It set him up, and after he had showered, shaved, and dressed he came downstairs hungry for breakfast.

He was met by a butler who said, "It's a beautiful morning, Mr. Gray. Would you like breakfast on the terrace?"

"That's a good idea. I'll have it out there, yes."

"What would you like?"

Tommy told him and then found a place on the terrace where he could see the sea beyond the lawns and trees. He had just begun to eat when Bill Carter joined him. Bill looked like a poster in white flannels, white shirt, and blue sweater.

"Good-morning," he said. "How come you're up so early?"

"I sneaked," said Tommy, "at one o'clock. How about you?"

Bill grinned boyishly. "At one-thirty. I was just too damned tired. I explained to Mrs. Tomlinson and she sent me to bed like the big-hearted darling she is."

The butler appeared with Bill's breakfast and a newspaper. "This is the *Herald-Tribune,*" he said. "Would one of you gentlemen like the *Times?*"

"Oh, don't bother," Tommy told him. "We'll split this one. Which half?" he asked Bill.

"It doesn't make a bit of difference. You keep the news section. I'll read it at home tonight. Just give me anything." He leaned forward and pulled out a section of the newspaper. Then he laughed. "The society section. Fate smacks the gigolo plunk in the eye. Oh well, it'll do. . . ."

Tommy let his eye run down the first page. The *Herald-Tribune* was going to make a hero out of Landon or bust a font of type, that was plain. They must know he hadn't half a chance. Roosevelt had the Middle West bought and paid for.

A strangled gasp from Bill made him look up. "What—" he began, and then stopped. Bill's eyes and mouth were both opened wide; his face was suddenly pale; and he seemed frozen in position while he stared at the newspaper.

Bill stared at the newspaper and Tommy stared at Bill until he could endure the silence no longer and asked, "Bad news?"

Bill started. "Bad news?" He shook his head in a vague negation.

Tommy suspected that he hadn't really understood the question. Certainly the news could not be good. He seemed absolutely stricken, and now that his fixed stare was broken, he was obviously reading and rereading an item. Finally he closed his eyes and let the paper fall to the floor. His young mouth was tight with pain.

Tommy was confused and embarrassed. He did not know what to do or to say, if there was anything he could say or do under the circumstances. Carter had been reading the society section. What in the world could there be in it to upset him like this? Some girl he cared about getting married? Girl getting married. . . ? Then with absolute certainty he knew, and he felt a rush of sympathy for Bill Carter. Mary had been cruel.

"It's about Mary and Tyckman, isn't it?" he asked.

Bill nodded slowly. *"You* knew?"

"Yes, but you mustn't think anything about that. Mary felt she had to tell me because I happened to have brought them together. She said nobody else knew. I'm sorry she let you get the news this way. I was afraid she wasn't being fair." Tommy was at the moment so concerned with Bill's distress that he did not realize how much his remarks implied.

Bill glanced at him miserably and bit his lips. Finally,

his voice husky and uneven, he asked, "She's talked to you about me?"

Damn! He'd let the cat out of the bag. Well, there was no getting it back in now; he might just as well be honest. "Yes," he admitted. "I wish I could say she hasn't, but there's no use lying."

Bill stood up and turned his back while he looked at the sea. When he turned again, his face was set, his look determined.

"Gray," he said, "I want to talk to you. I have to. I don't know what Mary's said to you, but I can guess. Are you very good friends?"

"Yes, but I don't want you to think that even that made Mary talk to me about you. I'm sure she's never said a word to anybody else. It was just chance. She did it the first time she saw me—and she never expected to see me again. It was on the train and all rather anonymous, you see. She's told me since how sorry she was she had said anything. She's proud, you know. She doesn't talk about intimate things to people."

Bill accepted the explanation without comment. If it gave him comfort, he gave no sign. "I'm glad she did," he said, "because now there's somebody I can talk to—and there hasn't been anybody." He looked around. "Won't you take a walk with me? The first thing we know somebody'll be barging in—and I couldn't stand that just now. This Tyckman business has knocked me clean off my feet. You'll be doing me a great favor. . . ."

"Of course," Tommy agreed, standing up. "If I can help I'll be glad to—but don't bust over and then be sorry."

"I won't be sorry, and I have to bust over."

They walked down the steps side by side, across a wide lawn, passed a fountain, and cut through a grove of trees. Neither spoke. Bill was setting a fast pace as if he had to get somewhere at once, and he was looking straight ahead. Tommy glanced at him and wished fervently that none of this had ever come up. It was going to be pretty bad. . . .

They came to a semicircular marble bench. Bill pointed to it. "Let's sit here," he said. "Nobody'll be around."

When they sat down, the curve of the bench brought them almost face to face. The sunshine was warm, and Tommy, comfortable in his body and most uncomfortable in his mind, waited. Bill stared at the grass. Then he lifted his eyes to Tommy's and spoke:

"Mary told you, didn't she, that I was a bootlicker, a climber, and an ungrateful pup?" He cleared his throat and looked away. "Or something like that?"

"Well, something," Tommy admitted. Mary had used a stronger epithet. What was it? Louse? Yes, that was it. She had called Bill a louse. "Mary," he added, hoping to soften the admission, "uses strong words, you know."

"I know." Bill fumbled in his sweater pocket, found a package of cigarettes, offered one to Tommy, took one himself, and lighted both. Inhaling deeply, he looked past the trees for minutes, and then once more he looked into Tommy's eyes.

"Gray," he began, "I'm going to try to tell you the whole story. This is the most important thing in my life, and there's never been a single person I could mention it to. I've worried about it until I can't think straight. Most of the time I just try to justify myself over and over again—or I just hate myself, and I don't know why. And now Mary's going to marry Tyckman. That spills it. . . ."

He bit his lip, dropped the half-smoked cigarette on the grass, stepped on it, and stared fixedly at his foot. At last he looked up and began:

"I guess Mary told you our folks died eleven years ago. I was thirteen then and Mary was twenty-three. Did she tell you about our father?"

Tommy shook his head.

"He was an accountant. I think he was a kind of thwarted genius. I remember him perfectly, of course—Mother, too. He had black hair and blue eyes and was as homely as hell.

He was half Irish, and I've always thought Mary and I must look like some Irish ancestor. Mother was pretty, all right, but we don't look like her. Well, Father was one of those men with a thousand talents that got all twisted up with his emotions. He lacked something and liked liquor—and I know damn well Mary thinks I'm like him.

"He and Mother were killed in an automobile accident. Mary was in New York then and she was already making a good deal of money. She came out to Ohio and took charge of me. She wouldn't let any of the relatives say boo. I was going back to New York with her and that was all there was to it." He smiled a little and added, "You know Mary. You can imagine."

"Yes," said Tommy, "I can imagine."

"Well, Mary and I had always been nuts about each other. It was only natural, I guess. She was big enough to take care of me when I was a little kid, and she petted the life out of me—and of course I thought that was swell. I was crazy to come to New York with her.

"We got along perfectly. You've got to understand that. I did what she wanted me to because I thought everything she did and said was exactly right. When I was about fourteen I began to write poetry. Lots of fellows do, I guess, and mine was pretty good. Mary was tickled to death. She was taking me to concerts and galleries and things like that already, but when I started the poetry, she set out to educate me—really educate me. I learned hundreds of poems by heart, and I wrote and wrote and wrote. And she studied every word I wrote. I know now I wouldn't have written so much if I hadn't had such a perfect audience—and if I hadn't wanted her approval so much.

"I can't tell you everything she did. She made me take singing lessons, though I haven't much of a voice. She taught me to draw and paint. I liked that, as any kid would—but I didn't have any talent really, and she had to admit it. She took me to all the good shows and bought books by the dozen for me, and she read poetry to me hour on end. Have you ever heard Mary read?"

"No, but it ought to be wonderful with that voice of hers."

"It is wonderful. God, she'd keep me spellbound. Well, never mind that. I made a swell record in school, and then we had our first argument. I wanted to go to N.Y.U. at Washington Square so I could be with her, but she wouldn't stand for it. She was making plenty of money by then—ten or fifteen thousand a year, anyway, maybe more, and I had to go to Yale and have a trip abroad and everything. The best was none too good for me—in her mind it wasn't good enough. I had to have the best clothes, everything!

"Well, with me, what Mary wanted, went. If it would make her happy to have me in New Haven, I was going; but you ought to have seen me running down to New York every week-end I could get away the first two years. I was lost without her, and I was scared as all get-out. You see, at the end of my first term I knew I didn't want to be a writer. Without Mary around, writing didn't mean a thing to me. Oh, I enjoyed turning out verses when I got worked up over a girl or something, but it made me sick to think of writing all my life. Besides, I didn't seem to be able to write any more. When Mary wasn't right there waiting to see what I'd done—oh, damn, I don't know how to put it! I mean—"

"You mean, don't you," Tommy interrupted, "that Mary's interest made the writing important and that it didn't have any importance without her?"

Bill's head bent in a grateful nod. "That's exactly it. But I didn't know how to tell her. I tried to once or twice, but she just laughed at me. You don't know how a kid can suffer over something like that. Gray, I used to lie awake nights composing letters to her. They'd seem perfect, but the next day I couldn't write them. But by the time I was a junior I had to do something, and I finally got up my courage and told her I was going to make economics my major."

He shivered. "God," he muttered, "what a scene!" Then his voice grew stronger and he spoke directly to Tommy again. "I tried and tried to make her understand, but I couldn't get anywhere. She said I was selling out. She said I was going soft because I was associating with a lot of weak-kneed rich fellows who didn't have any integrity or ambition. Rich fellows! Hell, the depression was going good and plenty of the rich fellows were looking for jobs to get through college. But that didn't mean a thing to Mary. I couldn't make her see that I couldn't be a writer just because she thought I could."

Suddenly he jumped up and walked back and forth from one end of the bench to the other. He thrust his hands in his trousers pockets, stopped before Tommy, bent forward, and said passionately:

"A man's got to know two things: He's got to know what he's like and what he wants out of life. I thought I knew. I still think I did. Mary thought writing was wonderful, that it was romantic and thrilling. To her, business is just making money, but to me it's more exciting than any play on Broadway. I mean business in its big sense—not the kind of thing I'm having to do to get started; but any work has its dull side, and the big side of business is bigger than almost anything else. The world lives by business, and it isn't like a book, an isolated thing; it touches the whole world. Why, sometimes, Gray, it seems to me like a great dragon coiling and coiling around the world and around it and around it. One part of the dragon moves—just one, and the shiver goes through the whole dragon, affecting every part. Steel slumps five points in the Exchange and they feel it in France and Italy and Egypt and China—everywhere! A movement in business touches everywhere, and a movement anywhere touches business. It's as big as the world and as sensitive as an eye. Drama? The dramatists can't touch business; it's so goddamned much too big for them they can't touch it. Do you see what I mean?"

"Yes," said Tommy, "I see what you mean; and when a man feels as you do, he belongs in business. But Mary couldn't see that?"

Bill shook his head and dropped again to the bench. "No," he said forlornly, all the excitement suddenly gone from him; "no, she couldn't see it. She never really listened. I'd broken her heart, I guess, and she couldn't listen. Nothing has been the same since then. My last two years in college were ruined. I'd never thought of asking her up to New Haven my first two years because I was always running down to New York—and—and my last two years I was afraid to. She fairly scorched me every time I mentioned my friends, and I didn't know what she'd say to them. She didn't even come to my graduation. I just took it for granted she would come, you know, but she didn't. I told her what was going to happen and she listened and didn't say anything. Then she didn't turn up. I—oh hell, you might as well know the whole thing. I bawled—I bawled like a kid."

Tommy was afraid he was going to bawl again, so deep was the pain in his eyes, so obvious the trembling of his lips. But Bill did not cry. He looked away for a moment, fought for control, found it; then he continued:

"Everything's been wrong. I know now that I spent too much money my senior year, but Mary never gave me a hint. She sent me my allowance and paid the bills I sent her and acted as if she had just as much money as ever. I've kicked myself a thousand times for not using my head. I ought to have known! But I was so used to—well, taking her for granted; I guess that's the way to put it—just taking things from her that I didn't think. And I had such faith in her that it never even occurred to me that any depression could get her down. I did a lot of things I shouldn't have done, but I was a spoiled kid who didn't know he'd been spoiled.

"Now I'm afraid every time I go near Mary, and I don't dare go very often. No matter what I say, she takes it the wrong way every time. She asks me how I'm doing, for instance. I tell her not so good—and then I can see she thinks I'm hinting for help. She thinks that no matter what I say, and she makes it so plain I get hot and then I say the wrong thing. And she keeps making nasty cracks about my friends. I hate the lice that crawl around her studio bumming off her, and I say things. It all goes wrong, every time. I can't make her see . . ."

His voice trailed off and tears came into his eyes. "Gray," he said huskily, "Mary's everything I've got in the world. She's father, mother, sister, and brother to me—and—and— well, I guess I worship her. I've kept hoping and hoping I'd get her back some day, but now I never can. When she marries Tyckman—" He lifted his hand in a weak gesture that suggested infinite futility—"when that happens, she'll think—she'll be sure . . ."

Tommy could stand Bill's groping no longer. "Don't try to explain," he said gently; "I'm sure I understand. You and Mary have loved each other so much; you've been so proud of each other, so ambitious for each other that—well, your emotion has got in the way of your understanding, and you're both terribly emotional. You're so much alike. That's the main trouble, I think."

"I suppose," Bill murmured, his head drooping.

Tommy studied the handsome, distressed young man opposite him. To interfere in a thing like this, to become a part of anything so personal, so painfully intimate, was repugnant to him; yet he could do something that needed to be done, something of overwhelming importance to both Bill and Mary, and apparently only he could do it. He hesitated; then placing a firm hand on his instinct to evade, he said:

"Carter, I think you've done a lot better job of understanding Mary than she has of understanding you. But this is only a misunderstanding. Neither of you has *done* anything irrevocable. I believe you when you say you can't explain to Mary; but if you want me to try, I think I can."

Bill looked up and stared. "You mean—why, I didn't intend; I never thought . . ."

"I know you didn't. But I honestly think I can make everything clear to Mary, and I know how happy she'll be if I succeed in doing it. Do you want me to try?"

Bill Carter stood up, placed both hands on Tommy's shoulders, and looked deep into his eyes. "If you do that," he said, his voice tense with eagerness and hope, "I'll do anything in the world for you. I'll—I'll—"

"You needn't," said Tommy, horribly uncomfortable before such emotion. "I'll be entirely satisfied if I make a decent job of it."

## IV

Bill returned to the city at once. "Make my excuses to Mrs. Tomlinson for me, won't you?" he asked Tommy. "If you say I'm sick, you'll be telling the exact truth. I'm licked. I've got to be alone."

"You have no roommates, then?"

"Two, but one's on his vacation and the other's out of the city for three days—and I'm damn glad of it. I'll have the apartment to myself. Maybe I can rest, or maybe I can think, but, anyway, I won't have to talk to people."

Tommy reached his own apartment at six that evening. He telephoned to Mary immediately.

"Are you busy?" he asked.

"Not really. Nick's here. He got back to town this afternoon. We're having what he calls high tea. Out from where I come from we call it a Sunday evening snack. Want to join us?"

Tyckman there. . . . That made a difference. Or did it? Wouldn't it actually be better perhaps to have him there?

"No, thanks," he said. "I'll have a bite and come along a little later, if you don't mind. I wouldn't intrude, but I have something rather important on my mind."

"Important? What is it?"

"I'll tell you when I see you. It's nothing to worry about."

He went at once to see Hollis. "Have something to eat with me," he asked urgently. "I had an emotional morning, and I'm going to have an emotional evening. Come along and pump courage into me."

"What happened?"

"I'll tell you while we eat. I haven't much time."

They went to a quiet restaurant in the neighborhood and Tommy told her the story. Hollis listened and said gravely when he had concluded:

"So much needless suffering, but it's all so understandable. She's hardly mentioned her brother to me, and I've never met him. You hate the whole thing, don't you?"

"Hate it? There're no words . . ."

"I know, but you're going to feel awfully good after it's over."

"Am I? I doubt it. Besides, there's more than half a chance Mary won't believe me. She's terribly sure about him. She's so bitter I'm not sure she'll listen."

"Will you stop in at the club on your way home and tell me how you come out?" Hollis asked.

"You really want me to?"

"Why, Tommy, don't be stupid. Of course I want you to."

v

It was eight o'clock when he reached the studio, and he found that his talk with Hollis had done nothing to give him confidence. This was going to be horribly difficult, and even if Mary listened to him and believed him, she would get emotional. She was bound to! The prospect frightened him. Bill's emotion had been bad enough; Mary's would be worse. He wished fervently that he was less given to kindly impulses.

Mary and Tyckman welcomed him warmly. He offered

Tyckman his congratulations and liked the way in which the man received them. Tyckman was all right. His manner might seem arrogant to strangers, but it was only a defense. Essentially, he was kind and genuine.

Once the amenities had been observed and they had seated themselves, Tommy turned to Tyckman and said, "Unless I miss my guess, in about three minutes you're going to get up and offer to leave. Please don't. I think you ought to hear what I have to say—and it will save Mary an explanation later."

"What are you talking about, Tommy?" Mary demanded. "You sound terribly serious and mysterious."

"I'm not mysterious, but I am serious. Mr. Tyckman—"

"Nick to you," Mary interrupted.

"Yes, please," said Tyckman.

Tommy smiled and said, "Thank you. I like that. Very well, then—Nick will feel what I have to say is so personal to you that he ought to leave, but I'm sure you'll want him here." He paused and rubbed his forehead. "I've thought and thought about what salesmen call the approach, but I can't find it; so I'll just have to blurt out that I want to talk to you about your brother."

"Bill!" exclaimed Mary. "Why, what about him? He isn't hurt or anything?"

"Oh no! I happen to know that he's quite all right."

"I meant to ask you about him, Mary," Tyckman interposed. "He's been left out in a curious way. I ought—"

"Wait, please," said Tommy. "You'll understand in a minute. That," he said, turning to Mary, "is what I want to talk about—and I'm going to ask you to let me do the talking. I know you'll want to interrupt and explain, but please try not to."

Mary looked at him, looked at Tyckman. She lighted a cigarette and puffed at it nervously. Tommy noted her tenseness and rather frightened air of expectancy. If she would only hang on. . . .

"I can't imagine what you're getting at," she said. "You say nothing's wrong with Bill. What is it, then?" Tommy frowned and she promised penitently, "All right; I promise to keep quiet."

Tommy turned again to Tyckman. "The first time I met Mary," he began, "was on a train. We happened to sit together. We talked as strangers will, you know—more frankly, I mean, than they ever would if they expected to see each other again. When we stopped at New Haven Mary told me about Bill. She landed on him with both feet and a club.

"Now, it happens that Bill and I were on the same week-end party, and we sat together going down to the Tomlinsons' place. Mary had prejudiced me against him, but I couldn't help liking him."

"I've found him attractive," said Tyckman.

"He is. Let's skip that for the moment, though. First, let me tell you about him and Mary. They—"

Mary jammed her cigarette into a tray. Her color had deepened and her eyes were brilliant with the suspense. "But, Tommy," she protested excitedly, "surely I can tell that better."

"No. I'm sure you can't. Let me. Later you can modify any of my statements you want to."

She opened her lips to object further; then with a sudden movement of defeat, she murmured, "All right. All right. Go on."

"Mary and Bill," Tommy explained to Tyckman, "were left orphans eleven years ago. Mary is ten years older than Bill, and she brought him here to raise. They were devoted to each other. It's easy to imagine what a charming kid Bill must have been."

"He was the sweetest thing in the world," Mary said. "Absolutely the sweetest."

"That's what you thought, Mary, and he thought you were the most wonderful. Well, Nick, Bill showed a gift for poetry and Mary was delighted. She couldn't make a singer or a painter out of him, but she thought he had the makings of a writer. She gave everything she had to him—sent him off to Yale when he wanted to go to Washington Square and stay here with her. She had the best tailors make his clothes, gave him a good allowance, sent him to Europe."

He glanced at Mary and then carefully held his gaze on Tyckman. Mary was leaning forward tense in her chair, her eyes wide in a stare of wonder and anxiety. Tommy was grateful for Tyckman's presence. Talking to him made the problem easier; he didn't have to battle directly with Mary's emotion.

"The first two years Bill was in college," Tommy continued, "he came to New York every chance he got because he wanted to be with Mary. But by that time he knew he couldn't be a writer and that he didn't want to be one. Without Mary's constant interest to excite him, he had no literary ambitions. It wasn't because he lacked imagination. He's got a world of it, but it wasn't fired by writing. Business fired it. He saw business as a great romance, a world-wide adventure. He tried to explain to Mary and failed hopelessly. She was sick with disappointment. She said things. Probably he did, too. Then they began to grow apart. She was so scathing about his Yale friends that he was afraid to invite her to New Haven, but he expected her to come to his graduation—and she didn't. He has never got over that.

"Now, because he is much like Mary, as proud and emotional as she is, he can't make his position clear to her—and he suffers. He said to me, 'Mary is everything I've got, mother, father, sister, and brother.' That's the way he feels."

"Tommy!" Mary cried. "You mean—"

Tommy glanced at her again, and again turned his eyes to Tyckman. Mary's face showed too plainly her agony of hopefulness, and the tears were streaming unheeded down her cheeks.

"Wait, please. Let me finish. He worships Mary. That's

not too strong a word. But Mary thought he was a climber
and a weakling. She couldn't see that his week-ends in the
country and so on were just good sense, the sort of thing a man
in a broker's office has to do if he wants to get along. Bill's
got a level head, and he's neither a weakling nor a sycophant.
He's playing the game he has to play because he sees big
things beyond, but he hates a lot of it just as much as Mary
would.

"Now comes the hard part of it. Mary was so hurt and disappointed that she didn't tell Bill of her engagement because
she thought he would make capital out of his relationship
to a Tyckman. I was with him when he saw the announcement in this morning's paper. I've never seen any one more
stricken. He knew instantly what Mary would think—and
her silence told him just how far apart they were. And he
knew there was no way he could make her understand. She
wouldn't believe him. I thought I might be able to explain."
He forced himself to look at Mary. "That's what I've been
trying to do, Mary, and if I've ever been sure of anything I'm
sure Bill Carter is absolutely honorable and self-respecting,
and I can't possibly tell you how grateful he is to you and
how utterly he adores you. But he's broken-hearted over
your engagement. He feels that it has separated you forever."

Mary hid her face in her hands and sobbed. Tyckman half
rose to go to her and then sank back into his chair. The sobs
frightened Tommy. He did not know where to look, what to
do. Probably he'd gone at the whole thing the wrong way,
been brutal about it. . . .

Finally Mary lowered her hands. Her face was swollen,
wet with tears.

"Where is he now?" she asked, her voice breaking.

"Home, I think—at the apartment."

Mary's eyes opened very wide; a brightness flashed in
them, an excited determination. She stumbled to her feet,
rushed to the telephone. Tyckman looked at Tommy and

lifted his eyebrows questioningly. Tommy understood and nodded.

Mary did not see them leave, but as they closed the door behind them, they heard her cry: "Oh, Bill, Bill darling— come, come right away!"

# CHAPTER XVII

## I

MARTIN TUCKER returned from Europe, and a few days later Jonathon Winchester returned from Maine. Then Tommy felt free at last to take a vacation. "I'm going to the White Mountains," he told Hollis, "and walk. I've thought it over. It's strange, I want to be alone; I *need* to be alone—and that's really funny after all my fear of aloneness for the past five years."

"Isn't it," Hollis asked, "that you're making plans now, and you weren't making any during all those years? Isn't that the reason?"

"In a way, yes, though I'm not making plans. That isn't it. I hardly know how to explain. I'm not making plans, but I'm trying to all the time; I'm wanting to. Bill Carter said something that set me going. I think he gave me the starting-point I've been looking for all along. But, anyway, my head is buzzing, and I want to get away from everybody and everything and just walk and think. I want to talk to myself—if you know what I mean."

"Yes, I know. I think we're all like that sometimes. We like to ask ourselves questions just because we know the answers, or think we do."

Tommy touched her hand gratefully. "Hollis," he said, "you don't know how comforting it is to have you always understand what I'm getting at. You let me talk and talk to you, and you never seem bored and you never miss what I mean even when I can only half state it."

Hollis smiled at him as if she were enjoying a delightful secret that she had no intention of sharing. She was very lovely these days, he thought, even after the long hot summer. Maybe it was the new clothes that she was slowly accumulating, but they could hardly account for the brightness that so often made her eyes beautiful or the smile that so often lighted her face. Quiet as always, she somehow seemed vital and gay.

"I'm not in the least clairvoyant," she said, "and I'm not very wise. I suspect you've never given any one else a chance to understand you."

"That's true," he admitted, "but I've never known any one else who I thought would understand."

## II

He was gone two weeks. When he returned there was a new look of determination on his face, a sternness in his eyes that had not been there before. He had written to Hollis that he would be back on a certain date and please to hold that evening open. "I started," he wrote, "and I've gone somewhere. I'm almost frightened at the lengths to which my thinking has taken me, but I'm sticking right on the path, just the same; I think it leads to where I want to go."

She was waiting in the lounge when he entered the club.

"You look different," she said at once. "You're brown and healthy and hard, but it isn't that. You look so determined you look almost mean, and you look keyed up."

"I am," he said, holding tight to her hand. "I know I am, but I don't care. I've done nothing but think since I've been gone, walk and think. I've torn handfuls of cobwebs out of my mind. And I've made up my mind, too. I want to talk to you, Hollis; I've got a world of things to tell you." He glanced at the several people in the lounge. "Where can we go where we'll be alone?"

"Why not to your apartment?"

"Of course! Why didn't I think of that?" The doubts that had troubled him in the summer never arose at all. He did not even remember them. There were a hundred thoughts that he wanted to share with Hollis Graham, a dozen plans, and he thought of nothing else. Kiss Hollis? He did not think about that possibility.

They talked for hours, Hollis on the davenport, he in a chair opposite. They talked and smoked, argued, debated, analyzed.

"But, Tommy," Hollis objected, "it's all so drastic. You may be sorry."

"Well?" he demanded combatively.

"I don't want you to be sorry. Don't think I don't understand. I do. And I agree with everything you've said. I agree so much that I'm suspicious. I'm afraid I'm doing wishful thinking."

"Suppose you are. Suppose I am. What of it? The point is that it's *wishful*. Do you see? Wish—ful. That's what matters, isn't it?"

"To me it does, but you're the only one who knows about—"

She broke off, and he looked at her questioningly. Tommy waited, but she did not speak. Instead she looked at him, laughter in her eyes.

"What were you going to say?" he asked. "Why are you smiling like that?"

Her cheeks grew pink and the smile deepened. She seemed to be waiting for something. Perplexed, Tommy stared at her, and then understanding came. For a passing instant there was an answering smile as his eyes lighted; then he grew quiet and serious.

"Hollis, my dear," he said tenderly, "I know now what you're waiting for. I've based all this talk, haven't I, all my plans on the assumption that we're going to get married? I had no right to do that, I know; but that's my faith in you— my faith that you can never fail me. I think you knew I loved you before I did. You wouldn't have let me open my heart to you if you didn't love me, too. Isn't that right?"

She moved from the davenport to his arms without a word. Tommy held her, incredulous before his own happiness. He had felt sure of Hollis; yet when she actually came to him, he could hardly believe in his own good fortune.

They murmured the things they had wanted so long to say, gave the kisses they had wanted so long to give. And finally they merely sat embraced and let themselves drift in a dream of happiness.

Something occurred to Tommy. He lifted Hollis from his knees and set her gently on the davenport.

"My dear," he said, "I've just thought of something I want you to have. Wait a minute." He went into the bedroom and returned with a small box.

"I want to make a speech," he began when he had sat down again in the chair opposite her. "I want to tell you—no, that's not it. I can't tell you. There are no words for my hope and peace and happiness. It's just this, Hollis: I married Freda without thought. There was no question of faith or understanding. There wasn't anything but emotion. But you—you are my faith. All the plans and hopes I've told you about would be nothing without you. I thought I'd never dare love again, because I never dreamed a girl lived who could give me what you've already given me. Nobody has ever had me as you have; I don't believe anybody ever could."

He opened the box and revealed a ring of yellow gold holding a large diamond surrounded by small ones.

"This," he said, "was my great-grandmother's, my grandmother's, and my mother's. Will you wear it for me?"

"Tommy," she breathed; "oh, Tommy . . ."

### III

Tommy read the note twice. It solved something for him, something that had been troubling him in the back of his mind for days. Yet, strangely, he didn't know what it was. Here, what was it Maribelle said? He read the note for the third time. Maribelle was resigning with regrets. "You is the kinnest gennelmum I ever worked for." She was going to get married and her husband-to-be would permit her to work for no one. He had a store, Maribelle wrote proudly, on 125th Street and made plenty of money. He was going to rent a four-room apartment and maybe get an automobile. "He luves me turrible and he says I ant goin to work no more but I think mebbe hes talkin pritty big bout that car cause he ant as rich as he pertends he is."

Well, this meant more than losing Maribelle. She offered to find a girl to take her place. There wouldn't be any need of that. He'd have to let her know. Yes, but there was something else. He could do something. Funny, how he couldn't get his mind to form the thought, present it directly to him. Or maybe he was just imagining there was something . . . There really couldn't be. He hadn't dreamed that Maribelle was going to get married. Lord, no; he hadn't been thinking about Maribelle at all. Just his own marriage and Hollis. . . .

Ah, that was it! Wait a minute . . . He'd been wondering . . . Now, what was it he'd been wondering about? The two poles were there, and suddenly the mental spark bridged the gap. He knew. Of course! Of course! The perfect thing. Smiling with satisfaction, he picked up the pencil and wrote rapidly on the pad:

"Dear Maribelle: I'm very glad you are about to make such a fortunate marriage, and I offer all my good wishes for your happiness. I want to talk to you, though, before we part company. I'll telephone from the office tomorrow morning about 10:30, and if you're here I'll come over. T. Gray."

True to his promise, the next morning Tommy called his own number. A soft voice answered.

"Is this Maribelle?" he asked.

"Yassuh, Mistah Gray; it's me."

"Can you wait a little while?"

"Yassuh. I'll wait jes' as long as you wants me to."

"Good! I'll take a taxi and be over right away."

Tommy had often wondered what Maribelle was like, whether she was youngish or oldish, fattish or thinnish, black, brown, or yellow. While in the White Mountains he had thought about her for a long time one day, and he felt that he knew her. For five years and more she had been revealing herself to him through her work; but as he rode eastward that morning he wasn't curious about Maribelle's character. That he had already determined on; it was her appearance and personality that were really unknown to him. He was genuinely anxious to meet her.

She was in the living-room when he opened the door. For a moment they stared at each other, and Tommy would have confessed to more than a little embarrassment. It was a trifle upsetting to have Maribelle turn instantly from a miraculous jinnee into a person.

His first thought was, "Why, she's younger . . ." And his second was, "No, she's not . . ." He couldn't tell. Maribelle might have been twenty or thirty-five or any age in between. She was most surprisingly small and surprisingly slender. He had expected a plump mammy in a blue dress and a big white apron, some one fat and chuckling and comfortable. Later, he realized that he had expected Maribelle to be a composite of all the mammies of popular literature, posters, and song.

She wore no apron and her dress was black silk. Her hair had been de-kinked, carefully parted on the side and wound into a small knot at the nape of her neck. Her grandfather or great-grandfather, Tommy decided, had almost certainly been a white man. Her skin wasn't quite black, and it lacked the shine he associated with full-blooded negroes. Furthermore, her lips weren't as full as he had supposed they would be, her nose wasn't as broad or as flat. Maribelle came within a hair's-breadth of being pretty.

"Hello, Maribelle," he said, closing the door behind him. "I'm glad to meet you at last."

Maribelle giggled. "I'se awful glad to meet you, Mistah Gray."

"Sit down, will you? I want to talk to you." Tommy motioned to the davenport and selected a chair for himself. "I'm glad, you know, to find out you're real. I had begun to think you weren't."

"I'se real, all right, Mistah Gray, and you allus seemed real to me. You looks jes' the way I thought you would."

"I do? Well, you don't look the way I thought you would. I thought you'd look like Georgia and you look like New York. You don't sound like either, though."

"I ain't either. I comes from Delaware."

"Maybe that explains it." He hesitated. The night before his plan had seemed perfect and altogether simple to put into operation; but now that he was face to face with Maribelle he began to feel doubtful. He hadn't expected to find any one so young and trim.

"I have something on my mind," he began, "and I don't know quite how to tell you about it. You see, I shan't want anybody to take your place. I'm giving up this apartment."

"You is!"

"Yes. My lease is up and I'm moving out in a few days. The truth is, Maribelle, you're not the only one who's going to get married. I am, too."

Maribelle's smile transformed her into the person he had imagined she was, and her soft chuckle was strictly according to tradition. It seemed to him that he had never seen so many milk-white teeth at once or heard so much amused pleasure in a sound.

"I'se glad," she said. "I didn't want no other girl takin' care of yo' 'pahtment."

"I didn't either, Maribelle; so I rushed right out and found me a wife. I'll have to explain to you that I was married before I came to New York. When my wife and I were divorced, she took only her personal belongings with her and left everything else to me. Besides the things here in the apart-

ment there's a good deal down in the basement, a trunk full
of linens and a barrel of dishes, some dining-room furniture
and things like that. Now, I've been wondering what I was
going to do with everything."

"It's all good," Maribelle said. "It's puffect."

"Yes, I know, but it has associations for me that I don't
want to take with me. I don't want to mix up my first marriage with my second. You know what I mean by those associations, Maribelle?"

Again she chuckled. "Yassuh, I know. 'Deed I know! I got
an ol' stew-pan I ain't takin' with me when I marries Dewey.
I got 'sociations with that stew-pan."

"You have?"

"Yassuh. It allus makes me think of 'Gustus. It's got a big
dent in it. I put it there once with 'Gustus's head. He jes'
set too long."

Tommy joined in her laughter. Now he felt quite at ease,
sure of himself. Maribelle would understand.

"I never bent any furniture over my wife's head, but it
reminds me of her. Besides, I think my new wife ought to
have the right to select her own things. But I didn't want
to sell these furnishings, Maribelle. I didn't want to at all.
In the first place, I wouldn't get anything for them—and in
the second place, well, I just didn't want to. Then last night
I found your note and I knew what I wanted to do. I wanted
to give them to you for a wedding present."

Maribelle could not speak. She stared almost in fear at
Tommy, as if he had turned into a ghost or a madman. When
he smiled at her astonishment, her eyes rolled and the whites
showed. Tommy wanted to laugh, but he stifled the impulse.
Maribelle might look funny, but she had earned the right
to be taken seriously.

"Don't look so surprised, Maribelle," he said. "It really
isn't so surprising. You've taken perfect care of me for a
long time, and I'd want to give you a present, anyway. Now
you have solved a problem for me. I really want you to have

these things. You see, I know you will take care of them and that you'll like having them. That pleases me."

"But, Mistah Gray," she protested weakly, "it's so much. You don' mean *everything?*"

"Everything, Maribelle."

"Not the *pi*-anna?"

"Yes, the piano. Everything except a couple of pictures and, of course, my books. The linen, the silver, the piano, the draperies, the cooking things, everything. Have you found your apartment?"

Speechless, she could only nod.

"Then in a few days we'll call a truck and transfer everything from here to there. That is, of course, Maribelle, if you're willing. I don't want to force you."

"Willin'! Mistah Gray, o' course I'se willin', but how can you—? You's sure you ain't sick or nothin'?"

Tommy laughed. "No, Maribelle, I'm not sick. If you think about these furnishings as your stew-pan, you'll understand. I have a good reason for what I'm doing, and please remember it's going to make me happy to know you have these things. I have a lot to thank you for." He stood up. "Now I must get back to the office."

"Mistah Gray," said Maribelle, standing up too, "I don' know how to thank you. I jes' don'."

"Then don't try to. I'm glad to have the problem off my mind, and I'm glad you're pleased. That makes it perfect."

"Yassuh." Maribelle ducked her head and then looked up with a shy smile. "I hopes you're goin' to be awful happy, Mistah Gray."

Tommy held out his hand. "I think I'm going to be. Thank you, Maribelle."

### IV

That evening Tommy reported to Hollis. "I'm afraid she thinks I'm a little cracked," he said. "The *pi*-anna was too much for her. And, to tell you the truth, sweetheart, I feel a

little cracked myself. I'm a descendant of Yankee horse
traders, and giving away things with reckless abandon doesn't
come naturally to me."

"I don't think you were reckless," said Hollis. "I think
you were a shrewd Yankee, and I think you know you were.
Leaving out your own reasons altogether, you made Maribelle happy and you wanted to do that—and you made me
eternally grateful whether you wanted to or not."

"Well, I didn't think about gratitude, but I hoped you'd
be pleased."

"Of course, I'm pleased. I'll always be a little jealous of
Freda, anyway. I know that, but you couldn't have done anything that would have reduced my jealousy to a minimum as
giving away the furniture has done. In your own shamefaced way, Tommy my darling, you're very wise."

Tommy held her close. "Am I? I thought maybe I was
sentimental and foolish."

She rubbed his cheek tenderly with hers. "I can stand
lots of that kind of sentimentality and foolishness. Besides,
I think there's lots more wisdom sometimes in being sentimental and foolish than in being sophisticated and cautious."
She drew back in his arm so that she could look in his eyes.
"But I don't want you to have regrets, Tommy. Giving away
things isn't anything to what you're planning to do. I know
I've asked you before, but I've got to ask you again before it's
too late. You're sure?"

"As sure, Hollis, as I am of you—and nothing could be
surer than that. I've thought and thought and thought.
Maybe I'll have regrets now and then. Who can tell? But
if my life isn't worth the chance to me, I can't imagine what
is. And remember, darling, you're taking the same chance."

"Oh, no, I'm not!" she cried. "It doesn't matter to me. I
mean it matters to me only because it matters to you. I don't
care where we are or what plans you make as long as you're
happy. It's your life—but, Tommy, Tommy dear, you're
my life."

# CHAPTER XVIII

## I

AT Tommy's request the partners were meeting in conference. The telephone girl and the secretaries had been told that none of the partners would receive calls or callers. Now Mr. Jonathon was sitting behind his own desk, Tucker, Mr. Frederick, and Tommy in comfortable arm-chairs in a semicircle facing him. They had often sat together thus in the last year, and Tommy shrank from the task he had set himself. It hurt to think that he would probably not meet with these men again, and it hurt to tell them that he would not. But the cord had to be broken, and only he could break it.

"Well, Tommy?" Mr. Jonathon asked. "What's on your mind?"

Tommy smiled at him and shook his head dubiously. "So much, sir, that I hardly know where to begin. I ought to know exactly what I want to say. I suppose I do know, but it's damnably hard to say it."

"Why, what do you mean?" Martin Tucker demanded, studying Tommy shrewdly. "I hope I'm wrong in guessing—"

"That I'm about to resign from the firm? No, Mr. Tucker, you're right." Tommy felt a moment's weakness from having actually said the words he had dreaded so much to say.

There were exclamations of surprise, regret, and actual unbelief from all the partners. They asked what was the matter: was he ill, was he in trouble, was there anything they could do? Tommy could only make vague gestures of negation and try not to look as moved and unhappy as he felt. This was going to be bad. . . .

Mr. Jonathon tapped with his pencil on the desk. "Wait," he commanded. "This is getting us nowhere. We must let Tommy talk. Tell us about it, my boy. You've given us a great shock. I hope we haven't failed you."

"Failed me? Oh no, Mr. Jonathon. None of you have failed me. I hope you won't think I've gone suddenly insane if I say I don't think I'd resign if I were less contented here."

"You sound a trifle cracked, of course," Tucker remarked, "but you're one of the most cautious young men I've ever known. You don't indulge in paradoxes for pleasure. You have a reason, I'm sure. Let's hear it."

Mr. Frederick rubbed his round cheek and smiled in his gentle way. "You know I have a simple mind, Tommy," he said. "Go easy; don't confuse me."

"I'll try to be clear, though I can't state my reasons in plain words. They're too involved." Tommy paused, looked at each man in turn. "I'm offering my resignation, but I don't expect you to accept it if you don't approve of my reasons. I know I'm not being sensible—not as we generally use that word, anyway; I may even be acting quixotically. I don't know. It's for you to decide. I'll ask you to hear me out; then if you feel I'm wrong or foolish, I promise to withdraw my resignation if you want me to."

"That," said Mr. Jonathon, "is the kind of fair attitude we've come to expect from you."

"Thank you, sir." Tommy thought deeply, then began: "In the first place, I want to say this: I know I'm not necessary to the firm. I'd like to think I am, but this firm existed before I was born, and it will go on with or without me. Please don't think I don't feel a responsibility to the firm. I do, the strongest kind of responsibility, but I'm trying hard to consider facts—and the fact is that I'm not at all a necessity.

"I want you to understand, too, that I was tremendously proud and happy when you made me a partner. I felt I was

all set, though it did not occur to me at that time to ask
myself what I was all set for. That came later. Just remember, please, that I knew you had done me an honor
and that I prized it. I still do."

He hesitated, looked out of a window, and then, fighting
an impulse to evade speaking the words that must be spoken,
he continued: "It isn't easy for me to talk about myself. I
think I must have been born reticent, and I was brought up
among reticent people. I have never been able to confide in
others easily, but now I'm going to try to confide in you. I
know I shan't be entirely successful. It just isn't in me to
break loose and reveal myself entirely, but I'm going to do
my best."

"If some people said anything like that, Tommy," Tucker
interposed, "I'd be halfway down the hall already, but I
feel quite safe with you." He smiled. "Can you break over?"

Tommy grinned in obvious embarrassment. "I'm going
to try to—and you'll have to stand it, Mr. Tucker, because
you're directly responsible for some of what's coming. You
put some of the ideas in my head. As a matter of fact, I think
you supplied the largest plank in my platform. I thought
over those ideas while I was tramping through the White
Mountains—those and others. That's what I went for." He
hesitated. "I'm starting at the wrong end. Let me go back.

"I'll have to indulge in some autobiography, but I'll make
it as brief as I can. My life, you see, really divides itself very
sharply into two parts, though they're quite unequal. The
first part takes in my first twenty-five years; the last part
takes in the last five. I can't say I was always happy until I
was twenty-five, but I suspect I was happier than most. Anyhow, life was extremely significant to me. It had meaning.
Since my divorce five years ago it has had almost none. During the last year I have been struggling hopelessly to find
some meaning. Now I think I can do it. That's why I'm
resigning."

"That sounds like a *non sequitur*," said Mr. Jonathon, "but I'm probably missing your major premise. Never mind that now. Go on, please."

"Logically it may be a *non sequitur*," Tommy admitted, "but I don't think it is emotionally. Where was I? Oh, yes; I know. Well, it seemed very silly to me for a man like me to find life flat, stale, and unprofitable. I had everything supposedly that makes for happiness. I had freedom and health, an assured income—and since my mother's death it has been doubled; I had work I liked enormously and that paid me well, enough to give me everything I wanted. I had an income and didn't need it. To millions of people that would sound like heaven, and I knew that there must be something wrong with me. It was easy to say the times were out of joint, but it was too easy; it was only an evasion—and, besides, saying it didn't make life even a little bit more meaningful."

Tucker was leaning forward in his chair. "I'm beginning to understand, Tommy," he said softly. "I have an idea I'm 'way ahead of you already. Go on. I think you mean, don't you, that you had everything to give you pleasure but you could find no happiness? Is that it?"

"That's it exactly. Now, I have a real gift for pleasure. I can enjoy all kinds of things. I can play any game like a kid and enjoy it just as much. I love music, and nobody gets greater pleasure out of a good concert than I do. Toscanini sends me out of Carnegie Hall in a kind of blind daze of happiness. I like to go to the theater. I'm gregarious; I like people and I get along with most of them. I like pictures, and I get great pleasure out of going to the galleries. I can get crazy excited at hockey matches or prizefights. I like to dance. In other words, I can have a good time almost any time—and I've had lots of good times in the last five years, lots of them in the past year.

"But they were just good times. I didn't look back on

them with any particular pleasure, and I didn't look forward to new ones with that anticipatory eagerness that's half the fun. They began and ended; that was all. That was true of my work, too. I enjoyed it while I was doing it, but it gave me no satisfaction to take home with me. It ended when I left the office and began again when I returned the next morning. You might say everything I did was without connotation.

"I've tried to express the emptiness to myself over and over again, but I've failed. I can't find any metaphor that satisfies me. The best I can do is to say that my work and my friends and pleasures were like a lot of shining bricks that were—well, just bricks. I couldn't build a house with them. I had no mortar and no plan. Mind you, I was desperate, and I was willing to build on sand if I could get the shining palace Edna St. Vincent Millay wrote about, but I couldn't even do that. I tried it a few times—and ate the sand. No, I couldn't build at all; there was no foundation, no plan, nothing."

"I'm not sure I understand," said Mr. Frederick, wrinkling his forehead in thought. "Aren't you just saying you were lonesome as any unmarried man is likely to be—especially a man who has been married?"

Tucker answered before Tommy could. "No," he said quickly. "No, he isn't just lonesome. It goes far beyond that. You've always had your mortar, Frederick. For one thing, you helped build this firm. Tommy can't do that. It's built. He can only help continue it. You've had your family, your home, your garden that you're so crazy about, and your studies. Your mind, I'll wager, is never empty. You have a great deal to look back on, and I'm sure you're still looking forward."

"Yes," Mr. Frederick agreed; "that's all true, Martin. That's what I'm saying. If Tommy were married—"

"I'm going to be," Tommy interrupted. He did not give the partners time for congratulations but continued without a break. "And that's what's made me resign now. I know I can find temporary satisfaction out of marriage—temporary significance, and I'm afraid it will satisfy me enough for a while so that I'll be caught forever."

"I know exactly what you mean," Tucker said, "exactly. Go on, Tommy. Explain. Frederick and Jonathon will see, too."

Encouraged, Tommy took a deep breath and went on: "This is a tremendously exciting world we're living in, but I wasn't excited. I couldn't get excited. I'm a part of that world, but I couldn't—I can't—feel a part of it. There's a war being fought, and the world is getting ready for a greater war. Sometimes I almost wished it would come, because all my difficulties would be solved. I wouldn't have to think any more."

"That's right," said Tucker. "A soldier doesn't think—not if he's a good soldier. He has no responsibilities except to do what he's told. Life is reduced to its simplest terms—and death waits around the corner."

"Yes, that's what I mean. There's no need for worry, and the imminence of death is enough to give life significance. Of course, I knew I was only hunting for another escape when I gave over to thoughts like those, but my knowledge of my own weakness didn't make it possible for me to care about what is happening in the world. I was interested in a way, but my interest was entirely outside my emotions; it was entirely academic. For example, I think Nazism is about the most despicable thing that has ever come upon this earth, but I can only use strong terms in talking about it; I can't feel strongly. Do you see what I mean?"

"I see," said Mr. Jonathon, "but I don't understand. Nazism makes me boil. There's something about it that outrages every decent American instinct in me."

"That's the way I ought to feel," said Tommy; "that's the way I think I should feel. I ought to be emotional about Communism the way my friend Steve Austin is. It means something to him. Now, I don't happen to agree with him, but that makes no difference. The point is that there is no feeling in my disagreement; I just think quite placidly that it would be most unfortunate for us to adopt it. I'm the same way about Mussolini's Fascism; I'm even like that about the New Deal and the election. I get mildly irritated at the *ad hominem* arguments men put up when they discuss politics, but the poor logic at least comes mostly from passionate interest. Politics mean something personally to people who put up *ad hominem* arguments. They may not think as logically as I do, but I'll gladly resign some of the logic if I can gain a little of the passion. I want politics to matter to me. I want to be a part of something, not isolated as I am now."

Tucker smiled and asked half-teasingly, "You wouldn't care about loving if you could just hate? Is that it?"

Tommy smiled in return and shook his head. "Not really. I want to do both. I was thinking about all these things when I was walking in the mountains, and I decided that a lot of the general confusion was due to the fact that man had changed the world faster than he could change himself—if he can change at all. That was borne on me when I flew back from California last spring. I left there on a marvelous day— people in light clothes, their heads bare, flowers everywhere, green grass, warm sunshine. The next day I was back in a bleak, cold rainstorm. I couldn't adjust myself. I actually suffered from the suddenness of the change. The world is suffering the same way, I think. We weren't made for the pace we've set. We're trying to run a lifetime as if it were a hundred-yard dash.

"I'm not made for that pace, anyway. Of that I feel sure. And here in New York you're at the center of the wheel. That, I knew, had something to do with my problem. But that wasn't enough. I asked myself how other people found a continuing purpose in life—that mortar I was talking about that held their work and pleasures and experiences together, made some kind of whole of them, formed them into some kind of pattern.

"Well, I thought of several things. Some people have religion. Charlie Lovett has, for example. I think there's no doubt that his faith is the unifying force in his life. In a way it is for Mae Vadney, too. When I was helping Mae find a boy, I asked her one day about her religion because she had mentioned the church several times. Well, her religion isn't like Charlie's, though it's just as unquestioning. As I see it, she hasn't any religion in the sense he has, but she has the church. It is the center around which her world swings. Why, when she moved to East Orange she found her church before she was half settled. Her life moves for six days and comes to a focus on Sundays. She repeats the creed without thinking what it means. And I doubt if she listens to the sermons—certainly she doesn't listen to them critically. It's just the routine, the institution of church itself that matters to her—and for her it does great work."

"There's a great deal in what you say," Mr. Jonathon remarked judicially. "At least, I know how it is with me. Intellectually I'm an agnostic, but I formed the habit of church-going when I was a child, and it has always stayed with me. I couldn't give it up if I would, though it's something more than a habit. The church itself has a meaning in my wife's life and mine."

"But you see, sir," said Tommy, "it has never had a meaning in my life. I went to a Unitarian Sunday-school when I was a child, and that was all. Charlie Lovett said to me once that he was taught to believe—and he was taught, you may be sure, by people who believed with absolute faith. Therefore he does believe. I wasn't taught, and I don't. I'm probably no more agnostic than you are, sir," he said to Mr. Jonathon, "but the church has never been a part of my life at all. It isn't that I've rejected it; it's just that I've never had it. And to tell you the truth, I don't miss it. I don't miss religion, either. Some people need some kind of mysti-

cal faith; others don't, but I think the people who adopt
a faith in their maturity always had it down in their hearts;
they've merely gained assurance and joined a church. They
aren't really converted, most of them—not people like T. S.
Eliot and G. K. Chesterton. They just put an emotion into
words and argue about it publicly. Probably they're trying
to reassure themselves or keep themselves reassured. I don't
know, and it doesn't matter."

He paused and smiled rather deprecatingly. These generalizations would have to be controlled; he was using them
almost by instinct to avoid the personal revelation he had
promised.

"I hope you understand," he explained, "that I realize
that all my remarks and arguments are *ad hominem;* but
that's my only excuse for straying so far afield. I'm not
really trying to solve the problems of the world. I'm trying
to solve my own problems, and I'm mentioning the bigger
ones because they affect me—or ought to."

"Oh, we understand that," said Mr. Frederick. "You
needn't apologize. But, Tommy, I'm still in the dark. I
still don't see what you hope to accomplish by resigning.
You say you're going to be married. Well, then, why not
take a place out our way in Westchester and go on as we've
been going?"

"Because, Mr. Frederick, that's exactly what I'm afraid
of—that I'd go on as I've been going, I mean. If I had something like religion to tie the facts of my life together, perhaps I might just as well do what you suggest as anything
else, but I haven't religion and I never expect to get it."
He looked at Tucker. "You said one night in my apartment
that your generation had taken faith away from mine. I
think probably you're right. Whether you were or not, the
fact remains that most of my generation lack the faith our
elders had. And most of us don't miss it very much. We
admit that we don't know anything about God and let it
go at that.

"But we haven't given up an interest in ethics. I remember once when I was in college I thought I might be on my way to religion. I had written a sophomoric essay ridiculing Christianity. The professor read it and smiled at me. 'Gray,' he said, 'how long is it since you've read the Sermon on the Mount?' It had been years. I hadn't an idea what was in it. He opened a Bible and made me read it then and there. I was astonished, to put it mildly, and I admitted to him that I could accept almost everything in it. 'Well,' he said, 'that's Christianity.' Then and there I almost decided I was a Christian, but, of course, I wasn't. I could accept the ethics, but I gagged on the theology. It mattered to me then. Now I'm merely indifferent.

"But I didn't mean to talk about religion. All I wanted to say was that it does the work for some people. Ambition does it for some people. They want to get very rich or become very powerful or very famous. I'm not like that. I'm like most people. We have dreams when we're youngsters, but when we're a little older, if we dream we know we're just dreaming. We lack the egotism or drive or something —or maybe we aren't sufficiently out of balance. Anyway, whatever the reason, we accept the fact that we're not going to make any great mark in the world, and our hearts aren't broken.

"Of course, there are sycophants who seem to get all the thrill they need just out of being near famous people. To me, though, they seem diseased and they don't matter. But somebody like Robert Constant does matter; at least, he has mattered a lot to me. He's been like a prophecy to me—a prophecy of what I might become if I didn't watch out."

"Nonsense!" Mr. Jonathon exclaimed. "Constant has given up."

"Well, what was I doing? I was giving up, too; all I was doing was going through the motions. These other people aren't."

"Yes, of course," said Tucker. "Some live in their work,

some in their families, some in both, and so on. Your point is that you lack all those things, but you're young and healthy and intelligent and there ought to be something that would make you look back and look forward. It isn't as if you lacked intellectual or physical vitality."

"Yes," said Tommy gratefully, "that's it. There ought to be some sting to life while one's young. I'm thirty, and I've lost five years. I can't afford to lose any more. I was filled with bitterness five years ago when my marriage blew up, but I haven't even got that any more. Of course, now that I'm going to get married again, I have hopes and dreams, but I'm not satisfied to let it go at that. I want to give them a chance of fulfilment, and as I stand I'm a poor bet as a husband. When I'm married I shan't be lonely, but that's a negative virtue as I am now."

Mr. Frederick said something about being too modest. Other virtues were necessary in marriage, and Tommy had those virtues. But Tommy hardly heard. He was afraid he was doing a bad job of explaining himself. He had an uncomfortable suspicion that he wasn't explaining himself at all. He must be more personal.

"Thank you, sir," he said to Mr. Frederick. "I hope what you say is true, but I think the virtues you mention hardly make for happiness, though they are a necessary part if the marriage is to be a success." He smiled apologetically. "I'm afraid I'm going in circles. I wish now I'd made the notes I thought of making, but I couldn't bring myself to make a formal speech to you three."

"Oh, take your time, Tommy," said Mr. Jonathon, "and ramble to your heart's content. This is all interesting to all of us and important to all of us. Get at it in your own way."

"Well, I'll make another try—go at it from another direction, I mean. I'll tell you what sent me off to the mountains. I was at an absolute standstill, though of course I only half realized that. And I'd lost most of my courage, too. I half realized that—but only half. I was in love, and I was afraid to admit even to myself that I was. I was afraid to take another chance at marriage. I was so afraid, I realize now, that I was subconsciously doing my best to keep from being in love. I was in a vacuum and hating it, and I was afraid to escape from the vacuum. I wasn't thinking at all. I was just feeling, and most of the time I was just feeling sorry for myself.

"Then a few weeks ago I met a young man on a house party. There's no need to tell you about him, but he was in a bad jam through no fault of his own. He was suffering, but he had courage—and he said something to me that was like a kick in the teeth. It was something I'd known so long that I had learned to ignore it, if you know what I mean. He said, 'A man's got to know what he's like and what he wants out of life.' At the moment I let it pass for a platitude, but later it came back to me. Then I remembered something you'd said once." He addressed Martin Tucker directly. "You said a platitude wasn't necessarily untrue because it was a platitude. Remember?"

"No, I don't remember, but I probably said it because I think platitudes are more often true than not."

"So do I—now. Anyway, I began to consider that platitude. Then I realized that I didn't know what I was like, and I didn't know what I wanted out of life. I gave up self-analysis a good many years ago. I associated it with adolescence or undue vanity, and I liked to think of myself as mature. And I'd always taken it for granted that I was progressing very nicely along the only road I wanted to travel. But now I suspected I'd been all wrong. It was time for me to do some thinking, and so I went off to the mountains where I could be alone and think.

"For the first few days I got nowhere; or, rather, I didn't think I was getting anywhere. My mind kept going back to my childhood and dredging up all kinds of things I'd thought I'd forgotten. Later I knew they were important; that is, they'd all gone to make me what I am today.

"Don't worry; I'm not going to break out with an analysis of me. Only the conclusions matter. In the end I realized that I had never come to grips with life at all. Everything up to the time of my marriage had been simple, all settled for me, neatly marked out. I lived in a community where my family had made a place for itself generations before I was born. Then when my father's death might have made serious problems for me, they were taken care of by the routine of prep school, summer camps, and so on. Later there was the routine of college and travel. Then law school, and the job in Albany. And there was always plenty of money, and there was every indication that there always would be.

"If my marriage had failed because I had been at fault or if my wife had been, I might have been able to find some understanding about it. But neither of us had really been at fault, and when I finally realized that, I was simply stunned. I had no experience and no philosophy that would take care of such a situation.

"Then you took me in, and I liked both the office and the work enormously. There was dignity and a complete escape from the sordid side of the law. I liked that. No fireworks, no publicity, no digging into the dirt of people's lives. I didn't realize until recently that for me it was just an escape from life. It was like my unwillingness to quarrel with people. I know now that I never let myself get close enough to people to quarrel with them. I don't involve myself in their lives or permit them to involve themselves in mine. I've broken in on people only twice in years and years. One was Mae Vadney, and the other was the young man I mentioned a few minutes ago."

"That was a fine thing you did for Mae," said Mr. Jonathon. "You've made her into a happy woman."

"Yes," said Tommy, "she is, and I've done a lot of thinking about Mae. Theoretically she's pitiable; actually she is enviable. She gets up early, does a lot of housework, rushes over here, works hard all day, and then rushes back to cook supper for that boy, mend his clothes, and so on. But she's happy. And that," he said with a smile for Martin Tucker, "brought me to another platitude."

"You mean, don't you, that to gain one's life, one must lose it?"

"Yes. That's exactly what I mean. Mae and I were the antipodes. She gave her life utterly and got life in return; I had mine entirely to myself—and I didn't have anything. You know, I found I couldn't begin to think until I had gone back to those platitudes we sneer at so smugly. This is the era of the wise-crack, and whether I like it or not, I'm a part of my era. We're suspicious of the homely old saws that people used to quote and believe in. And our thinking is largely governed by writers who make a business of originality and disillusionment and sophistication. That's especially true here in New York, I think. Those writers preach emptiness and futility, and it's too easy to agree with them; it's too damn comforting. They offer you a ready excuse for your emptiness and supineness. Of course, there's a world of truth in what they say, but there's truth on the other side, too. I think they do good work in showing us how rotten and weak and aimless human kind is, but they make cowards of us; we're afraid to examine old truths and we're afraid of sentimentality."

"Tommy," said Mr. Frederick, "I'm beginning to understand you at last. I enjoy reading Aldous Huxley. He's truly brilliant, and he's as bitter as only an idealist can be. I usually agree with him, but when my little granddaughter climbs on my lap and loves me, none of it matters. I'm sentimental about her, I suppose, but that sentimentality is more real and precious to me than anything else. I'm willing to admit that mankind is vile, but she isn't."

Tommy nodded. "That's what I mean. The sophisticates make us ashamed of an emotion like that. We hardly dare mention it. They make us ashamed to be trite in our thinking, and I've come to believe that the truths that matter are trite. We're afraid to quote the Golden Rule. We associate it with the simplicity of country churches. We're afraid to quote: 'This above all, to thine own self be true; thou canst not then be false to any man.' We're even afraid of admitting to ourselves that marriage is a spiritual experience. We talk in a superior manner about the biological urge, and we're so busy admitting that sex can be filthy that we're ashamed to admit that it can be beautiful. I think we've turned into emotional cowards. We run away from honest emotion or try to hide it. Then somebody like Mae who doesn't read sophisticated books shows us up to ourselves. She takes a waif and loves him and doesn't care who knows it. She hasn't any theory of futility. She doesn't know whether she's sentimental or not, and she doesn't care. She just gives with all her heart, and I don't see how anybody can call the happiness she finds futile or meaningless. It wouldn't be to me, anyway."

"All of us," said Tucker, "are old enough to agree with you without argument. We're not the futilitarians—not my generation or Jonathon's and Frederick's. It's yours."

"I know it. Well, I'm still a futilitarian to a certain extent. I'll confess that I don't know what life means. Wasn't it Browning who said that life means intensely and means good? I'm too much a part of my generation to be sure that it means good or that it means anything, but I do think it can, and does, mean intensely to individuals—and that's what I'm getting at. I'm determined to make it mean something to me; and I know from long experience that isolated pleasures won't give it the meaning."

"No," said Mr. Jonathon, shaking his head; "no, isolated pleasures will never do it. As men go, I think I've had a happy life, but it hasn't come from even a stream of isolated pleasures. One has to travel a long road."

"And want to travel it?" asked Tommy.

"Yes—and want to travel it."

"And with some kind of goal?"

"Don't be afraid to quote Emerson," said Tucker, laughing softly. "He said something, you know, about hitching your wagon to a star. And how about dear old Victorian Tennyson's admonition to follow the gleam? Even the Greeks had a word for it."

"Probably," said Tommy, smiling at Tucker, "the cave men did. It's so basic, so damned elementary, that we ignore it. It took me a long time, though, to realize that we must want something out of our lives and make a try for it. Like lots of other people, I've been getting along with a half-formulated code. It isn't enough. It may save you from shame or regret, but those are only negative virtues. I've got to the place where I have to have something positive, something real."

"Do you really know what you want?" asked Mr. Frederick. "Or are you merely reversing your position?"

"That's a hard question to answer," Tommy admitted, "and 'reversing your position' is so pat it hurts. I know I want to *feel* alive. I feel alive now, and you don't know how wonderful it is after five years of merely existing. And, above anything imaginable, I want to keep the feeling. I want the satisfaction of looking back and the anticipation that comes with looking forward—the way I am now, I mean. That's when you're really living with every ounce of you, when you're looking forward like a kid and waiting for something with all your heart and soul. I'm waiting like that—and I can't tell you; I can't even begin to tell you. . . ." His emotion rose, stopped him. Embarrassed, he lowered his eyes and then went on more quietly: "I'm going to try to arrange my life so that things'll keep on mattering. Maybe I'll fail, but just trying will give me something to look forward to all the time, and I've found recently that I'm capable of looking back if I give myself a chance. I suppose I'd better explain that.

"Well, I've looked back on finding that youngster for Mae with all the satisfaction in the world, and while I was hunting for him life didn't seem purposeless and insignificant. During that time I wasn't concerned with myself. The other time is different. The young man I mentioned was in a jam. He couldn't do anything about it, but by a coincidence I could. I didn't want to. Anything but. I hated the mere thought of mixing into other people's lives, intruding on their emotions. But I couldn't escape. I could do the job, and I was the only one who could. So, hating it all like hell, I did it. I don't deserve any happiness out of doing a duty I couldn't escape, I suppose, but I find happiness every time I think of the happiness I helped bring about.

"That taught me something. I know now that I can't evade other people's lives if I want to have a life of my own. I know I've got to live close to people—close enough to hate some of them, probably—if I'm going to have any permanent satisfaction out of being a human being. I've got to care, really care, and be cared about. I've got to hurt and take a chance of being hurt. I've got an enormous number of pleasant acquaintances. I never intrude on them, and I'm pretty darned skilful about keeping them from intruding on me. Now I want some of the happiness that comes from real friendship. I've evaded that happiness because I've been so careful to avoid the confusion and pain that come from living close to people. Well, I'm going to take that chance. I'm going to arrange my life so I'll have to take it. And the first thing I've got to do is get out of New York."

"Get out of New York?" asked Jonathon Winchester. "Why? What has New York got to do with it?"

"It's got a lot," Tommy replied, feeling sure of himself at last. "One thing I've always liked about New York is the ease with which you can escape people you don't like. You aren't always bumping into them the way you are in smaller places. Of course, sometimes you're cooped up with them in offices, but there's no doubt that the evasion is easier here than it is even in a city like Boston. But the

same thing is true of people you do like. The city itself
separates you. You have to take thought and make a real
effort to get together. Wait! I'll give you a perfect example.

"You may not believe it but I've had a negro girl taking care of my apartment for more than five years and
I never saw her until day before yesterday. We left notes
on the ice-box."

"Oh," said Mr. Frederick, "I've heard and read of things
like that. Has all your communication really been by ice-
box notes?"

"Yes. Her brother was the janitor when I took the apartment. I engaged her through him. Now, her notes and
her work made me really admire her. She had standards
and pride and loyalty and humor. I was sure Maribelle
was a real person, though it was hard when I never saw
her to believe she was real at all. Now, the point is this:
I've met her, but in order to do it, I had to write a note,
telephone, and take a taxi trip. That, Mr. Jonathon, is
New York."

"Such things happen here, of course," Mr. Jonathon
agreed, "but they're not common. So far as friendship is
concerned, it's no different from San Francisco or Squee-
dunk. People are people in New York or Singapore.
Friendships aren't dependent on places. I was born in
Manhattan, and two of my closest friends were my friends
when we were ten."

"I know, but you're a New Yorker; I'm not." Tommy
paused and rubbed his cheek. "I wonder if I can make
you understand. I guess I'll come at it from a tangent.
Last fall, you'll remember, I went up to Hanover for a
few days. Well, I didn't accomplish what I went for at all,
but I had a talk with one of my old professors and—" He
broke off and stared blindly at the wall, his lips parted in
a smile of utter unbelief.

"What's hit you?" Tucker asked. "Have you seen a sudden light?"

Tommy blinked. "No, not a light, but I just realized something. All I'm saying now goes directly back to that trip to Hanover. Listen to what happened. On the way back a girl sat with me. I didn't know her. She just happened to choose that seat at Springfield. I liked her and called on her later. She's Mary Carter, the girl Tyckman's going to marry."

"She is!" the Winchesters exclaimed together.

"Yes, and I introduced them to each other. Tyckman, it happens, introduced me to her brother—and he's the one who started me thinking by saying a man had to know what he's like and what he wanted out of life. But wait; that's not all. Mary Carter introduced me to Hollis Graham, the girl I'm going to marry." He paused again and shook his head wonderingly. "I suppose we could trace back practically everything we do to a chain of circumstances like that, but it's a little startling to realize suddenly that several lives have been changed because a girl happened to sit by me on a train, especially when there wasn't any particular reason for me to be on that train or in that seat."

Tucker smiled grimly. "In 1914," he said, "a man who happened to be a grand duke was shot by a fool who happened to have a phobia. That altered my whole life and the lives of millions and millions of others. Don't get to speculating about the links of coincidences that make up the chain of your life, Tommy. That way madness lies."

"I suppose so," Tommy agreed, "but it dumfounded me to see all those links so suddenly. Where was I? Oh, yes, I was going to tell you about Kingston, the professor. He seemed happy to me. He loves teaching. His contacts with the students give him constant and lasting satisfaction. He admits to disappointments, but he expects them, accepts them, and goes on hopeful of a vicarious success in the lives of the fellows he helps.

"That didn't seem to have any significance for me at

the time, but from what I've already said, you can see the significance it has for me now. Then when I was in California I called on an old college friend, Cal Cameron. He teaches in Berkeley—science—and he finds students just a bother. He's interested in research. He's a bilious, irritable sort of person, but I suspect he's happier than most, too. He's a nut on gardening. And Powers is even a worse nut, and he *is* happy; you know that the minute you see him. Now, I don't mean those men are happy because they like to garden, though—"

"Oh, I know!" Mr. Frederick broke in, his fat cheeks growing pink with his pleased excitement. "Don't I know! Why, a garden is the biggest satisfaction in the world. There's absolutely nothing like it. When spring comes—"

"Now, Freddy," his brother interrupted mildly, "you restrain yourself. You're going to tell us about your chrysanthemums and that new mulch you found so wonderful and about your double nasturtiums. Haven't I been listening to you for years?"

"But I understand how these men feel. I can explain that satisfaction."

"Tommy understands that satisfaction," Mr. Jonathon said.

"No, I don't understand it," confessed Tommy, "but I want to. I'm going to have a garden to see if I can't find it. Probably I'll try so hard to be enthusiastic that I'll miss the mark entirely, but, never mind, I'll be trying. But it was something that Cameron said that really resolved all my thinking into a plan. He said, 'A man needs to get his hands into the dirt.'

"I remembered that when I was walking in the mountains, and then things began to clear up—about me, I mean. I'm a country boy. I was born in the country, went to a prep school in the country, a college in the country. Even Cambridge has a country atmosphere. It's a town of homes and gardens; it's a community, the kind of community I've always been accustomed to. Even Albany is a lot like that.

"Then just at the wrong time, I realize now, I came to New York. I thought it was marvelous on account of the concerts and the theaters and the galleries, and it is marvelous—in many ways, I suppose it's the most marvelous city the world has ever seen. But it isn't a community. It's been made so great and wonderful by human beings that it's unfit for human beings. It defies nature. It's up in the air and under the ground—but never *on* the ground. There's no dirt for a man to get his hands into. It's a total denial of nature, and human beings are a product of nature. At least, I am. Hundreds and hundreds of thousands of New Yorkers are, too. They don't live in New York even in spirit; they merely work here. It's a gigantic ant-hill. The human ants swarm here in the morning, swarm up cell after cell, swarm down at night, and swarm away to some other spot where they can find enough strength from nature to swarm back again the next morning.

"Look at me! I never touch earth. My apartment is on the fifth floor. I'm suspended in the air. This office is on the fifteenth. Again I'm suspended in the air. I get here over macadam or asphalt or concrete. Why, I even have to lean back to see the sky. I don't breathe real air but a man-made mixture of smoke and gases.

"Well, I've decided that I'm like Antæus; I have to touch the earth. When I'm in the woods, I feel alive; in New York I never really do. I feel alive in any town where there are trees and grass and flowers and space. Cameron was right; a man *does* need to get his hands into the dirt. New York is built on the principle that one doesn't need to—and look at the people you see on the streets and in the subways. Well, they're still human beings, but I wonder what they'll be in a few generations."

He paused, lifted his hand and let it fall to his knee. "Well, there you are. I know I've got to get out of this great city. I'm going to make myself a part of a community. Notice, please, that I said *make* myself a part. Hereafter that word *make* is my motto. Honestly, I think I spent most of a day up there in the mountains thinking about that word. If you let yourself go with it, there's no stopping."

"I don't understand," said Mr. Jonathon. "You needn't give us a day of exposition, but give us a hint at least."

Tommy leaned forward in his chair and talked eagerly. "I think *make* is the most important word in our language. You and Mr. Frederick made this firm; Mr. Frederick makes a garden; you make a home, a family, a career —you make anything that counts, and as long as you're making something, you're safe; and you're likely to make happiness for yourself if you're making several things at once, home, family, garden, career. There's just one thing you can't make."

"Pleasure," said Tucker quickly. "You can't make pleasure. You can prepare for it, enjoy it, look forward to it and back on it; but you can't make it. Am I right?"

"Dead right. And there's the answer to Robert Constant. Believe me, I was glad to find the answer, too. That man had haunted me. So long as he was making a career and a home, he was somebody. Then he threw them aside and set out to make fun. Well, I don't believe he's getting it. Happy people don't rot, and he's rotting. No, you can't make a good time, not really, but if you're making other things, the good times come often of their own accord."

"I agree with you from here to everywhere," said Mr. Jonathon, "and making things is the best fun of all usually. You, I take it, are planning to make things?"

"Yes. As I said before, I'm going to make myself a part of a community. I'm going to have neighbors, not strangers existing in cells alongside of my cell. Hollis and I are planning to go to California—not because it's beautiful, but because it's new to us and different. We don't know where we'll settle, maybe in San Rafael where Powers lives, maybe in Berkeley, maybe somewhere else in Northern California. I don't know or care very much right now just where, so long as it's a community and not just an adjunct to a larger place like most Westchester towns. And I'm going to make myself a part of that community the way my father and his father were a part of the community where I was born."

"I can understand that desire, Tommy," Mr. Jonathon said. "Tell us, just what are your plans?"

"Hollis—Hollis Graham, my fiancée, I mean—is leaving tonight for her home in Iowa. Just as soon as you can spare me, I'll go out there and we'll be married. Then, as I said, we're going to California.

"I'm going to practice law, but not this kind of law. I'm going to open an office and scratch for business, and I'm going to take whatever business comes my way. I'm going into court and fight for my client. I like the kind of law we practice here because it's reticent. Now I'm going into law that's human. I shan't like a lot of it, I know, but I'll learn to like it. I'm going to put myself in a position where I'll have to like it. And I'll know the satisfaction of winning, and I'll have to learn how to take a licking."

He smiled and looked a little shamefaced. "Now I'm going to confess something that goes against the grain. I'm afraid you'll think I'm quixotic, but I'm going to come clean. I haven't saved any money until this year since I've been in New York. This year, of course, I've put away a few thousand, but in the previous four years I gave away everything I didn't need to indigent relatives—and what a lot of them turned up! I didn't know I had so many relatives. I gave a lot to charity too, but, of course, there was no need to save, and my giving involved no sacrifice. Altogether now I have about six thousand a year from investments—and that's all I'll have when I end my connection with this firm. It's enough, of course, but that's just the point; it's enough—and I've decided it's bad for me to have enough.

"Well, I haven't reached the point where I'm willing to give all my goods to the poor. I'm the kind of person who feels that selling government bonds except under the stress of absolute need is as sinful as rape, but I'm going to sell government bonds. I'm going to buy land and build a house—a house that I'll have to support. I'm going to furnish it, buy a car. In other words, I'm deliberately going to establish a standard of living beyond the income I'll have left. I'm going to put myself in a position where I'll have to support my home and wife and, I hope, a family. I'm not willing to throw away the security that my income will give us, but I'm not willing to slump back on that security, either. I shall have to make money. I'm going to make the practice of law a necessity. I shan't come to the office as I do here and find the business brought in by a reputation other men have made."

"And," asked Mr. Frederick in his gentle way, "you're going to have a garden?"

"Real and symbolical, Mr. Frederick, and I'm going to cultivate both myself."

## II

Back in his own office, Tommy felt very tired. The long explanation had been a great strain, and the affectionate things the partners said to him when at last he was done had added to it. He slumped in his desk chair weak with weariness.

The door opened and Martin Tucker appeared.

"I'd like to see you a minute alone, Tommy," he said.

"Come in, please."

Tucker stood by the desk, placed his hands on it, and looked at Tommy. The lines in his face were even deeper

than usual, and the bright light was gone from his small
eyes. He looked long at Tommy before he spoke.

"Some day," he began, "when things get tough, you'll
be sorry. You'll have lots of moments of regret. There'll
be irritations and failures and disappointments, worry, too
—everything you're escaping now. But you're doing the
right thing, Tommy. I know. Frederick and Jonathon
can't quite understand, because they belong just where
they are; but the war and—and something else broke my
life in two just as your marriage broke yours. I came in
here as to a sanctuary, and I've found it a pleasant prison
—and I realized too late that it was a prison for a man
like me. I'm glad you've found out soon enough, though
a year ago I was the one who suggested that you be taken
into the firm. I thought you were temperamentally ideal
for it. But I understood you no better than you did."

"No," said Tommy, "I didn't understand. I'm afraid I
understood almost nothing. Now I'm so full of hope I'm
almost afraid. I'm in love, and that's frightening. I'm doing something reckless, and that's frightening, too. It isn't
easy for me to be reckless—to take chances I don't need
to take, but I know it's worth it. I've got to believe it's
worth it."

"It is." Martin Tucker's eyes, always so full of disillusionment and world weariness, grew soft. "It is," he repeated. "Life's worth suffering for. You've got to believe
that or it isn't worth living. Other people are worth suffering for, no matter how much they hurt you. Most of the
time I think mankind is too foul and too stupid to be
worth saving, but that's because I haven't had the courage
to escape my own weaknesses. You're making a brave
start—and you're in love. That ought to sustain you."

Tommy said nothing. He was thinking of Hollis, and
he could not speak.

Tucker waited. Then he said, "You have St. Paul's trinity,
you know—and that's everything. You remember?"

Tommy looked at him questioningly and shook his head.

In a voice hardly more than a whisper, Tucker quoted: "But now abideth faith, hope, love, these three; and the greatest of these is love."

### THE END